THE GOSPEL OF LOKI

Also by Joanne Harris

The Evil Seed

Sleep, Pale Sister

Chocolat

Blackberry Wine

Five Quarters of the Orange

Coastliners

Holy Fools

Jigs & Reels

Gentlemen & Players

The Lollipop Shoes

Blueeyedboy

Runemarks

Runelight

Peaches for Monsieur le Curé

A Cat, a Hat and a Piece of String

WITH FRAN WARDE

The French Kitchen: A Cook Book
The French Market:
More Recipes from a French Kitchen

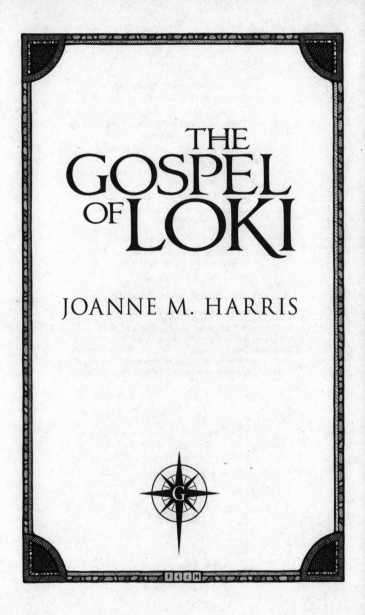

THE GOSPEL OF LOKI

JOANNE M. HARRIS

The right of Joanne Harris to be identified as the author
of this work has been asserted by her in accordance with the
Copyright, Designs and Patents Act 1988.

First published in Great Britain in 2014 by Gollancz
An imprint of the Orion Publishing Group
Orion House, 5 Upper St Martin's Lane,
London WC2H 9EA
An Hachette UK Company

This edition published in Great Britain in 2014
by Gollancz

5 7 9 10 8 6 4

A CIP catalogue record for this book
is available from the British Library.

ISBN 978 1 473 20316 7

Typeset by Input Data Services Ltd, Bridgwater, Somerset

Printed in Great Britain by Clays Ltd, St Ives plc

The Orion Publishing Group's policy is to use papers
that are natural, renewable and recyclable products and
made from wood grown in sustainable forests. The logging
and manufacturing processes are expected to conform to
the environmental regulations of the country of origin.

www.joanne-harris.co.uk
www.orionbooks.co.uk
www.gollancz.co.uk

To Anouchka, again, again.

ACKNOWLEDGEMENTS

Heartfelt thanks to everyone who has helped this book cross over from Dream and onto your Kindles and bookshelves. To Jon Wood of Orion Books goes the rune of persistence, humour and enthusiasm. To Gillian Redfearn from Gollancz, the rune of energy and imagination. To Jenn McMenemy, the rune of success (which is also the rune of chocolate), and to Jemima Forrester, the rune of communication. The rune of fabulous artwork goes to Andreas Preis, and the rune of getting important things done to Sophie Calder. To Anne Riley, the rune of staying afloat when the paperwork threatens to drown us all; to Becca Marovolo the rune of believing in oneself, even when no-one else does; and to Mark Richards, the rune of putting things in their rightful places. To Peter Robinson goes the rune of quietly turning the Worlds when everyone else has gone to sleep, and to Kevin and Anouchka, the rune of Mexican food, big hugs, hot tea and always knowing where you belong.

It takes Nine Worlds to make a book, or so it seems from my side of the desk. Editors, copy-editors, proofreaders, designers, artists, sales and marketing teams, book reps, booksellers, website designers. And you, of course. The readers; the tweeters; the bloggers; the dreamers; the fans - all the people who open the door and step inside these worlds that we build. Without each other, we wouldn't be here. The last rune goes to all of you. You know what it is. Use it carefully.

CHARACTERS

These are the people you're going to meet in the pages of this book. A word of advice before you start: don't trust *any* of them.

The Gods
(aka the Popular Crowd)

Odin – aka One-Eye, Allfather, the Old Man, the General. Leader of the Aesir. Knows how to sell himself (and others). Would throw his brother to the wolves (and did) for a percentage.

Frigg – Odin's wife, the Seeress. Stepmother of . . .

Thor – the Thunderer. Likes hitting things. Not a fan of Yours Truly.

Sif – his wife. Nice hair. Also not a fan of mine.

Balder – god of peace. Yeah, right. Known as Balder the Fair. Handsome, sporty, popular. Sound a little smug to you? Yes, I thought so too.

Bragi – god of poetry. Two words: *expect lutes*.

Idun – wife of Bragi. Likes fruit.

Freyja – goddess of desire. Vain, petty and manipulative. Will sleep with practically anyone as long as jewellery is involved.

Frey – the Reaper. Twin brother of the above. Not a bad guy, but a fool for blondes.

Mani – the Moon. Drives a cool car.

Sól – the Sun. Drives a hot car.

Sigyn – handmaid of Freyja. Adoring wife. Possibly the most annoying woman in the whole of the Nine Worlds.

Heimdall – the Watchman. Not a fan. Has it in for Yours Truly.

Hoder – Balder's blind brother. A better shot than you might think.

Mimir – the Wise. Odin's uncle. Apparently, not wise enough.

Honir – the Silent. Never shuts up.

Njörd – father of Frey and Freyja. God of sea. Nice feet. Married to . . .

Skadi – the Snowshoe Huntress. Not one of my biggest fans. The words 'forgive and forget' don't feature in her vocabulary. Has a thing about bondage. And snakes.

Aegir – god of the storm. Married to . . .

Ran – custodian of the drowned. Strangely enough, likes to party.

Týr – god of war. Brave, but not bright.

Others

(including: demons, monsters, warlords,
freaks and other undesirables)

Yours Truly – Your Humble Narrator. Otherwise known as the Trickster; the Father of Lies; Loki; Lucky; Wildfire; Dogstar and various other epithets, not all of them flattering. Not the most popular guy around.

Hel – his daughter, guardian of the Dead.

Jormungand – the World Serpent, demon offspring of Yours Truly.

Fenris – aka Fenny, demon wolf, also the demon offspring of, etc.

Angrboda – or Angie. Mother of the three above. So shoot me. Turns out I'm not naturally monogamous.

Dvalin – a smith. One of the sons of Ivaldi.

Brokk – a smith. Good at sewing.

Thiassi – a warlord. Skadi's father. Likes: ice-fishing; torture; foreign travel.

Thialfi – a fanboy.

Roskva – a fangirl.

Gullveig-Heid – the Sorceress. Renegade of the Vanir. Mistress of runes. Shapeshifter extraordinaire. Greedy, clever and spiteful. All my favourite qualities . . .

Lord Surt – ruler of Chaos. Or whatever you call the lord of a place that, by definition, *has* no rules.

FOREWORD

I know a tale, o sons of earth.
I speak it as I must.
Of how nine trees gave life to Worlds
That giants held in trust.

OK. *Stop.* Stop right there.

That was the Authorized Version. The Prophecy of the Oracle, as told to Odin Allfather by the Head of Mimir the Wise, and dealing, in thirty-six stanzas, with all of the history of the Nine Worlds, from 'Let there be light' to Ragnarók.

Pretty neat, don't you think?

Well, this *isn't* the Authorized Version. This is *my* version of events. And the first thing you have to understand about this little narrative is that there *is* no real beginning. Or real end, for that matter; although, of course, there have been many of both. Multiple endings, multiple beginnings, woven together so tightly that no one can tell them apart any more. Endings, beginnings, prophecies, myths, stories, legends and lies, all part of the same big carpet; especially the lies, of course – which is what you knew I'd say, me being the Father and Mother of Lies, but this time it's at least as true as anything you'd call *history*.

See, this is the thing about history. *His* story. That's all it is. The Old Man's version of events, which basically the rest of us are supposed to accept as the undisputed truth. Well, call me cynical, but I've never been one to take things on trust, and I happen to know that history is nothing but spin and metaphor, which is what all yarns are made up of, when you strip them down to the underlay. And what makes a hit or a myth, of course, is *how* that story is told, and by *whom*.

Most of what we know as history came to us from a single text: 'The Prophecy of the Oracle'. It's an old text, in an old language, and for a long time it was pretty much all the knowledge we had. From beginning to end, the Oracle and the Old Man had it all worked out between them; which made it all the more galling that we only found out what it *really* meant when it was too late for all of us.

But we'll get to that soon enough.

'Sticks and stones may break my bones', as they say in the Middle Worlds, but with the right words you can build a world and make yourself the king of it. King, or even god – which brings us back to the Old Man; that master storyteller; keeper of runes; lord of poetry; scribe of First and Last Times. Creationists would have us believe that every word of his story is true. But 'poetic licence' was always the Old Man's middle name. Of course, he has a lot of names. So do I. And because this isn't *history*, but *mystery* – *my* story – let's start with me for a change. Others have already had their chance to tell their version of events. This is mine.

I'm calling it *Lokabrenna*, or in rough translation, *the Gospel of Loki*. Loki, that's me. Loki, the Light-Bringer, the misunderstood, the elusive, the handsome and modest hero of this particular tissue of lies. Take it with a pinch of salt, but it's at least as true as the official version and, dare I say it, more entertaining. So far, history, such as it is, has cast me in a rather unflattering role. Now it's my turn to take the stage.

Let

    there

        be

           light.

BOOK 1

Light

That was the first Age, Ymir's time.
There was no land or sea.
Just void between two darknesses,
No stars by which to see.

Prophecy of the Oracle

LESSON 1

Fire and Ice

Never trust a ruminant . . .

Lokabrenna

ALL OF US CAME FROM FIRE AND ICE. Chaos and Order. Light and dark. In the beginning – or back in the day – there was fire coming out of a hole in the ice, bringing disruption, turmoil and change. Change isn't always comfortable, but it is a fact of life. And that's where life as we know it began, as the fires of World Below pierced the ice of World Above.

Before that, there were no Middle Worlds. No gods, no Folk, no wildlife. There was only Order and Chaos then, pure and uncorrupted.

But neither Order nor Chaos is very hospitable. Perfect order is immovable; frozen, unchanging and sterile. Total Chaos is uncontrolled; volatile and destructive. The middle ground – basically, lukewarm water – created the perfect environment for another kind life to emerge among the frozen Wilderlands and volcanoes erupting under the ice.

The Authorized Version goes like this, supported by the Oracle. From the meeting of Order and Chaos there came a giant being called Ymir, the father of the Ice Folk, and a cow, Audhumla, which licked at the salt that was in the ice and brought out the first man, Buri. From this I think we can all

5

conclude that the cow was the primary instigator of everything that followed – war, Tribulation, the End of the Worlds. Lesson One: never trust a ruminant.

Now the sons of Buri and those of Ymir hated each other from the start, and it didn't take long for them to go to war. Buri's three grandsons, the sons of Bór – their names were Odin, Vili and Ve – finally killed old Ymir and made the Middle Worlds from what was left of him; the rocks from his bones; the earth from his flesh; the rivers from his steaming blood. His skull became the Firmament; his brains the clouds; his eyebrows the division between Inland and the Outlands.

Of course, there's no way of proving this – let's face it – rather unlikely hypothesis. All of the possible witnesses have disappeared, except for Odin, the Old Man, the only survivor of that war; architect and chronicler of what we now call the Elder Age and, as it happens, the only one (except for me) to have heard the fateful prophecy, delivered to him by Mimir's Head when the Worlds were fresh and new.

Call me cynical if you like. But it all sounds a bit too convenient. The Authorized Version of events leaves out a number of details, which Creationists seem content to ignore. I personally have my doubts – not least about the giant cow – although even now you have to beware of how you express these sentiments. At one time, even to suggest that Odin's account of things might have been metaphorical instead of literal would have resulted in cries of heresy and a good deal of personal discomfort for Yours Truly, which is why, even then, I was always careful to keep my scepticism to myself.

But that's how religions and histories make their way into the world, not through battles and conquests, but through poems and kennings and songs, passed through generations and written down by scholars and scribes. And that's how, five hundred years later or so, a new religion with its new god came to supplant us; not through war, but through books and stories and words.

After all, words are what remain when all the deeds have been done. Words can shatter faith; start a war; change the course of history. A story can make your heart beat faster; topple walls; scale mountains – hey, a story can even raise the dead. And that's why the King of Stories ended up being King of the gods; because *writing* history and *making* history are only the breadth of a page apart.

Not that there was much of *that* when Odin was fighting the Ice Folk. There were no runes to write with then, and nothing but rock to write upon. But metaphor or otherwise, this is as much as I believe: that the world came into being through Change, which is the servant of Chaos; and only through Change has it endured. Much like Your Humble Narrator, in fact; adapting to suit the circumstance.

The snow hare changes its coat to white to go unseen in winter. The ash tree drops its leaves in the fall, better to survive the cold. All of life does the same – even gods – turning their coats to suit the turning seasons of the world. There should be a name for that kind of thing – in fact, it should be one of *my* names. Let's call it *Revolution*.

LESSON 2

Aesir and Vanir

Never trust a wise man.

Lokabrenna

THE WORLDS ARE ALWAYS CHANGING. It's their nature to ebb
and flow. That's why, in the old days, the Middle Worlds were
smaller than they are today – later, they expanded in the years
of the Winter War, then receded again like pack-ice, only to
expand again when Order came to claim them. That was always
the way of things; that shift between Order and Chaos. And
between the two, there was Yggdrasil, the pole that keeps the
Worlds apart; known to some as the World Ash, and to some as
Odin's Steed. Trust the Old Man to get his name in there somewhere, as always, although that tree (if it *was* a tree) was planted
long before Ymir was even a glint in Audhumla's eye.

Some claim it wasn't a tree at all, but some kind of cosmic
metaphor. Its roots, they said, were in Netherworld, plunged in
the Cauldron of Rivers, where the waters boil with ephemera
born from the primary source of Dream. Its topmost branch was
the branch of stars that crosses the sky on clear nights. There
was no World through which it did not grow; it had a hold
even in Chaos, where serpents and demons worked tirelessly to
undermine its living roots. Ratatosk, the squirrel, carried news
all over the Worlds by way of the great Tree's branches – as did

Odin One-Eye, of course; the ultimate collector of news, hoarding and distributing.

Some might suspect that the Old Man and Ratatosk might actually have been one and the same; certainly his business was all about gathering and disseminating information. It's how his legend was born, as you know, and how it survived for so long. It's also why he was the first to see the turn of the seasons; the waning of our influence and the beginning of our end.

Because it all has to end, of course. Everything dies – even Worlds; even gods; even Your Humble Narrator. From the moment the Worlds came to life, Ragnarók, the End of All Things, was written into every living cell in runes more complex than any we know. Life and Death in one package – with Order and Chaos acting not as two forces in opposition but as a single cosmic force too vast for us to comprehend.

I'm telling you this so you'll understand how this story's going to end; that is, not well for any of us. It all begins so hopefully, but these Worlds we build for ourselves are all just castles in the sand, waiting for the evening tide. Ours was no different. Odin knew that. And still, he kept on building. Some folk never learn.

So . . .

Having hacked out the Worlds from Ymir's remains (literally or otherwise), Odin and the sons of Bór set out to allocate its territories. The Ice Folk claimed the Outlands, in the frozen North of the Worlds. The Rock Folk claimed the mountains that ran like a spine through Inland. Mankind – what we now call the Folk – made the valleys and plains their home, in the heart of the Middle Worlds. The Tunnel Folk ('Maggots', we called them) lived in the darkness of World Below, mining for precious metals. Darker creatures – werewolves, hags and nameless things released through the river Dream – found their way into Ironwood, the sprawling forest that cut across much of the south of Inland, before it tailed off into marshland, salt flats, and finally, the One Sea.

The sky, too, had its territories. Sun and Moon – which, Odin said, were fragments of fire released from the forges of Chaos – rode in the sky in their chariots, each trying to outrun the other. The night sky was ablaze with stars; silent, ordered and serene. And as for the gods – because by then Odin had awarded himself divine status – there was Asgard, a citadel with its head in the clouds, overlooking the Southlands; linked to the Middle Worlds by Bif-rost – a long and narrow bridge of stone that gleamed in the sky like a rainbow.

Of course, they weren't quite gods. Not yet. Another tribe, the Vanir, had pretensions to godhood. The Vanir were bastard Firefolk, born from the dregs of Chaos and the promiscuity of Mankind, but they had powers that Odin's people – the Aesir – could neither grasp nor duplicate. What's more, the Vanir had *runes* with which to write down their own version of history; runes that, cunningly used, could ensure that their tribe lived forever in memory.

From the beginning Odin, whose ambitions lay that way himself, coveted these mysterious runes – letters from a secret script – and the powers that came with them. But the Vanir, predictably, weren't interested in sharing.

There followed a series of skirmishes. The Aesir, though weaker in numbers, were by far the better tacticians but the Vanir had glamours and runes on their side, and managed to resist them. The Old Man tried to negotiate, promising gold in exchange for the runes, and for a while it almost seemed as if they would come to a peaceful arrangement.

The Vanir sent an envoy to Asgard to begin discussing terms. She was Gullveig-Heid, the Sorceress, and she was ready to take on the gods for every piece of gold they had. She was a mistress of the Fire; a witch, like all the Vanir; a shapeshifter; a worker in runes; an oracle; a wielder of glam. She frightened them a little, I think, except perhaps for Odin, who watched her show off her powers with increasing amazement and jealousy.

She came to them as a beautiful woman, clothed from head

to foot in gold. Gold was in her unbound hair, and gold were the rings on her fingers and toes. She was the very glow and incarnation of Desire – and when she walked into the room, even Odin wanted her. She showed him the runes of the Elder Script tattooed on the palms of her hands and how she could use them to write his name on a sliver of stone, and then she showed him what *else* they could do, and promised to teach him – for a price.

Well, with Gullveig, nothing came free. Greed was in her nature. The price of peace with the Vanir was gold; every scrap the Aesir possessed. Otherwise, said the Sorceress, the Vanir would use their glam – their runes – to raze Asgard to the ground. And then Gullveig changed her Aspect from that of a beautiful woman to that of a grinning, gap-toothed crone, and laughed in their faces, and said to them:

'So which one will it be, boys? The golden girl or the viper-snake? I'm warning you, they both have teeth, and *not* where you're expecting them.'

The Aesir – never subtle – were outraged by this arrogance. That the Vanir should have chosen a woman to deliver their challenge was already insult enough, but her insolence and pride (both qualities I respect and admire) were enough to make Odin and his men lose control of what wits they had. They grabbed hold of Gullveig and threw her into the massive fireplace that burned in Odin's banquet hall, forgetting that she was a child of the Fire, and couldn't come to any harm.

Shifting to Fire Aspect, she laughed and mocked them from the flames and spat and promised retribution. Three times they tried to burn her up before the idiots realized the truth, by which time it was pretty clear that their chance at peace was over.

And yet the transition from dog to god is only a revolution away, and Odin was just getting started. The more he heard about the runes, the more he wanted them for himself, and the more frustrated he became. Because, as Gullveig had shown them, the runes were so much more than just a means of writing history. They were fragments from Chaos itself, charged with its fire and energy. The very language of Chaos was in those sixteen symbols; and with it, an awesome power.

Power to change the Worlds; to shape; to build; to rule; to conquer. With runes and the right kind of leadership, the Vanir should have made short work of Odin and his little band of revolutionaries. But they were Chaotic by nature, and had no proper leadership, while the Aesir had Odin as General, whose ruthlessness was almost as great as his cunning.

For decades the two sides were at war without either one gaining the upper hand; between them they scorched the Middle Worlds and reduced Asgard's walls to rubble. Gullveig saw the futility of waging war with the Aesir and left, with a handful of renegades, to establish herself in the mountains. She had no intention of ever sharing the runes with Odin and his people and so she went to the Ice Folk, who lived in the far North of Inland, and threw in her lot with them instead.

The Ice Folk were a savage race, directly descended from Ymir. They hated all the Aesir, who had driven them into the Northlands and stolen their birthright – the new World, built from Ymir's legacy. They hated the Vanir almost as much, but they respected Chaos, the fire of which ran through their veins, and when they heard Gullveig's proposal, they accepted it eagerly. Unlike the Aesir they were a matriarchal people and they had no problem accepting a woman's authority. Gullveig gave them a share in her glam and in exchange they taught her everything they knew about hunting, fishing, weapons, boats and survival in the cheerless North.

Under Gullveig's influence, the Ice Folk grew in power and strength. They were many in number, while the Aesir and Vanir were few. They created strongholds in the mountains, with fortresses built into the rock. They carved valleys through the glacier ice and made roads through the mountains.

Some of them moved from the Northlands into the forest of Ironwood, only a stone's throw from Ida, the plain above which

Asgard stood. They used Gullveig's runes to shift Aspect, taking the forms of animals – snow wolves, hunting birds – to hunt and spy on their enemies. They preyed on Aesir and Vanir alike, growing in malice every day, until at last the General realized that unless they worked together, both Aesir and Vanir would fall to this new, unexpected threat.

But, after years of conflict, neither side trusted the other. How could they hope to keep the peace without assurances of faith? Odin's solution seemed simple.

'We'll make an exchange,' he told them. 'Your people, your expertise for ours. We can learn a great deal from each other if only we cooperate. And if either side betrays the other, they'll have a handful of hostages to deal with as they see fit.'

It seemed like a reasonable idea. The Vanir agreed to the exchange. They would give Odin the runes while he would share with them the art of war and provide them with leaders who would teach them the value of order and discipline.

And so after long discussion, the Vanir accepted to hand over Njörd, the Man of the Sea, with his children, Frey and Freyja. In exchange they got Mimir the Wise, Odin's uncle, good friend and confidant, and a handsome young man called Honir (nicknamed 'The Silent' in the hope that one day he might take the hint), whom Odin had chosen, not for his skills, but precisely because he was the least likely of the Aesir to be missed when the inevitable happened.

For a while, the arrangement worked. The three guests taught the General the runes – the sixteen letters of the Elder Script. First, they taught him to read and write, ensuring his place in history. Then came the occult side of the runes – their names, their verses, their fingerings. Each of the Vanir had one special rune that governed his or her Aspect; this gave the Vanir their power, and allowed them to direct the runes, each in his own, individual way. And so Odin passed on his new-found skills to the rest of the Aesir, allocating to each of them a rune according to their nature. Thus Odin's son Thor got *Thúris*, the

Thorny One, rune of strength and protection; Thor's wife Sif got *Ár*, rune of plenty and fruitfulness; Týr, Odin's war chief, was given *Týr*, the Warrior; Balder the Fair, Odin's youngest son, had *Fé*, the golden rune of success; and Odin himself kept two runes: *Kaen*, Wildfire – more of that later – and *Raedo*, the Journeyman, a humble rune at first glance, but which gave him access to places where the others never ventured, even to the Lands of the Dead and the borders of Pandaemonium.

Meanwhile, back in the Vanir camp, Mimir and Honir stalled for time, spying, finding out secrets, whilst giving out false information about Odin, the Aesir and their tactics. Mimir was clever enough in his way, but not enough to win the game. And Honir *looked* the part all right, but every time he opened his mouth (which he did rather a lot) he confirmed what the Vanir suspected; that there was a lot less to him than met the eye.

Of course, the idiots bungled it. They should have seen it coming. In those days Odin was far from being the subtle schemer he was to become. But he *was* ruthless even then; willing to sacrifice his friends to get whatever he wanted. He must have known that by sending them into the enemy camp to spy, he'd practically signed their death warrants. Remember *that* when you find yourself starting to think the Old Man's on the side of the angels. Remember how he got where he is. And never turn your back on him unless you're wearing a metal shirt.

In the end, the Vanir lost patience. They started to suspect their new friends. And Honir, never the most discreet, kept letting information slip. Finally, they understood that Odin had had the best of the deal; he'd learnt the secret of the runes without giving anything in return, and left them with a spy and a stooge and a lot of unanswered questions.

Of course, by then it was too late to review terms. And so the Vanir, in revenge, grabbed Mimir and cut off his head, and sent Honir back with it to Asgard. But the Old Man took the Head and, using his newly acquired skills, preserved it with runes, and made it speak, so that Mimir's well of knowledge was passed onto the General, and Odin the Ruthless became Odin the Wise, unchallenged and beloved by all – except perhaps by Mimir's Head, which he kept in a cold spring that led straight down to the River Dream.

But in the end Odin paid for sacrificing Mimir. The first down-payment was his eye, as part of the spell that kept Mimir alive. The rest, well. More of that later. Suffice it to say at this point: never trust an oracle. And never trust a wise man to do the work of a felon.

If I'd been in Asgard then, I'd have stolen the runes *and* kept my head and saved us all a lot of unpleasantness. Wisdom isn't everything. Survival requires an element of trickery; Chaos; subterfuge. All qualities I possess (if I may say so) in abundance. I would have been in my element spying for the Aesir. I would have taught them a trick or two that even the Vanir didn't possess. Mimir the Wise wasn't wise enough. Honir 'The Silent' should have kept shtum. And Odin should have known from the first that perfect Order does not bend; it simply stands until it breaks, which is why it rarely survives for any meaningful length of time. The General didn't know it then, but what he needed was a friend; a friend whose morals were flexible enough to handle the moral low ground while Odin lorded it on high, keeping Order, untouchable . . .

Basically, he needed *me*.

LESSON 3

Blood and Water

Never trust a relative.

Lokabrenna

Now I'm not claiming Odin *made* the Worlds. Even Odin doesn't say that. The Worlds have ended and been rebuilt so many times that no one knows how they came about. But Odin certainly *shaped* them. To the Folk of the Middle Worlds, that kind of power meant godhood, and with Asgard and the runes on his side, the Old Man was unstoppable. From the shores of the One Sea to the banks of the river Dream, everything was under his command, and his rivals – the Rock Folk, the unruly Ice Folk – were, if not *entirely* subdued, at least obliged to watch his triumphant ascent in sullen, angry silence.

But with power comes responsibility. And with responsibility comes fear. And with fear, comes violence. And with violence comes Chaos . . .

This is where Yours Truly comes in. Time to pay attention. Till then I'd existed in Chaos, of course, in the world of Pandaemonium. Chaos, the pure; Chaos, the wild; Chaos, the unpolluted. Ruled by Disorder in its primary Aspect in the form of Lord Surt, the Destroyer; Father of glam; Master of Change; the original wellspring of the Fire. The Vanir were only bastard Firefolk, living off the scraps of glam that fell from Lord Surt's table. But I was Wildfire incarnate; a true son of Chaos; happy and free.

Well, maybe not *entirely* free. Or even entirely happy. Lord Surt was a jealous master; pitiless; all-consuming. There was no reasoning with Surt; he was, by nature, unreasonable. You might as well try reasoning with an erupting volcano, or a thunderstorm, or the pox. And we were formless, innocent, hostile to *everything* that lay beyond the borders of our world, and that was how Surt meant us to stay; perfect Chaos, unfettered by form, blissfully free of all the rules of god, mankind or physics.

I, on the other hand, was perverse. It was, after all, my nature. And I was curious to know more about the other Worlds that lay beyond our boundaries; Worlds in which Order and Chaos met and sometimes co-existed; where creatures kept to the same shape, and lived and died without tasting the Fire.

Of course I'd already heard of the gods. The warring parties – well, most of them – had put aside their differences, and the survivors of that war – twenty-four Aesir and Vanir in all – were living together in Asgard. It wasn't an easy alliance. Some of the Vanir had refused to accept Odin as their General, and had broken away to join forces with Gullveig in the Northlands. Others allied themselves with the Rock Folk, some buried themselves in World Below, some fled to the forests of Inland and hid away in animal form. Thus were the old runes scattered and lost; divided between our enemies, bastardized and gone to seed like grain reverting to wild stock.

Of course, in time this bastardization had its effects in Chaos. Runes have their primal source in the Fire, and every time Aesir or Vanir used a piece of their stolen glam, every time they shifted Aspect or cast a rune at an enemy, every time they dipped a toe into the river Dream, or wrote down a story, or even carved their name into the trunk of a fallen tree, Chaos shivered in outrage and I grew increasingly curious. Who were these people, whose influence I could feel across the Worlds? How was it that I could sense them, and did they even know I was there?

Meanwhile, in Asgard, the twenty-four remained in a citadel blasted by war; torn by petty rivalries; arguing incessantly; easy targets for anyone who fancied trying for godhood. I saw them mostly through their dreams, which were small and unimaginative but which nevertheless gave me food for thought. Perhaps even then a part of me knew how badly they needed a friend, and how much I could help them, if only they could put aside their puny little prejudices.

In those days the General liked to travel in Journeyman Aspect throughout the Worlds. His blind eye, sacrificed to the runes, saw much further than his living one ever had, and he was obsessed with exploration and the pursuit of knowledge. He was a great traveller in Dream – that river that skirts our borders, flowing alongside Death itself, dividing this world from the next – and he would often watch our realm from the far side of the river, muttering cantrips to himself and squinting through his blind eye.

He didn't look all that impressive back then – a tall man in his fifties, with unruly grey hair and an eyepatch. But even then I sensed that he was something out of the ordinary. For a start, he had glam – that primal fire stolen from Chaos, which the Folk later came to call *magic* and to fear with a superstitious awe. I could see it in the colours swirling all around him and by the signature he left, as unique as a fingerprint; a broad blaze of kingfisher-blue across the bleakness of rocks and snow. I'd seen that signature in dreams that were bigger and brighter than the rest and now I could almost *hear* him, too; his soft and coaxing voice; his words:

Loki, son of Laufey.

Son of Farbauti – Wildfire—

We didn't have much need for names back in Pandaemonium. Of course I *had* them – everything does – but back then they had no power over me. As for my family, such as it was – well, demons have no family. My father was a lightning-strike and my mother was a pile of dry twigs (no that's *not* a metaphor), which, to be fair to Yours Truly, made for pretty poor parenting.

In any case, Wildfire is hard to control: volatile; unpredictable. I'm not making excuses or anything, but it's in my nature to be troublesome. Surt should have known it; Odin, too. Both got what was coming to them.

Leaving Chaos was strictly forbidden, of course, but I was young and curious. I'd seen the man so many times staring into our domain, watching us from Dream and beyond, working his primitive glamours. To be frank, I felt almost sorry for him; as a man sitting by a roaring fire might feel for the beggar sitting outside, trying to warm his hands with a match. But this beggar had a noble look, for all his rags and shivering. It was a look that told me that, sooner or later, he meant to be king. I rather admired his arrogance; I wondered how he would do it. And so, that day, for the first time, in defiance of Surt and of all the laws of Chaos, I left my fiery Aspect and ventured out into World Above.

For a moment I was disoriented. Too many sensations, all of them new, enveloped my new Aspect. I could see colours; I could smell sulphur; I could feel the snow in the air and see the face of the man before me, cloaked in glam from head to foot. I could have chosen any form: that of an animal, or a bird, or just a simple trail of fire. But, as it happened, I'd assumed the form with which you may be familiar; that of a young man with red hair and a certain *je ne sais quoi*.

The man stared at me in amazement (and, dare I say, admiration). I knew that behind my human disguise he knew me for a child of the Fire. A demon, if you prefer the term; although to be honest, the difference between god and demon is really only a matter of perspective.

'Are you real?' he said at last.

Well, of course, that's a relative term. *Everything*'s real on some level, you know, even (maybe especially) dreams. But

I wasn't used to speaking aloud. In Chaos, such things are unnecessary. Nor had I been expecting the sheer impact of physicality; the sounds (the wind; the crunch of the snow; the thumping of a snow hare on the side of a nearby hill); the sights; the colours; the cold; the fear . . .

Fear? Yes, I suppose it was fear. It was my first real emotion. Chaos in its purest form is free of all emotion, working on instinct, and instinct alone. Pure Chaos is without thought. That's why it only ever takes shape when in the face of the enemy, taking its form from the enemy's thoughts; its substance from his deepest fears.

Still, it *was* an intriguing experience – if somewhat claustrophobic – to keep to a single physical form, constrained by its limitations; feeling the cold, half-blind with the light, assailed by all those sensations.

I flexed my limbs experimentally, tried the speaking-aloud thing. It worked. Still, with hindsight, I can't help thinking that if I'd *really* wanted to try and blend in, I should have thought myself up some clothes.

I shivered. 'Gog and Magog, it's cold. Seriously, are you trying to tell me that you people *choose* to live out here?'

He fixed me with his one eye; blue and chilly and none too kind. Behind him, his colours showed no fear, just wariness and cunning.

'So. You're Loki, are you?' he said.

I shrugged my new shoulders. 'What's in a name? A rose by any other name would smell just as pink and virginal. And speaking of which, if you could find your way to lending me some *clothes* . . .'

He did – some breeches and a shirt, taken from his backpack, and smelling rather strongly of goat. I put them on, grimacing at the smell, as my new acquaintance introduced himself as Odin, one of the sons of Bór. I knew him by reputation, of course. I'd followed his career from afar. I'd watched his dreams. I wasn't what you'd call impressed – and yet his ambition and ruthlessness were not without potential.

We talked. He explained his position as General in Asgard; painted a pretty picture of the Sky Citadel and its inhabitants; spoke of Worlds to conquer and rich rewards to be won, then moved onto the subject of a possible alliance with my folk against the Ice People, the renegade Vanir, Gullveig-Heid and the warlords who occupied the Outlands.

I had to laugh. 'I don't think so.'

'Why not?'

I explained that Lord Surt was really not an alliance kind of guy. '"Xenophobic" doesn't begin to cover how much he despises strangers. It's bad enough that your kind of life emerged from the ice in the first place, but you'll never get him making a deal with a race of people that entered the Worlds naked and covered in cow-spit.'

'But if we could talk—' Odin began.

'Surt doesn't talk. He's a primal force. He reduces Order in all its forms into its component particles. From the mightiest warlord to the tiniest ant, he hates you all impartially. Simply by virtue of being alive and conscious, you're already an offence to him. You can't talk him round. You can't *par-lay*. All you can do, if you've got any sense, is simply to keep out of his way.'

Odin looked thoughtful. 'And yet *you* came.'

'Shoot me. I was curious.'

Of course, he didn't understand. The closest he'd ever got to Chaos was through Dream, its ephemeral sibling. And primitive people always imagine their gods to be something like themselves; at best, a kind of warlord, with a warlord's mentality. For all his intelligence, I could tell that Odin would never understand the scale and the grandeur of Chaos – at least not until the End of the Worlds, by which time it would be too late.

'I'm going to rule the Worlds,' he said. 'I have power, gold, runes. I have the finest warriors the Worlds have ever seen. I have the Sun and Moon. I have the wealth of the Tunnel Folk—'

'Lord Surt isn't into possessions,' I said. 'This is Chaos we're talking about. Nothing has substance, or order, or rules. Nothing even keeps to the same physical Aspect. These things you care so much about – gold, weapons, women, battlements – I've seen them all in your dreams, and none of that means a thing to him. To Surt, it's all just cosmic debris; flotsam and jetsam on the tide.'

'Forget Lord Surt for a minute,' he said. 'Maybe you're right. But what about you? It seems to me that someone like you could be a big hit in my camp.'

'I bet they could. What's in it for me?'

'Well, freedom, to begin with. Freedom and opportunity.'

'Freedom? Do me a favour. Do you think I'm not free?'

He shook his head. 'You think you are? When there are Worlds to discover and shape, and you have to stay in one place all the time? You're no more than a prisoner of this Surt, whoever he is.'

I tried to explain. 'But Chaos is, like, the hotbed of creation. Everything else is just overspill. Who wants to live in a septic tank?'

'Better a king in the gutter,' he said, 'than a slave in an emperor's palace.'

You see, that silver tongue of his was already making mischief. And then he started to talk to me of the Worlds he'd visited; of the Middle World, abode of the Folk, where already the people of Asgard were beginning to be worshipped as gods; of the Tunnel Folk of World Below, toiling to bring out gold and gems from the darkness; of the World Tree, Yggdrasil, its roots in the depths of the Underworld, its head in the clouds of Asgard; of Ice Folk; of the One Sea; of the Outlands far beyond. All ripe for conquest, Odin said; everything new and up for burning. All that could be mine, he said, or I could go back to Chaos and spend an eternity shining Surt's shoes . . .

'What do you want from me?' I said.

'I need your talents,' said Odin. 'The Vanir gave me their knowledge, but even runes aren't everything. I brought this world out of blood and ice. I gave it rules and a purpose. Now I must protect what I've built, or see it slide back into anarchy. But Order cannot survive alone; its laws are too fixed; it cannot bend. Order is like ice that creeps, bringing life to a standstill. Now that we're at peace again, Aesir and Vanir, the ice will creep back. Stagnation will come. My kingdom will fall into darkness. I cannot be seen to break my own rules. But I do need someone on my side who can break them for me when necessary.'

'And what do I get in return, again?'

He grinned and said: 'I'll make you a god.'

A god.

Well, you've seen the Prophecy. Odin was already tacitly taking credit for the creation of the Worlds as well as the birth of humanity. Thus:

> *From the Alder and the Ash,*
> *They fashioned the first Folk from wood.*
> *One gave spirit; one gave speech;*
> *One gave fire in the blood.*

Folk have a tendency to assume that the third one, the fire-giver, was Your Humble Narrator. Well, I may be guilty of many things but I'm not taking the blame for the Folk, or anything to do with them. Wherever they came from, it sure as Hel wasn't a couple of trees and Yours Truly. And whatever the Oracle *really* meant, it was not to be taken literally. Still, it was a common tale, and did no harm to Odin's burgeoning reputation as the daddy of us all.

For now, back to the story, and Odin's promise of godhood. *Well . . .*

He had a point about Chaos, I thought. There are advantages to being an independent entity. In Pandaemonium, I knew I would always be a spark in a forge; a flicker in a bonfire; a drop in an ocean of molten dreams. In Odin's new world, I could be anything I wanted to be: an agent of change; a firebrand; a worker of miracles. A god.

Which all sounded quite appealing, but . . .

'Of course, you could never go back,' he said.

I thought about that too. He was right. Chaos may not have *rules* as such, but it does have *laws*, and I knew its lords had ingenious ways of dealing with people who broke them. Still . . .

'How would they even know? Like you said, I'm a drop in the ocean.'

'Oh, I would need assurances of your good faith,' said Odin. 'Look at it from my point of view. It's going to be hard enough for me to explain your presence to the Aesir. I need to be sure of your loyalty before I open Asgard's gates.'

'Of course,' I said.

Oh, please, I thought. Loyalty, honour, truth, good faith – all those things belong to Order. The children of Chaos neither need nor fully understand them.

But somehow the Old Man had read my mind. 'I'm not going to ask for your word,' he said. 'But all the same, I'll need something. A mark of allegiance, if you like.'

I shrugged. 'What kind of a mark?' I said.

'*This*,' said Odin, and suddenly, I felt a searing sensation in my arm. At the same time, something hit me so hard that I fell onto my back in the snow. Colours blazed around me. Later, I learnt that this was called *pain*. I already knew I wasn't a fan.

'What in Pandaemonium was *that*?'

Of course, in my fiery Aspect I'd never experienced physical pain. In some ways, I was still very innocent. But I *did* recognize some kind of attack, and leapt back into my primary form, ready to rejoin Pandaemonium.

'I wouldn't do that if I were you,' said Odin, seeing my intention. 'My mark is on you now. My glam. We're brothers, whether you like it or not.'

I jumped back into physical form, and – dammit – I found I was naked again. 'No *way* am I your brother,' I said.

'We're brothers in blood,' said Odin. 'Or brothers in glam, if you prefer.'

I touched my arm. It still hurt. But now, on the new pink flesh, there was a mark, a kind of tattoo, which gleamed a soft violet against my skin. The sting was fading but the mark, the shape of a broken twig, endured.

'What's that? What did you do to me?'

Odin sat down on a rock. Whatever he had done to me had taken a great deal of glam from him. His colours had faded considerably, and his face was almost colourless.

'Call it a badge of loyalty,' he said. 'All my people have one now. The Vanir taught us their names and their use; yours is *Kaen*, Wildfire. Quite appropriate, I thought, given your demonic nature.'

'But I don't need a badge,' I said. 'These runes of yours' – I indicated the violet mark – 'they're just some of the letters that make up the language of Chaos. I don't need runes to do what I do. I can tap Chaos at the *source*.'

'Not in this World, or this body, you can't. Your Aspect determines what you can do.'

'Oh.' I should have thought of that. Of course, glam in its purest form exists only in the realms of Chaos and Dream. Here, I'd have to work for it. *Work*. Like *pain*, I sensed that this was an experience I would want to avoid as often as possible.

'That wasn't part of the deal,' I said. But I knew the old fox had me cold. As soon as he gave me that runemark, some part of his glam and mine had merged. If I returned to Chaos now, they'd know I had betrayed them. And now, I had no other choice but to go with his offer of godhood.

'You bastard. You knew this would happen,' I said.

Odin gave a wry smile. 'Then that makes us brothers in trickery. But I told you the truth,' he said. 'I'll never forget what I owe you. I'll never take a drink of wine without first seeing your goblet filled. And whatever your nature drives you to do, I promise that none of my people will ever lay violent hands on you. You'll be as close as a brother to me. As long as you promise to serve me, of course.'

What choice did I have? I gave him my word. Not that a promise means much to a demon – or a god. But I *did* serve him. I served him well; though half the time even he didn't know what he really needed. And even when he reneged on the deal . . .

But more of that later. Suffice it to say: never trust a brother.

LESSON 4

Hello and Welcome

Never trust a friend.

Lokabrenna

AND SO I CAME TO ASGARD, where Odin introduced me to my new friends, the twenty-three Aesir and Vanir. All of them burnished, sleek and well-fed, dressed in furs and silks and brocade, crowned in gold and gemstones and generally looking rather pleased with themselves.

You've probably already heard of Asgard. The Worlds were already full of tales about its size; its magnificence; its twenty-four halls, one for each god; its gardens, cellars and sports facilities. A citadel built on an outcrop of rock so high above the plain below that it seemed part of the clouds themselves; a place of sunlight and rainbows, accessible only by the Rainbow Bridge that linked it to the Middle Worlds. That's the story, anyway. And yes, it *was* impressive. But in those days it was smaller, protected by its location; a cluster of wooden buildings surrounded by a palisade. Later, it grew, but at that time it still looked like a pioneer stronghold under siege – which was *exactly* what it was.

We met in Odin's hall, a sizeable, warm, vaulted space with twenty-three seats, a long table set with food and drink, and Odin's gilded throne at the head. Everyone had a seat but me.

It stank of smoke and ale and sweat. No one offered me a drink. I looked at the cold faces around me and thought: *This club isn't taking new members.*

'This is Loki,' the Old Man announced. 'He's going to be one of the family, so let's all make him welcome, and no picking on him because of his unfortunate parentage.'

'*What* unfortunate parentage?' said Frey, the leader of the Vanir.

I gave them all a little wave and told them I was from Chaos.

A second later I was flat on my back, with two dozen swords jabbing at the parts of me I've always preferred to keep intact.

'Ouch!' Unlike the rest of my newly acquired physical sensations, the pain thing wasn't getting any more fun. I considered the possibility that this might be some kind of an initiation ceremony, more of a game than anything else. Then I looked at those faces again; the narrowed eyes; the bared teeth . . .

No doubt about it, I told myself. *These bastards really don't like me.*

'You brought a *demon* into Asgard?' said Týr, the General's war chief. 'Are you out of your mind? He's a spy. Probably an assassin, as well. I say slit the little rat's throat.'

Odin gave him a quelling look. 'Let him go, Captain.'

'You're kidding,' said Týr.

'I said, let him go. He's under my protection.'

Reluctantly, the hedge of blades was withdrawn from around Yours Truly. I sat up and tried a winning smile. No one around me seemed to be won.

'Er, hi,' I said. 'I know it must seem strange to you that someone like me should want to hang out with people like you. But give me a chance and I'll prove to you I'm not a spy. I swear it. I've burnt my boats by coming here; I'm a traitor to my people. Send me back, and they'll kill me – or worse.'

'So?' That was Heimdall; a flashy type, with golden armour and teeth to match. 'We don't need a traitor's help. Treachery's a crooked rune that never flies straight, or hits the mark.'

That was typical Heimdall, or so I came to realize later. Pompous, rude and arrogant. His rune was *Madr*, straight as a die; boxy and pedestrian. I thought of the mark of *Kaen* on my arm and said:

'Sometimes crooked is better than straight.'

'You think so?' said Heimdall.

'Let's try it,' I said. 'My glam against yours. Let Odin decide the victor.'

There was an archery target outside. I'd noticed it as we came in. The gods were predictably keen on sports; popular types so often are. I'd never used a bow before, but I understood the principle.

'Come on, Goldie,' I said, and grinned. 'Or are you having second thoughts?'

'I'll give you this,' he said. 'You can talk. Now let's see how well you perform.'

Aesir and Vanir followed us out. Odin came last, looking curious. 'Heimdall's the best shot in Asgard,' he said. 'The Vanir call him Hawkeye.'

I shrugged. 'So what?'

'So you'd better be good.'

I grinned again. 'I'm Loki,' I said. '*Good* doesn't enter into it.'

We stood in front of the target. I could tell from his colours that Heimdall was sure of beating me; his golden smile radiated confidence. Behind him, all the rest of them stared at me with suspicion and scorn. I'd thought that *I* knew prejudice, but this lot redefined it. I could see them itching to spill some of my demon blood, even though it ran through the veins of a dozen or more of them. Heimdall himself was one of them – a bastard child of the primal Fire – but I could see he wasn't about to celebrate our kinship. There are races that hate each other on sight – mongoose and snake; cat and dog – and though I didn't know much of the Worlds, I guessed that the straightforward, muscular type would be the natural enemy of the lithe and devious type who thinks with his head and not his fists.

'How far? A hundred paces? More?'

I shrugged. 'You choose. I couldn't care less. I'm going to beat you anyway.'

Once more, Heimdall smiled. He beckoned two servants forward and pointed at a distant spot right at the end of the Rainbow Bridge.

'Stand the target there,' he told them. 'Then, when Loki loses his bet, he won't have quite so far to walk home.'

I said nothing, but only smiled.

The servants set off. They took their time. Meanwhile I lay down on the grass and pretended to have a little nap. I might even have slept a little, if Bragi, the god of music and song, hadn't already been working on a victory chant for Heimdall. To be fair, his voice wasn't bad, but the subject matter wasn't entirely to my taste. Besides, he was playing a lute. I hate lutes.

Ten minutes later, I opened one eye. Heimdall was looking down at me.

'I've got pins and needles,' I said. 'You go first. Whatever you do, I promise I can do better.'

Heimdall bared his golden teeth, then summoned the rune *Madr*, aimed and fired. I didn't see where the rune struck – my eyes weren't nearly as good as his – but I could see from the flash of his golden teeth that it must have been good.

I stretched and yawned.

'Your turn, traitor,' he said.

'All right. But bring the target closer.'

Heimdall looked puzzled. 'What do you mean?'

'I said, bring the target closer. I can hardly see it from here. About three dozen paces should do.'

Heimdall's face was a study in confusion. 'You say you're going to win – against *me* – by bringing the target *closer*?'

'Wake me up when you've brought it,' I said, and lay down for another nap.

Ten minutes later, the servants returned, carrying the

target. I could see Heimdall's strike now, the rose-red signature of *Madr* stamped right in the bullseye. The Aesir and the Vanir all clapped. It *was* a fairly impressive shot.

'Hawkeye Heimdall wins,' said Frey, another handsome, athletic type all gleaming with silver armour. The others seemed inclined to agree. I guess Frey was too popular for them to contradict him – or maybe it was the runesword balanced suggestively at his hip that made them want to stay friends with him. An elegant piece, that runesword. Even at that early stage I found myself wondering if he would be as popular without it.

Odin turned his one eye upon Your Humble Narrator. 'Well?'

'Well – not bad. Bird-Brain can shoot,' I said. 'But I can beat him.'

'It's *Hawkeye*, actually,' said Heimdall, between clenched teeth. 'And if you think you're going to win by standing right *next* to the target—'

'*Now* we turn it round,' I said.

Once more, Heimdall looked confused. 'But that would—'

'Yes. That's right,' I said.

Heimdall shrugged and gestured to the two servants, who obediently turned the target around so that the bullseye was on the back.

'*Now* try to hit the bullseye,' I said.

Heimdall sneered. 'That's impossible.'

'You're saying you couldn't?'

'No one could.'

I grinned and summoned the rune *Kaen*. A fiery rune, a quick rune, a shapeshifting, clever, *crooked* rune. And instead of shooting it straight at the target, as Heimdall had done, I flicked the rune to one side, sending it into a wide curve to double back on itself, ricochet, then strike the bullseye from behind, obliterating *Madr* in a blaze of violet. A trick shot, but a nice one.

I looked at the Old Man. 'Well?' I said.

Odin laughed. 'An impossible shot.'

Heimdall snarled. 'A trick,' he said.

'Nevertheless, Loki wins.'

The other gods were forced to agree, with varying degrees of grace. Odin clapped me on the back. Thor did too – so hard, in fact, that he nearly knocked me over. Someone poured me a cup of wine, and from the first mouthful I realized that *this* was one of the few things that made my corporeal Aspect worthwhile.

But Heimdall stayed silent. He left the hall with the dignified walk of a man with a serious case of piles and I knew I'd made an enemy. Some people would have laughed it off, but not Heimdall. From that day on till the End of the Worlds, nothing would ever make him forget that first humiliation. Not that I *wanted* to be friends. Friendship is overrated. Who needs friends when you can have the certitudes of hostility? You know where you stand with an enemy. You know he won't betray you. It's the ones who claim to be your *friends* that you need to beware of. Still, that was a lesson I was yet to learn. Then, I was still hopeful. Hopeful that in time I might be able somehow to prove myself; that one day, they might accept me.

Yes, it's sometimes hard to believe that I was ever *that* innocent. But I was like a puppy who doesn't yet know that the people who have adopted him will keep him chained in a kennel all day and feed him nothing but sawdust. I find it takes a little time to learn that kind of lesson. So, until then, remember this: *Never trust a friend.*

LESSON 5

Bricks and Mortar

Never trust a labourer.

Lokabrenna

AND SO, Your Humble Narrator received a grudging acceptance, though it was hardly the warm welcome that the General
had promised me. It wasn't just that I was racially different, or
physically less imposing, or radical in my opinions, or unfamil-
iar with their ways. It was simply (and I say this in all modesty)
that I was a whole lot *cleverer* than the rest of the folk in Asgard.
Clever folk aren't popular, by and large. They arouse suspicion.
They don't fit in. They can be useful, as I proved on a number
of occasions, but among the general population there's always a
sense of vague mistrust, as if the very qualities that make them
indispensable also make them dangerous.

There were a few compensations to having corporeal Aspect.
Food (jam tarts were my favourites); drink (mostly wine and
mead); setting things on fire; sex (although I was still extremely
confused by all the taboos surrounding this – no animals, no
siblings, no men, no married women, no demons – frankly, it
was amazing to me that *anyone* had sex at all, with so many
rules against it). There was also sleep, which I enjoyed; and
flying above the battlements in hawk Aspect (and occasionally
shedding a well-aimed load onto Heimdall's golden armour as

he stood watch on Bif-rost). This, I discovered, was *humour*, another new sensation for me – and in its way even better than sex, although here again, it was hard to know where to draw the limits.

By then, I had already found out that there was as much xenophobia in Order as in Chaos, especially among the Vanir, of which Heimdall was the worst. In my experience, it's always the mixed-race types who are the most sensitive, and being half-born of Chaos themselves, they felt a special need to express their moral superiority over such scum as Yours Truly.

Among them, besides Heimdall, there was Frey, the Reaper, and his twin sister Freyja, a bold-eyed hussy to whom Odin had given the title of Goddess of Desire. Both were tall, bronze-haired and blue-eyed and drawn to reflective surfaces.

Then there was Bragi, the Bard, and his wife, Idun the Healer, keeper of the Apples of Youth – both lute-playing crystal-gazers of the most tiresome kind, who believed in the healing power of song and liked to wear flowers in their hair. Then there was Njörd, the Fisherman, who spent much of his free time standing in rivers, tickling trout; and Aegir, the Sailor, who, with his glaucous wife Ran had assumed the role of Lord of the Waves. Their hall was underwater, guarded by luminous jellyfish, and they ruled there on thrones made of mother-of-pearl, their long hair waving like seaweed.

On the side of the Aesir, there was Odin's eldest son Thor, known as the Thunderer (I assumed at first for his unruly bowels), a muscle-bound oaf with more beard than brain and a love of sports and hitting things. His wife was Bright-Haired Sif, a blonde prone to excess poundage, whom Odin had accorded (not without humour, I thought) the title of Goddess of Plenty.

Then there was Frigg, the Enchantress, Odin's calm, long-suffering wife; Honir, nicknamed the Silent for his apparent ability to speak without ever stopping for breath; Týr, the god of War, a strong and mostly silent type with an underbite like a bulldog's; Hoder, Odin's blind son; and his brother Balder, nicknamed the Fair, whom I hated on sight with a particular intensity.

Why Balder, do you ask? Some things are just instinctive. It wasn't that he disliked *me* – that, after all, was hardly unprecedented. It wasn't that women adored him, or that men all wanted to *be* him. It wasn't even that Balder was handsome, brave, good and true, or that if he as much as farted, birds sang, flowers bloomed and small, furry animals gambolled and frolicked around him in joyous abandon. To tell the truth, I don't really know *why* I hated Balder. Perhaps because people *liked* him so much; perhaps because he'd never had to struggle for acceptance. Face it, the guy was born with a whole set of golden cutlery in his mouth, and if he was good, it was only because he'd never had to be otherwise. And to make matters worse, it was *he* who first poured me a cup of wine, put a garland on my head, and told me I was welcome.

Welcome. The snivelling hypocrite.

Welcome? Hardly the welcome that Odin had led me to expect. And in spite of Balder's efforts to make me into one of the boys – to rope me into sporting events, to introduce me to unmarried girls, to generally encourage me to let my hair down and 'chillax' – I could tell that most of Asgard still secretly despised me. At last they had a whipping boy; someone to despise, to blame. And blame me they did, for *everything*.

If Freyja got a spot on her nose, it was always Loki's fault. If Bragi's lute was out of tune, if Thor lost one of his gauntlets, if someone farted audibly during one of Odin's speeches – ten to one I'd get the blame.

All the others had halls of their own. I was stuck in a backroom with no running water, miles away from anywhere, damp and gloomy and in a draught. I had no servants, no fine clothes, no rank. No one offered to show me around. Call me picky if you like, but I'd hoped that Odin's new brother might have had

35

a more royal treatment.

Still, you'll notice that history doesn't reveal what happened to Odin's *other* brothers, the legendary Vili and Ve. Probably buried under a patio somewhere, or scattered across the nine Worlds. In any case, there I was, regarded with veiled hostility by most of my new friends – except for the ladies, from whom I received a slightly warmer reception.

Well, don't blame *me* for being attractive. Demons are, for the most part. Besides, it wasn't as if the competition was especially tough. Sweaty, hairy warlords with no polish and no address, whose idea of a good time was to kill a few giants, wrestle a snake and then eat an ox and six suckling pigs without even taking a shower first, whilst belching a popular folk song. Of *course* the ladies gave me the eye. A bad boy is always appealing, and I'd always had a silver tongue.

One of Freyja's handmaidens seemed especially taken with me – Sigyn, a motherly type with a soupy expression and a not-unpleasant figure, which she hid under a series of demure floral housedresses. Even Thor's wife, Bright-Haired Sif, wasn't entirely immune to my charm, which ran more to witty conversation than merely hitting things, a welcome change in Testosterone Central.

Nevertheless, I began to sense that tensions were running against me. I'd been with the Old Man some time by then, and I still had to prove my worth to him. Not that he'd said so in as many words, but there was a kind of chill in the air whenever he and I were alone, and I sensed that sooner or later he would start to put the screws on me. Besides, we'd had trouble from the North: the Rock Folk had attacked us twice; first taking the lower flanks of Asgard's mountain, where there was a flat ledge on which they could build and shelter, then by flinging huge rocks at us by means of giant catapults.

This was a first for the Rock Folk; we knew they were excellent builders, carving great halls from the mountains, but we'd never seen them build engines before, or come at us in such numbers. Odin guessed that there must be a new warlord on the scene, maybe working with Gullveig-Heid, with aspirations of godhood. The Ice Folk were also restless – they often were in summertime – and had moved down from the Northern lands to gather on the outskirts of Ironwood. From Asgard, they looked like packs of wolves circling; wary at first, awaiting their opportunity. But Odin knew the Ice Folk to be more of a threat than they appeared. Many had fragments of rune lore bartered from the renegade Vanir, and they were masters of shapeshifting, often travelling in wolf, bear or eagle Aspect. They were less organized than the Rock Folk, living in smaller communities, often warring among themselves, but if at last they had decided to put their rivalries aside, as the Aesir had done with the Vanir . . .

Suffice it to say that Odin was more than a little concerned about this; and although so far neither tribe had managed to reach the Sky Citadel, their numbers were growing alarmingly. The warriors of Asgard – Thor, Týr and Frey – had made short work of the rock-slinging engines of the Rock Folk, but the enemy had not withdrawn as far as we had expected. Instead they remained around Ironwood, mostly hidden from our eyes, which made the Old Man all the more cautious. The perfect time of crisis, in fact, for me to show my value to the gods. All I needed was the right opportunity.

This finally came when Heimdall – who, by token of his keen vision, had appointed himself Watchman for the rest of us – saw a figure on horseback slowly approaching Asgard. The Ice Folk never used horses – horses don't thrive in the far North. The Rock Folk did, but not often, and besides, the lone rider didn't look as if he was trying to stage an attack. He was too slow, to start with. Dressed like a rustic from the Lowlands, he was both unarmed and unburdened; his signature showed no trace of glam, and he approached us openly across the plain, without any apparent concern.

This plain was called Ida, and in those days was a barren, arid wasteland, scattered with the fragments of Asgard's war defences, levelled during the conflict between the Aesir and Vanir. No one crossed it without intent – usually malevolent – and the gods all watched with suspicion as the rider neared the Rainbow Bridge.

Thor was all for hitting first and asking questions afterwards.

Týr, who was even less subtle than Thor, was of the opinion that hitting first, and then hitting some more afterwards, was probably the best way to go.

Heimdall thought it might be a trap, and that the stranger might be hiding a powerful glam behind his humble appearance.

Balder, who always tried to believe the best in everyone – until proved wrong, at which point he would look pained, as if he'd been personally betrayed – said *he* thought the man might be delivering a message of peace from our enemies.

Odin gave no opinion. He simply glanced at me briefly, then gestured at Heimdall to let the man pass. Twenty minutes later, the stranger was standing before Odin's high seat, with all the gods around him.

Closer inspection revealed him to be a broad-shouldered man with iron-grey hair, as slow and massive as his horse. He wouldn't give his name. Nothing surprising about *that* – names, like runes, are full of power. Instead he looked around at the hall – which was solidly built from ancient oak – then around at all of us. It was clear he wasn't impressed.

Finally, he spoke up. 'Well, so this is Asgard,' he said. 'What a mess. What a cowboy job. One big puff could blow it down.' (At this I winked at Heimdall, who bared his golden teeth and growled.)

'Are you out of your mind?' said Thor. 'This is Asgard, the home of the gods. We've withstood *decades* of warfare.'

'Yes,' said the man. 'And it looks it. Wood's all very well

for a *temporary* settlement, but if you're looking for permanence, stone's by far the best way to go. Stone stands in all weather. Stone has a rugged authority. Stone is the future, you mark my words. *That's* where the smart money's going to be.'

Odin looked at the stranger through his blue, unflinching eye. 'Is this a sales pitch?'

The stranger shrugged. 'I'd be doing you a favour,' he said. 'But I can build you a fortress with walls so high, so massive that nothing – not the Ice Folk, not the Rock Folk, nor even Lord Surt himself – will get through. It'll be a great investment.'

It sounded like a great idea. I knew how anxious Odin was about safeguarding his position. 'How soon could you build it? And what's your price?'

'Oh, eighteen months, give or take a few. I'm only a one-man outfit.'

'And your price?' repeated Odin.

'It's high. But I think I'm worth it.'

Odin stood up. From his high throne he looked about twenty feet tall. 'You'll have to give me an estimate before you start the work,' he said. (That's how you talk to builders.)

The builder grinned. 'So this is the deal. I'm going to need the goddess Freyja as my wife. *And* the Sun and the Moon Shields.'

Freyja was the most beautiful of all the goddesses in Asgard. Red-gold hair, skin like cream; she was Desire incarnate. *Everybody* wanted her – even Odin wasn't immune – which was why all the gods were outraged at this suggestion (though unsurprisingly, the goddesses seemed willing to negotiate).

As for the Sun and Moon Shields, these had been put in place when Sól and Mani, the sky charioteers, had been assigned their duties. Born from the fires of Chaos itself, bound with runes and glamours, the shields gave their riders protection from the minions of Surt, sent to recover their stolen glam and to return it to Chaos.

To give up Freyja would have been bad enough, but to give

up the Sun and the Moon Shields would have been disastrous. Mani, the Moon, who happened to be awake and off duty at the time, went even paler than usual, and Odin smiled regretfully and shook his head.

'I'm sorry. No deal.'

'You'll regret it. One day, Lord Surt will leave his realm to purge the Worlds of you and your kind. You people are going to *need* stone walls around you, when the time comes.'

Odin shook his head. 'No deal.'

A hubbub of voices ensued. Freyja was wailing; Thor was arguing; Heimdall was gnashing his golden teeth. Some of the lesser goddesses seemed keen to keep the debate alive: the man had a point; without a doubt, Asgard needed defences. The recent attacks by the Ice Folk and Rock Folk had been proof enough of this. They'd been relatively disorganized until now, but with Gullveig-Heid still out there, stirring unrest and selling her runes to the highest bidder, they would soon possess the skills to pose an increasingly serious threat. After that, all it would take was a General with a basic knowledge of strategy, and the gods would be in deep trouble.

Finally I took pity on them. 'Hang on,' I said. 'I've got an idea.'

Twenty-three pairs of eyes, plus one, turned to look at Yours Truly. We sent the builder to see to his horse, and I explained the plan in private.

'We shouldn't dismiss this idea,' I said, 'just because the initial estimate seems a little unreasonable.'

'*Unreasonable!*' Freyja shrieked. 'To sell me into marriage with a . . . with a *labourer*!'

I shrugged. 'We need stone walls,' I said. 'And so we need to agree to his terms.'

Freyja burst into noisy tears.

I passed her my handkerchief. 'I said we need to agree with his *terms*. Actually paying his *price* remains an entirely different matter.'

Heimdall gave me a scornful look. 'We can't renege on a deal. We're gods. We're bound by our word. We'd have to pay.'

'Who says we renege?' I grinned. 'We just make sure that the terms we set are impossible for him to fulfil.'

'You don't mean we should *cheat*?' said Balder, opening his blue eyes very wide.

I grinned. 'Just think of it as maximizing our winning potential.'

Odin thought about this for a while. 'What are you suggesting?'

'Six months. From the first day of winter to the first day of summer. Not a day more. No extra help. And then, when he fails to finish, we declare the contract null and void, and we've got at least half of our fortress built for free, without a care in the Nine Worlds.'

The gods exchanged glances. Heimdall shrugged. Even Freyja looked impressed.

I shot a grin at the Old Man. 'Isn't this why you brought me here? To come up with solutions?'

'Yes.'

'Then trust me,' I said. 'I won't let you down.'

'You'd better not,' said Odin.

After that, all I had to do was present my wholly unreasonable offer to the builder. He took it rather well, I thought. Perhaps I'd underestimated his intelligence. He listened to our terms, shook his head, then looked at the Goddess of Desire.

'I'd be cutting my own throat,' he said. 'But gods, for a prize like that . . . I'll take your offer.' He spat in his hand, ready to shake with the Old Man.

'Let's make sure we've got this straight,' I said. 'Six months. Not a day more. And no sneaky sub-contracting, either. You do the job yourself, right? Alone and single-handed.'

The labourer nodded. 'Just me and my horse. Good old

Svadilfari.' He patted the flank of the big black horse that had carried him over Bif-rost. Quite a nice-looking horse, I thought, but nothing out of the ordinary.

'It's a deal,' I told him.

We shook. The race against time had begun.

LESSON 6

Pony and Trap

Never trust a quadruped.

Lokabrenna

THE NEXT DAY AT DAWN, the job began. First, the dragging of fallen masonry; then the quarrying of new stone. The horse, Svadilfari, was exceptionally strong, and by the end of the first month he and his master had accumulated more than enough to begin.

Then came the placing of stone blocks; once more aided by his horse, the mason was able to hoist them to a great height. One by one, the wooden halls of Asgard were remade in stone, with strong, round arches, massive lintels, walls of granite so full of mica that they shone like steel in the sun. There were courtyards paved in stone, turrets, parapets, stairways. The work progressed with an eerie speed that the gods viewed at first with amazement, then, as winter deepened, with dread. Even I began to feel a little nervous as the walls of Asgard grew; most builders underestimate the time it takes to finish a job; in this case it looked as if six months might have been over-generous.

But the long winter was on our side; snow began to fall in drifts. Still the mason and his horse went on dragging stone up from the plain. Gales and snowstorms and biting cold seemed to have no effect on them; too late, we started to suspect that the mason and his horse were not everything they seemed to be.

Months passed with dizzying speed. The plain of Ida began to thaw. In Idun's garden, snowdrops bloomed. Birds sang with sickening regularity. And day by day, Asgard's walls grew bigger and more impressive.

Spring approached and, unfairly, all the gods blamed *me* for the fact that the work was getting on so fast. Freyja was especially scathing, pointing out to all her friends that *this* was why you should never trust a demon, and even suggesting that I might be in league with the stonemason, as part of a treacherous plan by Surt to take back the fire of the Sun and the Moon and to plunge the Worlds into darkness.

Balder took the moral high ground and said that folk should give me a chance, whilst assuming that hurt-puppy look of his and asking me if I didn't feel *just a little bit* responsible?

Others were less delicate in pointing out my guilt. No one used actual violence – Odin had made his orders plain – but there was a good deal of sneering and spitting whenever I happened to be around, and even the General, whose people were giving him serious aggravation about his new brother-in-blood and his reasons for adopting me, started to look at me differently, the light of calculation in his one blue eye.

Well, I wasn't completely naïve. I knew the Old Man needed to show his authority. There was no point in having an impregnable wall around the Sky Citadel if there was rebellion within. Heimdall was especially combative (besides which, he hated me), and I knew that if Odin showed weakness, then Goldie would be there to take his place as fast as thrice-greased lightning.

'You're going to have to make a stand,' I told him, as the deadline approached. 'Call a meeting of the gods. You have to assert some discipline. If you show weakness now, you'll never get your people back again.'

To do him justice, the Old Man knew exactly where I was

44

coming from. Which made me suspect that perhaps he'd been having exactly the same unquiet thoughts. What made mine less so was the fact that I already had a plan, which I'd been keeping under wraps for maximum dramatic effect. I prepared for a killer performance.

So, on the eve of winter's last day, the Old Man called his people to an emergency council meeting. The outer wall was almost complete – only the giant gateway remained half built, a massive arch of raw grey stone. One more trip to the quarry would be enough to finish the job, after which the mason could claim the reward I'd promised him.

That evening, the gods and goddesses all assembled in Odin's hall. No one wanted to sit near me (except for Balder, whose sympathy was almost as bad as their mistrust), and I felt a little hurt that their faith in me had been so easily lost.

I don't wish to brag, but really, folks, the day that I don't have a plan is the day Hel freezes over. Still, it had to be done in a way that gave Odin back his authority. I knew I was never going to be anything but an outsider in this camp, but as long as Odin was on my side, I was safe. I knew where I stood.

The meeting began – in Odin's new hall – and all the gods had plenty to say. The Old Man let them vent for a while, watching through his living eye. The atmosphere darkened progressively as Thor clenched his hairy fists and growled and one by one, my fickle new friends turned their vengeful gaze on me.

'This never would have happened,' said Frey, 'if *you* hadn't listened to Loki.'

Odin said nothing and did not move, silent on his high throne.

'We all thought he had a plan,' Frey went on. 'Now he's lost us the Sun and Moon, and Freyja into the bargain.' He turned on me, drawing his runesword. 'Well, what do you say? What are we going to do now?'

'I say make him bleed,' said Thor, taking a step towards

me.

Odin gave him a look. 'Hands off. No violence from my people.'

'What about *my* people?' said Frey. 'The Vanir never made any promises.'

'Too right, we didn't,' said Freyja. 'I second Thor.'

'Me too,' said Týr.

At that I started to back away. I could feel the temperature rising. The little hairs at the back of my neck started to prickle with cold sweat.

'Guys, come on,' I protested. 'We all agreed to the deal, right? We *all* agreed to the stonemason's terms—'

'But you were the one who told him that he could use his horse,' Odin said.

I looked up, startled. The General was standing behind me, tall and stern as the World Ash. His hand fell onto my shoulder. He was wearing iron gauntlets. He tightened his grip, and I recalled how deceptively strong he was.

'Please, it's not my fault!' I said.

Freyja, cold as carrion, eyed me with a baleful glare. 'I want to see him suffer,' she said. 'I want to hear him screaming. I'll wear a necklace made from his teeth when I go walking down the aisle . . .'

Odin's grasp on my shoulder was really hurting now. I winced. I'd set up this situation myself, but even so I was afraid.

'I swear, I've got a plan!' I said.

'You'd better, or you're toast,' said Thor.

The gauntleted hand on my shoulder gripped me harder than ever now, forcing me to my knees. I yelped. 'Please! Give me a chance!' I said.

For a moment the grip held fast. Then, to my relief, it relaxed.

'You'll have your chance,' said the General. 'But your plan had better work. Because if it doesn't, I promise you'll be in Nine Worlds of hurt.'

I nodded, dry-mouthed. I believed him. What an actor.

Painfully, I got to my feet, rubbing my aching shoulder. 'I told you I had a plan,' I said, feeling quite rightly resentful. 'I promise, by tomorrow night we'll be in the clear, with nothing to pay, honour and promises intact.'

The gods looked openly cynical, with the exception of Idun, the Healer, whose view of the world was so sunny that she even trusted *me*, and Sigyn, Freyja's handmaid, who just looked soupier than ever. Everyone else muttered and glared. Even Balder turned away.

Freyja gave me a scornful look. Heimdall showed his golden teeth. And Thor hissed at me as I passed: 'Till tomorrow, demon boy. Then I'm going to kick your ass.'

I blew him a kiss as I went out. I knew I was in no danger. The day a cowboy builder takes Loki for a ride is the day that pigs fly over the Rainbow Bridge and Lord Surt comes to Asgard for tea and little fairy cakes, wearing a taffeta ballgown and singing mezzo-soprano.

Just saying, in case you had any doubts. Yes, folks. I'm *that* good.

The next day I got up early and high-tailed it from Asgard. Or so people thought – those doubters who didn't believe I had a plan. Meanwhile, the mason and his horse set off across the grassy plain, now only piebald with patches of snow. Spring was trembling in the air. Birds sang, flowers bloomed, tiny furry animals scampered and scurried in the fields and the black horse Svadilfari seemed to have a gleam in his eye that had been absent all winter.

Above him, Asgard glittered in the sun, its granite walls spackled with mica. It looked truly magnificent; its shining rooftops, turrets, walkways, gardens, sunny balconies. Its twenty-four halls were all different (you notice *I* still didn't have one); each made to the specifications of the god or god-dess who lived there. Odin's was the largest, of course, towering dizzily over the rest, with his high seat – a kind of crow's nest

– lost in a ballet of rainbows. The only unfinished section was that massive entrance gateway. Three dozen blocks of stone, no more, remained to quarry and hew into shape – a morning's work, if that, I thought. No wonder the mason looked cheery, whistling between his teeth as he started to unpack his tools.

But just as his master was about to start work quarrying the last of the stone, the black horse raised his head and neighed. A mare – a very *pretty* mare – was standing on the far side of the quarry. Her mane was long, her flanks were smooth, her eyes were bright and inviting.

She whinnied. Svadilfari replied, then, shaking free of his harness, ignoring his master's angry commands, he ran to join the pretty mare as she galloped off across the plain.

The mason was furious. He spent all day chasing his horse from one stand of trees to another. No stone at all was quarried that day. Meanwhile, the horse and the little mare celebrated the coming of spring in the usual time-honoured fashion, and the mason tried to complete the gate with ill-fitting pieces of leftover stone.

By nightfall, the horse had still not returned, and the mason was incandescent with rage. He stormed up to Allfather's hall and demanded to see the General.

'You must think I'm an idiot,' he said. '*You* sent that mare to entrap my horse. *You* tried to renege on our deal!'

Coolly, Odin shook his head. 'You failed to complete the building in time. That makes our agreement void. Just chalk it up to experience, and we'll part on amicable terms.'

The mason looked round at the assembled gods and goddesses, watching him from their shining thrones. His dark eyes narrowed. 'Someone's missing,' he said. 'Where's that little red-haired rat with the freaky eyes?'

Odin shrugged. 'Loki? I have no idea.'

'Cavorting with my horse, that's where!' shouted the mason, clenching his fists. 'I knew there was something about that mare! I could tell from its colours! A trick! You've tricked me, you two-faced bastards! You slags! You sons and daughters of bitches!'

And at that he lunged at Odin, revealing himself in true Aspect at last as one of the tribe of the Rock Folk; massive, savage and lethal. But Thor was upon him in seconds; a single blow from the Thunderer's fist was enough to crack the giant's skull. All Asgard trembled from the blow. But the walls held fast – the mason's claim had not been an empty one. We had our citadel at last – minus half a gateway – and for a very affordable price.

As for Your Humble Narrator, it was some time before I returned to Asgard, and when I did, I was leading a colt – a rather unusual eight-legged colt of a fetching strawberry hue.

I blew a kiss at Heimdall as I approached the Rainbow Bridge.

The Watchman gave me a sour look. 'You're revolting, d'you know that? You seriously gave *birth* to that thing?'

I gave him my most fetching smile. '*I* took one for the team,' I said. 'I think you'll find that the others will be more than happy to welcome me back. And as for the General . . .' I patted the colt. 'Sleipnir – that's our little friend's name – is going to be very useful to him. He has his father's powers and mine; the power to cross over land or sea; to travel with a foot in each World; to span the sky in a single step, faster than the Sun and Moon.'

Heimdall grunted. 'Smartass.'

I grinned. Then, taking Sleipnir by the bridle, I stepped onto Bif-rost and crossed home into Asgard.

LESSON 7

Hair and Beauty

Never trust a lover.

Lokabrenna

Aᴏᴛᴇʀ ᴛʜᴀᴛ, I was more or less accepted into Asgard's fold. I already knew I would never be part of the popular crowd. But my little escapade had bought me some goodwill, at least, and the chilliness of previous months was replaced by a kind of tolerance. I was back in with the General, and the rest of the gods followed his lead, except, of course, for Heimdall (did I mention he hated me?) and Freyja, who hadn't yet forgiven me for promising her to one of the Rock Folk.

Still, I'd cut myself some slack, and made a reputation. People called me 'Trickster' now and forgave me my misdemeanours. Aegir invited me to his place for drinks. His almond-eyed wife asked me if I wanted to learn how to swim. Balder magnanimously offered to include me in the next Aesir versus Vanir football tournament. Odin promoted me to the rank of Captain, Bragi wrote ballads about me and the ladies enjoyed my company to such an extent that Frigg, Odin's motherly wife, started to drop less than tactful hints that I should find a wife of my own before some jealous husband decided to teach me a lesson.

Perhaps it was the threat of wedlock that made me overstep

the mark – or perhaps the Chaos in my blood rebelling against the unnatural peace. Either way, the General should have seen it coming. You don't bring Wildfire into your home and expect it to stay in the fireplace. And Thor should have seen it coming as well; you don't leave a wife as alluring as Sif to fend for herself day in, day out. And . . .

All right. I confess. I was angry. Thor had treated me roughly over that business with Asgard's wall, and I might have been looking for a chance to pay him back in some way. He just happened to have a pretty wife – Sif, the Golden-Haired, she was; the Goddess of Grace and Plenty. Very pretty, but not very bright, with a promising streak of vanity that made her easy to cajole.

Anyway, I wooed her a little, spun her a little yarn or two, and one thing led to another. Fine. Thor had a place of his own to sleep, far from Sif's bedchamber, so the lady's reputation was safe – that is, until the moment at which Yours Truly decided (in an early-morning moment of madness) to mark his victory by taking a trophy – in the form of the sleeping lady's hair, which spilled across the pillow like grain.

So shoot me. I cut it off.

To be fair, I assumed she could grow it back, or change her Aspect the way I could. My mistake. How could I have known? Apparently, the Aesir can't change their shape like the Vanir can. But the Goddess of Plenty has a great deal tied up, so to speak, in her hair; it's where most of her powers lie, and without knowing it, in a single snip, Yours Truly had robbed her, not only of her beauty, but also of her Goddess Aspect.

Of course that wasn't *my* fault – but after due consideration I decided it might be wise to leave before the lady woke up. I left the hair on her pillow; perhaps she could make it into a wig, or something. Or maybe I could make her believe that the damage was somehow the result of one too many peroxide treatments. Either way, I figured that she wouldn't dare tell Thor about our night of passion.

Well, I was right about *that* part. But I hadn't counted on the fact that Thor, arriving home from one of his trips to find his wife sporting a pixie crop some five hundred years before they came into vogue, would instantly (and unfairly) conclude that I was the probable culprit.

'What happened to the presumption of innocence?' I protested, as I was dragged without ceremony to the foot of Allfather's throne.

Odin gave me his dead eye. At his side, Sif, in a turban, fixed me with the kind of stare that blights crops at a distance.

'It was a *joke*!' I told them.

Thor picked me up by the hair. 'A joke?'

I considered shifting to Wildfire Aspect, but Thor was wearing his fireproof gauntlets. That meant no escape for Yours Truly, whatever form I tried to take.

'You don't think she looks kinda cute?' I said, looking appealingly at Sif. Some women look good with short hair. But even I couldn't bring myself to say that Sif was one of them.

'All right. I'm sorry! What can I say? It's the Chaos in me.' I tried to explain. 'I wanted to see what would happen if—'

Thor growled: 'Well, so you know. The first thing that's going to happen is that I'm going to break every miserable bone in your body. One by one. How's that for a joke?'

'I'd really rather you didn't,' I said. 'I'm still not good with the pain thing, and—'

'That's just fine by me,' said Thor.

I looked at Odin. 'Brother, *please* . . .'

Odin shook his head and sighed. 'What do you expect me to do?' he said. 'You cut off his wife's *hair*, for gods' sakes, and you deserve to pay for it. Pay, or get out of Asgard. It's up to you. I've done what I could.'

'You'd throw me out of Asgard?' I said. 'Do you know what that would mean? I can't go back to Chaos now. I'd be helpless, at the mercy of every one of the Rock Folk who felt like getting payback for what I did to cheat their friend out of the price of building a wall.'

Odin shrugged. 'Your choice,' he said.

Some choice. I looked at Thor. 'You wouldn't prefer an apology?'

'As long as it's deeply felt,' said Thor. 'And I promise, you'll feel it deeply.' He raised a fist. I closed my eyes . . .

And then came inspiration. 'Wait!' I said. 'I have an idea. What if Sif could have new hair, better than she had before?'

Sif gave an indignant grunt. 'I'm not wearing a wig, if that's what you're suggesting.'

'No, not a wig.' I opened my eyes. 'Hair extensions, made of gold, that would grow just like your natural hair. And it wouldn't need curling, or styling, or bleach, and—'

Sif said, 'I *don't* bleach my hair!'

Thor said, 'I'd rather hit him.'

'And let her hair grow back on its own? Well, if you're happy to wait that long . . .'

Thor gave an indifferent shrug. But I could see that Sif was intrigued. She wanted her Goddess Aspect back, and knew that the fleeting satisfaction of seeing me bite the dust was never going to compensate for the loss.

She gave me a look that could have stripped paint, and put her hand on Thor's shoulder. 'Before you give him a pounding, dear, let's just hear what he's offering. You can hit him *anytime* . . .'

Thor looked doubtful, but let me go. 'Well?'

'I know a man,' I said. 'A smith. A genius with metals and runes. He'll spin Sif a new head of hair in no time, and probably throw in some extra gifts for us as a token of goodwill.'

'He must be a very good friend of yours.' Odin looked at me thoughtfully.

'Er, not exactly a *friend*,' I said. 'But I think I can persuade him to help. It's just a matter of offering the right kind of incentive – to him, and to his brothers.'

'You're really that good?' said Thor.

I grinned. 'Better,' I said. 'I'm Loki.'

LESSON 8

Past and Present

Never trust an artist.

Lokabrenna

AND SO I WAS REPRIEVED – for a time – and I left Asgard on foot to go in search of the man who would save my skin. Dvalin was his name, and he was one of the sons of Ivaldi, the smith, and he and his three brothers had their forge in the caverns of World Below. They were the Tunnel Folk, delvers of gold, and their reputation was unmatched. More importantly, they were also half-brothers to Idun, the Healer, and I figured that if I claimed friendship with her, they would be sure to oblige me.

Now geography, like history, is subject to cyclical changes. In those days the Worlds were smaller than they are today, and less subject to physical rules. Don't believe me? Look at the maps. And we, of course, had our own ways of crossing between the boundaries. Some involved working with runes – for instance, *Raedo*, the Journeyman, opens up many a door between Worlds – and some were simply a matter of footwork, wingwork and clever orientation. I set off on foot to convince the gods of the sincerity of my remorse, but as soon as I had crossed Ida's plain and entered the forest of Ironwood, I found myself a shortcut. The river Gunnthrà ran through it; it was one of the tributaries that linked the nine Worlds to their primal source, and a direct link to World Below and the Worlds that lay beyond: Death, Dream and Pandaemonium. Not that I planned to go *that* far, but the Tunnel Folk enjoyed their seclusion, and it took me the best part of a day on foot to reach their fetid empire.

I found the smiths in their workshop. A cavern, deep in World Below, where a series of cracks in the earth gave vent to a seam of molten rock. This was their only source of light; it was also their forge and their hearth. In my original Aspect, I would not have suffered, either from the fire or the fumes, but in this body I was unprepared, both for the heat and for the stench.

Nevertheless, I approached the four smiths and gave them my most winning smile. 'Greetings, sons of Ivaldi,' I said, 'from the gods of Asgard.'

In the light of the fiery forge, they turned their faces towards me. The sons of Ivaldi are almost identical; sallow-skinned, hollow-eyed, stooped and scorched with labour. Tunnel Folk rarely go aboveground. It interferes with their vision. They live, work, sleep in their tunnels, breathe the foulest of air, eat maggots and beetles and centipedes, and live only for the things they make from the metals and stones they find in the earth. Not much of a life, I thought. No wonder Idun had left them, taking with her the apples of youth made by her father as a wedding gift.

But now, as my eyes adjusted to the half-light, I saw that the cavern was filled to the roof with examples of the craftsmen's work. All around there were objects of gold: jewellery, swords, shields; all embossed and gleaming with the soft sheen of beautiful things kept in darkness.

Some were merely decorative – bracelets, rings, headpieces – some intricate to the point of obsession, some starkly, deceptively simple. And some were virtually buzzing with glam; carved and filigreed with runes so intricate that even I could only guess at their purpose.

I've never cared that much for gold, but in the hall of the Tunnel Folk I found myself feeling covetous; eyeing those bright and beautiful things, planning and wishing to make them mine. It was a part of their glam, I suppose; the glam that runs through World Below like a seam of precious metal. It makes men greedy and women corrupt; blinds them with the light of desire. Too long in this place could drive a man mad – the gold, the glam, the fumes from the forge. I had to get out of there, and quick. But not without Sif's golden hair. And if I could manage to persuade them to give me a little extra . . .

I took another step and said: 'Greetings, too, from your sister, Idun the Healer, Idun the Fair, Keeper of the Golden Fruit.'

Ivaldi's sons all looked at me, their eyes shining and skittering like beetles in their sunken sockets. Dvalin stepped forward. I knew him by reputation, and by the fact that his right foot was twisted and lame – an accident, the circumstances of which I may tell in some later tale (not that Yours Truly was involved . . . well, not *very* much, at least). I hoped he didn't bear a grudge, or better still, that he didn't recognize me in my current Aspect. I said:

'Greetings, Dvalin, to you and yours. I bring you marvellous news from Asgard. You and your brothers have been chosen, among all the craftsmen of World Below, to carry out a delicate task, for which your names will be celebrated and your work be known throughout the Worlds. For a limited time only, this opportunity will allow *you*, the sons of Ivaldi, to share in the glory of Asgard; Asgard the golden, Asgard the fair, Asgard the eternal—'

Dvalin said: 'What's in it for us?'

'Fame,' I said with my broadest smile. 'And the knowledge that you're the best. Why else would Odin have chosen you, of all the smiths in World Below?'

That was the way to draw them in. I knew it from the old days. The Maggots can't be bought in the regular way, they already have all the wealth they need. They have no passions beyond their craft, but they are very ambitious. I knew they wouldn't be able to resist a challenge to prove their superior skill.

'What do you want?' said Dvalin.

'What have you got?' I said, and smiled.

It took the Tunnel Folk some time to prepare themselves for the task I'd set. I explained about Sif's hair – omitting the reason for its loss – and the smiths all laughed in their sour way.

'Is that all?' said Dvalin. 'Any child could make that for you. It isn't a proper challenge.'

'I also want two special gifts,' I said. 'One for my brother Odin, leader of the Aesir, and one for Frey, leader of the Vanir.'

This was a political move on my part; Frey, the Reaper, was in fact only one of the Vanir leaders, but he was influential. In favouring him – over Heimdall, for instance – I would be giving him the edge over his friends. With luck, he would remember that when it came to rewarding me; besides, he was Freyja's brother, and I needed to get her back on my side.

Dvalin nodded and set to work. His brothers and he worked as a team, smoothly and gracefully. One handled the materials; one cast the runes; one tended the forge. One hammered out the hot metal; one finished the piece with a polishing cloth.

The first of the gifts was for Odin; a spear. It was a lovely piece of work, straight and light and beautiful, carved down the shaft with a ladder of runes. It was a regal weapon, and I grinned inside as I pictured the Old Man's surprise and pleasure as he received it.

'This is Gugnir,' said Dvalin. 'She always flies true, and never fails to hit her mark in battle. She'll make your brother invincible, as long as he keeps her by his side.'

The second gift looked like a toy; a little ship, so dainty that it made you wonder how Dvalin, with his big, clumsy hands, was able to handle it with such ease. But when it was finished, he said with pride:

'This is Skidbladnir, greatest of ships. Winds will always favour her. She will never be lost at sea. And when the journey's done, she can be folded up so small that she'll fit into your pocket.' And then he uttered a cantrip, and the ship folded up like paper, fold after fold after fold, until it became a silver compass that he dropped into my hand.

'Nice,' I said. I knew Njörd's son would appreciate this gift most of all. 'And now for Sif's hair, if you don't mind.'

At this the sons of Ivaldi brought out a shapeless piece of gold, and while one of them held it in the forge's heat, another used a wheel to spin it into the finest thread. Another cast runes; another sang, in a voice as sweet as a nightingale's, cantrips and spells to bring it to life. Finally, it was finished; gleaming and jewelled and fine as spun silk.

'But will it grow?' I asked Dvalin.

'Of course. As soon as she sets it in place, it will become a part of her. More beautiful than ever before, rivalling even Freyja's.'

'Really?' I grinned again at that. Freyja was rather protective of her position as fairest of all. I filed the knowledge away for possible use at a later date. Everyone has a weakness, and I make it my business to know them all. Dvalin's was pride in his handiwork, and so I praised him to the skies as I picked up the three precious gifts.

'I have to say I doubted you,' I told him as I prepared to leave. 'I knew you were good, but not *how* good. You and your brothers are masters of all the craftsmen in World Below, and that's what I'll tell them in Asgard.'

Well, a little flattery never hurt, I told myself. Now to get home with the loot. It was time. I turned my face towards World Above. I was sick as a dog with the fumes from the forge, and I needed a wash like never before, but I was flushed with triumph. This ought to show the General, I thought. And as for that smug bastard Heimdall—

But as I was about to leave, I found a figure blocking my way. It was another craftsman, Brokk, one of Dvalin's competitors. A squat little bulldog of a man, with eyes like currants and arms like logs.

'I heard you gave Dvalin some work,' he said, looking at me from under his heavy brows.

I admitted I had.

'You were satisfied?'

'More than satisfied,' I said. 'He and his brothers are incredible.'

Brokk sneered. 'Call that incredible? You people should have come to us. Everyone knows my brother and I are the kings of World Below.'

I shrugged. 'Talk's cheap,' I told him. 'If you want to prove yourself better than Ivaldi's sons, go ahead and match their work. Otherwise, as far as Asgard's concerned, you're just another amateur.'

I know. I shouldn't have baited him. But he was getting on my nerves and I was eager to get out.

'An amateur?' he said. 'I'll show you who's the amateur. A wager. I'll make three gifts for you, Trickster, and come back with you to Asgard. Then we'll see whose work is the best. Let your General decide.'

All I can say in my defence is that World Below must have clouded my brain. All that gold and glamour – and now was a chance to get some more, and for free. Besides, the children of Chaos can never resist a wager.

'Well, why not? I'm in,' I said. Three more gifts for the Aesir, at minimal risk to Yours Truly. I'd be a fool to pass by the chance. 'And what shall we wager?'

Brokk scowled at me. 'You've damaged my reputation,' he said. 'All of World Below now believes Dvalin's work to be better than mine. I need to make a point.'

'How?'

'I'll wager my work against your head.' He gave me a very nasty smile.

'Really? That's all?' I was beginning to feel a little uncomfortable. These artist types can be very intense, and besides, what would he do with my head?

'I'd use it as a doorstop,' said Brokk. 'That way anyone coming in or out of my workshop would know what happens to anyone who dares to disparage my craftsmanship.'

Nice, I thought. But a bet was a bet. 'Fine,' I told him. 'But you'll have your work cut out.'

He smiled, if you can call that a smile. His teeth were like pieces of amber. '*I'll* be doing the cutting,' he said. 'If you're lucky, I'll use a knife. If not—'

'Just go ahead,' I said.

Not really the best choice of words, come to think of it. But I was feeling confident. I had a few more tricks up my sleeve, and besides, when I walked into Asgard, I knew I'd be the blue-eyed boy, and therefore immune to everything.

Just proves how wrong you can be, I guess.

LESSON 9

Hammer and Tongs

Never trust an insect.

Lokabrenna

Brokk's workshop was not at all like that of Dvalin and his brothers. For a start, he had a regular forge, fed with regular fuel, and therefore had none of the natural advantages enjoyed by the sons of Ivaldi. His brother Sindri, whom I'd rather expected to be the brains behind the outfit, looked little more than a halfwit. There were no objects on display here; no weapons, no jewellery; only a pile of raw materials: metals, pieces of sacking, animal skins, lumps of wood and other pieces of detritus more suited to a ragman's cart than to an artist's studio. And it stank; of sweat and goat and smoke and oil and sulphur. Hard to imagine that out of this mess could ever come anything beautiful.

However, I was suspicious. I watched the two brothers carefully as they began work, and saw that, although they both seemed boorish and slow, Sindri had very nimble hands, and Brokk's arms were very strong as he worked at the giant bellows that would bring the forge to sufficient heat.

This gave me a sudden idea. 'I'm going outside for some air,' I said. 'Call me when you've finished.'

I went into the passageway and shifted my Aspect to that of a fly. A gadfly, to be precise; quick and sharp and annoying.

I flew back into the workshop unseen and watched from the shadows as Brokk picked up a piece of raw gold and flung it into the heart of the forge.

Sindri was casting runes into the fire. His style was eccentric, but he was fast, and I watched with curiosity as the piece of gold began to take shape; spinning and turning over the coals.

'Now, Brokk,' said Sindri. 'The bellows, quick! If the piece cools before its time . . .'

Brokk started to pump the giant bellows for all he was worth. Sindri, with his delicate hands, was casting runes as fast as he could.

I was starting to feel a little nervous. The piece that hung between them was looking quite impressive. Still in my gadfly Aspect, I buzzed up to Brokk, with his bellows, and stung him sharply on the hand. He cursed, but didn't flinch, and moments later the piece was complete: a beautiful golden arm-ring, worked and chiselled with hundreds of runes.

I flew back into the passageway, assumed my human Aspect again and rapidly pulled on my clothes.

A moment later, Brokk came to find me and showed me the golden arm-ring.

'This is Draupnir,' he said, with a grin. 'A gift from me for your General. On every ninth night, she'll give birth to eight rings just like her. Do the maths, Trickster. I've just given your people the key to unending wealth. Quite a princely gift, don't you think?'

'Not bad,' I shrugged. 'But the spear makes Odin invincible. Which one do you think he'll value most?'

Brokk went back into the workshop, muttering. I resumed my gadfly Aspect and followed him.

This time, from the pile of materials, Brokk selected a pigskin and a fist-sized lump of gold, and flung them both into the fire. While his brother shot runes at the work in progress, Brokk wielded the bellows, and something big began to emerge; something that growled and grunted and snarled and glared with burning amber eyes from the golden heart of the forge.

Once more I flew towards Brokk and stung him on the neck. He yelled, but never stopped working the bellows. A moment later, Sindri pulled out a giant golden boar from the forge, and I fled back to get dressed again.

'This is Gullin-bursti,' said Brokk, as he showed me result of their work. 'He'll carry Frey across the sky on his back, and light the way ahead.'

I noticed that he gave the word 'ahead' an inflexion I didn't like at all. But I shrugged again, and said: 'Not bad. But the sons of Ivaldi have given Frey mastery of the ocean. And what about the Thunderer? You'll have to work harder to please Thor. The sons of Ivaldi have given him a wife whose beauty will be the envy of every woman, and the desire of every man. Can you and your brother offer more?'

Brokk glared and went inside without a word. In gadfly Aspect I followed him, and watched as, still glaring, he pulled from the pile of raw materials a piece of iron as big as his head. He threw it into the heart of the forge, then, as Sindri started to shape it with runes, he wielded the bellows, his face turning red with the effort.

I could already see that this third artefact was shaping up to be something unique. What was it? A weapon? I thought it was; shaped like the rune *Thuris* and snapping with glam and energy. I had to make sure that this time it failed; and so I flew into Brokk's face and stung him right between the eyes, stung him hard enough to draw blood. He gave a roar of anger and raised a hand to sweep me aside – and for a moment, a second, no more, he loosened his grip on the bellows.

Sindri cried out; *'No! Don't stop!'*

Brokk redoubled his efforts. But it was too late; the weapon that had taken shape in the forge was already losing its substance. Sindri cursed and started to cast runes at an incredible speed. Could he salvage the delicate work? I was inclined to believe he could not. Even if he managed to save it somehow, I knew it wouldn't be perfect.

I flew back into the passageway, resumed my Aspect (and my clothes). I was waiting when Brokk came out, blood still trickling down his face and something, wrapped in a cloth, in his hands.

'Well?' I said.

'Well, this is it,' said Brokk, unwrapping the object.

It was a warhammer, I saw; heavy and brutal and laden with glam from its nose to the tip of its handle – a handle that was rather short, the only flaw in a weapon that even I could tell was wholly unique; unique and uniquely desirable.

'This is Mjølnir,' said Brokk, with a snarl. 'The greatest hammer ever forged. In the hands of the Thunderer it will protect all of Asgard. It will never leave his side; it will always serve him well; and when a show of modesty is required, it will fold up like a pocket knife and—'

'Excuse me,' I interrupted. 'A show of modesty? Are we still talking about a hammer?'

Brokk displayed those awful teeth. 'Of course Thor loves his wife,' he said. 'But when it comes to impressing his friends, a giant weapon is all he needs.'

I pulled a face. The Maggots rarely manage humour, and when they do, it tends to be coarse.

'We'll see about that, shall we?' I said. 'As for your weapon, it seems to me to be a little – ah, short in the shaft.'

'It's what you do with it that counts,' growled Brokk. 'Now, shall we get going? My brother and I have a wager to win.'

I led the way to Asgard.

LESSON 10

Needle and Thread

Basically, never trust anyone.

Lokabrenna

I WAS FEELING QUIETLY CONFIDENT as we arrived in Odin's hall. Sif was already waiting for me (her head still wrapped in a turban); Thor at her side like a thundercloud. Odin was watching from his throne, his one eye gleaming with anticipation. Heimdall was looking slightly put out – I guess he hadn't expected me to make good my promise to return. And the goddesses – especially Sigyn, who had been making eyes at me since I arrived – were watching me expectantly, no doubt wondering whether I would manage to save the day once again.

Brokk, looking (and smelling) all the more repulsive for being in the daylight, stood at my side with his three gifts, with the golden boar Gullin-bursti growling at the end of his chain, and the hammer sticking out of his waistband.

'Who's this?' said the Old Man.

Brokk said his piece and explained about our wager.

Odin raised an eyebrow. 'Well, let's see these gifts of yours,' he said. 'We'll vote on their merit afterwards.'

I shrugged. 'I think you'll find—' I began.

'Let's see them, Trickster,' said Odin.

I presented my gifts. Brokk offered his. After what seemed

like an unnecessarily lengthy interval, Odin gave his judgement.

'Ivaldi's sons have done well,' he said. 'Their work is quite remarkable.'

'Isn't it?' I winked at Sif, who was already wearing her new head of hair. True to Dvalin's promise, the hair extensions had bonded perfectly with Sif's own hair, restoring her Goddess Aspect.

She gave me a grudging look. 'It's all right.'

'And what about the spear?' I said. '*And* the compass that turns into a ship . . .'

Odin nodded. 'I know,' he said. 'But Brokk's gifts are also remarkable. The hammer, Mjølnir, especially.'

'What? That little stubby thing?'

Odin gave a chilly smile. 'It's true, the handle's a little short. But even so, it's a magnificent piece, more impressive than my spear, or the Reaper's runesword. And in Thor's hands, it could mean the end of all our current defence issues.'

Thor was holding Mjølnir protectively in the crook of his arm. 'I agree. Brokk wins.'

Odin turned to the other gods. 'What do you think?'

Frey nodded. 'I say Brokk.'

'Heimdall?'

'Brokk.'

'Njörd?'

'Brokk.'

'Balder?'

Golden Boy sighed. 'Oh, dear. Honestly, I'm afraid it's Brokk.'

Aesir and Vanir, one by one, voted Brokk's gifts the superior. All except Sif, who was plaiting her new hair, Idun, who didn't like weapons, Bragi, who was already working on my death anthem and Sigyn, who was watching me with a disturbingly motherly look, as if at any moment she might be impelled to put a soothing hand on my forehead.

I was revolted. 'Seriously?'

Odin shrugged. 'I'm sorry. You lost.'

Brokk's dark eyes lit up. 'I win.'

'That's right,' I told him. 'You're the best. Now about that silly wager—'

'Your head belongs to me,' said Brokk, pulling out his knife from its sheath.

'I'll give you its weight in gold instead,' I said, retreating a step or two.

'No deal,' said Brokk. 'I want your head. That way, anyone walking into my workshop will know how highly I value my reputation.'

'How about double or quits?' I said, taking another step backwards.

He grinned, once more showing his disgusting teeth. 'Tempting . . . but no. I'll take the head.'

'I guess you'll have to catch me, then,' I said, shifting into my Wildfire Aspect. In less than a second I was out of the hall, trailing smoke behind me. But Thor was even quicker than that, and he was wearing his gauntlets.

'Oh no, you don't. Shift back,' he said.

I struggled and cursed in Thor's big fist, but knew I had no chance of escape and resumed my habitual Aspect. Now Yours Truly was covered in soot and clad in nothing but his skin. *Not* my finest moment.

I appealed to the Old Man. 'Odin, please . . .'

'A bet's a bet. You lost. It's out of my hands,' he said.

'Frey? Njörd? Anyone?'

No one seemed ready to intercede. In fact, I thought that a number of them showed signs of a callous enjoyment. The bastards were enjoying the show. Heimdall's eyes were gleaming, and Týr had actually brought snacks.

Thor dropped me at Brokk's feet; beaten, exhausted, abandoned by all. But brilliance in extremis has always been one of my attributes.

I put up my hands. 'All right. I give up.'

I heard Sigyn gasp.

'Brokk, be my guest.'

Brokk raised the knife. He pulled back my hair, exposing my throat to the wicked blade . . .

'Er – hang on a minute,' I said. 'I thought our deal was for the head.'

Brokk looked nonplussed. 'Well, so it is.'

'But you were going to slit my throat,' I said, with feigned indignation. 'Fair's fair, the head belongs to you. But no one promised you the neck. In fact, the neck is out of bounds. Totally and utterly. Put as much as a scratch on the neck, and the deal's off. A bet's a bet. Don't you agree, everyone?'

For a moment I watched as Brokk struggled with this new information. 'But how do I . . .?'

'Not the neck,' I said.

'But—'

'You set the stakes,' I told him. 'You were the one who insisted.'

'But I can't take the head without the neck!'

'Fine by me,' I said, and grinned.

Brokk's face darkened. Behind him, the Aesir and Vanir began to smile. Even Thor, who had a rudimentary sense of humour at best, was looking amused.

Brokk turned to Odin. 'That's not fair! You can't let him get away with this!'

'I'm sorry, Brokk,' Odin said. 'You made the bet. It's out of my hands.' His face was stern as granite, but I knew that inside he was smiling.

For a moment longer, Brokk tried to find words to express himself. His fists clenched. His body shook. His dark face darkened still more with rage. Then he turned on me, eyes smouldering like the coals from his forge.

'You think you've outwitted me, Trickster,' he said. 'Well, maybe I can't claim your head. But since it now belongs to me, I can at least make some improvements.'

'What? Are you going to cut my hair into a more flattering

style?'

Brokk shook his head. 'No. But that smart mouth of yours can be taught a lesson. I can do that, if nothing else.'

And from his pocket he pulled out a leatherworker's awl and a long, thin leather thong.

I said: 'You can't be serious.'

'You'd be surprised,' said Brokk, with a grin. 'We Tunnel Folk aren't such humorists as you seem to believe. Hold his head, someone.'

And so, while Heimdall held me down (of course, it *had* to be Goldie, and I could tell he was enjoying himself), Brokk sewed my lips together. It took nine stitches, each of them like being punched in the mouth by a fistful of wasps.

But much as it hurt, it didn't hurt as much as did their laughter. Yes, they *laughed*, my so-called friends; they laughed as I struggled and whimpered, and no one moved a finger to help, not even Odin, who had sworn to treat me like a brother – but we all know what happened to *them*, don't we? Bragi, Njörd, Frey, Honir, Thor – even goody-two-shoes Balder joined in the laughter, succumbing to peer-group pressure like the weakling he secretly was.

And it was the sound of their laughter that followed me back to my bolt hole, where I pulled out the stitches and howled in rage and swore that one day I would pay them back – *all* of them, and especially my loving brother – in full. In blood.

The stitches healed quickly. The pain went away. But Brokk's awl was a magical tool. It left a permanent mark on me. Nine neat little cross-stitch scars that faded silvery with time, but never vanished. After that, my smile was never quite as true, and there was something in my heart, a barbed thing, like a roll of wire, that never ceased to trouble me. The gods never suspected it. Except perhaps for Odin, whose eye I often felt on me, and whose morality, I knew, was almost as dubious as my own.

As for the rest of them, they thought I'd forgotten. I never did. 'A stitch in time saves nine', or so goes the saying among the Folk. Well, I could have saved the Nine Worlds. I could have halted Ragnarók. But the gods, in their arrogance and greed, had clarified my position. I would never be one of them. I knew that now. I was alone. I would always be alone. I'd learnt my lesson for good, this time.

Basically, never trust *anyone*.

'Every dog has his day', as the old Middle-Worlds saying goes. Every dog and every god, and now I began to long for the day when our roles would be reversed, and I would be the one looking down on all of *them* as they pleaded and cried. That day would come, we all knew that. Change is the wheel on which the Worlds turn, and the time would come when gods would be dogs, howling as everything they had built came down in ruins around them. Power always comes at a price, and the higher they climb, the further they fall. I meant to engineer that fall, and to laugh as they came tumbling down.

Till then, I bided my time, and smiled as sweetly as my scarred lips would allow, until the day I would take my revenge and bring the gods down, one by one.

BOOK 2

Shadow

The Aesir meet in council.
But oaths are to be broken.
The Sorceress has done her work.
The Oracle has spoken.

Prophecy of the Oracle

LESSON 1

Gold

All men are one-eyed when a woman's involved.

Lokabrenna

Aɴᴅ ꜱᴏ I ʙᴇᴄᴀᴍᴇ ᴛʜᴇ Tʀɪᴄᴋꜱᴛᴇʀ, despised and yet invaluable, hiding my contempt for them all behind my scarred and twisted smile. I found my appeal undiminished among the ladies, who seemed to find that scarred smile quite attractive – but that wasn't the point, of course. Chaos is unforgiving. And in spite of my defection, I was still a child of Chaos.

Isn't it funny, how quickly things change? Nine little stitches, that's all it took for me to suddenly realize the truth: that whatever I did, whatever I risked, however much I tried to fit in, I would *never* be one of them. I would never have a hall, or earn the respect I so clearly deserved. I would never be a god; only ever a dog on a chain. Oh, I might be of *use* to them now and then, but as soon as the current crisis was done, it would be back to the kennel for Your Humble Narrator, and without as much as a biscuit.

I'm telling you this so you'll understand why I did the things I did. I think you'll agree I had no choice; it was the only way I could retain what little self-respect I had. There's such purity in revenge, unlike those *other* emotions I'd had to endure in Odin's world. Envy, hatred, sorrow, fear, remorse, humiliation – all of them messy and painful and quite spectacularly pointless – but now as I discovered revenge, it was almost like being home again.

Home. See how they corrupted me? This time, with nostalgia, that most toxic of their emotions. And perhaps with some self-pity as well, as I started to think of all the things I'd given up to join them: my primal Aspect; my place with Surt; my Chaotic incarnation. Not that Surt would have understood or cared for my belated remorse – that too was the product of their pernicious influence. Hence my hunger for revenge, not because I expected a reconciliation with Chaos – not *then* – but because the urge to destroy was really all that I had left.

My first and purest impulse was to seek out the enemies of the Aesir. Just as Gullveig-Heid had done in the days of the Winter War, I thought to find refuge among the renegade Vanir, exchanging my skills for their protection. The problem was, I'd been *too* good. My reputation preceded me. I was known throughout the Worlds as the Trickster of the gods, the man who'd given Odin his spear; Frey his ship; Thor his hammer. I was the man who'd built Asgard in stone and cheated the builder of his reward. In fact I'd cheated *everyone* – including Death itself – with the result that no one would trust me, or believe I meant business.

And so I decided to bide my time. There were perks to living in Asgard. The food was good, there was plenty of wine and the view was the best in the Nine Worlds. War with the Aesir would change all that. Living under a grubby tent, or in a cave in the mountains; no Idun to heal my wounds; growing old; getting fleas; looking up at Asgard and remembering what I could have had . . .

No, I decided. That wasn't my style. Better to live as a dog in Asgard than as a god anywhere else. Better to work undercover for now; undermining them one by one; spreading discord among them; working to find out their weaknesses; taking them down one at a time. Then, when they were ready to fall . . .

Boom!

*

I started with Freyja. No reason, except that she was the weakest link in the chain. Odin had a soft spot for her, and if my plan worked, I meant to cut him as deeply. Now the Goddess of Desire was vain and, since my encounter with the Tunnel Folk, had never ceased to question me about their treasures, especially the jewellery I'd seen on my visit to World Below.

'Tell me more,' she would say, lounging on her silken couch, eating fruit, attended by her maidens. One of them was Sigyn, whose interest in me seemed to increase the less attention I paid to her. Next to Freyja she looked plain, which I guess was Freyja's intention. Freyja herself was peerless, of course; creamy skin, red-gold hair, a rack like you wouldn't believe. Her amber-eyed cats purred at her feet, the air all around her was scented. No one – not even I – was wholly impervious to her charms, but I preferred the wilder type, and besides, I had more important things on my mind than romance.

'Well,' I began, helping myself to a grape. 'The sons of Ivaldi may not have been judged the best craftsmen in the Nine Worlds – although I still dispute this – but they are undoubtedly the finest goldsmiths I've ever seen, as I'm sure you'd agree, if you'd seen their work. I'm talking about *gold*, Freyja. Necklaces, bracelets, the lot – shining like scraps of sunlight. And there was one particular piece – a necklace like you've never seen. A choker, broad as the length of your thumb, made up of links so delicately crafted that it might almost be a living thing; moulded to every curve of your neck; gleaming, reflecting, perfecting—'

Freyja gave me a sharp look. 'Perfecting?'

'Sorry. My mistake. Of course. My lady, you're perfect already.'

I grinned inside. The lure was thrown. After that, it was only a matter of time before Freyja went in search of it. I watched her from afar. Not for long. Sure enough, as I'd anticipated, I saw her leave Asgard one morning – on foot, without her chariot, without even a single handmaiden to assist her – and cross the plain of Ida in search of the Sons of Ivaldi.

I followed her in bird form, soaring high above her head, and when she entered World Below through the Forest of Ironwood, I changed myself into a flea and dropped into her cleavage, to find out just what kind of deal she was ready to make with the Maggots.

The first time I'd been in that workshop, my own head had almost been turned by the potency of all that gold. Freyja, who lived for beautiful things, I knew would be bedazzled. And so she was. In spite of the stink, and the heat of the forge, that necklace, displayed against a backdrop of rock, blazed out like the light from the sun. I saw her eyes widen; her lips part. She held out her hand to touch it . . .

Dark against the orange glow, the Sons of Ivaldi watched her. I told you they worshipped beauty; they'd never seen anything like her before. Desire, unveiled and in Aspect; as I said, even Odin, married to Frigg and a seemingly happy father-of-three, had been known to lust after Freyja, although he kept his feelings at bay and hidden to all but Yours Truly.

The Sons of Ivaldi had no such restraint. Their dark eyes shone; they practically drooled.

Dvalin stepped forward. 'To what do I owe . . . ?'

'How much is that necklace?' said Freyja.

Dvalin shrugged. 'It's not for sale.'

'But I want it,' said Freyja. 'I'll give you gold. Whatever you want.'

Once more, Dvalin shrugged. 'I have all the gold I can use,' he said.

'Well, surely you must need *something*?' Freyja gave him her sweetest smile and touched him on the shoulder. 'Besides, it would please me so *very* much. Don't you want to please me?'

Slowly, Dvalin nodded. His brothers stepped forward to join him. From the shadows I saw them, hungry and filled with longing. 'Oh, yes. I want to please you,' he said.

Freyja's smile grew broader. She reached out to touch the necklace; studded with gemstones; gleaming with runes; lithe and light as a golden snakeskin.

'I'll give you the necklace,' Dvalin said. 'In payment for four nights of pleasure.'

'What?' said Freyja, the smile fading.

'One night for each of us,' Dvalin said. 'We made the necklace together. It's unique. It's stitched through with glam. The wearer's beauty will never fade. Nothing will ever spoil it – or *you*. That's my price. Now what do you say?'

Freyja bit her lip. A tear, burning gold in the light of the forge, ran slowly down her cheek.

'Four nights,' said Dvalin. 'After that, the necklace is yours for ever.'

OK, so I watched. Is that so bad? Besides, it was a Hel of a show. I knew that Freyja was shallow, but until that moment I hadn't been sure how far she would go for the sake of personal adornment. Well, folks, she went *all* the way, *every* way – and not just once, but four times, with four uncouth and demanding men who hadn't had a woman in years. Still, she got what she wanted, and I watched as the Sons of Ivaldi fastened the necklace around her neck, leering and smirking and touching her all over with their horny hands. I followed her as she fled back home to Asgard and a long bath – and then I made for Odin's hall and told him everything I'd seen.

They say 'never trust a one-eyed man'. But some might say that where women are concerned, *all* men are one-eyed, and even that eye doesn't see much. Odin's one eye narrowed in rage when I told him the sordid details, but he couldn't seem to stop listening. I know. I'm a good narrator. And the story I was telling him was almost irresistible.

When I had finished, he vented his rage, flinging his goblet of wine to the floor. 'Why did you tell me all this?' he said.

'Hey, don't shoot the messenger. I thought you might want to know, that's all. That Freyja, our beautiful Freyja, sold herself to the Maggots. *I* didn't sanction it. *I* didn't encourage her. She's a responsible adult, and I guess she knew what she was doing. Still, *some* people might say that her actions could have endangered all of us. Or that she had a duty to inform you if she was leaving Asgard. I said *some people*. I don't judge. Still, I thought you ought to know.'

Odin gave a low growl. 'Get me the necklace,' he told me.

'What, me?'

'You know how to do it,' he said. 'Don't think I don't know what this is. This is payback for Brokk, and that awl.'

I feigned innocence. 'Payback?' I said. 'Why would I need payback? You're my brother. We swore a pact. And as for that silly business with Brokk . . .' I smiled. My mouth was almost healed by then. 'You know, I'd almost forgotten that. You really don't need to feel guilty. Although, *some* might say that the things we do sometimes come back to haunt us. There should be a word for that, don't you think? Something poetic. I'll think of one.'

Odin's growl grew more menacing. 'Get me the necklace, Loki,' he said.

I put up my hands. 'I'll give it a try.'

I waited till Freyja was asleep. Then I entered her chamber, once again disguised as a flea. Freyja was wearing the necklace in bed – and nothing else, I noticed – but, regaining my Aspect, I found that she was lying on the clasp. I couldn't reach to unfasten it. And I couldn't afford to wait until the goddess turned over in her sleep. My mission might have Odin's blessing, but if I were caught next to Freyja's bed, naked, in the middle of the night, the Vanir wouldn't hesitate to gut me like a mackerel.

And so I returned into my flea Aspect and bit her on the eyelid. She gave a sigh and turned over, exposing the clasp of the necklace. Assuming my Aspect once again, I reached for the necklace and, very gently, unfastened it and slid it off. Then I crept to the chamber door and unlocked it from the inside, blew the sleeping Freyja a kiss, and prepared to head back to Odin's hall, where the Old Man was waiting grimly for proof of her betrayal.

But as I was reaching for my clothes (which I'd left at the door as I shifted, of course), I became aware of a figure standing in the passageway. It was Heimdall, snooping around as usual, who must have spotted my signature from his vantage point on Bif-rost.

He drew his mindsword, a cantrip of *Týr* – a flickering blade as deceptively fast as a moth's wing, and as sharp as my tongue.

'This is not what it looks like,' I said.

He smiled, exposing his golden teeth. 'Let's see what your insides look like.'

I shifted to my Wildfire Aspect and started to race down the passageway, dropping the necklace onto the flags. But Heimdall cast the rune *Logr* – water – and I found myself suddenly, painfully quenched.

I returned to my habitual Aspect, shivering, drenched and *au naturel*.

'You don't know what you're getting into,' I gasped. 'The Old Man sanctioned this himself.'

He laughed. 'I knew you were a liar,' he said, 'but this tops it all. The General asked you to break into Freyja's rooms? Why would he do that?'

I shrugged and picked up the necklace again. 'Let's go. You can ask him yourself.'

They tell you revenge isn't worth it. I say there's nothing finer. I reached Odin's hall in a headlock, naked, wet and covered in soot. Heimdall, looking like a golden retriever triumphantly bringing one of his master's slippers, flung me at the General's feet.

'I found this little weasel sniffing around Freyja's bedroom,' he said. 'I know that for some reason he entertains you, but—'

'Get out,' Odin said.

'But, Allfather—' began Heimdall, confused.

'I said, get out,' snarled Odin. 'You've done quite enough for one night. And unless you want to bring even more shame onto Freyja and the Vanir, keep your mouth shut about what you saw. Loki has shown more loyalty than any of your people. Lay a hand on him again, you overgrown canary, and I'll knock you off your perch for good. All right?'

Heimdall's jaw dropped. 'I don't underst—'

'Bye-bye, Goldie,' I said, and grinned. 'Don't say I didn't warn you.'

He left, grinding his golden teeth so violently that sparks flew.

'You got the necklace,' Odin said, turning back to me.

'Of course.'

'Let me see it.'

I kept a straight face but inside I was grinning.

Oh, the Old Man was sweet on Freyja, all right, in spite of his comfy marriage to Frigg. Freyja liked to encourage it, as she encouraged everyone – but saving a special smile for him, and cultivating a girlish flutter whenever Odin was around. His admiration gave her status, of course. And even Allfather wasn't immune to a little flattery.

I affected an air of sorrow as I handed over the necklace. There was no denying either its beauty or its value. The runes that held it together shone like captive shards of starlight, and the many gemstones spun into the work gleamed like the tears in a woman's eyes.

'What are you going to do?' I asked. 'Keep it? Wear it? Give it back?'

Slowly, Odin shook his head. Behind him, on the back of his throne, his ravens – Hugin and Munin, the physical manifestations of Allfather's thoughts in bird form – clicked their beaks and glared at me.

'Leave me alone. I need to think.'

I grinned and sauntered back to my rooms, where I slept like a babe for the rest of the night. I doubt whether Odin did, but then, that was kind of what I was going for.

I woke with the sun, showered and shaved, and was just contemplating a spot of breakfast when I heard a terrific commotion coming from Allfather's hall. Freyja had discovered the loss of her necklace and, finding the doors to her chamber unlocked, had rightly suspected Yours Truly.

'Where is my *necklace*?' she was screaming as I wandered into the hall.

Odin was sitting on his throne, a bird on either shoulder. His face was stony. Only the birds moved.

Freyja saw me come in. '*You!* You broke into my chamber!'

'Who, me?'

Freyja turned to Odin. '*Yes!* Loki stole my necklace. He crept into my room, like a thief, and stole it from me as I slept. I want him punished. I want him *dead*. And I want my *necklace*!'

'What, this?' Odin said, pulling it out of his pocket.

Freyja coloured. 'Give it to me.'

He shrugged. 'It's a pretty bauble,' he said. 'Was it very expensive?'

Now she grew pale. 'Hand it over,' she said.

'Four nights. That sounds like a bargain,' said Odin in his cold, silky voice. 'Ivaldi's sons got a good deal.'

Freyja's expression hardened. 'You don't own me, Odin,' she said. 'You can't tell me what to do. The necklace is mine. I paid for it. Now give it back.'

He did not reply. On his shoulder, one of the birds scratched its dark head with a claw. Nothing else moved. The Old Man might have been carved from granite.

Freyja started to cry then. She could do that at will, golden tears to melt the heart of the sternest of men. 'Please,' she said. 'I'll do anything . . .'

'I think we've established that,' I said.

Odin gave a little smile. It wasn't a good smile, but Freyja must have taken it as a sign of capitulation. She draped herself on Odin's arm and peered at him through her lashes.

'I'm yours,' she said. 'If you want me . . .'

The smile became a skull's grin.

'Oh yes,' said Odin. 'I want you. But that rune you bear – the rune *Fé* – is more than just the desire for gold. I'm giving you a new Aspect, Freyja. Desire cuts both ways, like a double blade. It can mean love. But it's also the lust that drives a man to his own death, the lust for blood and violence. Henceforth, you will spread that desire everywhere in the Middle Worlds; you'll set men against each other, you'll lie, you'll use your charms to deceive, to betray, and even then they'll worship you. Even as they bleed and die, they'll only want you even more, with a desire that only Death can satisfy for ever.'

'What about my necklace?' Freyja said.

'Yes, I'll give it back,' he said. 'In fact, you'll never take it off. I want you to wear it so neither of us will ever forget what happened here.'

'Whatever,' said Freyja. 'The necklace, please.'

Odin handed it over.

And that's why the Goddess of Desire has two Aspects: the Maiden, ripe and beautiful as a golden peach in summertime; and the Crone, the carrion demon of battle, hideously beautiful, gloved in blood to her armpits and screaming with unsatisfied lust.

LESSON 2

Apples

An apple a day keeps the doctor away.
No one's immune to bribery.

Lokabrenna

IT WAS A VERY SMALL REVENGE, but it pleased me, nevertheless. I hadn't been planning to challenge the gods, just cause as much distress as I could without arousing suspicion. And the business of Freyja's necklace had already caused its share of distress – to Freyja and the Vanir, of course, but also to Heimdall, whose position of trust I'd undermined; to Frigg, Odin's wife, whose loyalty had taken a hit; and, of course, to Odin himself, who had revealed himself to be an old fool of the most classic kind, losing his head over a girl.

And the greatest thing about it? They'd brought their sorrow on themselves. All I did was tell the truth and let their nature do the rest. Greed, hatred, jealousy – all the corrupting emotions with which Odin had infected *me* – coming home like pigeons to roost. I tell you, it was beautiful.

But that was only the start of it. An appetizer, if you like. One day I meant to have them all at my feet, begging for help, just so I could kick them aside and laugh as they went tumbling . . .

Still, all in good time, I told myself. It takes more than a couple of stones to bring down an enemy fortress. And I had all the time in the Worlds to bring the Old Man to his knees. I decided to play it safe for a while, to try and play at being one of the guys until a new opportunity arose. As for Odin, as far as he was concerned, I'd paid him back for Brokk and the awl, and now he figured we were square.

But as time passed, I realized that the business with Freyja had changed him. He became increasingly moody and withdrawn. He'd always been fond of travelling but now he left Asgard more often than ever – alone, except for Sleipnir, his horse – and often for weeks and months on end. No one knew where he went during those long absences, but I knew he favoured the Middle Worlds, and most especially Inland, where he walked unseen and in disguise and the Folk told all kinds of tales about him.

True, he spread most of them himself, posing as a travelling storyteller, but he liked them anyway, and he enjoyed the way in which the Folk expressed their devotion. What he enjoyed less was the fact that Thor was by far the more popular, at least as far as the Folk were concerned. I suspect there may have been a little friction between father and son; Thor's muscle provided excellent protection for Asgard, but secretly Odin was dismayed that he and his son were so different. As for his youngest son, Balder – well. Frigg adored him, but Odin – well. Suffice it to say that whenever Balder was around, Odin always found an excuse to be somewhere else.

I could see why. There was darkness in Odin, a darkness that only I understood, and I could see how it preyed on him, eating him from the inside. Still, that's the price of godhood, folks. Maintaining Order isn't easy, especially in a world in which Chaos is always struggling to regain the upper hand. The little world of Inland gave the Old Man comfort, somehow; that's why he went there so often, although he also ventured as far as the realms of the Rock Folk and Ice Folk, always in secret and in disguise, telling no one where he went, not even Frigg

– not even me.

Meanwhile, back in Asgard, things had settled down for a while. Heimdall still hated me from afar, but after his last humiliation he was afraid to say too much. Thor had his hammer to play with, Bragi was learning the bagpipes, Balder was working his pectorals and Frey was engaged on a romantic quest. More of that later. But Yours Truly had time on his hands for exploring the Worlds, and Odin was more than happy for a temporary change of scene.

You recall he liked to travel alone? This time, he wanted company. I was more than willing; besides, I was getting restless too. There's only so much a man can achieve within four walls. I needed air. I needed new sensations. I was finally coming to terms with my current Aspect, and with the fact that bad smells, pain, cold and some of the more disgusting requirements of my physical body could be tempered by its insatiable capacity for pleasure.

Women and food I already knew – I had an appetite for both – but I guessed that the Worlds outside might contain considerably more than that. Besides, if I was to bring down the gods, I wanted to know their enemies. As it turned out, I got to know some of them just a little *too* well – but I'll get to that later.

And so, when Odin suggested a little trip out of Asgard, I was happy to oblige. There were three of us: the General, Honir and Yours Truly. Remember Honir the Silent? The same young man that Odin had sent with Mimir to spy on the Vanir long ago. A vapid, indecisive type, better at sports than at thinking. Basically, an expendable, which was why Odin chose to take him along. As for myself, I like to think that Odin valued my company; or maybe it was just to make sure I didn't cause trouble while he was away.

We crossed Bif-rost into Inland, the centre part of the Middle Worlds, and, using the rune *Raedo* for speed, made our way through the Ridings, keeping to the less-travelled roads, until we reached the Northlands. It was an area Odin liked for some reason; I personally found it too cold, but Wildfire *is* my nature. In any case, we found ourselves travelling through mountains; huge, looming, dark mountains with slices of narrow valley between and winds that cut like razors. Beyond lay the realm of the Ice People; another area of incomprehensible fascination for the General. Perhaps he had a mistress there – the Old Man had a roving eye – or maybe it was just his way of keeping track of his enemies.

We travelled for days; Odin morose; Honir talking constantly – about the scenery, the sheep in the fields, the funny dream he'd had last night, speculating on whether we were there yet, how many leagues we must have travelled, or how long it was to lunchtime . . .

Odin had his horse with him, but Sleipnir too was in humbler Aspect, and the steed with a foot in eight of Nine Worlds was now just an ordinary roan, vaguely red in colour, with only the standard number of legs. It meant we had to take turns to ride, which I for one thought rather a waste, but Odin would have it no other way, and so I endured the discomfort and hoped he appreciated my sacrifice.

Our supplies had long since run out, and all of us were hungry. There was clearly to be no nipping back to Asgard for lunch, riding Sleipnir in full Aspect. So, finding a herd of wild oxen grazing in one of those narrow valleys, we killed one, butchered it, lit a fire and started to roast the animal in pieces among the hot coals.

Odin sat down on his bedroll and lit his pipe (another habit of the Folk he'd picked up on his travels).

'See how simple all this is? Just the three of us and the fire, with the open sky overhead.'

I looked up. I didn't see that the sky looked any different from the sky we could see in Asgard, but when Odin was in poetic mood, there was no reasoning with him.

'Is the meat cooked?' Honir said.

Odin shook his head. 'Just wait. Listen to the sound of the

wind. Don't you think it calls to you?'

I could have told him that the only thing that was calling to me was that haunch of beef over the fire, but then I thought better of it.

And so we waited. And waited. I was getting very hungry. Of all my new physical sensations, eating was one of the ones I preferred, but actual *hunger* – I wasn't a fan. The scent of roasting flesh was so good that my mouth was watering. My stomach was cramped with anticipation. We waited until we were sure it was ready, then raked the meat out of the ashes, only to find it was still cold.

'What's this?' I said. 'That beef should be cooked.'

Odin shrugged. 'Put it back. It can't have been cooking for as long as we thought.'

We put the meat back on the fire and covered it in hot coals. Night began to fall. The icy mist that during the day had kept mostly to the mountaintops began to roll down into the valley.

Honir asked: 'Is it ready yet?'

'How the Hel should I know?' I said.

'Should we check? I think we should check.'

I pulled a haunch out of the fire. I like my beef pretty rare, and I was more than ready for lunch. But the piece of meat was as cold as ever, not even seared on the outside.

I cursed. 'This isn't right,' I said.

'Do you think someone's using glam?' Honir said.

'Well, *duh*.'

I looked around. And we saw, above us, in a tree, a giant eagle watching us. *Bjarkán*, the rune of true vision, revealed it to be no ordinary bird; its eyes gleamed with evil intelligence.

It saw us watching and gave a croak, flexing its powerful wings.

'*Ark.* Share your meal with me,' it said, 'and I'll make sure the meat is cooked.'

I could see the glam around the bird; he had a powerful signature. A demon, I guessed, or a scavenger; or maybe one of the Ice Folk in bird Aspect, flying south to explore the terrain. In any case, our position was weak and it didn't seem wise to dispute him a share of the spoils.

'I think we should share,' Honir said. 'Don't you agree that we should share? I mean, if we share we'll get to eat soon. And birds don't have much of an appetite. Don't the Folk say "he eats like a bird" when someone doesn't have much of an appetite?'

Odin agreed to the bargain. The ox was a good size, he said, and besides, as Honir suggested, how much could an eagle eat?

Turns out that particular eagle could eat almost a whole one. As soon as the ox was ready, it grabbed both haunches and the rump, leaving us with little more than the carcass. Then it took the pieces onto a nearby outcrop of rock and began to tear at the flesh, noisily and with relish.

Let me explain for a moment here. I was very hungry. I'd had a long and exhausting day. I'd had to listen to Honir's inane conversation for hours. I was cold and frustrated, and the only food for miles around was fast disappearing into the gullet of a great, greedy bird. So shoot me. I lost my temper.

I picked up a length of branch.

The eagle kept on eating, tearing at the pieces of meat with its brutal, bloodstained claws.

I raised the branch with both hands and aimed a swipe at the eagle. It struck. But the moment the blow connected, I felt a sudden surge of glam run through my body and my arms. At the very same time, I found that my hands were frozen onto the piece of branch, which in its turn stuck to the eagle. A blaze of runelight surrounded us both. I sensed that maybe I'd been just a *little* unwise.

'What's happening?' said Honir.

I ignored him and tried to shift Aspect. But whatever glam was affecting me had robbed me of my power to change. I was trapped; my hands were caught, and now the bird spread its powerful wings and, rising above the outcrop of rock, lifted me with it into the air.

'Hey!' I yelled. 'Hey! Let me down!'

The eagle said nothing but rose higher, now flying in a steep diagonal towards the rocky mountainside. Its wings beat with smooth and vigorous strokes; helplessly I just hung on. Below me, the figures of Odin and Honir receded into the rolling mists.

I started to feel a little scared.

'All right! I'm sorry I hit you!' I said.

Still the eagle did not speak. My arms were hurting.

I said: 'Come on. A joke's a joke. Put me down and finish your lunch. You can even have my share if you like.'

The eagle made no response but continued its trajectory, angling low towards the scree that covered the flank of the mountain. I saw the ground approach at speed and braced myself for a hard landing.

But the eagle did not land. Instead it dipped low across the scree, dragging me along the ground. My hands were still caught; I couldn't escape. I tobogganed across the scree, the stones and rocks and boulders.

That pain thing again. I'm not a fan. I howled and struggled and begged for release; cracking my ribs against a rock; skinning my backside on the gravel; barking my shins and ankles repeatedly over a xylophone of little stones.

'Why me? What did I do?'

Still, the eagle did not reply, but concentrated on giving Yours Truly the ride of his life; first along the skirt of scree, then up through a narrow chimney of rock, then through the topmost branches of a sizeable stand of trees, that whipped and tore and flailed at me as I was dragged through the canopy.

By then I was screaming for mercy. My clothes were torn; I'd lost my boots; I was bruised and bleeding. I felt as if I'd been beaten, first by a dozen men with cudgels, then by the same dozen men with whips, then set alight, and then beaten out like a dusty carpet.

'Please!' I said. 'I'll do anything!'

Finally, the eagle spoke. '*Ark.* You will?'

'I swear!' I said.

'*Ark.*' The voice was harsh and dry. 'Swear you'll bring me Idun, and her golden apples. Then I'll let you go.'

'Idun?' Too late, I saw the trap.

'And the golden apples. *Ark.*'

I started to protest. 'But how? How could I even do that? She never leaves Asgard. Bragi's with her all the time. She's— *Owwww!* That was unnecessary!'

That was the tip of a young poplar, right in the spot where even a god feels it keenly.

'Please,' I said, when the power of speech finally returned to me. 'It can't be done. It's impossible.'

'*Ark.* I suggest you find a way,' said the eagle, making for the next patch of scree. 'Unless you want to experience the world's worst case of road-rash.'

My throat was dry. I swallowed.

'Um. I might be able to think of something.'

'You'll have to do better than that,' he said. 'I want your word. Your binding oath.' And he started to plummet towards the ground, folding his wings to increase his speed.

I closed my eyes. 'All right! I swear!'

The eagle unfolded his wings again.

'Swear on your name. Your true name.'

'Please! Do I have to?'

'*Yes!*'

So shoot me. I swore. What else could I do?

The eagle's trajectory broadened out and we started a long and lazy descent back. As we reached the valley floor, some thirty miles or so from the place where Odin and Honir had made their camp, finding my frozen hands free at last, I dropped the last dozen feet to the ground and lay there, exhausted and hurting.

'Remember your oath,' said the eagle. 'Idun, and her apples.'

I flipped him the bird. Even doing *that* hurt.

The eagle just laughed as it flew away; a nasty, croaking,

rusty sound. It knew I couldn't break that oath; my true name bound me to obey. I had no glam left to shift Aspect, or to hurl runes at the fleeing bird, or even to cast the rune *Bjarkán* to identify my abductor. Instead I lay where I was for a while until I was strong enough to stand, then pulled myself painfully to my feet and started the long walk back to camp.

It was near dawn when I arrived. I'd had to walk for most of the night. I was starving; I was sore; I was limping badly. Though it was no consolation, I saw that the others had also spent a sleepless night. Odin in particular was looking weary, and Honir, fresh as the morning dew, was talking nineteen to the dozen.

He stopped when I reached the camp.

'Loki! What happened?'

'Nothing,' I said.

'It doesn't look like nothing to me,' said Honir. 'Odin, what do you think? I think something happened. In fact, I'm pretty sure something happened. Loki looks terrible. Don't you think Loki looks terrible?'

'Shut up, Honir,' Odin said, and, summoning Sleipnir's true Aspect at last, prepared to carry the three of us back to civilization.

Arriving at the Sky Citadel on nothing but spleen and will power, I first ate three roast chickens, a mutton pie, a haunch of beef, a salmon and four dozen jam tarts that Sigyn had left to cool on a ledge. Then I drank three bottles of wine and slept for forty-eight hours.

I awoke feeling somewhat better, if not completely recovered, took a hot shower, shaved and dressed and went off in search of Idun. I found her in her garden, singing softly to herself. Her blonde hair was woven with daisies; her feet were bare in the damp grass. Her basket of apples was at her side, ready for immediate use.

'Loki, you look terrible,' she said. 'Are you hurt? Did you get in a fight? Is there something I can do?'

I guess it was common knowledge that I didn't make much of a habit of hanging around in gardens. Besides, as Idun had pointed out, I'd taken a lot of punishment, and even after a long sleep I wasn't exactly Balder the Beautiful.

'I had some trouble in the North,' I said. 'But that's not why I'm here. Imagine, Idun, while I was there, I saw a tree in the heart of a wood, and on it were apples just like yours!'

'Like mine?' said Idun. 'Really?'

'The very same,' I told her.

'Did you bring some back?'

'No. I was otherwise engaged at the time in single-handedly fighting off a giant eagle that had attacked our camp. But as I limped back home, I thought, I bet Idun would want to see these. Maybe these golden apples have similar properties to hers. If so, I thought, it's my duty to check. And so I came here straight away.'

Idun cut me a sliver of fruit. 'Eat this. It'll make you feel better.'

It did – Idun's golden apples were known throughout the Nine Worlds. They were Ivaldi's wedding gift to her when she moved in with Bragi, and as well as conferring perpetual youth (always a bonus when applying for godhood), they also acted as a kind of universal tonic, healing most ills, from warts to the pox, and all but the most lethal of wounds. My cuts and bruises healed at once; the pain in my body disappeared; my glam was restored to its usual strength.

'Thanks. That hit the spot,' I said. 'Now about that tree . . .'

She looked at me with eyes that were innocent as summer sky. 'Shouldn't we tell Bragi first? Or Odin – he'll know what to do.'

'What, and disappoint them if the apples *don't* turn out to be like yours? No, let's just go and check for ourselves. Then, if it's good news, we'll all celebrate.'

I told you she was innocent. No sense of threat or danger

at all. It was like abducting a kitten – but then, I was already running so many risks that the last thing I wanted at that point was a challenge.

I shielded us with the rune *Ýr* as we passed Heimdall's lookout post on the Bridge. Then I led Idun as fast as I could into the plains of the Middle World. It wasn't easy – she stopped to sniff every flower on the way and to listen to every bird – but at last the enemy found us. In eagle Aspect he tracked us down, then, swooping from the leaden sky he picked up Idun, basket and all, in his talons and flew away.

I cast the rune *Bjarkán* as he left and focused on his signature. As I'd suspected, my avian friend was one of the Ice Folk – one of the worst. His name was Thiassi, and he was a warlord of the far North, an ally of Gullveig, armed with her runes, and I'd just given him what he most craved – Idun's apples, eternal youth, and the chance to make a serious bid for godhood.

Well, so far so good, I thought. Perhaps my misadventure could be turned to my advantage. After all, if I wanted to bring down the gods, Thiassi could be an ally – except that he had already got what he wanted from me by then, which rather reduced my bargaining power. Besides, the Ice Folk hated me; I'd earned a reputation by then as the Trickster of the gods, and it wouldn't be easy to convince the enemy of my change of heart. I didn't blame them. Frankly, I wouldn't have trusted me either.

I walked back home, released from my oath, but feeling slightly guilty. Idun was the one person in Asgard who had never done a thing to me, and who'd been kind when I was hurt. Still, I'd sworn a binding oath, a real one, on my true name, and no one reneges on a binding oath without some radical consequences. I'd had no choice, I told myself – besides, the sliver of apple that she'd given me would last a while, at least until the other gods started to notice her absence . . .

It didn't take long. The apples of youth, like all cosmetics, work on a cumulative principle. Meaning: once you stop, you drop. And that's what happened in Asgard. Before you could say *an apple a day*, everyone was the worse for wear. Even Golden Boy, Balder the Fair, started to look distinctly less than glamorous. As for the others – well, you can imagine. Wrinkles, hair loss, middle-aged spread, incontinence, forgetfulness, piles . . . you name it – and that was just the goddesses. Except for Your Humble Narrator, of course, which meant that sooner or later they would put two and two together.

That was all right. That was my plan. Another little revenge – this time, hitting the gods where it hurt them the most, right at the heart of their vanity. And the beauty of it was that I would be the one to save the day – because when Asgard fell, I promised myself, it wouldn't be at the hands of some hairy warlord from the hills, but in style, and with maximum effect, and with Yours Truly holding the whip. I wasn't about to hand my revenge to someone like Thiassi; a renegade whose ambition extended to nothing more than sitting in Odin's high seat and assuming the name of Allfather. No, if I was ever to regain my place in Chaos (an almost impossible dream, to which I turned in my darkest moments), I would have to do something spectacular. Nothing short of the total destruction of Order would satisfy Chaos. That meant Asgard; the gods; the Worlds. And even then, it might not be enough . . .

Eventually, they figured it out. Heimdall, whose eyesight had dimmed perceptibly since his supply of fruit was cut off, remembered seeing me coming back over the Bridge furtively a few weeks before. The rest of the gods searched their memories and concluded that this was the last day that anyone had seen Idun. And so they found me and dragged me in front of the Old Man, who was looking older than ever by then, white-haired and craggy-faced, and prepared to do very bad things to me.

'Is this true?' he said. *'Why?'*

'What does it matter?' said Heimdall. 'Let's just kill him now, before we all forget why we brought him here.'

'Wait a minute,' I said, and explained everything that had happened. Odin listened in silence, while his ravens clicked their beaks and everyone mumbled and dribbled in rage.

'You see?' I went on. 'I had no choice. That eagle was no ordinary bird. It was Thiassi, the Hunter, and he would have killed me if I hadn't agreed.'

'We'll kill you now,' said Heimdall. 'Slowly and *very* painfully.'

'What? And lose your only chance of getting Idun back?' I said. 'Use your brain, Goldie. I know it's not as sharp as it used to be, but—'

Odin interrupted. 'You think you can get Idun back?'

I shrugged. 'Of course. I'm Loki.'

Heimdall protested. 'Seriously, Allfather, you're going to let him go *again*? How can you know if he'll even come back? He might decide to throw in his lot with Thiassi and the Ice People.'

'If he'd wanted to do that, don't you think he'd have done it before?' said Odin. 'Besides, we don't have a choice. Let him go.'

And so, they released me.

I stretched my limbs. 'Where would you be without me now?' I grinned at the angry circle of elderly gods and goddesses. 'I'll try to be quick,' I told them. 'Try not to die of old age while I'm gone.'

Then I looked at Freyja. 'Lend me your falcon cloak,' I said. 'I need to fly to the Northlands.'

'But you can do that anyway,' protested Freyja, whose shapeshifting skills were as good as my own, but who rarely shifted Aspects unless she really needed to. Thus the cloak; a marvellous thing of feathers bound together with runes, allowing the wearer to fly like a bird, without arriving naked at his destination.

I have to admit, that appealed to me – it was cold in the Northlands, and I didn't want to freeze to death. But, more importantly, the cloak would allow me to carry the apples home;

plus I couldn't cast runes while I was in bird Aspect, which would make me extremely vulnerable if Thiassi were to come after me.

'Are you going to argue?' I said, giving Freyja my broadest smile. 'Or shall we wait another few days, till your hair falls out and your teeth go black?'

Freyja handed over the cloak.

'Thanks,' I said. 'Now, the rest of you. Keep watch. Look for my signature in the sky. Collect all the firewood you can – dry wood, shavings. You'll know what that's for if the time comes. And try to stay awake, won't you? I might be in a hurry.'

Odin said nothing, but nodded. I pulled on Freyja's feather cloak. An interesting sensation, though I had no time to enjoy it just then. I took flight at once, leaving them to watch me, open-mouthed, as I flew, and made my way back to the Northlands, shielding myself with runes all the way.

I tracked Thiassi back to his stronghold – the Ice Folk are careless with signatures – a castle built into the rock in the cleft between two mountains. It was bleak and very cold – even with Freyja's feather cloak I was half frozen in the air – but luck was on my side, because I found Idun almost at once; alone and shivering by the fire in one of the castle's many rooms.

I stepped out of the feather cloak.

'Loki!' she cried, and hugged me. 'I *knew* you'd come to rescue me!'

I said, 'Where's Thiassi?'

'Gone ice-fishing with his daughter, Skadi. I don't like her,' Idun said.

I thought that if *Idun* didn't like her – Idun, who thinks that wolves and bears are cute and that even Your Humble Narrator has a soft side – then Skadi must be something else. I made a mental note to avoid her.

'All right,' I said. 'Then let's go.'

A single cantrip and I'd changed her into something a falcon could carry. Then I swept her basket of apples underneath my falcon cloak and let it transform me once again. A moment later, we were off; a falcon, flying hard and high, carrying a hazelnut.

This time, I wasted none of my glam trying to go unseen, but simply concentrated on speed. How long before Thiassi and Skadi returned? How long would it be before Idun was missed?

I knew that Thiassi's eagle form was more than a match for a falcon. I was fast, but he was faster, which meant that even with a head start, I could expect him to catch up with me long before we reached Asgard. In fact, I was three-quarters of the way there when I saw the speck in the sky, hunting me, observing me.

I waited until he was close enough, then shot him with the rune *Hagall*. The eagle dropped back for a mile or so, then started to creep back again. I gave him the fire-rune *Kaen* as I fled, and folded my wings to increase my speed. Thiassi tracked me for an hour that way, keeping his distance, but close enough to move in for the kill as soon as I showed any weakness. I was getting tired by then, and my glam was weakening. I gave him a blast of the rune *Thuris* and felt myself flagging in mid-air; Thiassi saw it at once and began to circle me from above.

But I could see Asgard, ten miles away, shining and gold in the sunset. If only I could reach it in time. Ten miles . . .

'Hold tight,' I said to Idun in her hazelnut form. Then I increased my speed again, leaving nothing in reserve. The seconds passed. The hunter drew close. By the time I'd reached the Rainbow Bridge, I could actually feel him on my tail.

But the Old Man had done as I'd asked; with my bird-vision I could see bundles of firewood stacked on the battlements and barrels of dry shavings drenched in oil, just ready to burn. My body, under the feather cloak, was trembling with exhaustion and fear. I folded myself into a dart and made a final lunge for the walls . . .

'Light it up! Light it up!' I yelled as I shot past the battlements.

I hit the ground with more urgency than grace, rolled and

flung off the feather cloak. Idun, still in hazelnut form, bounced across the cobblestones. I freed her with a cantrip, then collapsed in exhaustion, drained of every scrap of glam.

If my plan had failed, that was it. I was totally helpless.

But I hadn't failed, of course. The fires were burning fiercely. The combination of dry wood and oil had caused the blaze to leap up fast and Thiassi, hot on my tail, had found himself heading, not for battlements, but for a massive firewall.

Wings alight, he lost control and fell in flames to the parapet. After that, they finished him off – old as they were, with sticks and rocks – and that was the end of Thiassi. The greatest hunter who'd ever lived; flame-grilled like a chicken and killed by a gang of old-age pensioners.

Gods, I told myself, *I'm good*.

Then I got up, still shaky, and took a bow. 'Thank you, ladies and gentlemen. Refreshments are available. Form an orderly queue, please . . .'

Idun gave out her apples.

LESSON 3

Feet

Laughter disarms the fiercest of men.

Lokabrenna

IT WASN'T TOO LONG before the news of Thiassi's death reached the Middle Worlds. I may have had something to do with that; after all, it isn't every day that Yours Truly turns out to be a hero. The best part of revenge, I found, was earning the enemy's gratitude: Bragi wrote songs about me; people sang them in roadside inns. Soon, it was common knowledge that Loki had lured the Hunter to an ignominious death. Before I knew it I was famous; my name was on everyone's lips. Women loved it – though I'll admit I could have been more careful.

As it was, I'd forgotten about Thiassi's daughter, Skadi. She must have heard what had happened, because some three months afterwards, she arrived at Asgard's gates, armed and ready for combat, demanding recompense for her father's death and threatening the gods with war.

I have to say, she had a point. Killing Thiassi in battle was one thing. A worthy end for a would-be god. But to be slaughtered and grilled like a chicken – well. It was no less than he deserved for what he'd done to me, of course, but the Ice People were a proud lot, and it must have rankled.

Odin could have sent Skadi packing, of course, but he didn't want war with the Ice Folk. A friendly foothold in the North would make far more sense than another set of enemies. And so he invited her to talk, and to see if they couldn't come to some kind of agreement.

It didn't start well. Skadi was not what you might call the approachable type. One of those chilly blondes; cropped hair, the runemark *Isa* – ice – on her arm. She arrived all in furs, wearing snowshoes, and carrying a runewhip – crafted from thousands of shining strands of woven glam, and barbed with the cruellest of runes – which slithered and hissed in her hand like a snake.

I've never been a fan of snakes. And so that whip did nothing to endear her to me. Nor did the fact that when she arrived, she demanded my execution.

'Why me?' I protested.

Skadi gave me a poisonous look. The whip in her hand hissed and slithered. 'I know who you are,' she said. 'You're Loki, the Trickster. Everyone's saying you planned the whole thing. You lured my father into a trap and then you disgraced his memory.'

'It wasn't *exactly* like that,' I said.

'Really? You weren't as modest when you were spreading the tale around the Middle Worlds.'

'That was poetic licence,' I said. 'Bragi uses it all the time.'

Odin smiled. 'Now, Huntress,' he said. 'You should know better than to listen to rumours. Stay here a while – have a rest, drink our mead – and we'll discuss how best to handle this.'

Skadi shot me a sideways look. Her runewhip crackled like lightning. But she accepted a cup of mead, and when we sat down all together to feast, she ate six whole carp to herself, and half a barrel of salt herring. Clearly grief hadn't interfered with her appetite, although she never smiled from one end of the meal to the other.

Still, I thought her attitude softened just a little – the Old Man had gone out of his way to show respect, seating her by his side, with the men, next to Thor and Balder. As you know, Balder was popular; being athletic, smooth-skinned and with more teeth than brainpower. Ladies liked his floppy hair; men liked the fact that he was good at sports and otherwise nicely unthreatening. I'd never seen the appeal myself, but even I had to concede that the guy was doing a pretty good job of melting Skadi.

She'd downed a good half-barrel of mead on top of the carp and the herring. I reckoned if that didn't soften her, then nothing would. The women were bringing in dessert – honey-cakes, dried figs, giant baskets of fresh fruit – and Bragi was getting out his lute in preparation for some after-dinner entertainment when Odin turned to Skadi and said:

'I'm sorry for your father's death. I'll like to offer you something.'

She took a handful of figs and said: 'Whatever you offer won't bring him back. Or lift the shame of his passing.'

Odin smiled. 'I've always found that gold covers shame, if used in sufficient quantities.' I thought he was looking at Freyja as he said it, but that might have been a trick of the light.

Skadi shook her head. 'Gold? My father's hoard belongs to me now. So does his empty castle. Gold won't buy me company, or make me laugh as *they* do.' She looked enviously down the table towards the seated goddesses, all of them beautiful, carefree, at ease.

Odin looked thoughtful. 'Is *that* what you want?'

Skadi's eyes flicked towards Balder. 'If I had a husband, then perhaps I could learn to laugh again.'

Balder looked distinctly nervous. 'A husband? Really?'

Skadi said, 'Yes. If I could choose one of the Aesir . . .'

For a moment Odin considered it. Skadi looked at Balder again. I grinned inside as Golden Boy began to look uncomfortable.

'Well?' said Skadi. 'Is it a deal?'

Odin nodded. 'All right. As long as this ends the hostility.'

Skadi's eyes lit. 'All right. Then I choose—'

'I'll let you take your pick,' he said. 'But on one condition. We'll stand all our eligible men behind a screen, with only their feet on display. Then you'll choose. You'll choose your husband by his feet. Agreed?'

I stared at him. I mean, really. *His feet?* What new perversion was this?

But Skadi nodded and said, 'Agreed.'

I guess she must have been thinking how much you can tell from a man by his feet. Or maybe she wasn't thinking at all. I've seen that look on faces before; that soupy, soft, idiotic look. Oh, Skadi was falling for Balder, all right. Skadi had it big-time. I have to say, I was just a *little* disappointed. I'd thought better of Thiassi's daughter. And, although I'd already discarded the idea of allying myself with the Ice Folk, an alliance with the Aesir would make that all the more difficult. I had to hand it to the General: it was a very neat little move.

And that was how, at the end of the meal, all of us found ourselves lined up behind a screen, with nothing but our bare feet on show, while Bragi played power chords on his lute and Skadi moved slowly down the line, trying to work out which pair of feet was Balder's.

Finally, she came to a decision. 'I choose *him*,' she said, pointing.

Please. Not me. Not me, I thought.

'Are you sure?' Odin said.

Skadi nodded, her iceberg gaze starting to melt as the screen was removed. And then she found herself face to face . . . not with Balder, as she'd assumed, but with Njörd, the Fisherman – whose feet, like those of all fishermen, were clean and white and shapely.

'But I thought . . .'

I began to laugh. Beside me, Golden Boy's relief was almost as great as my own.

'But I thought . . .' she said again.

The gods saw her dismay, and smiled.

'I'm sorry,' said Odin. 'But that was the deal. You chose Njörd. Be good to him.'

Skadi's face darkened. 'Is this a joke? Do you see me laughing?' she said. She lifted the runewhip again, its serpent coils seething angrily. 'I said I wanted to laugh again,' she said. 'You promised me laughter. Now, either someone makes me laugh, or I'll take the next best thing. Hand to hand combat, here and now. All together or one at a time. I don't care. Who wants a fight?'

Odin looked at me. 'Loki.'

'What, *me*? You want *me* to fight her?'

'Of course not, idiot. *Make her laugh.*'

It was a Hel of a challenge. A sense of humour's one of those things that you either have or you haven't, and nothing I'd seen of Skadi thus far suggested any sign of one. But laughter disarms the fiercest of men, and besides, there was no way I was going to take on that runewhip. And so I marshalled all my wits and prepared for some stand-up comedy.

There was a little white goat nearby, tethered to a wooden beam. I guessed that Idun had brought it in – she was partial to goat's milk, and rarely dined on anything more substantial. I untied the leash and stepped forward, bringing the little goat with me.

'Got milk?'

That earned me a snigger from Thor, but Skadi was unaffected. I could see this was going to be a somewhat difficult audience.

I put on an air of innocence. 'Lady, I can explain,' I said. 'I was taking this goat to market . . .'

I yanked at the leash. The goat yanked back.

'See what she's like?' I said. 'Typical goat. Never does what she's told to do. Plus I had this basket of fruit . . .' I took one from the table and demonstrated the problem. Every time I brought the basket into the goat's range, the goat would try to go for the fruit. It was a lively young goat, and I was hard put to control it.

I looked at Skadi. She still wasn't smiling. I said:

'I need to tether the goat – but to what?' I pretended to look around. 'What I could use is some kind of, *um* – appendage – um, about *this* long . . .' I held out my finger and thumb about six inches apart.

Thor, never subtle, sniggered again.

I continued to feign puzzlement. 'But *where*?' I searched my person. Pockets, waistcoat, belt . . .

I paused. Dropped my gaze an inch or two.

Around me, expectant laughter.

I went on with my story. 'So – I tethered the goat securely to the only suitable – *ahem!* – I could find.' I demonstrated with the leash. Once more the little goat tugged on it.

'*Ouch!*'

Thor's big face went red with mirth.

'Will you *stop* that!' I yelped at the goat, yanking at the leash in my turn. Some fruit fell out of the basket. The goat danced nimbly towards it, dragging me along with it.

'*Ouch!*' More fruit fell out of the basket. I yelped. 'Owwoww! My plums! My plums!'

Now *all* the gods were laughing. Even the icy Skadi joined in. Turns out the one thing that could make her laugh was the sight of Yours Truly, tied by the balls to a nanny goat.

I only saw her laugh again once. As it happens, in tragic circumstances, at least for Your Humble Narrator. But that's another story, one for a darker, colder day.

And so the Huntress joined our ranks – though not for long, as it turned out. She missed the snow of the far North, the howling of wolves and the icy wastes. As for Njörd, in spite of his wish to make a success of the marriage, he found that he was incapable of living so far from Asgard and his hall overlooking the One Sea, with the sound of the waves and the cries of birds and the soft clouds gathering overhead. And so they agreed to live apart, though Skadi was always welcome in

Asgard, and would sometimes call round, in animal Aspect; an eagle or a white wolf or a snow leopard with ice-blue eyes.

I wasn't sorry to see her go. My clowning around had saved me once, but there was a nasty look in those eyes. I suspected she was the kind to bear a grudge, which made me think that the further I got from her – and from that runewhip – the happier I was likely to be.

Turns out I was right, of course – but more of that later. For the moment, suffice it to say that though laughter may be the best medicine, there are some folk who can *never* be cured. Skadi was one, and Lord Surt was another – there is no laughter in Chaos, except for the desperate laughter of those imprisoned in Surt's Black Fortress. But that was a lesson I had yet to learn. And of course, the more time I spent in this world of laughter, hate and revenge, the smaller my chances of ever returning to my primal state of grace . . .

LESSON 4

Love

Love is boring. Lovers, even more so.

Lokabrenna

Y OU'D HAVE THOUGHT that after *that* close shave, the folk of
Asgard might have been a little more careful with their affec-
tions. But love was in the air that year, perhaps because of Idun's
return, and suddenly it seemed that all the gods were thinking
of marriage. That was fine by me, of course. Marriage means
discord, generally, and Discord is my middle name. It's so much
easier to stir up trouble between a married couple than between
single, healthier types.

Take Frey, for instance. After having lavished him with gifts
from the Tunnel Folk – and at considerable personal risk – I'd
expected at least a word of thanks. Not so – he'd accepted them
as no more than his due, which made me feel that perhaps he
deserved a little lesson in gratitude.

I had been lying low for a while, trying to live down my new-
found celebrity. It was all very well being famous, I thought, but
my reputation had grown so fast that it was starting to hinder
me. Trickery and subterfuge are best performed in stealth, I
find, and the new, high-profile Trickster was finding it hard
to go unseen. The Folk of the Middle Worlds were the worst,
pointing at me as I went by, trying to get me to tell jokes, asking

me to sign my name on amulets, weapons and pieces of rock. I found that the only way to prevent rioting wherever I went was to adopt a disguise – a hat, a cloak, another Aspect – which, apart from being tiresome, made my ongoing, secret quest for allies against the General all the more difficult to pursue.

Besides, my own list of enemies was growing daily. The Ice Folk still blamed me for Thiassi's death. I could expect no help from them – or mercy, if they caught me. The same was true of the Rock Folk and the Maggots – not to mention Chaos, of course. I decided to suspend my activities abroad until my notoriety had abated, and to concentrate on the simpler task of undermining the gods, one by one. I'd already scored a few decent points, but my methods were opportunistic, rather than part of a plan, which was one of the reasons I'd managed to stay so far ahead of the game. I'd drawn on my new-found knowledge of weaknesses and emotions and come to the conclusion that, although greed, fear and jealousy are powerful motivators, there's an even greater one. *Love.*

Can't say I understood it, myself. Of all the emotions I'd learnt about during my time on the corporeal plane, this one seemed the most pointless, painful and complicated. It's all about *giving*, apparently. Seems like *taking* isn't enough. There's also a lot of random stuff about poetry, flowers and lute music, plus kissing and cuddling (lots of this), wearing similar outfits, talking incessantly about the current object of devotion, and generally losing one's faculties. As far as I could understand, love made you weak and boring. Balder, who by that token must have been in love *all the time*, told me, with his pitying look, that it was one of life's greatest joys. I guessed he'd never experienced revenge, a threesome or Sigyn's jam tarts.

Still, back to the story, and arrogant Frey, and how I used love to bring him down.

Now, Odin had the power to see anywhere in the Nine Worlds; it was a power for which he'd paid dearly, and he was unwilling to share it. That was why the high seat in Asgard was reserved for him alone; it was where he kept Mimir's Head, bound by glamours, and where he came to be alone, and to think, and to plan his strategies.

Frey had no business sitting there, and probably wouldn't have thought of it, if I hadn't given him the idea. But marriage and love were in the air – Idun was back with Bragi, and their happiness together was almost enough to make a man gag. Plus Balder had just got married to Nanna, a doe-eyed milksop who thought he was a genius and deferred to him in every way –I guess his blind date with Skadi must have given him an extra push. Anyhow, Frey was bored (and restless, and randy) and feeling unloved. The pool of available goddesses in Asgard wasn't what you'd call plentiful, and when you ruled out his sister and his various cousins among the Vanir, there wasn't much left to work with.

Enter Yours Truly, with sympathy and the hint that Odin was getting his sexual kicks from spying on women throughout the Nine Worlds.

'You can see *everything* from that throne,' I told him, over a jar of mead. 'Women undressing, bathing, the works. No wonder Odin spends so much time there. It's like an old man's wet dream.'

'Really?' said Frey. 'Despicable. Women undressing – bathing, you say? Shocking. Honestly, I'm shocked.'

'Me too,' I said and grinned.

We finished the mead in silence.

I found Frey a few days later, sitting in one of the gardens, listening to Bragi playing his lute and looking glummer than ever.

'What's wrong?' I said.

'Oh, everything.'

Well, there's only one thing that can make a man want to listen to lute music. Turns out he'd sneaked into Odin's high seat, and seen the girl of his dreams there. He'd spied on her, watched her undress, and now he was desperately in love.

Whatever. Love is boring. People in love are even more so, and I had to pretend to listen while Frey ranted on about his girl; her beauty, which was like radiant stars, her laughter, which was like nightingales, and all kinds of other quite frankly nauseating details, until he got to the bit where he was going to die if he didn't get to meet her in person.

I tried to keep a straight face. 'Well, why don't you go out and get her, then?'

'It isn't as easy as that,' said Frey. 'If I tell Odin, he's sure to ask how I found out about her in the first place. And there's another thing . . .'

'Really?' I said.

'She's the daughter of one of the Rock Folk. A relative of—'

'Let me guess. The builder who gave us our battlements. Oh, dear.' I feigned sympathy. '*His* blessing's out of the window, then.'

'I've got to have her,' said Frey. 'I'll die if I can't have her.'

Well, *that* was a bit of hyperbole. No one dies of sexual frustration. Still, he looked pretty miserable, which made me increasingly cheerful.

'I'll see what I can do, shall I?' I said, and went off to do some matchmaking.

First I went to the father. Gymir was his name, and he was as hairy and unpleasant a man as ever sired a daughter. The daughter was called Gerda, and I guess she took after her mother because she was fragrant and beautiful and smooth in all the right places.

I went in disguise, with a fake beard. I introduced myself as Skirnir, Frey's servant, and informed the uncouth Gymir that Frey was desperately in love. Predictably, the father told me to perform an impossible sexual act but, on reflection, understood that he was more likely to benefit if he considered the offer.

Frey was the perfect mark, I said: ready to give up anything for the sake of gratification. I pointed out to Gymir that this was his chance to capitalize. If he refused, then he and I knew that Frey would take Gerda anyway, in which case her father would lose, both the girl, and any chance of recompense.

'This way,' I said, 'you name your price. Go on. Ask for anything.'

Some people have no vision. When I say 'ask for anything', I expect to hear something better than a pigskin filled with gold, some sheep or a lifetime's supply of dung. Still, the Rock Folk weren't what you'd call the most sophisticated of people, and I sensed I might have to guide him.

I started by telling him something about Frey, the chief of the Vanir. I stressed his good looks, his flashy armour, his wealth of gold and treasures. I spoke of the ship, Skidbladnir, that folds up into a compass, and of the golden boar Gullin-Bursti, and of the runesword made for him in the early days of the war between Aesir and Vanir. Most of all, I described that sword, chased in silver and gold and fizzing with glam from point to hilt; that runesword, symbol of his might, his manhood, his authority . . .

'Name your price. *Any* price,' I said to Gerda's father. 'Don't be afraid to speak up for yourself. A daughter is worth more than gold. More than cattle. More than rubies.'

Gymir scowled. 'All right,' he said. 'My price for Gerda is Frey's runesword. That is, *if* she wants him. If not . . .' He shrugged. 'I'm warning you. My daughter's unusually headstrong.'

I hid my smile behind my hand. 'Sir, you drive a hard bargain,' I said. 'Still, Frey *did* say he'd pay *anything*.'

Now to persuade the daughter, I thought. It shouldn't be too difficult. A little flattery and charm; some baubles; a little poetry . . .

I found the girl in her father's hall. A blonde and haughty piece of work – just Frey's type, in fact. Blue eyes, creamy skin, legs that just went on and on. And that look that men like Frey seem to find irresistible; a look that says, *On your knees, scum, because you know I'm worth it.*

Well, I gave her the works. I wooed her. Lutes, flowers, perfume, the lot. But Gerda was impervious. Nothing seemed to entice her. Not gold, nor presents, nor flattery, not even the golden apples of youth. The woman was incorruptible. Seems she'd caught sight of Frey once and he just really wasn't her type.

Well, I sympathized with *that*. But I'd told Frey I'd win the girl, and besides, I had my plan to consider. And so I went back home to Frey, to tell him the girl was *practically* his, barring a little paperwork.

'Paperwork?' repeated Frey. He was learning to play the lute, and doing it rather badly.

'Well, formalities,' I said. 'The man has to check your credentials before he entrusts his daughter to you. Plus, his asking price was unreasonably high.'

'Oh, pay him and be done with it!' said Frey. 'I'm going crazy here.'

I shrugged. 'All right. It's your funeral. But when Odin finds out about all this, as you know he will, I want you to remember that giving up your runesword to your prospective father-in-law was entirely *your* idea, and that I opposed it.'

'Whatever,' said Frey. 'It's *my* sword. Odin has nothing to do with this.'

See what I mean? Love makes us weak. That runesword was beyond price. A triumph of runes and glamours, it rivalled Odin's spear in strength and even Thor's hammer in accuracy. It was a true indication of how badly Love had got him that Frey hardly even glanced at me when I told him Gymir wanted it.

'Just as long as no one blames me,' I said. 'You know what people are like.'

Frey waved an impatient hand. 'What am I, a child?' he said. 'I make my own decisions. Now go and take the sword with you, and don't come back without Gerda.'

Well, what else was I to do? The man had spoken. The promise was made. No one could doubt I'd done my best to talk Frey out of this impulsive decision, as disastrous to the rest of the gods as it would prove to Frey himself. That sword was life insurance to them, and when the End of the Worlds came around, as I never doubted it would, Frey and the others would soon find out that there's only so much you can do with a lute. Still, that was for later. For now, all I had to do was simply deliver the sword and win Frey's girl.

Win her? That implies fair play. I, of course, was planning to cheat. There's more than one way of skinning a cat, strangling a snake or winning a girl, and even Gerda, obstinate as she was, would be no match for my persuasive tongue.

Having failed to win her with flattery, poetry or jewellery, I moved onto some basic threats; dire warnings of worse to come; painted a bleak but convincing picture of Gerda, alone and abandoned by all, shunned for her rejection of Frey, growing old and cursing herself for missing the opportunity. I reminded her that Death was long and that worms would dance in her cooling flesh, while all her peers would laugh at her for going to the grave a virgin.

Then I spoke of the prejudice that had blinded her to Frey's charm. I spoke of tribes divided by war; of the romance of love at first sight; of the fact that of all the girls in all the caves in all the mountains of the Middle Worlds, it was *she* who had caught his eye. Surely that meant *something* to her?

When it became clear that it didn't, I followed up with a desperate and colourful depiction of Frey's magnificent hall in Asgard, with its formal gardens, its topiary, its ballroom and its ornamental fountains.

'Really?' said Gerda. 'A topiary?'

Funny how even the most determined of women can be swayed by the prospect of nicely clipped hedges.

'Absolutely,' I said. 'Plus a rose garden, a lawn, a conservatory, some garden statues, a pond and a whole area devoted to decking and container plants. You'll be mistress of the finest house in all of the Nine Worlds, and your friends will be green with envy.'

And so she and Frey were married, and Gymir got the rune-sword. Not such a wise investment for Frey, who realized when love's pink haze died down that he'd just delivered his most treasured weapon into the hands of the Rock Folk, but by then there was nothing to be done. 'Marry in haste and repent at leisure', as the old wives of Inland say, and, let's face it, they should know. It's an open secret that old wives really run *everything*.

Odin was furious, of course. But even he could hardly blame me for what had happened. He took to spending even more time alone, with only his ravens and Mimir's Head for company. Sometimes I heard him talking in a low and urgent voice – though whether it was to the ravens, to himself or to the Head, I could only speculate. As for myself, I'd managed to carry out another covert act of sabotage, and I was feeling pleased with myself – at least until the hammer fell, taking me wholly by surprise . . .

LESSON 5

Marriage

They don't call it 'wedlock' for nothing.

Lokabrenna

Yᴇꜱ, ᴛʜᴇ ʜᴀᴍᴍᴇʀ. I should have known that Odin would find a means of, if not actually punishing me for my part in Frey's misadventure, then at least of restraining me for a while. This time, the blow was delivered by Frigg, Odin's wife, the Enchantress, who, in the wake of Frey and Gerda's nuptials, now turned her matchmaking eye on me.

'Loki's just a little wild,' she said. 'He needs a good woman.'

I didn't see the danger at first, or expect the disastrous consequences. It was only when the General announced that he was giving me a wife that I realized how neatly I'd been caught, and how hard it would be henceforth for me to get away with *anything* without attracting the vigilance of my new and eager spouse . . .

It was Sigyn, of course. Who else? She'd had her eye on me from the start. What was more, she'd confided in Frigg, who had confided in Odin. The result was one of those female conspiracies that men are powerless to resist, and I found myself under attack from both sides, and helpless.

Of course I protested. But the damage was done. And Odin made it abundantly clear that his generous gift was both non-returnable *and* non-negotiable.

Frigg was delighted. As far as she was concerned, Wildfire had been tamed by love. Sigyn, too, was delighted, and prepared for a life of domestic bliss. Freyja was rather less happy – she'd just lost her favourite handmaid, the plain one she liked to keep around because she made Freyja look prettier. As for Yours Truly, he was in shock, stunned at the speed of his downfall, trying to work out just *how* he'd been caught, and how he might manage his escape.

For a start, until that point I'd had no idea how much women *talked* to each other. Nothing was private any more: my personal habits, opinions, tastes and every intimate detail that a loving wife could discover and share with her various cronies.

Was I ungrateful? Perhaps I was. But Frigg, who was wise enough in other ways, had totally failed to understand my nature or, indeed, my needs. A month of living with Sigyn in her little place in Asgard, all chintz and roses round the door, of eating Sigyn's home-made cakes, of listening to Sigyn's views on Life, of sleeping with Sigyn (lights out, of course, and veiling her charms beneath an assortment of almost impenetrable flannel nightdresses), was enough to confirm my initial belief that Frigg was wrong and that what I *really* needed was the love of a very *bad* woman.

And so I went in search of one, telling my wife that I needed space; that it wasn't her fault, it was me; that I just needed to find myself; and, in my bird Aspect, I ventured out as far as the forest of Ironwood, that stretches over a hundred miles between the plain of Ida right up to the shores of the One Sea.

Ironwood was a good place to hide. Dark as night, and teeming with predators and demons. Most of them had glam of some kind, stolen scraps of Chaos, bartered from other realms or brought into the Worlds through Dream. The river Gunnthrà ran through it; it was swarming with snakes and ephemera. It was a dangerous place, but it was as close as I was ever likely to get to Chaos again, and I made for its shelter with relief.

My quest was not a romantic one. While I was among the Rock Folk, I'd heard a rumour that Gullveig-Heid, the renegade Sorceress of the Vanir, had established a stronghold in Ironwood in the hope of attacking Asgard. I thought that if I could contact her, then maybe we could join forces – but Ironwood was a vast place, hissing with glam and signatures, and Gullveig – if she was there at all – had shielded herself with so many runes that finding her trail was impossible.

But I did come across someone else. Angrboda, the Witch of Ironwood. Mad, bad and dangerous, she lived in the heart of the forest, half in and half out of Chaos. Like me, she had left the primal Fire to explore the emerging Worlds; like me, she enjoyed new sensations; and, like all demons, she was alluring. Dark-skinned, long-haired, a ring on every finger and toe, eyes like red-hot embers and every muscle, every nerve charged with a sexual energy that I hadn't known I craved until the craving was satisfied.

We spent a number of nights together, both in our human form as well as in various animal Aspects, cavorting through Ironwood, hunting, destroying and generally raising Chaos, until exhaustion got the better of me. Angie's tastes ran to violence, and every inch of me was sore. Not that I was complaining but I needed time to recover.

And so I returned to Sigyn's arms, her cooking, her love of Bragi's lute-playing, her attentions and her curious affinity with wildlife of all sorts – Sigyn's most annoying trait, which meant that she was often surrounded by little woodland creatures, birds, raccoons, squirrels and so on – teeming and twittering constantly.

'Now, sweetie, be *nice* to my little friends,' she would say as I swiped at a fieldmouse climbing up the curtains. 'You never know, one day you might *need* that little mousie.'

Yes, before you condemn my faithlessness, that's what Sigyn was like, folks. And all in all, with Angie's help, I think I managed to cope pretty well. I lived in Asgard most of the time, and when domesticity became too much for me, I fled to my mistress in Ironwood. The concept of monogamy was not unknown to me, of course, but, like pain, lutes and poetry, I just didn't see the point.

Sigyn bore with my faithlessness rather well, on the whole, I thought. Of course she liked to complain to her friends about my beastly appetites, but I don't think she was all that surprised. In Sigyn's world, men often stray, but always return to their faithful wives, who show their forgiveness by baking cakes, tending wounds and placing hands on fevered brows. Vengeance comes later, in the form of bedtime headaches, snide remarks and that business with the snake – yes, I'll be getting to that soon enough, so don't think I got away scot-free. Odin knew what he was doing, all right, when he handed me over to her. But at the time, I was pleased with myself. I thought I'd managed to reconcile my two opposing natures. I tolerated Sigyn whilst enjoying Angrboda and managed to persuade myself that frolicking with her in Ironwood constituted some kind of secret rebellion against the Old Man.

I know; I lost focus. Perhaps that's what Odin intended. Perhaps he was trying to stop me from doing any more mischief by keeping me in a perpetual state of sexual exhaustion.

But, idyllic as it was at first between Angrboda and myself, it was inevitable that, in time, our . . . activities . . . would bear fruit. Demons often tend to . . . let's say *exotic* progeny, and in Angie's case, this was especially true. Over our twelve-month liaison, she presented me with three offspring: a cute little werewolf called Fenris, an undead half-corpse-daughter called Hel, and Jormungand, an enormous snake, which proved to be the final straw between me and Angrboda.

So shoot me. I can't stand snakes. But she liked to push the boundaries. We argued – well, *she* argued. She said that I needed to take responsibility for my actions; accused me of fearing commitment; said she felt violated and used and finally screamed at me to go back to my wife, whom I obviously was never going to leave, and with whom she wished me a long and happy future. And so I went back to Asgard for good, feeling more or less relieved, and leaving Odin to figure out what to do with Fenny, Hel and Jormungand.

Well, the snake was the easiest. By the time we reached a decision he'd grown so large that only the One Sea could safely hope to contain him. So that was where we threw him, to lounge in the ocean mud and feed on fish for the rest of his days, and he became the World Serpent, spanning the Middle Worlds with his girth, tail in his mouth, biding his time till Ragnarók.

As for Hel, by the time she was grown, everyone wanted rid of her. It wasn't that she was evil, as such, she just wasn't a social animal. She could clear a room in two minutes; her conversation was minimal; everywhere she went, there was gloom; parties fell flat as storm-blown tents.

Even so, Odin tolerated her for my sake, at least until she was in her teens, when, as well as developing the most shocking case of adolescent acne, she also developed an equally bad case of puppy-love towards Asgard's favourite Golden Boy, aka Balder the Beautiful. It eventually got so embarrassing that at last Odin made a decision and gave Hel her own realm, the Land of the Dead, on the near bank of the River Dream, and waved her merrily on her way.

It was only fair, given that her brother already ruled the One Sea. As for Fenris, for the next fifteen years he lorded it in Ironwood, dismembering small creatures and generally running amok. They had to restrain him later, of course, though for the time being he was considered insufficient threat to count. But Hel was smart, and had to be dealt with a little more sensitively.

Odin made it sound as if she was performing a crucial task on behalf of the gods and gave her a runemark of her own – *Naudr*, the Binder – and almost unlimited power – but only within her realm, of course. The Old Man was planning to avoid Death for as long as he could, but even then, in his prime, he was already laying the foundations for a possible alliance – with a view to finding a loophole when the inevitable occurred.

As for Angrboda – well. She went her way, I went mine. I hoped there were no hard feelings, although, with Angie, you never could tell. Sigyn's arms were always open, and she was endlessly forgiving, but what with the chintz, and the animals, the cooking, the nagging, the lutes, the scented candles, the pot-pourri and the cuddling, I would have lost my mind if I'd stayed. And so I fled the domestic scene and returned to my digs in Asgard.

No, I didn't abandon her – Frigg would never have let me do *that* – but I managed to convince her that I needed my personal space. By then she was pregnant anyway, and her energies had been channelled into knitting bootees and little hats. A good time for me to make my excuses, I thought – and after that, she had the boys to occupy her.

Yes, the boys. My twin sons, Vali and Narvi, with my green eyes and my temperament, whom Sigyn (wrongly, as it happened) assumed would awaken my sense of responsibility. In fact, they had the opposite effect, with the result that over the next few years I took every excuse to travel as far and as often from my loving family as possible.

What can I say? It's my nature. Besides, what role models did I have? An absent father in Chaos, and an absent mother in World Above. That's hardly a wonderful start in life. Still, if I'd done things differently . . .

But no. Regrets are for losers. What's done is done, and there's no point in wishing for anything else. Didn't I pay for it in the end? Maybe I even deserved it. And maybe I should . . . but none of that now. It's easy to be wise *after* the Worlds have ended. The Black Fortress of Netherworld is filled with that kind of wisdom.

And so I went through fatherhood like a grain of wheat through a goose, unscathed and unremembered. And if there ever was a time when I wondered what it might have been like to play a game of catch with my sons, or teach them to fly, or shift

Aspects, or educate them in such essential life skills as lying, cheating and treachery, I wisely kept the thought to myself. And yet, I was conscious that *something* had changed. Something inside me had shifted. The knot of barbed wire inside my heart was suddenly less intrusive. I could spend whole weeks and months without even thinking about revenge. One day, I flew into Asgard from one of my jaunts in hawk Aspect and saw my sons, aged seven or eight, playing on the battlements. And just for a moment, I almost felt . . .

Yes. I almost felt *happy.*

I should have known there was something wrong. Face it, it wasn't natural. But after years of trying, at last, Odin had corrupted me. No, it wasn't *love*, of course, but it *was* a kind of contentment. Suddenly, I wasn't alone. Suddenly, I had people. And suddenly, the End of the Worlds couldn't be too far away, as I looked at my sons from afar and thought: *Perhaps this was what I was missing. Perhaps I belong here after all . . .*

LESSON 6

Bridesmaids

Something borrowed, something blue.

Lokabrenna

AFTER THAT there came a stretch of generally crisis-free existence. Not that I was slowing down, but it was Asgard's summertime, and all of us felt the sunshine. We were at our zenith then; worshipped throughout the Middle Worlds. Anything we wanted, we had. Gold, weapons, wine, women. Odin and Thor were the popular ones – along with Golden Boy, of course – but even Yours Truly had his share of songs and sacrifices. Ice Folk and Rock Folk were both at peace; Frey was happy with his bride and Skadi was on one of her trips to the North, meaning that there was no one there to cast a damper on the festivities.

Something, sometime, was bound to go wrong. We had all become *far* too complacent. Suspicion and Survival are twins – lose one, and the other soon follows.

One morning after a drunken night, Thor awoke in his empty hall to find that his hammer was missing. For a while he assumed that Sif had tidied it away, then that one of the others had maybe hidden it for a joke, but when everyone denied knowledge and finally, Yours Truly was called and accused of having stolen it, we realized we had a problem.

'What in Hel's name would I want with your hammer?' I

said.

Thor shrugged. 'I dunno, I thought—'

'Don't try to think,' I said, and cast *Bjarkán*, the rune of true vision. It revealed a shielded signature – the colours of which I recognized immediately. 'That signature belongs to Thrym, one of the chieftains of the Ice Folk. He must have found his way in here – he likes to travel in eagle form – and stolen it when you were asleep.' I looked at Heimdall. 'Where were you? Drunk again? Gods, the security in this place . . .'

'Watch your tongue,' Heimdall growled. 'Or I may relieve you of it.'

I arched an eyebrow. 'Go ahead. Enjoy yourself while you still can. Because as soon as the news gets out that Thor's lost his hammer, we're going to get pounded on all sides by every little warlord who fancies his chances against us.'

There was silence, as everyone realized that I was right.

I turned to Freyja. 'Your falcon cloak.'

She nodded. Even she knew what would happen if Mjølnir were lost. It wasn't just the hammer, but the loss of credibility. Odin's empire was built on bluff and the knowledge that no one dared to strike, but our enemies were like wolves around a bonfire: at bay, but let them scent blood, just once, and they'd be on us before we knew it.

Odin watched as I flung on the cloak. 'Talk to Thrym,' he told me. 'Find out what he wants from us. And, Loki – please. Be careful.'

I was surprised. It had to be the first time that the Old Man had shown any interest in my personal safety. I guessed he knew they'd need my skills if they were to retrieve the hammer. I'll admit, I felt rather flattered; Odin had put his trust in me, and I was looking forward to showing him what I was capable of. And so I flew to the Northlands and found old Thrym in his courtyard, making collars for his hounds and looking very pleased with himself.

I flew down to join him and perched on a branch, just out of reach of his big hands.

'Loki,' he said, and showed his teeth. 'You're looking very chirpy today. How are the Aesir? The Vanir?'

'Not so good,' I told him. 'Not now you've stolen Thor's hammer.'

Thrym gave a broad grin. 'Have I?' he said.

'I thought you knew better than this, Thrym,' I said. 'Do you really want to see the whole of the Nine Worlds at war over a hammer? It won't just be Asgard in trouble, you know. What you've done is likely to destabilize Order and Chaos. You'll have Lord Surt on your doorstep before you can say "death wish". So give Thor back his hammer, and we can all go back to staying alive. What do you say?'

He grinned again. 'I don't want Thor's hammer.'

'That's nice. So what *do* you want?'

'I'm in love,' he said.

I cursed. 'Oh, gods. Not you as well?'

'I've buried the hammer in World Below. You'll never find it in time,' he said. 'But you can have it back as soon as I get the Goddess of Desire as my bride. You have nine days to deliver.'

Freyja! Gods. I should have known. That woman was nothing but trouble. So I flew back to Asgard as fast as I could – time was short – and found the Thunderer waiting, rather impatiently, in his hall.

I took off Freyja's feather cloak, ready to drop with exhaustion.

'Well?' said Thor.

'Well, a drink would be nice. I've been flying for days, you know.'

Thor grabbed me by the throat. *'Well?'*

'Well,' I said. 'I talked to Thrym. And he's happy to return the hammer, on condition that we agree to give him Freyja as his bride.'

Thor gave the matter some three seconds' thought, then said: 'Fine. We'll tell her.'

We called a meeting of the gods – all of them – in Odin's hall. 'There's good news and slightly less good news,' I said. 'The good news is, I persuaded Thrym to give back Mjølnir. The slightly more ambivalent news is . . .' I smiled dazzlingly at Freyja. 'Now, before you shoot me down in flames—'

'You'd better not be about to say what I think you're about to say,' said the Goddess of Desire, through her teeth.

'Ah, come on,' I said. 'Be fair. Thrym's a decent guy at heart. And he's a king, for gods' sakes. It's not like I'm trying to pair you up with a labourer. Think about it. You'll be Queen of the Ice Folk. You'll have a crown of diamonds and a wedding dress of mink.'

She gave me one of her looks. 'No. I'd rather go to war.'

'With *what*? Thrym has Mjølnir, in case you'd forgotten.'

'I don't care. I'm not marrying one of the Ice People. They're ugly, and uncouth, and all of them smell of fish.'

'What's wrong with the smell of fish?' said Njörd.

Freyja looked appealingly at Odin. 'You can't want me to do this,' she said, fluttering her eyelashes.

But since the business with Dvalin and the necklace, Odin had been a lot less indulgent with Freyja. Most of the time he didn't let his anger show, but I knew him too well to misread the signs.

'We need the hammer, Freyja,' he said.

'Meaning you don't need *me*?' She started to cry, which was her usual way of dealing with adversity. In this instance, no one seemed to care much. Freyja dried her tears. 'I see. You'd rather see me sold, like a whore.'

I hid a grin behind my hand, but not before she'd seen it.

From his throne, Odin caught my eye. I knew what he was thinking, and so did Freyja. Anger made her tremble. She started to shift to her Carrion form – that monstrous personification of all-consuming, selfish Desire – and in the violent discharge of glam, the golden choker around her neck broke apart, scattering its links and gems all around Odin's high seat.

'My, *that's* appealing,' I said, and grinned again.

Freyja gave an anguished scream. 'I hate you all!' she said, and ran out.

I said: 'I'll take that as a no.'

The gods exchanged uncomfortable glances.

'We still have to deal with Thrym,' I continued. 'The King of the Ice Folk, in his stronghold, surrounded by his people, armed with runes and all kinds of local knowledge – not to mention Thor's hammer . . .' I paused to allow time for this to sink in. 'Thrym wants a bride. We have no choice. I say we give him one.'

There was silence. Everyone looked glum.

Frey said: 'Freyja won't have him.'

'I see her point, of course,' I said. 'But we have to give him *someone*. And, wrapped in a wedding veil, covered in gems, one bride looks a lot like another.'

'You think you can fool him?' Heimdall sneered. 'As soon as he finds out he's been duped, he'll slit the bride's throat.'

'Not if she slits his first,' I said. 'It all depends on who we send.'

Everyone was looking at me now. I grinned again and turned to Thor.

'You'd better not be thinking what I think you're thinking,' he growled.

'I'm thinking floor-length taffeta under a cloak of snow-white mink. Plenty of skirts to make your hips roll. And your hair tucked under a sweet little cap . . .'

'No way,' said Thor dangerously.

I ignored him. 'We'll fix Freyja's necklace,' I told them. 'It's her signature piece, and Thrym will be expecting to see it. And we'll hide his face under a veil, and walk him right into Thrym's place without anyone suspecting a thing. Then, when Thrym brings out the hammer . . .'

Odin was smiling now. 'It could work.'

'No *way*,' said Thor again.

I said: 'I'll be your handmaid, Thor. Don't worry, I won't steal your thunder. You'll make a *gorgeous* bride.'

Thor growled.

'And don't worry about the wedding night. I'm sure Thrym will be very gentle. I'll tell him it's your first time—'

His blow, had it connected, would have left nothing of me but a smear on the floor. As it was, I evaded it easily and danced away, still grinning.

'We don't have the choice,' I told him again. 'It's this, or lose Mjølnir. What do you say, folks?'

They all agreed. And that was how, eight days later, the Thunderer, dressed in one of Freyja's gowns, drenched in her perfume, arms and legs waxed, fingernails gilded, wearing Freyja's necklace and an expression of murderous rage (happily, hidden under the veil), set off on the road to the Northlands with Your Humble Narrator at his side.

His chariot left a furious trail of scorch-marks and pot-holes behind it, visible for miles around. It was Thor's usual way of travel, of course, but a purist might have condemned it as a little too aggressive for a lady on her way to her forth-coming nuptials. I'd managed to shield the signature that would have proclaimed his presence in a broad red stripe of glam all the way from Ida's plain into the northern glaciers, but there was nothing I could do about the collisions on the way, or the grinding of Thor's teeth under the jewelled bridal veil.

On arrival, I explained to our host: 'Freyja was keen to arrive, Lord Thrym. Besides, we women charioteers . . .' I shot him a smile from beneath my handmaid's headdress. I make a more convincing woman than Thor and, being beardless, had no need to wear a veil. In any case, Thrym seemed to approve, and chucked me under the chin, and said:

'If the mistress is half as pretty as the maid, I think my luck is in tonight.'

I giggled. 'Oh, *you*! Get *away*!'

Then, avoiding Thrym's roving hands, I ushered the fake bride into the banqueting hall of the Ice Folk, where tables had been laid for a feast. Haunches of meat, whole salmon, pies, mountains of cakes and candied fruit. Branches of candles everywhere, giving the place a festive glow. And mead, lots and lots of mead; enough for an army of drinkers.

I could hear Thor muttering to himself, and hissed at him, 'Be quiet. All right? Let me do the talking.'

Thrym's people led us to our place at the table, on Thrym's left side. I cleverly manoeuvred Thor away from the place where the warriors sat, and settled him with the women.

Thrym was nearby, but not near enough for any hanky-panky. The man had wandering hands, all right, and I didn't want Thor losing his temper – at least not until we had the hammer, at which point Thor was free to run amok as much as he liked.

'Just try to eat something, *my Lady*,' I hissed, poking Thor in the ribs. Then, turning to Thrym, 'She's a little shy. I'm sure she'll unbend when she's eaten.'

Well, Our Thor has always had a more than healthy appetite. On this occasion he surpassed himself, managing to put away a whole roast ox, eight salmon and *all* the little delicacies – sweets, cakes, biscuits, candied fruit – that had been put out for the women. I tried to warn him, but Thor and food are friends that can't be parted. And after that, he started on the mead, downing three whole horns of the stuff before I managed to make him see sense.

Thrym watched him in astonishment. 'She likes to eat, doesn't she? How does she keep her figure?'

I giggled and fluttered my eyelashes. 'Oh, Lord Thrym, but my mistress hasn't eaten or drunk *a thing* since your flattering proposal. For eight days she's been on a strict fast, she was so worried about fitting into her wedding dress.'

Thrym smiled fondly. 'Ah, bless,' he said. 'She doesn't need

to diet for me. The bigger the cushion – now don't be shy . . .'
He made a lunge for Freyja and managed to peek under her
veil.

What he saw there seemed to make him uneasy.

'Freyja's eyes . . .' he stammered.

'What?' I patted his arm and smiled up at him.

'They're so fierce – they burn like embers!'

'Oh, but my mistress hasn't slept for eight nights,' I explained.
'She's been so keen for her wedding night – her wedding night
with *you*, my Lord.'

'Oh,' said Thrym.

I smiled. 'She's heard all about you, my Lord,' I said. 'Your
vigour, your handsome looks, your *size* . . .'

'Really?' said Thrym.

'Absolutely,' I whispered. 'Look at the way she's watching
you now. She's practically *squirming* with anticipation.'

'Bring the hammer at once!' said Thrym. 'I want to be married *right now*!'

It took a few minutes for servants to bring the hammer into
the dining hall. Meanwhile, Thor waited impatiently, while
Thrym's sister, who had been watching the fake bride throughout the meal, came to sit down next to us, eyeing the rings on
Thor's hand. They belonged to Freyja, of course, and – of course
– they were very beautiful.

'You'll need a friend round here,' she said. 'Give me those
rings on your fingers, and I'll show you the ropes.'

Thor said nothing, but I could tell he was reaching the end
of his patience. I ushered the sister away from him, promising
her as many rings as she liked as soon as the wedding was
over.

'I think we should leave Freyja alone,' I said, with a quelling
glance at Thor. 'She's very shy and nervous, you know. Let's
respect her modesty.'

At last, the hammer was carried in, with every tedious piece
of ceremony you can imagine. Speeches, toasts, and I could

practically *feel* Thor's temper, frayed to the point of combustion.

'And now,' said Thrym, who was very drunk, 'we can all agree that Freyja has made the right choice. Mjølnir is a mighty weapon, but I think we both know there's a mightier one. I hear she can't wait to try it out.' And he staggered up to Freyja and winked, and placed the hammer on her lap.

Thor's reaction was immediate. He stood up, grasping the hammer, and flung away his disguise. Unveiled and in Aspect, he was fearsome; his red beard bristled; his torso bulged; his eyes were alight with fury. I just kept out of his way; it's really the only thing to do when Thor's on one of his rampages.

Thunder crashed; lightning blazed; the hammer did its deadly work. 'Something borrowed, something blue' – well, they'd borrowed the hammer, I guess, and soon the happy multitude were all going to be as blue as anything . . .

Within five minutes the hall of Thrym was piled with broken corpses. You had to admit he was good – not smart, but a death machine on two legs. Men, women, servants, dogs. All fell beneath Mjølnir. And then, when the bloodlust subsided at last, we went back to Asgard together, not speaking a word until we arrived within sight of our battlements.

Freyja was waiting for us there. Thor gave her back her necklace.

Bragi was standing by with his lute. He said: 'What's Thrym like?'

'Dead,' said Thor.

'And the in-laws?'

'Dead,' said Thor.

'I guess you got your hammer back, then. That's going to make a great ballad,' he said. 'Or a celebration chant. Or what would you say to a chorus, maybe in the Classical style?'

Thor turned his gaze on Bragi. Reaching out his big hand, he picked up the lute and wrung its neck.

'If ever I hear a single *note* of a song about this,' he said softly, 'a song, or a poem, or even a *limerick* . . .' He paused to drop the lute on the floor. There came a sad little splintering sound. 'In fact,' Thor said, 'if you say another word, I'll string you across the Rainbow Bridge and use your guts as a guitar. Is that clear?'

Bragi nodded, wide-eyed.

And that was the last time anyone dared to mention the episode again.

LESSON 7

Celebrity

*Killing your fans. Never the most efficient way
to build on your public image.*

Lokabrenna

AFTER THAT, QUITE SUDDENLY, Yours Truly became almost popular. I'd always been notorious, but now my fame spread through the Middle Worlds like a dose of wildfire. People *loved* that story – the business with Thor in the wedding veil, and Yours Truly disguised as a bridesmaid – and in spite of the fact that Bragi was under strict orders not to spread it around, it became a word-of-mouth success.

Thor had *always* been popular. Big and strong and good-natured and about as bright as your average Labrador, he was a man the Folk could admire without feeling threatened by his intellect. I was just the opposite: no muscles, but too damn smart, and the Folk mistrusted me.

All that changed after Thrym, though. We were now a double-act. People stopped us in the street and demanded their favourite anecdotes. His muscle and my brain were suddenly a winning combination, and I have to admit that I for one felt a certain amount of pressure to duplicate our most recent success.

No, I hadn't forgotten how much I resented the gods. But being a part of the popular crowd was a new experience, and in spite of everything, I was rather enjoying it. I despised them still, and yet I now had a kind of reflected shine; an unexpected attraction; an aura of celebrity. Doors that would have been closed to me were suddenly flung open. Total strangers gave me gifts. Women offered themselves to me – and with their husbands' blessing. I found that I could get away with all kinds of misbehaviour for which I would have been condemned before – drunkenness; deception; acts of malicious vandalism; theft; outrageous practical jokes – and when the culprit was revealed, people shook their heads and laughed and said: 'Oh, that's so Loki', and actually seemed to be *flattered* when they found out I'd taken advantage of them.

This unexpected tolerance even extended to Asgard. There, too, I found my behaviour was suddenly more acceptable. People smiled at my antics, rather than took offence at them. Thor told the story of Sif's hair as if he'd seen the joke from the start and bellowed with laughter as he did, roaring and clapping me on the back. Bragi reworked the ballad of Idun and her apples so that my character came across more as a victim than a traitor. Even my dalliance with Angie and tales of our monstrous progeny had only served to reinforce my reputation as a sexual athlete. Meanwhile, my twin sons were growing fast – the image of their father now, with my red hair and weird eyes. Not that I felt any more paternal for that. But it kept Sigyn happy, which was all to the good, besides raising my status among the gods.

Heimdall never warmed to me, though; and Skadi – who still came and went in and out of Asgard, spending six weeks in the mountains, then three or four days in Asgard before going back to her hunting grounds – sometimes looked at me coolly from those blue-gold eyes of hers, and I sensed that she was wondering exactly what part I'd played in the death of her father. I might have made her laugh once, but she was still a chilly piece, cold as the heart of the mountains, deadly as a killer whale, and I tried to avoid being *too* popular whenever Skadi was around.

Odin didn't seem surprised at my new-found popularity. My brother already knew about fame; its fickleness; its transience. And maybe it suited him for me to be a little bedazzled – in fact, thinking back to that time, I wonder if Odin wasn't the one who'd spread word of my exploits. His ravens, Hugin and Munin, flew off every morning, scouring the Worlds for gossip and news, while Odin himself remained aloof, alone except for Mimir's Head. Perhaps I should have asked myself just *what* that Head was telling him, and why he seemed so preoccupied with rumours and stories of all kinds, but this new corruption – celebrity – had taken such strong hold of me that I'll admit, I lost focus. Thrym had been my big break; my entrance into the premier league. And I had started to believe in the myth that had grown around me; to believe I deserved special treatment; that I was beyond the reach of the law. Pride, that most godlike of failings, had me by the short hairs, and I was blissfully unaware of the fall that awaited me . . .

It happened the time that Thor and I set off on a tour of the Middle Worlds. Touring, I'd found, was essential when trying to maintain a profile, and Thor was fond of travelling, while I was always happiest away from my wife's attentions. We took Thor's chariot out of Asgard, skirted Ironwood and went east, checking for activity among the Rock Folk. We skirted the Northlands, to ensure that the Ice Folk were still subdued. And then we crossed Inland in disguise, to hear what the Folk were saying about us and to spread a few more stories.

On our first night in Inland, Thor insisted on sampling local hospitality. He'd got it into his head that we should arrive at some hovel in human Aspect, to find out what kind of grass-roots support we really had in the area. I would have preferred a nice inn, with plenty to eat and a decent bed – and maybe some girls to warm it for me – but Thor wouldn't hear of it, and eventually chose a humble turf-roofed cottage on the edge of a stretch of moor.

It looked ghastly, and I said so. 'What's the point of being famous if you don't get to stay in the best accommodation?'

'Ah, come on,' said Thor. 'Salt of the Nine Worlds, these farmer types. Besides, imagine what they'll say when they find out who we are. They'll be telling the tale for *years*.'

And so we knocked, and asked to share the meal that the woman of the house was preparing. A bit of a clichéd approach, I know, but Thor was in charge, and in his mind that was the kind of things gods were supposed to do. We called ourselves Arthur and Lucky – Thor winking hugely at me whenever he used the alias, so that I was sure we'd be recognized before we sat down to dinner.

Turns out I was wrong about that. The people were rustics from the hills, unable to see behind our disguise. I started to feel impatient. But Thor kept nudging and winking at me, and by then night had fallen, so I resigned myself to spending the night in less-than-luxurious surroundings and concentrated on making the most of the little that was offered me.

The meal wasn't much. Some kind of stew. The beds were just straw mattresses. But the family seemed nice enough – a middle-aged couple, a teenage son, Thialfi, and a pretty daughter, Roskva – and so Thor had one of his brainwaves, offering to supply the meat that was so sadly lacking.

Now Thor had a couple of goats with him, picked up somewhere along the road. Carried away by his own generosity, he offered the goats to the little family, but warned them not to crack any of the bones – a test of obedience, if you like. Thor was very big on respect. I guess you can afford to be, when you weigh three hundred pounds.

Our hosts were touchingly overwhelmed by the gift of goat meat. The parents were stunned into silence, while the children asked all kinds of questions. Where did we come from? Were we rich? Had we ever seen the One Sea? Thialfi, the teenage son, especially, seemed very curious about Thor, while Roskva, the daughter, watched me from under her lashes.

Well, a good time was had by all, if you enjoy that kind of

thing. We ate, we slept, and in the morning Thor gathered up all the bones from the feast of the previous night and prepared for a breakfast of bread and bone marrow. But on investigating the discarded bones, he saw that a thighbone had already been split, and knew someone had disobeyed.

'What did I tell you not to do?' he said, revealing his true Aspect.

Thialfi opened his eyes very wide. 'Wow. Oh, wow. You're Thor,' he said.

'Yes I know that,' said Thor.

'I *knew* it!' said Thialfi. 'I mean, *the* Thor. The Thunderer. The thunder god.'

'Yes,' said Thor. 'And if you recall—'

'Oh, wow,' said Thialfi. 'I love your work. That time you dressed up as a bride—'

'*Don't* mention that!' said Roskva.

'Oh. Well, the time you rescued Idun from the Ice People, and—'

'Actually, that was me,' I said.

Roskva's doe eyes opened wide. 'Oh, my gods, you're Loki,' she said. 'You're absolutely my favourite of all the gods in Asgard. Thialfi, you dope, this is *Loki*. Loki, the Trickster in person. Thor and Loki, in our house, and we never even *suspected*!'

'Whatever,' said Thor, still irate. 'You disobeyed my specific command. You all deserve to pay with your lives.'

I pointed out that killing his loyal fans would hardly help his public image. By then all the family were bowing, scraping and *I-am-not-worthy*-ing as if they'd never seen a celebrity before. I was frankly revolted, but it seemed to have an effect on Thor.

'All right, all right. I'll let it pass.'

Thialfi and Roskva jumped for joy. Roskva brought out a little pink notebook and a stick of charcoal and asked me to write my name inside. Thialfi wanted to feel Thor's arms, to see if they were as thick as they looked.

'So, how do you get to be a god?' said the father of the family. 'Is it something that can be taught? Or is it something you're born with? Because my son's always saying that *he* wants to be a god someday, but I don't know if there's a career in it. Not like there is in farming.'

Thor assured him that there was.

'So, did you train?' said Thialfi. 'Or were you, like, recruited?'

Thor told him it was a bit of both.

'And where *do* you get your ideas from?' said the mother, addressing me. 'All those clever plans you make, I don't know how you think of them. Do they just come into your head?'

I smiled and told her yes, they did.

Father and mother looked impressed. 'Roskva's clever, for a girl,' said the mother fondly. 'Her head's so full of ideas, I don't know where she gets them from. And my Thialfi, he can run like the wind. I've never seen anyone faster. Do you think perhaps they might have – you know – *potential*?'

I could see where this was heading. I started to say something about not having enough time to nurture new talent, when I saw Thor's expression and cursed inwardly. It isn't often Thor gets an idea, and even less often a good one, but when he gets one into his head it's almost impossible to shift. And Thor had had an idea, I could tell: his eyes were bright, his face was flushed and his beard was bristling.

'Don't even think about it,' I said.

'Come on, Loki. They're so cute. I think I want to keep them.'

'Absolutely not,' I said. 'I mean, what would you *do* with them?'

'Thialfi could carry my weapons,' said Thor. 'Roskva could cook and clean for us. Come on, Loki. They're only kids. Besides, they think the Worlds of us.'

I pointed out that his *last* two kids had ended up as goat stew. Thor laughed uproariously.

'That's *so* Loki,' he exclaimed. 'Trust me, this is going to be *fun.*'

And that was how the two of us acquired a pair of followers. Thialfi was Thor's number-one fan, and Roskva was Yours Truly's. But in retrospect, I think you'll agree that it wasn't the wisest move ever made to take them with us into the unknown. Fans are as fickle as fame itself, and when we allow them to get too close, we risk revealing our feet of clay. First to the followers, then to the foe. And then we all come tumbling down.

LESSON 8

The Midnight Sun

The place in which the sun never sets is
a place where anything is possible.

Lokabrenna

Meanwhile, we were still wandering in the middle of nowhere. Mist had rolled thickly off the moors, and although at this time of year in the North the sun barely ever left the sky, it was cold, and bleak, and cheerless. I for one was beginning to wish for my hearth and Sigyn's home cooking but Thor was keen to make an impression on his eager new followers, and even I was reluctant to go back without putting on a bit of a show.

And so the four of us made our way over one last necklace of glaciers until we reached a strip of sea, beyond which we could see forest and a dizzying chain of white mountains.

This was Utgard – the Furthest North. We knew it by reputation, although as far as we knew, even Odin had never actually been there. For six months in the year, we'd heard, the sun never clipped the horizon; everything was frozen, and Northlights danced across the dark-blue winter sky. The summer was brief – barely three months – but during that time, Chaos reigned: the sun never set; monsters roamed; the vegetation grew rampant and, according to the legends, anything was possible.

To me, it sounded like a good place to avoid, but Thialfi and Roskva were watching us, their eyes like stars, and we felt their expectation – their *love* – like the weight of a yoke on our backs.

I suppose we both got carried away. I don't know how else to explain it. We were drunk on celebrity; willing to run the most foolish of risks rather than let down our worshippers. By the shore, we found an old boat, bleached white as bone, but still intact and, leaving Thor's chariot behind, we decided to cross the sea into the land of the Northlights.

The strait was mostly free of ice. We crossed it in less than twenty-four hours, landing on a broad white beach bristling with driftwood and the bones of long-dead animals.

We dragged the boat past the tideline, then picked up our packs and headed inland. The mountains seemed as far away as they had on the other side of the strait, and much of the land was forest; dark and deep and scented with pine and filled with plants and animals that none of us had ever seen. Here there were trees so straight and tall that they almost rivalled Yggdrasil; black squirrels that ran up and down the trunks; livid fungi as tall as a man. It was a strange and unsettling place, and as we moved further into the woods I felt more and more uneasy. Something out there was watching us. I could feel it in my guts.

'Frightened of wolves?' said Thor, and laughed. 'That's a good one. The Father of Wolves, getting jumpy about his relatives.'

I pointed out that just because I was Fenris's father, it wouldn't have stopped him snacking on me if the urge had taken him. Besides, if even mushrooms could grow this tall in this part of World Beyond, to what size could a werewolf grow – or even, gods preserve us, a *snake*.

'Snakes?' said Thialfi. 'You think there are snakes?'

I shrugged. 'Who knows? There might be.'

Thialfi shivered. 'I hate snakes. Especially those green ones that hide in the reeds when you're swimming, and the brown ones that lie by the side of the path and look almost invisible. Or the big ones that hang from the trees . . .'

This was when I realized that I might have found a travelling companion even more annoying than Honir. I considered closing his mouth with a cantrip of the rune *Naudr*, but he was Thor's number-one fan, and I feared that the Thunderer might object if I muted his number-one fan. And so we went on through the forest, Yours Truly feeling increasingly jumpy, Thialfi talking cheerily and incessantly about snakes.

At this point, it began to rain. The kind of steady, drenching rain that might go on for ever. It ran down our backs, flattened our hair, filled the forest with the scent of rotting wood and sour, damp earth. I was getting hungry but there was no sign of game, and I wasn't quite desperate enough to try eating one of the squirrels.

'I'm tired,' said Roskva. (I could tell from her trusting expression that she expected me to fix this.) 'Isn't it nearly time to make camp?'

I looked around and realized I had no idea how long we had been walking. I could still see daylight between the trees but this was the time when the sun never set, and I guessed it might already be late. I didn't like the thought of sleeping in the woods but there didn't seem to be any choice. There was no sign of habitation; no shelter, not even a woodsman's hut. We continued along the narrow path, until at last we came to a glade, in which there stood a building. It was a strange and shapeless building; not quite a hall, and not quite a cave; there were no doors or windows; and the opening, whatever it was, seemed almost as broad as the ceiling was high. It was a decent size, though, and although it didn't look (or smell) too welcoming, it would at least provide shelter.

'Let's sleep here tonight,' I suggested. 'It looks completely abandoned.'

The children looked at me doubtfully. Perhaps they'd

expected their gods to provide better accommodation. But we'd been walking for hours by then, and I was cold and exhausted. The cave – the building, whatever it was – would keep us dry till morning.

And so we slept for an hour or so, until we were awoken by a crash. There followed an ominous rumbling sound, the ground rocked like a boat in a storm . . .

'An earthquake!' said Thor.

'Terrific,' I said.

Thialfi and Roskva clung to each other. Both were pale and trembling. I made for the cave entrance, half expecting a rock-fall, but almost at once the rumbling died down, and so did the rocking movement. Soon, everything was calm again. If it had been a quake, it was over.

Outside, the rain continued unabated.

We debated leaving the shelter. Another earthquake might trap us inside the mysterious building. On the other hand, a night in the woods was hardly a welcome prospect.

'I don't see how outside is going to be any safer than inside,' said Thor. 'There may be wolves in those woods, or worse. I say we stay here tonight. Perhaps we can make a stand if something attacks. I've heard there are monsters in these parts.'

'*Now* he tells me,' I muttered.

And so we retreated to the back of the hall, where, in the semi-darkness, we found a kind of shallow cave leading off at an angle. It was warmer in there, and more secure; if it came to a fight, at least we'd have the wall at our backs. We slept there, but badly; twice more in the night there were sounds – a muffled bellowing. It might have been Thor breaking wind in his sleep, but on the whole I doubted it.

I pulled my cloak over my head and tried to ignore the weird sounds, but it was a tired and listless Trickster who, some four hours later, finally called it a night and crept to the entrance of the cave to see what might be happening.

The first thing I saw was a pair of feet as large as the average garden shed. Further investigation revealed them to belong to a sleeping figure; a giant of spectacular size, fast asleep and snoring.

I told Thor. 'That explains a lot. The rumbling, the earthquakes. Seems you're not the only one who farts in his sleep and snores like a pig.'

Thor went out to see for himself. I followed at a cautious distance. At Thor's approach the giant opened one eye (an eye as big as a barn door and grey as a freshwater oyster) and said: 'Why hello, little man.'

'Who are you?' said Thor, who didn't appreciate being called 'little'.

'Skrymir,' said the giant. His voice was as deep as the ocean. He looked a little more closely at the two of us. 'And if I'm not mistaken, you're Asa-Thor. And that's Loki, the Trickster.'

I had to admit that I was.

He grinned. 'I've heard the stories,' he said. 'But I thought you'd be bigger in real life. Has anybody seen my glove?' He sat up and looked around. 'Ah! There it is!'

That was when I realized that the hall in which we'd spent the night was Skrymir's glove; a stitched leather mitten of colossal size, with an extra space for the thumb. This space was the smaller cavern in which we'd spent the night – it also explained the strong smell of goat and the strange consistency of the walls, which were neither stone nor wood, nor any other building material I could identify.

Thialfi and Roskva had come out into the open and were watching Skrymir nervously; he put on his glove, shouldered his pack and stood up, ready to go on his way.

Then he seemed to have a thought. 'If you want to meet my folk, our stronghold isn't far from here. Utgard. I could show you the way.'

We thought about that for a moment. As I said before, Utgard had a reputation. There were rumours of a fortress, buried deep in the permafrost, built to rival Asgard and ruled by a master of glamours and runes. No one had ever gone far enough north to find out the truth of these rumours, though if there was any truth to the tale, it probably wasn't the wisest move for Thor and me to go in alone.

But Thialfi and Roskva were watching us, and – what can I say?

'All right,' said Thor.

'I'll lead you as far as I can,' Skrymir said. 'I'm not heading back to Utgard myself, but I'll show you to the city gates. Walk with me, and I'll carry your gear.'

And so we handed over our packs, with the last of our food, our dry clothes and all we had for the journey. Then we followed Skrymir – or at least, we tried to. But the big guy was moving far too fast, and with such giant strides that he soon left the rest of us behind. Even Thialfi, who was young and energetic, could only keep up with him at a sprint, and was soon exhausted.

But Skrymir wasn't hard to track; we heard his progress from afar and saw the trail he left through the woods; a broken line of fallen trees. We followed the trail throughout the day, getting hungrier and more irritable as the hours passed, and finally, we caught up with him under a stand of ancient oaks; sitting on his bedroll and finishing the last of a giant meal.

Thor strode up to him, looking grim.

Skrymir gave his giant smile. 'Oh, *there* you are, Asa-Thor,' he said. 'I was just about to turn in. I get so tired after a day in the fresh air.'

'What about our dinner?' growled Thor.

'Help yourself,' said Skrymir. 'The food's in my pack. I'm going to sleep.' And he wrapped himself in his bedroll, and was very soon snoring like thunder.

But the knots that fastened the giant's pack were deceptively complicated. Thor struggled with them without success, then turned to Yours Truly.

'Here, you try. You're good with knots.'

But even I couldn't open the bag. The knots were too tight,

145

too slippery. I handed the bag to Thialfi and Roskva, thinking that perhaps their small fingers would prove more agile, but even they failed to open the bag.

'Skrymir did this on purpose,' said Thor. 'He's been putting us down from the very first. He's trying to make us look small.'

I shrugged. 'Well, that's not difficult. For a guy the size of a mountain.'

Thor picked up his hammer. 'The bigger they are, the harder they fall,' he said, and hurled Mjølnir at Skrymir's head.

Skrymir awoke. 'What's that?' he said. 'Did a leaf fall onto my head?' He stirred and rolled over. 'Thor, is that you? Have you had your dinner yet?'

Thor was so taken aback at this that he just opened his mouth and stared.

'Then go back to sleep,' said Skrymir. 'I'll see you in the morning.'

Within two minutes, he was asleep again and snoring like an army of pigs. The rest of us exchanged glances, shrugged and prepared to go to bed hungry.

That turned out to be harder than I'd previously thought. Even in the shade of the trees, the peculiar light was unsettling. Midnight, yet the sun still shone redly through the treetops. It made it hard for me to sleep; besides which, Thor's stomach was rumbling almost as loudly as Skrymir's snoring. I was ravenous, and yet I knew I couldn't ask for Skrymir's help in opening the knapsack. For a start, Thor would kill me, then he would probably kill himself in a fit of mortification. Second, Thialfi and Roskva were there, and they expected better of us. And so I lay, hungry and sleepless, and wondered what I was doing here, when I had a wife in Asgard.

Yes, that's how far gone I was. I actually almost *missed* Sigyn.

Eventually, Thor sat up. I could tell he was making an effort but even so, stealth really isn't his thing. Through one half-open eye, I watched as he went over to Skrymir's side. He was carrying Mjølnir, and I could see he meant business. That botched attempt at killing the giant – *and* in front of his number-one fans – must have been preying on his mind. Once more, he raised the hammer and brought it down with a sickening *thud* . . .

Skrymir awoke. 'What's that?' he said. 'I'm sure I felt a twig drop on my head. Is that you, Asa-Thor? Why are you up? Is it morning already?'

Thor looked distinctly put out at this. 'It's nothing,' he said. 'Go back to sleep.'

And so the giant turned over again, and was soon as soundly asleep as before.

The next time Thor waited longer, but I knew he wasn't asleep. Thor isn't what you'd call good at hiding his aggression, and between the mutterings, the gnashing of teeth, the rumbling stomach and the animal sounds, I could tell he was feeling frustrated. At last, he got up, Mjølnir in hand, and, striding up to Skrymir, dealt him such a terrific blow right between the eyes that birds fell stunned from the sky, trees fell and the whole of the neighbouring countryside trembled with the impact.

Skrymir sat up. 'Is it morning?' he said.

Thor was visibly shaken.

'There must have been birds nesting in that tree,' said Skrymir, getting to his feet. 'I'm sure I felt something drop on my head. Still, never mind. I'm glad you're up. It's time to get on with our journey. Have you had breakfast?'

Thor just snarled.

'Then let's get going. My home isn't far. But – a word of warning. My people aren't used to strangers, and they won't take kindly to arrogance. You gods may think you're the bee's knees in Asgard, but here in World Beyond you're just cute little wannabes. Utgard-Loki and his men won't stand for any nonsense.'

'Utgard-Loki?' I said in surprise.

'He's the King of World Beyond. What? You thought you were the only Trickster in the Worlds?'

Then he stood up and prepared to move on. His previous good temper had gone, and this morning he seemed unaccountably surly.

'I'm going north, to the mountains,' he said. 'If I were you, I'd head back home. I don't see you cutting much of a figure among the folk of Utgard. But if you *do* want to visit – well. You'll find the city due east from here, not more than a day's walk.' And, picking up his pack (still with all our belongings inside), he started off through the woods again, scowling, without even saying goodbye.

'Wow. I miss him already,' I said. 'Can't *wait* to meet his family.' I turned in the direction from which we had come. 'This way, I think. We might reach the sea by morning.'

'We're turning *back*?' said Thialfi to Thor. 'After he belittled you?'

Roskva said nothing, but I could tell that she was with her brother.

I tried to explain that bravery wasn't the same as foolishness. A city of giants like Skrymir, impervious to Mjølnir's blows and ruled by a king who thought the gods were just cute little wannabes – this just happened to be high on my list of things to be avoided.

But Thor's eyes were cold as knives. 'We're going to that city,' he said. 'I want to meet that Trickster King. And *you're* coming with me.'

'I am?'

'You are.'

And so that's why we headed east, to Utgard, and our downfall.

LESSON 9

World Beyond

The bigger they are, the harder they fall?
Tell that to the mountains.

Lokabrenna

WE LEFT THE FOREST BY MIDDAY, under that strangely luminous sky, and found ourselves approaching a bare ridge, in which three curious valleys – all square, one deeper than the rest – appeared like missing teeth. Beyond that lay a plain, and the stronghold that Skrymir had promised us: Utgard; the largest fortress we'd ever seen, with walls that rivalled Asgard's in height. We approached and knocked at the huge iron gates, but there was no answer.

'Somehow I was expecting a warmer welcome than this,' said Thor.

'What? The fatted calf?' I said. 'Come to think of it, roast beef *would* be nice . . .'

Thialfi and Roskva looked at me with eyes like saucers.

'You think we can get in?' said the boy.

We looked through the bars at the giant halls; the dizzying spires of Utgard. Thor hammered on the gates with his fists; yelled for someone to open them; and finally rattled them as hard as he could – without success. No one heard, and the gates stood as unresponsive as before.

'Well, we can't force our way in,' I said. 'But size isn't always everything.' And I slipped through the iron bars of the gate and beckoned the others to do the same. The youngsters followed me easily, but Thor, who was bigger and broader, had to force two of the wrought-iron panels apart before setting foot in the city.

He made his way to the largest hall, a building hewn from massive chunks of white rock, with a door of whole oak trunks, iron-bound. The door was open; looking through we saw an assembly of giants: men and women; old and young; sitting around huge tables; lounging on benches; drinking and making merry. Their shields were positioned neatly all around the hall; the polished surfaces reflecting the light from a thousand candles.

One giant sat alone on a higher seat than the rest.

'That must be Utgard-Loki,' I said.

We entered. It took some time for the giants to notice our presence. Then they began to smile, then laugh. Thor squared his jaw aggressively.

'What's funny?' he demanded.

The giants only laughed some more. Thor gritted his teeth and ignored them, making his way down the long hall to the throne of Utgard-Loki.

'Greetings, Utgard-Loki . . .' he began.

'I know who you are,' said the king. 'News travels quickly in World Beyond. I'm guessing you're Thor, the Thunderer. You know, I thought you'd be taller?'

Thor made an inarticulate sound.

'Still, size isn't everything,' went on the king. 'Perhaps you have skills we don't know about. We don't usually allow people to stay here unless they're the best at something. What skills do you and your friends possess? Let's have a demonstration.'

By then I was totally ravenous. Skrymir had taken most of our food, and there had been nothing to eat on the way except for a few handfuls of cloudberries. In fact, I realized, my last decent meal had been that goat stew, days ago.

'All right,' I said. '*I* have a skill. I bet I can eat faster than any man in this hall.'

The giant king gave me a look. 'You think?' he said.

'I can certainly try.'

I reckoned that this way, at least, I would get to eat *something*.

And so the giants brought a long trencher of roast meat to a table. It smelt so good I could barely restrain myself from throwing myself headlong into it.

'Logi!' called the giant king, addressing a giant sitting at the back of the hall. 'Why don't you take the challenge?'

I looked at Logi, and for a moment I thought he looked familiar. Something about his colours, perhaps; a fleeting glimpse of Chaos.

Then I shrugged. So what? I thought. He wasn't so big. I was sure I could take him.

Utgard-Loki seated us on opposite sides of the trencher. The general idea was that we should eat from the trencher as fast as we could, and when we ran out of meat we'd see who had made the most progress.

Well, it started out all right. Thialfi and Roskva were cheering. I just got my head down and ate as fast as I possibly could. I couldn't ever remember a time when I'd been as hungry, and Logi – whatever his name was – had presumably not missed any meals.

I only raised my head when I met the guy in the middle, and for a moment it looked as if the race had been a dead heat. Then Utgard-Loki pointed out that, although I'd eaten the meat from the bones, Logi had eaten the bones as well – *and* most of the trencher.

'Nice try, loser,' Logi said, and slouched back to his table.

Thialfi and Roskva hung their heads.

I gave Utgard-Loki a look. I *really* didn't like the guy. It wasn't just that manner of his, or the fact that he shared one of my names, there was something about him that wasn't right; something in his colours. I tried to see them properly, using the rune *Bjarkán*, but the hall was so full of reflections from the giants' polished shields that I couldn't be sure of anything. One thing I *did* know – he was tricky. Tricky, and maybe dangerous.

The giant king looked at Thialfi. 'You look like one of the Folk,' he said. 'Is there something you can do that might be entertaining?'

'I can run,' said Thialfi. 'Back home, I've never been beaten.'

Utgard-Loki looked sceptical. 'All right,' he said at last. 'A race! We'll try you against young Hugi.' He beckoned to one of the younger giants who had been watching. 'Let's go outside and see who wins.'

There was a long, broad strip of grass right behind Utgard-Loki's hall. 'This is where we play sports,' said the king. 'Let's see what this young man can do.'

The race was in three stages. During the first stage, Thialfi ran well, but Hugi reached the end of the track in time to turn and welcome him.

'Not bad,' said Utgard-Loki. 'Now you've had a chance to see Hugi run, perhaps you'll make an effort next time.'

The second time, Thialfi sprinted even faster. I could see the effort in his face; his feet barely seemed to touch the ground. And yet Hugi ran faster; this time he reached the end of the track and waved at Thialfi as he approached.

Utgard-Loki smiled. 'That's not bad for one of the Folk. But I think you'll have to do something quite special this time if you want to match Hugi.'

Thialfi prepared for a third race. This time, if anything, I thought he managed to run even faster. But Hugi was faster still – a blur – reaching the end long before Thialfi was even halfway.

'Brave try,' said Hugi to Thialfi. 'But I think we all know who the winner is here.'

Now Thor, who had watched all this with clenched teeth, strode up to Utgard-Loki. I knew the signs better than most: the Thunderer was losing patience.

'Oh, it's you, Asa-Thor,' said the king. 'Have you a skill you'd like to display? I've heard all kinds of fanciful tales, but seeing your companions, I'm rather inclined to dismiss what I've heard. It's easy to swagger among the Folk and impress them with your boasting. But to pit you against *real* men . . .'

Thor snarled: 'I'll gladly out-drink any of you.'

The giant king raised an eyebrow. 'A drinking contest? Really?' he said. 'I'm warning you, we're serious drinkers in Utgard. Come winter, when the light goes, there isn't much else to do here.'

'Bring it on,' said Thor. 'You'll see. There's no one in Asgard to rival me, not even Allfather himself.'

'All right,' said Utgard-Loki. We followed him back into the hall, where a servant brought to his table a cleverly fashioned sconce-horn. 'Most of my people like to drink from this, my ceremonial horn. Our very best drinkers can drain it in a single draught. Most of the rest can drain it in two. Let's see what you can do, little Thor.'

Thor was red in the face by now. He wasn't used to ridicule, and jokes about his size were never likely to go down well. I looked at the horn. It was very long, but Utgard-Loki hadn't seen Thor drink. I thought that maybe this time, he'd underestimated the gods.

Thor took a deep breath and raised the drinking-horn to his mouth. Then he began to drink, taking giant gulps of the stuff inside. To me, it smelt like some kind of beer; weak; a little salty. I was sure that the draught would prove no match at all for the Thunderer. But when Thor put it down at last, gasping for breath, and looked inside, the level seemed barely to have dropped.

'Never mind,' said the giant king. 'That's still quite a

respectable draught for such a little man as yourself. Try again. Twice should do it. Even the women and children here can do it in three.'

Thor said nothing, but drank again. I could feel the rage coming off him. The muscles in his neck worked; he drank until he was red in the face . . .

But when he finally put down the horn, it seemed to me that the level of beer had barely dropped more than an inch or so.

Thor shook his head like an angry dog.

'Well, if that's the best in Asgard,' said Utgard-Loki with a smile, 'I wonder you've kept it safe for so long. Your enemies must be very gullible, believing everything they hear about your strength and prowess.'

'My strength!' said Thor. 'You can test it. What sort of weights do you have in here?'

Utgard-Loki looked amused. 'I'm not sure I should be encouraging you to make a fool of yourself this way. But some of our youngsters play a game called "Lifting the Cat". Perhaps you could try. I wouldn't normally suggest it to a man of your stature . . .' he smirked, 'but maybe you'll surprise us.'

He made a curious clicking noise, and a cat snaked out from under one of the tables. It was quite a large cat; black, with sleepy yellow eyes.

'What am I supposed to do with this?' said Thor.

'Why, lift it from the floor, of course. Don't do yourself an injury; it's a big cat, and you're a bit on the small side.'

Thor growled and squared his feet and grabbed the cat in both hands. Then he lifted it high in the air – but the cat just arched its back and purred, and its feet stayed firmly on the ground. Thor tried to get a better grip, but the cat seemed boneless; it rolled and squirmed and Thor had no more luck than before. At last, Thor grabbed the cat squarely around the body. Grunting and cursing with the effort, he lifted it right over his head and stretched his arms as far as he could . . .

The cat stopped purring and lifted one paw from the

ground.

Sarcastic applause from the giants. Thialfi put his head in his hands. Thor turned to Utgard-Loki in rage. 'I'll wrestle you,' he said. 'No tricks. No cats. No games. I'll wrestle *you*.'

'Who, *me*?' said Utgard-Loki. 'Oh, please. I thought you might have learnt a little humility by now. There's no one in this hall who'd agree to wrestle a little man like you. It wouldn't be fair – and it wouldn't reflect well on any of us to try.'

'You're afraid to fight me,' said Thor.

'Not at all,' said the giant king. 'But I might do you an injury. I'll tell you what – my old nurse sometimes likes to wrestle. She's tougher than she looks, and she's used to dealing with children.' He raised his voice. 'Elli! Come over here!'

A very old woman came into the hall. White-haired, bent like driftwood; bright eyes in a face that was nothing but wrinkles. Thor clenched his teeth so hard that it hurt to watch. But the old lady cackled and crowed when she heard that he wanted to wrestle.

'Fine!' she said, and threw down her stick. 'I haven't been this close to a man since my old husband died. Let's see what you're made of, big boy!' And she threw herself at the Thunderer.

'What about me?' hissed Roskva, who was watching the proceedings with interest. 'Don't I get a chance to compete?'

'Don't be silly. Girls don't compete,' said Thialfi, still breathing heavily. 'Girls are meant to sit and watch, and maybe bring their brothers a drink?'

Roskva kicked him, hard, in the shin.

'*Ouch!*'

For the first time that day, I grinned.

Meanwhile, Thor and Ellie were locked in earnest combat. To begin with, Thor had held back, afraid to do the old woman harm. But very soon he had realized that she was stronger than she looked. The crooked old body was far from frail, and when he tried to throw her, she held her position fast, and laughed, and worked her bony fingers around all his most sensitive pressure points, so that he was obliged to go on the defensive just to avoid being thrown himself.

Suddenly the old woman twisted, locking Thor's arm as she stepped behind him. Thor tried to escape the lock, but he had been thrown off balance; he fell to one knee.

The giants roared.

Thor went red.

Thialfi looked at Roskva and I felt their disillusionment. That terrible moment when a god turns out to be no more than a man – it was almost heartbreaking. I, too, was tarnished with failure; in the eyes of our young friends, we would never be gods again, just beaten, second-rate heroes.

Damn it, that hurt. I began to see that celebrity wasn't all hot girls and free beer. It's also the curse of expectation – and the bitterness of falling short. Perhaps that was why I'd always been so suspicious of fatherhood; perhaps I'd known instinctively how much that disillusion would hurt if I saw it in the faces of my boys.

'Enough,' said Utgard-Loki. 'We've tested our guests to their limits. Now it's time for us all to relax – it's getting late. We're all tired.'

We spent the rest of the evening eating, drinking and listening to music played by the king's servants. No lutes in Utgard, thank the gods, but lots of heavy guitars, playing complicated, interminable solos. In victory, Utgard-Loki was as genial as he'd previously been rude; offering us the best cuts of meat, the best seats at his table. We didn't enjoy the experience much – Thor and I were too ashamed, and Thialfi and Roskva were suffering from a serious emotional let-down – but the giant king was at pains to make the rest of our stay as pleasant as he could. We slept on soft beds covered in furs, and in the morning, when we rose, our host was there to greet us. Once more he plied us with food and drink, although the rest of his people were still asleep on the floor of the hall, and then he accompanied us out of the gates and back to the ridge of mountains.

'This is where I leave you,' he said, stopping at last to address us. None of us had been especially talkative on the way out of Utgard. Thor was still angry about his defeat; Roskva was sulking because no one had asked her to demonstrate her skills, and Thialfi was still limping. Face it, we'd all been humiliated, and we wanted to forget the experience as soon as we could.

'So, what did you think of my city?' said Utgard-Loki with a smile. 'What kind of impression do you think you made on me, and on my people?'

Thor shook his head listlessly. 'I think we're all more than aware we didn't exactly shine,' he said.

Once more Utgard-Loki smiled. 'Let me tell you this,' he said. 'If I'd known how strong you were, Asa-Thor, and how powerful the gods of Asgard were in comparison to my folk, I would never have let you within a hundred miles of the city. Do you know you were nearly the death of us all?'

'I don't understand,' said Thor, perplexed.

But I was beginning to guess at the truth. The city was filled with glamours. The great hall had been thick with them, far too many to identify. A game of smoke and mirrors, I thought; enhanced by powerful runelore. And the giant king? A trickster, Skrymir had told us; a trickster to rival even the Trickster himself.

'I think I do,' I told him. '*You* were Skrymir, weren't you?'

Utgard-Loki gave a smile. 'That's right. I was Skrymir. I saw you coming from afar, and wanted to find out who you were, and what kind of threat you might pose to us. Remember the pack with the food inside? I fastened it with the rune *Naudr*, the Binder, so you couldn't open it. And later, when Thor tried to smash in my skull with that pretty hammer of his – nice weapon, by the way, but it's what you do with it that counts – he *may* have thought he was striking me, but in fact he was aiming for that ridge – the one with the three square-shaped valleys.

The valleys are Thor's hammer-blows.'

Thor isn't what you might call especially quick on the uptake. He pondered the giant's words for a while, then frowned and said: 'And after that?'

'My man Logi, who beat Loki in the eating contest.' Utgard-Loki winked at me. 'That was Wildfire in his elemental Aspect, which is why he looked familiar – and why he ate the trencher as well as the food inside it. And Thialfi, who raced so fast that I could hardly believe his speed, was racing against Hugi, the speed of Thought. And as for you, Asa-Thor . . .' He turned once again to Thor, whose face was slowly turning red. 'The drinking-horn from which you took such great draughts – that was a funnel that led to the One Sea, and you'll see for yourselves when you return how far back the tide has receded. The cat was the World Serpent, that circles the Worlds with its tail in its mouth, and you lifted it so high into the air that you almost dragged it out of the ocean. And as for my old nurse, Ellie . . .' Utgard-Loki shook his head. 'That was an Aspect of Old Age, and she only wrestled you to one knee.' He paused and looked at us all in turn.

'That's why,' he said, 'this is goodbye. You'll never see me or my city again. My glamours will hide us for ever. Your people might search a thousand years and still you'd never find us. Let's chalk this up to experience, shall we? Live and let live, that's what I say.'

At this, Thor's face went purple. He grabbed Mjølnir and raised it. But before he could use it, the Trickster of Utgard shifted Aspect and disappeared, leaving nothing but a faint scent of burning and a signature that led deep into the earth. And turning back towards Utgard, we saw that where the gleaming city had stood – its walls, its gates, its shining spires – there was nothing but grasslands and plain, unmarked as far as the eye could see.

'Wow,' said Thialfi. 'Just – wow. Wait till I tell the people at home about *this*.'

I looked at him. 'If I were you, I'd keep that story to myself.'

Thor growled: 'This isn't over.'

I shrugged. It was, and he knew it.

'Face it,' I said. 'We've both been had. Any more fuss and the story will spread right across the Middle Worlds. Let's go home. If anyone asks, we were never here.'

And so we went back to Asgard as if nothing had happened. We dropped off Thialfi and Roskva at their parents' house on the way – we'd both had enough of celebrity, applause and expectation by then – and we drove home through the back roads, staying in human Aspect and keeping a low profile.

Neither of us mentioned our trip to the land of the midnight sun, though sometimes, looking at Odin, I wondered if he knew more than he was saying. In spite of that, the story spread all over the Middle Worlds, rivalling even that of Thor's wedding to Thrym in popularity. Soon everyone knew the tale of how the Trickster had been beaten at his own game. Some laughed; some jeered; some were sympathetic. And some seemed to take my defeat to heart, as if I'd deliberately let them down.

Thor's reputation did better, I think. After all, intelligence had never been his strong point. But mine never quite recovered. I'd shown myself to be fallible – never a good move for a god – and the grudging respect I'd earned had all too soon been eroded. That was all Thor's fault, of course. He was the one who'd insisted on picking up Thialfi and Roskva. He was the one who'd decided to go to the land of the midnight sun. And *he* was the one who'd demanded that we go to Utgard.

But just like that, the bubble had burst. That eerie sense of contentment was gone. My fame had once more become mere notoriety. The snarl of barbed wire was back in my heart, and whenever I looked at my twin sons, I saw their disappointment.

That was what did it. That look in their eyes. And that was why, as time went by, I became increasingly aware of my damaged mouth; my damaged soul; my damaged reputation.

I'd always been a man of words. Now, my words deserted me. I spent too much time in my hawk Aspect; I slept too little; I drank too much mead. And all the time two little words chased each other around my head like Odin's ravens.

Two words; one goal.

Get Thor.

LESSON 10

Feathers

A bird in the hand will leave you with birdshit on your fingers.

Lokabrenna

O<small>F COURSE</small>, that wouldn't be easy. Thor was almost indestructible. Even without Mjølnir, his fireproof gauntlets, his belt of strength, he was a force to be reckoned with. Not that I meant to *use* force; Thor's besetting weakness was trust, and *that* was what I meant to exploit.

The first step was to create the trap into which I was to lure him. This proved harder than I'd thought – not because Thor didn't have any enemies – in fact, the Worlds were littered with folk who were keen to do him harm – but because no one would believe that I could ever betray him. Our fame had given rise to some underserved rumours of friendship between us, besides which my own reputation as a master of deceit meant that whomever I tried to recruit would immediately (and unfairly) assume that I was not to be believed.

No, straightforward recruitment was out. I had to do something subtle. Something that would persuade the mark that *my* idea was *his* idea.

A long con, in effect.

And so I assumed my hawk Aspect and went to visit the Ice Folk. It was my first time in that region since Thrym's death, and the mark was Thrym's successor, a brutal warlord named Geirrod. I knew him by reputation; I knew that he was ambitious; I knew that he thought he was smart; I knew that he liked hunting with hawks and that he had an unusual way of snaring the birds he meant to train. I also knew that he hated Thor, who happened to have killed one of his relatives, which made him the ideal target for the plan I had in mind.

Still, after the deaths of Thiassi and Thrym, no warlord of the Ice Folk would have dreamed of making a deal. No, I had to approach Geirrod in a way that would lead him to believe that *he* had got the better of *me* – not an appealing prospect, I know, but you have to speculate to accumulate. And so I flew to Geirrod's camp, where the man himself was training hawks, settled on a branch nearby, and let events take their course.

The trap was simple, but effective. The hunter had spread a kind of glue onto the branches of the tree on which I'd chosen to rest a while. When I came to fly away, I found that my feet were stuck to the branch, and before I could react, I was caged. What a humiliation.

Of course, I kept to my hawk Aspect throughout the unpleasant procedure, biting and screaming and flapping my wings. Geirrod's keen, acquisitive eyes brightened as he looked at me.

'This one has spirit. I'll train him myself. I'll put him in jesses and feed him scraps. He'll make me a fine hunter.'

I glared at him. He looked amused. I didn't like being kept in a cage, or being put into jesses, but there was glam around Geirrod, and I knew he'd recognize me quickly enough. He called over his daughters, two rather plain girls called Gjalp and Greip, and together they stared into the cage at Your Humble Narrator.

'There's something funny about this hawk,' said Geirrod. 'Have a look at his eyes.'

I closed my eyes and tried to look asleep.

'Who are you?' said Geirrod. 'Name yourself.'

I, of course, did no such thing.

He tried a cantrip then – *a named thing is a tamed thing* – which, if I had been a regular bird, would have confirmed my innocence. But, though I did not reveal my name, my ability to hide it from him told Geirrod all he needed to know.

So he opened the cage again and grabbed me tightly by the throat. I struggled and tried to bite him, but Geirrod was used to handling hawks.

'I know you're no ordinary bird,' he said. 'Tell me your name, or you'll suffer.'

I guessed I'd suffer a whole lot more if he suspected he was being had. And so I continued to play dumb, and said nothing.

'All right,' said Geirrod. 'I can wait. We'll see how you feel in a week's time.' And he opened a massive, iron-bound chest and thrust me, struggling, inside. Then he slammed down the heavy lid and left me there, in the airless dark.

Not Yours Truly's finest hour. The chest was locked. I was hungry and scared. I couldn't change Aspect; my glam was low, and I was using all of it to conceal myself from my captors. I waited for them to release me, but time passed and I realized that Geirrod's threat had been sincere; he meant to leave me there for a week, starving and dizzy from lack of air, unless I agreed to cooperate.

It was like Thiassi all over again, except that this time I'd chosen my fate. I was exactly where I'd meant to be, but after a few days of captivity I was starting to wonder if my plan hadn't been a little foolhardy. Of course, I needed to make Geirrod believe that he'd broken me for real; the problem was, I wasn't sure whether I could last the course.

Days passed without reprieve. I was hungry; thirsty. Then, after seven days, Geirrod opened up the chest and grabbed me by the throat again.

'Well? Are you ready to show yourself?'

I took a desperate gulp of air. It felt good, but I was alarmed at how weak I'd become over seven days. Much more of this and

I wouldn't have the strength to go on. And yet I clung to my hawk Aspect, knowing that if he suspected my game, I would be helpless, in his power.

'All right. That's earned you another week,' he said, and slammed the chest shut again.

Now I don't do well with prisons. A free spirit like Yours Truly was never made to be caged like this. Once more, I sweated and starved, listening to the muffled sounds of voices from the outside. Seven days later, once again, my captor opened the iron-bound chest.

'Well? What do you say?' he said.

I blinked at the sudden sunlight and took a desperate gasp of air. I was very weak by now. Hunger and thirst tore at my guts; my feathers were broken and covered with dust.

'I'm counting to three,' said Geirrod. 'Then you can rot for another week. One. Two—'

'Mercy,' I said, resuming my current Aspect. I didn't need to fake this: I was in a bad way. Naked, starving, on my knees; my throat so dry I could hardly speak. 'Mercy, please,' I repeated.

Geirrod's dark eyes opened wide. 'I know you,' he said slowly. 'You're that weasel Loki.'

I tried to get up, but couldn't. Changing Aspect was out of the question. 'You don't want me,' I told him. 'I'm worth nothing. Look at me. No one will offer a ransom for me, or even notice that I'm gone. Let me go, and I'll make sure you're paid. Whatever you want, I can find it.'

Geirrod thought about that for a while. 'Anything?'

'I swear it,' I said. 'Money, girls, power – *revenge* – you name it, you've got it.'

Geirrod looked even more thoughtful. 'Revenge, eh?'

'Absolutely.' I hid a smile. 'My word on it.'

'All right,' said Geirrod. 'Revenge it is. I want you to bring Thor to my hall, without his hammer Mjølnir.'

I gave him a look of anguished appeal. Inside, I was grinning. 'But Thor's my friend,' I protested.

'You gave your word,' said Geirrod.

'I know. But does it *have* to be Thor?'

'Thor killed my kinsman Hrugnir. I want him to pay. In full. In blood.'

Yes, I know. I'm *that* good. Geirrod had taken the bait, and I had provided myself with an alibi, so that if things went wrong and I was found out, Geirrod and his daughters would swear that I'd given my oath under torture.

And so we agreed I'd deliver Thor, unarmed and unsuspecting. Then Geirrod's daughters saw to my needs; fed me and clothed me; gave me a bed. And in the morning, tired and sore, but secretly still grinning inside, I flew off back to Asgard.

Persuading Thor to come with me wasn't as hard as you might expect. I suggested a trip to see a friend, Geirrod, of the Ice Folk; a friend with two lovely daughters. It was still summer, which meant plenty of game, good fishing, and no snow in the valleys. Of course, Sif wouldn't approve, I said, but if Thor left his hammer behind, and went without his chariot, then we could be there and back before Sif even knew we were gone. It didn't hurt my case that Sif had been prickly of late, following the little fling Thor had had with Jarnsaxa, a warrior woman from the mountains. Much as he hated the Rock Folk, he had a thing for their slim, dark haired, strong and hot-blooded women (which might account for the number of enemies he'd made over the years), and Sif, never the patient type, was quick to comment when he strayed.

And so we let it be known in Asgard that we were going fishing, and then we crept over Bif-rost, Thor looking as guilty as sin, Yours Truly as innocent as a newborn babe. Which I was, if you think about it; if Thor had been faithful to his wife, my plan would never have got off the ground. Which was why, I told myself, if the Thunderer came to any harm on our adventure, it would not be my fault, but his. It's the kind of poetic justice that people like Thor tend to overlook, which was why I didn't mention it to him at the time (or later).

As always, Heimdall watched us go. I would rather he hadn't seen us, of course, but there was no hiding anything from the sharp-eyed Watchman. We travelled into the Middle Worlds, keeping to the main roads, crossed the realm of the Rock Folk and, as we neared the ring of peaks that marks the approach to the Far North, we stopped to rest by a mountain pass, where an old friend of Odin's happened to live.

Her name was Grid, and she lived alone in her cabin in the wilds. She was one of those outdoor, sporty types; all hunting and fishing, cropped hair and sensible shoes. She could eat and drink almost as much as Thor could, and with the belt of strength she wore – a present from the Old Man – she could wrestle a bear to the ground. She had a pair of gauntlets, too, fireproof and woven with runes, which looked a lot like the ones that I'd gone to such pains to persuade Thor to leave behind.

Meeting her was the worst kind of luck. You might almost suspect that the Old Man, seeing Thor and Yours Truly sneaking out of Asgard, had sent her to keep an eye on his son and make sure he didn't run into trouble. *Could* Odin have suspected me? The thought didn't exactly fill me with reassurance. Still, it was too late to change the plan. And so we accepted her offer of a night's hospitality and followed her back to her cabin at the edge of the pine woods.

There, she fed us on fresh-caught fish and made us two beds by the fireside. She offered us beer and honey-wine, but I wasn't in the mood for drinking. Something really didn't feel right. My nerves were ringing alarm bells, and when I finally fell asleep, it was thin, unsatisfying sleep, from which I was roused some time later by the sound of whispering.

I kept my eyes closed and listened. Grid and Thor were still awake. I was already feeling uneasy; then I caught Geirrod's name in the conversation, and sensed I might be in trouble. I continued to feign sleep; after a minute or two, Thor came over to where I lay, and stood there for a long time. Still I kept my eyes closed; then after a while he went to bed, and soon I heard him snoring.

In the morning, we set off again, and I watched Thor attentively, trying to work out how much he knew. I saw with growing discomfort that Grid had lent him her belt of strength and her iron gauntlets. I wanted to ask him why, but couldn't find a way to do it without arousing suspicion. There were two ravens flying above the canyon through which we were travelling; I suspected Hugin and Munin, and wondered – not for the first time – whether Odin was spying on us.

Why would Odin do that?

Well – Odin hadn't got where he was through honesty and openness. He'd chosen to recruit me *knowing* my volatile nature, and though he'd kept his promises of friendship and protection, he'd never really trusted me. Fact is, I don't think he trusted anyone – not even Thor, his own son – which, looking back, explains a lot about what happened later.

But those birds unsettled me. Besides, I knew that by this time Geirrod and his daughters would be watching my approach from afar, and if they saw the ravens, or suspected a double-cross, then I'd be in a world of hurt.

We travelled further north, beyond the Hindarfell pass, and soon approached the Vimur River. It was broad at that point, and fast, swollen by a long month of rains. Rocks and boulders made it worse; and as if that wasn't bad enough, there on the far bank stood Geirrod's muffin-faced daughter Gjalp, singing a cantrip of *Logr*, so that the river swelled even more monstrously, now rushing with filth and debris, threatening to sweep us both away.

Damn. Those ravens must have alerted them. I'd always known Geirrod was twitchy. Rather than stick with the original plan, he'd decided to try and dispatch us both before we reached his stronghold. The river kept on rising – Gjalp casting runes at it all the time – and the bank at my feet began to give way.

'Loki, who's this hag?' yelled Thor, above the roar of the water. 'Anyone you know?'

I wisely omitted to tell Thor that the lady on the far bank was one of the beauties I'd promised him. Instead I grabbed onto his belt for dear life as the rising water swept us away. Gjalp laughed as the river took us, and we were pelted and beaten and scratched by rocks and pieces of driftwood.

Thor grabbed hold of a dead tree that stuck out from the river bed, and hauling us both upright again, managed to struggle to the far bank. Gjalp fled, mouthing curses, and, wet, cold and filthy, we moved on towards Geirrod's hall.

'So, this Geirrod,' said Thor as we went. 'How well do you know him?'

'Not very well,' I said cautiously. 'But he offered me hospitality last time I was in these parts.'

'Really?' said Thor.

'Absolutely,' I said. 'Two weeks without lifting a finger. He'd have kept me another week, to be sure, if I hadn't insisted.'

Thor seemed mollified by this, and as evening approached we reached Geirrod's settlement. I was on my guard by then but saw no sign of imminent violence. Instead, a servant greeted us and led us to our quarters. In winter the Ice Folk build their homes from the ice itself; in summer, they live in wood-framed tents covered in animal skins, though Geirrod had a good-sized hall overlooking the river. Our tent was large, with a chair, a lamp and two beds covered in elk and deerskin.

I went off to wash in the stream, and Thor sat down on the chair and promptly went to sleep. Ten minutes later, I returned to find that, rashly, Geirrod's daughters had tried to ambush the sleeping Thor. One had looped a length of thin garrotting wire around his neck; the other was trying to hold him down while her sister finished him off.

Big mistake, girls, big mistake. You should have trusted Loki. The one thing not to do around Thor (except, perhaps, to mess with Sif's hair) is to disturb his naptime.

As I entered, Thor sat up, grabbing one of the daughters in each fist. Gjalp and Greip were cawing like crows, trying to shift Aspect, but Grid's borrowed gauntlets held them fast and all they could do was struggle.

I adopted the casual approach.

'Oh. I see you've met Gjalp and Greip,' I said.

'What the Hel?' roared the Thunderer. 'These crones were trying to strangle me!'

I quickly disposed of the length of wire. 'Thor, this is hardly chivalrous. Not when our host's lovely daughters were trying to give you a relaxing massage, using – er – the traditional *massage cord* for which the Ice Folk are famous.'

Thor made an explosive sound. '*Lovely daughters?*'

I had to admit *that* was quite a leap. I pointed out that, though muffin-faced, Greip *did* have quite a nice figure, and besides, not *everyone* finds body hair unappealing.

Thor looked a little more closely at Gjalp. 'Isn't that the hag who tried to drown us earlier?' he said in a piercing whisper.

'Oh, no, I don't think so,' I said. 'That one was *much* uglier.' Then, addressing the two beauties, I said: 'Perhaps we'd better go and see your father before we accept any more hospitality? I'm sure he's keen to welcome us.'

I looked at Thor, who reluctantly loosened his hold on the two hags, and now stood looking vaguely confused, as if alarmed at his own strength. Grid's belt might have helped him, but even without it, half the time, Thor has no idea of his power. Just looking at those hands of his in their iron gauntlets, I felt a growing discomfort, and I was about to suggest we left when Geirrod's servant re-entered the tent and announced that his master was ready.

'He is?' I said.

'Oh, yes,' said the servant. 'He thought perhaps you might like to join in a few games before dinner.'

'Dinner?' said Thor.

'Games?' I said.

It crossed my mind that the kind of games Geirrod liked to indulge in were probably not the kind of games I was likely to enjoy. But Thor, to whom the word *dinner* was like a clarion call to arms, was halfway out of the door by the time I could voice my objection.

I followed – what else could I do? – and as we entered Geirrod's place we saw that, instead of the usual fire, there was a row of furnaces all down both sides of the long hall. It was already sweltering inside; the light was red and treacherous. Just the way I like it, in fact, but Thor was squinting against the smoke.

I could just see the figure of Geirrod somewhere near the back of the hall; he was carrying a pair of blacksmith's tongs, and as soon as we entered, he picked something out of one of the furnaces and flung it straight at both of us. It was a massive iron ball, heated to a dull red, and I shifted quickly to avoid it, adopting my Wildfire Aspect. But Thor just caught the iron ball between those massive gauntlets and hurled it back with terrific force. It struck Geirrod midsection, and went on travelling right through him, crushing his ribs and smashing the wall behind him into kindling.

If this was a game, I was pretty sure Team Aesir had already won it, but you know Thor; once he sees red, there really is no stopping him. He smashed Geirrod's hall to rubble, leaving it littered with body parts. Then he went outside and did it there too, and when the worst was over, I saw him, bloody to the armpits, looking over the scene of carnage with an air of vague confusion, no doubt remembering my account of green meadows, blue skies and a host with two lovely daughters.

I decided not to stay around to compare recollections. Shifting to my hawk Aspect, I winged it back to Asgard, vowing to leave a healthy interval before my next meeting with Thor. He had a fearsome temper when roused, but he seldom bore a grudge. In a week or two he would have forgotten the details of our little adventure, and my skin would be safe once again.

The Ice Folk, however, were another matter. I knew that my part in the day's events, innocent though they might have been, would ensure that there would be no escape for me in that part of the Middle Worlds. I was quickly running short of places to hide – should I need them. And there was something in the air that told me the time was approaching . . .

LESSON 11

Ransom

Blood is thicker than water.
But gold – gold pays for everything.

Lokabrenna

I TOLD YOU the Worlds had ended before. Of course that isn't entirely true. The Worlds never really end – just the folk who have made it their own. And Order and Chaos never end, but the balance of power is in constant flux, which is why the General never slept well, and never relaxed his vigilance.

We'd had a pretty good run thus far. Decades of security, with only sporadic attacks from the bands of Ice Folk and Rock Folk who still had an eye on Odin's throne. Gullveig-Heid had gone underground; Chaos seemed to be sleeping. Order was firmly in command, and there was nothing but blue skies ahead.

Of course, these were always the times when Odin felt the least secure. The Old Man was perverse in so many ways, always believing the worst of folk; always suspicious; always on guard; never giving a thing away. When I got back from my trip with Thor, I found that Odin had been perched in his crow's nest for the entire duration of our absence, talking only to his birds and to Mimir's Head in its cradle of runes.

Why the fascination with a disembodied Head? Well, crossing back from the Land of the Dead gives a certain perspective.

Sometimes it gives the power to foretell the future – though you know what I always say: 'never trust an Oracle'. But Mimir's Head, understandably, resented having been brought back to life and kept in an ice-cold spring for years, and so, although Odin could make it speak, it rarely did so willingly. Hence the time he spent with it, whispering over the secret spring, tracing runes on the water, trying to see his way in the dark . . .

No one knows when the Oracle first delivered the prophecy. Did the General *force* it to speak, or was it Mimir's initiative? No one knows for sure any more, except the Old Man himself, and Mimir's Head, if it still survives. But those thirty-six stanzas changed the world in which we lived; eclipsed our sun and moon and sent Odin's ravens flying to the far roots and branches of Yggdrasil in search of . . . what, exactly? Understanding? Deliverance?

Death?

I had no problem with *that*, of course. As far as I was concerned, the gods had had it too easy for far too long. But my own position was hardly secure, and I was in no hurry to die, be it at the hands of the Aesir or in the bosom of Chaos. If Allfather *was* spying on me (of which I was becoming increasingly sure), then I needed to understand why. I mean, he'd always known what I was. What did he think I was guilty of?

And so, having failed to work on Thor, I started work on Odin. I thought that if I could talk him into leaving Asgard for a while, I might find out the reason for the growing distance between us. He'd always enjoyed our trips abroad, and so I suggested an outing into the valleys of Inland, for a little hunting and fishing.

I asked Honir to make up the party – he was annoying but at least he had no particular grudge against me, which made him unique among the gods. Besides, the three of us had often gone hunting together, back in Asgard's early days, and I hoped that Odin's nostalgia for those days when we were still friends might prompt him to confide in me – or at least, to let something slip.

To my surprise, the Old Man agreed that he needed a few days away from home. He was looking tired, I thought, and the long hair under the hat he wore seemed more than usually grey. And yet he seemed pleased to leave Asgard; to dress in his oldest, shabbiest clothes; to carry his ancient haversack; to pretend he was just a journeyman, selling his wares as far as World's End. Perhaps that was all he wanted, I thought; the illusion of normality. But that's the problem with being a god – you lose the knack of being human.

And so we crossed Bif-rost and set off on our way – I with a cheery little wave to Heimdall, who watched me go with clenched teeth and a look on his face that, if looks could kill, might have left me, if not dead, at least with some nasty bruising. We headed for the Northlands on foot, into our old hunting grounds, where summer was ripe for the picking and there was plenty of game to be had. We found the river Strond as it ploughed a furrow between the mountains, and walked down a gully of waterfalls into a shady forest. We'd come in the Aspect of three of the Folk, unarmed and without signs of status. And I'll admit, it was fun to leave Asgard behind, with all its tensions and politics, to hunt with a sling and a pocket of stones; to sleep on a blanket under the stars. It was fun to pretend to be someone else; someone who didn't matter. And yet, it was still a performance. Odin and I both knew it. It was a kind of play, a dream of how things might have been if he and I had been capable of trusting each other for a change. And so we hunted, and sang, and laughed, and told heavily edited stories of the good old days, while each of us watched the other and wondered when the knife would fall.

We followed the river, and as evening approached I managed to bag our dinner, using my sling and a single stone; a fine otter as it sat by the riverbank, eating its catch of fresh salmon. I picked up the dead otter and the salmon (which was almost as large as the otter itself), and, rejoining the others, suggested we stop and make camp.

'We can do better than that,' Odin said. 'There's a little farm not far away. Let's offer to share our food with them in exchange for a dry bed.'

That was typical Odin. Don't ask me why; he *liked* the Folk. Any excuse to talk to them, to pretend to be one of them, he'd take it.

I looked at my catch and shrugged. 'All right. Let's see what your friends say, shall we?'

Well, we knocked at the farmhouse door. The farmer's name was Hreidmar, and he welcomed us affably enough, until the subject of dinner came up, and he saw the otter. In a moment his eyes went cold, and he walked into the little house without another word.

'What's eating him?' I said.

Odin shrugged. 'I don't know. Let's find out,' he said.

We followed Hreidmar into the house. His two sons were sitting by the fire. Fafnir and Regin were their names, and they were no friendlier than he had been. They barely spoke as we settled ourselves in front of the fire, but glared at us in silence. I didn't care for it at all, and if Odin hadn't been so keen to spend the night under their roof, I think that in his place I would have taken my chances sleeping outside by the river. But Odin and Honir didn't seem to have picked up on the fact that we weren't entirely welcome.

Finally, I cooked dinner. No one else seemed about to. Our three hosts must have been vegetarians, because they barely touched the fish and wouldn't even look at the meat, but I just thought *well, more for us*, and finally unrolled my bed and settled to sleep by the fireside.

Odin and Honir did the same, and we slept deeply and dreamlessly – that is, until, some four hours later, when somebody slapped me awake and I found myself and my friends tied up hand and foot, with Hreidmar and his two sons watching us intently.

'What's this?' said Odin.

I tried to assume my Wildfire Aspect but found myself bound with runes as well as rope. The farmer and his two sons weren't quite as rustic as they looked; if only we'd checked their colours before accepting their hospitality.

Hreidmar bared his yellow teeth. 'Which one of you killed my son?' he said.

'Your *son*? We haven't killed anyone . . .'

He showed me the otter's skin in his hand.

'Oops,' I said. 'That was your son?'

'Yes, that was Otter,' said Hreidmar. 'He used to like to hunt by day. He often took that Aspect. In the evening, he'd bring home his catch to share with me and his two brothers.'

Well, I mean to say. Who wanders through the woods during the hunting season disguised as *lunch*, for gods' sakes? And why hunt as an otter when you can catch more salmon with a net? This Otter couldn't have been very bright. I was about to point this out when I saw Hreidmar's face, and decided against.

'Look, I'm sorry,' I started to say. 'Obviously, I didn't know who he was. If I had, do you think we'd have come here?'

Hreidmar drew his knife and grinned. 'Talk all you want. Otter's still dead. And now you'll pay for what you've done. In full. In blood.'

In blood. *That* again.

'Does it *have* to be blood?' I said. 'How much do you want? I'll raise it.'

Hreidmar's eyes narrowed. 'A ransom?' he said. 'I'm warning you, it won't be cheap.'

'Anything,' I said. 'I swear.'

Hreidmar and his sons conferred. Finally, he spoke up again. 'All right. I agree,' he said. 'If you can bring me enough red gold to fill this otter skin in my hand, and then to cover it completely, I'll let you and your friends go free. Otherwise . . .' He ran his knife over the ball of his thumb, and smiled. The blade made a nasty stropping sound.

'I get it,' I said. 'Just let me go. You can keep my friends here as hostages.'

Honir looked alarmed at this, but the General just looked inscrutable. I guessed he was trying to assess how likely it was that I would just opt to save my own skin and leave the two of them to face the music.

I turned to him. 'You can trust me,' I said. 'I'll be back as soon as I can.' And then as Hreidmar released the runes, I took hawk Aspect and flew away to find the gold that would ransom my life.

I know. I know what you're thinking. Why bother with a ransom at all? That was my chance to finish him; to strike at the heart of Asgard; to take the revenge that I'd so long desired . . .

Stop. Stop there a moment. Follow the thread to where it leads.

If Hreidmar killed the Old Man, the whole of Nine Worlds would hear about it. Thor would be quick to avenge him. And there would be no way to escape the fact that I was responsible for his death. The gods would be after me in force. They would hunt me wherever I tried to hide. They would never leave me in peace. They would slaughter my twin sons, just to make sure that neither boy grew up with thoughts of vengeance in mind. And when they caught me – and they would – they would torture me to death as sure as snakes are slippery.

So now you'll see why I didn't do what you might have expected. For all my resentment of the Old Man, he was still my protector. Without him, I would have been friendless, cast out of Asgard quicker than leftovers that are starting to stink. No, I needed Odin on my side. I needed him to be grateful. And how better to achieve all this than by saving his life at the risk of my own? If I'd known the power of Hreidmar's runelore I might not have entered his den quite so fast. But I knew his reputation as well as his appetite for gold, and I'd been certain that enough of it would cover Otter's unfortunate death.

Yes. I'll admit it. I planned the whole thing. I needed Odin's gratitude. And, for all his intelligence, he was so predictable – his affection for the Folk, his love for those little valleys and woods. Everyone has a weakness, and his was this sentimentality; it didn't take much for Yours Truly to guide him to the appointed spot, while letting him think it had been *his* idea.

The rest had been easy. A handful of stones can bring down more than you might think. An otter, a man – even a citadel can fall under a well-aimed stone. All I had to do now was find enough red gold to ransom my friends, and I too would be redeemed.

So – where was I going to find the gold?

At first, I considered World Below. The Tunnel Folk could always supply plentiful quantities of gold of all varieties, but this time I sensed that Ivaldi and Sons might not prove altogether willing. Instead I made for the One Sea, where Aegir, the storm god, and Ran, his wife, had their cavern under the waves.

I arrived in Aegir's hall dripping and naked. Not that they cared; the Undersea was hardly big on etiquette. Ran was the goddess of the drowned, and she and Aegir ruled the Deeps, while Njörd, the Man of the Sea, ruled the waves and kept them safe for fishermen.

Aegir's hall was cavernous, lit by phosphorescence; dripping with water and studded with undersea gems and pearly shells. On a throne made out of a single shell, Ran sat, pale as sea-foam, watching me with oyster eyes.

I went up to her throne and bowed.

'The General's in trouble,' I said. 'I have a plan, but I need your help. Please, will you lend me your drowning-net?'

The net was Ran's prize possession. Unbreakable and stitched through with glam, she used it to drag the ocean floor, to turn the tides and drown sailors who ventured too far into her realm. She handed it over – reluctantly.

'What are you fishing for?'

'Gold,' I said.

Net in hand, I left the cave and went to explore the Undersea. I found myself a cavern, lit by a long, vertical shaft that led back to the World Above, and cast the net into the sea. I happened to know that the Tunnel Folk had cousins all over World Below, and that one of them – Andvari, his name was – liked to mine the sea bed, which was rich in all kinds of minerals. With Ran's net of woven runes, it didn't take me long to sense Andvari's presence, then to snare him and haul him out, totally at my mercy.

Of course he'd changed his Aspect. I cast the rune *Bjarkán* and saw that a massive pike was caught in my net, flailing and thrashing and showing its teeth.

I spoke a little cantrip – *a named thing is a tamed thing* – and, using his true name, made him resume his true Aspect. Within seconds, the little guy was sitting on the cavern floor, whining in the folds of the net.

'What are you doing here? What do you want?'

He sounded both aggrieved and scared. I wasn't surprised; Andvari's folk were a lot less aggressive than Ivaldi's brood. They were smaller, too; more like the goblins that came to infest the Undersea and World Below after the end of the Winter War.

'I want your gold,' I told him. 'Yes, I know you've got a stash down here. Red gold, and lots of it, or I'll wring you like a rag.'

He took a little persuasion. But I can be pretty persuasive, and with the help of Ran's drowning-net I managed to convince him. Still snivelling, he led me to his secret smithy, where I packed his supply of red gold into a number of leather sacks. When I had finished, there wasn't a scrap of gold left in the chamber – except for a little ring on Andvari's finger, which I saw him trying to conceal.

'That too. Hand it over,' I said.

Andvari snivelled and protested, but I wasn't taking no for an answer. I added the ring to the pile.

'It's cursed,' said Andvari sullenly. 'You'll never live to enjoy your theft. Bad luck will follow you everywhere.'

I grinned. 'So much the better,' I said. 'As I'm not planning to keep it myself.' And then I picked up my sacks of gold and set off on foot back to Inland.

'You took your time,' said Odin, when I got back to Hreidmar's place. The prisoners were still bound fast; they looked dishevelled and hungry and tired. It would make a good story, I thought, knowing that Honir would spread the tale; and then there was Ran, who would tell it to Aegir and all their cronies; how Loki had bravely come back into the wolf's lair to ransom his friends . . .

I grinned. 'Here comes the cavalry. I think, when you have a look at all this, you'll find that Otter has been suitably ransomed.'

Now Hreidmar untied the prisoners, as his sons counted the gold. They stuffed the otter's skin with it, then heaped it over the bursting remains like a barrow of strawberry gold. Odin watched them in silence, rubbing his sore wrists. I guessed he was as angry as I was at having been caught and humiliated – but he said nothing, just watched them silently through his one eye.

At last, the skin was packed full and covered nose to tail with gold. Only a whisker protruded –

'There's no more gold,' said Odin.

'Then I'll make up the rest in blood,' said Hreidmar, once more drawing his dagger.

'Wait, there's this.' I pulled off the ring I'd taken from Andvari. I'd hoped to slip it to Odin, of course, but needs must, when Wildfire drives.

'Will this cover it, do you think?' I bent down and covered the whisker with the ring of blood-red gold.

'Close,' said Odin.

I smiled at him. 'Did you doubt me?'

'No. Not even for a second.'

And so our very reluctant host was obliged to let the three of us go. As I crossed the threshold, I looked back over my shoulder at him.

'By the way, Andvari's curse lies on the ring I took from him. I hope you enjoy it. Serves you right for holding my brother to ransom.'

Odin gave me a sideways look. 'You're full of surprises, aren't you?' he said.

I shrugged. 'Just remember I saved your life. You know you can rely on me.'

He smiled. 'I know I can,' he said.

And just for a moment, I *almost* believed that neither of us was lying.

Funny, how the things we say come back to bite us, like rabid dogs we once made the mistake of feeding. Although we didn't know it then, our summertime was running out. The seasons had begun to turn, the shadows to lengthen, the sun to set. That rosy light is deceptive; it shines on the faces of those around you and makes them look like friends. They're not. In ten minutes' time, the sun will have set, and it will be merciless . . .

BOOK 3

Sunset

I see your fate, o sons of earth.
I hear the battle calling.
Odin's folk prepare to ride
Against the shadows falling.

Prophecy of the Oracle

LESSON 1

Death

The dead know everything, but don't give a damn.

Lokabrenna

AND JUST LIKE THAT, it was over. A golden age of godhood, gone, like apple blossom on the wind. I don't pretend to know much about love, but that's how great loves come to an end, not in the flames of passion, but in the silence of regret. And that's how my brother Odin and I reached the end of our fellowship; not in the heat of battle (though that would come round soon enough), but in lies, and polite smiles, and protestations of loyalty.

He never told me *how* he knew. But the Old Man knew everything. All my petty treacheries: how I'd tried to set up Thor; how I'd lost Frey his runesword. If I hadn't given away the ring I'd taken from Andvari, I might have assumed that the Maggot's curse was the cause of my turning luck, but I'd left that ring with Hreidmar as part of Otter's ransom. No, this was something different, something more unsettling. I could see his disappointment, his pain in the way he looked at me, although he never said a word – to me, or any of the gods.

I think I'd have preferred it if he'd simply punished me. That, I could have dealt with. A world built on Order has *rules*, so I'd learnt, and breaking them has consequences. I'd been living in Odin's world for long enough to understand, if not to approve, the principle. But this didn't seem to be Odin's plan. It made me quite uncomfortable.

Don't get me wrong. I had no regrets. Odin's corruption-by-sentiment hadn't brought me quite *that* low. And don't go believing those stories about how I really cared for him, and how our tragic friendship became a kind of passion-play acted out over centuries. Take it from me, it wasn't. All right? But I was feeling insecure. I felt the hammer about to fall, and I had nowhere to run. I needed to know the Old Man's mind. I needed to know what his plans were. And so I looked to the sky for help – and Hugin and Munin, Odin's birds.

They were no ordinary birds, of course. They were Odin's ravens, trained to carry the Old Man's thoughts anywhere in the Nine Worlds. That was a part of his power, those birds; manifestations of his Spirit and Mind – with their help, he saw everywhere. But it also meant that he was never at peace. If anyone ever thought too much, it was the Old Man, always alert, always scrutinizing the Worlds for the hint of a threat to his empire. It isolated him. It set him apart from the rest of the Aesir.

It suited him to be that way, but I knew he was lonely. Power had taken its toll on him, and knowledge was eroding the rest. Perfect knowledge was what he'd craved, but with perfect knowledge, illusions die, including such perennials as friendship, love and loyalty.

Think about it for a while. How can you hope to have any friends when you spy on everything they do? How can you enjoy the present when you can see the future? Most of all, how can you love when you know Death lies in waiting?

And Death was where they led me first. Or rather, Hel, Death's Kingdom. *Not* a realm I frequented much, in spite of having fathered its ruler, and not the kind of place in which I felt my unique skills would best be utilized. But that was where the ravens led, and that was where I picked up their trail – through Ironwood, and then underground, travelling on foot through World Below for much of the way, not being privy to their trick of simply crossing directly through Worlds – until, days later, I arrived onto the dusty plain of Hel.

Not my favourite place in the Worlds. Hel's own kingdom is cold and bleak. Unbound by the conventional rules of size, or scale, or geography, it stretches out in all directions; a colourless desert of sand and bone under an arch of colourless sky. Nothing grows here; nothing lives – even Hel was a half-corpse – and those who come here are either dead, doomed or simply desperate. I told myself that my daughter would surely agree to see me – but it *was* her kingdom. If she chose, she could have me wait at her pleasure for weeks or months; or until the desert swallowed me and I became one of the dead, dust on a wind that blew ceaselessly under that strange, subterranean sky.

I found my daughter waiting, drawing circles in the sand. She'd grown since I last saw her, though, sadly, she hadn't improved much. She'd always been moody and intractable, even when she was a child, and now she looked at me askance through her single living eye (the other one was dead as bone under a wisp of white hair).

'Why, it's dear old Dad,' she said. 'Fancy seeing you here.'

I sat down next to her on a rock. Around me, the hot dry wind of Hel stirred the souls of the departed into a kind of half-sentience. I could feel them drawn to me, sensing the warmth of a living being. *Not* a pleasant feeling. I made a mental note to myself to try to avoid Death as long as I could.

'I thought I'd say hello,' I said. 'How's the job shaping up?'

Hel raised a single eyebrow.

'Well?'

'Well – *Dad*. You've seen this place. What do you think?'

'It's . . . interesting.'

She made a sound of contempt. 'You think? Sitting here, day in, day out, surrounded by nothing but the dead? *Not* what you'd call *exciting*.'

'Well, it's a job,' I told her. 'It isn't meant to be exciting. Not at the start, anyway.'

'You mean you think it's going to improve?'

I shrugged.

'I didn't think so,' she said. 'So what do you want?'

'I'm hurt,' I said. 'What makes you think I want anything, other than to pay a visit to my daughter?'

'Because you never visit,' said Hel. 'And because the General's birds were here only a couple of hours ago. I'm guessing you want to know why.'

I grinned. 'That may have crossed my mind.'

She turned her living profile away, subjecting me to the full impact of her dead face. The eye that gleamed from the socket of bone was horribly, darkly sentient. The binding-rope of runes that she wore twisted around her narrow waist reminded me uncomfortably of Skadi's runewhip.

'You're none of you immune to Death,' she told me in her grating voice. 'The General knows that only too well. Death takes everyone in the end. Heroes, villains, even gods – you'll all end up as dust one day. Even the General,' she said, fingering her binding-rope. 'One day Death will take him too, and there'll be nothing left of him, or of Asgard, or of you.'

This was beginning to sound unnecessarily morbid to me, and I said so.

Hel gave me her twisted half-smile. 'Balder's been having dreams,' she said.

'Dreams of what?'

'Of me,' she said.

'Oh.' I was starting to understand. Ever since she'd first seen him, Hel had been crazy for Balder. Balder the Beautiful; Balder the Brave; Balder, Asgard's Golden Boy. Well, there's no accounting for taste, but there was no denying that a certain type of female found him irresistible. Skadi was one; Hel, another. But while Skadi had long since accepted that Balder would never belong to her, I guessed that Hel still hoped to see Balder at her side one day.

Of course, he'd have to die for that – but as she said, everyone dies.

'So, Golden Boy's been having nightmares?' I grinned at Hel's expression. 'He always was on the sensitive side. Though what that has to do with Odin . . .'

'Frigg has been having dreams as well,' said Hel. 'Forebodings of Balder's death. She wants to know how to protect him. That's why Odin sent his birds.'

'And?'

She gave me a look from her dead eye. 'Odin made me who I am,' she said. 'He gave me Death's dominion. I take my role very seriously, and I can't make exceptions. Not even if I wanted to,' she added, with the hint of a smile, most gruesome on that half-dead face.

'But why would Balder die?' I said. 'He doesn't fight. He doesn't play dangerous sports. He rarely, if ever, leaves Asgard. The only risk he ever takes is that of choking on his own smugness. So tell me, why the anxiety?'

Hel shrugged a shoulder. 'I don't know.'

Of course, Death and Dream are very close. Their territories intersect, which is why we so often dream of the dead. They dream of us, too, in their watery way, and sometimes they can tell us things; things about the future.

She was drawing in the sand again. Not a circle this time, but a little heart shape with the runes *Hagall* for Hel and *Bjarkán* for Balder written inside. I found it frankly nauseating, but summoned up a sympathetic look.

'How badly do you want him?' I said.

She looked up. 'I'd do anything.'

'*Anything?*'

That dead eye again. 'Anything,' said my daughter.

'All right,' I said with a little smile. 'I'll help you if I get the chance. But not a word to anyone. And you'll owe me a favour. Agreed?'

She gave me her living hand.

'Agreed.'

And that was how the Queen of the Dead promised me a favour. I couldn't foresee when I'd cash it in, but I sensed the changing seasons, and I knew that, like Ratatosk the squirrel, it was time for Yours Truly to put away a few supplies for the winter. Everything dies eventually, of course. The operative word is 'eventually'. And if I could somehow reshape events to suit my own agenda . . .

Well. Isn't that what Odin himself did, when he reshaped the Worlds from Ymir's corpse? Isn't that what *all* gods do, in their various ways, to survive?

LESSON 2

Deception

So shoot me. It's my nature.

Lokabrenna

THE NEXT PORT OF CALL for Odin's birds was the forest of Ironwood, where the second of my monstrous children was causing concern among the wildlife. I hadn't seen the Fenris Wolf since his mother and I had parted on less than amicable terms. Now he was no longer a cub, but fully grown and ferocious. Although he shared my ability to take a human Aspect, he tended to favour his wolf form, which was why Odin had sent his ravens to check out the danger he might represent.

This wouldn't have troubled me at all (I'd never been close to Angie's brood), except for the underhand way in which the General approached the problem, going behind my back without as much as a word to me. And now, as his ravens brought back news of my son in Ironwood, Odin declared the wolf a threat and called for him to be neutralized.

'Neutralized?' I said. 'Does that mean like Jormungand was neutralized? Or were you thinking more of a permanent solution?'

Odin remained expressionless. I went on:

'I mean, after all this time you suddenly think my son's a

threat? Who to? Since when has he done anything except run amok in Ironwood catching squirrels and, let's face it, the Worlds could always do with fewer of *those* . . .'

No one had mentioned Balder's dreams, but the connection was obvious. Balder was a Mummy's boy, spoilt and overprotected; I sensed his mother's influence now, as Odin outlined his demands.

'I need to see the Wolf,' he said. 'I need to know whose side he's on.' He fixed me with his coldest stare. 'Captain, I hope you're not going to be obstructive about this.'

'Me? Obstructive? Of course not. But I wish you'd tell me what this is about.'

'Later,' said Odin. 'Just bring the Wolf.'

And so I promised to bring my son to Asgard for assessment. I figured that if I helped him out, then Odin might confide in me – or if things went the other way, I'd have a friend in my corner. Besides, I hadn't seen Fenris in years and, like the Old Man, I wanted to know just how powerful he'd become, and what loyalty (if any) I could expect from the Wolf and his mother.

And so I flew to Ironwood, in my falcon Aspect. On my arrival, I found Angrboda waiting for me, looking alluring as always, with Fenris, in wolf form, at her side, looking rather less so.

'I should have known *you'd* be around,' she said, as I shifted back into Aspect. 'You and the General always were as thick as thieves. When I saw those birds of his I knew you wouldn't be far behind.'

That was unfair. I pointed out, as I had to Hel, that I needed no self-serving excuse to call on my nearest and dearest.

'Is it so hard to believe,' I said, 'that I might have wanted to see you? You *are* the love of my life, you know. And dear little Fenris . . .' Fenris snarled. 'How could you think I'd stay away?'

Angie arched an eyebrow, through which an emerald stud gleamed. 'Don't give me that. After fifteen years, you decide to come over all paternal?' She gave me one of her smouldering looks. 'What do you *really* want?'

'Well, apart from the obvious . . .' I looked down at my state of undress. 'Some clothes would be nice. Unless you feel like—'

Angie growled. 'Not in front of the children, dear.'

Once more I glanced at Fenris. I remembered him as rather cute – in a slavering kind of way. Now he just looked malevolent and generally unappealing. Still, teenage werewolves are typically foul; hairy, smelly and monosyllabic. Not unlike the human kind, when you come to think of it, although most human youngsters would be incapable of tearing your head off with their bare hands and making it into a buttock sandwich.

'So, what are you into nowadays?' I asked him, with little enthusiasm.

Fenris just growled again, showing his teeth. There were rather a lot of them, and his breath was distinctly rank.

'Mostly devouring things,' Angie said. 'Although he quite enjoys killing things, too.'

'Can't he speak for himself?' I said.

She gave the wolf an indulgent smile. 'You know what they're like at that age. Fenny, be nice and say hello to your father.'

The werewolf gave a beastly shrug and shifted Aspect oh-so-slightly, becoming a sullen-looking young man with a bad case of acne and thick fur on the palms of his hands. The stench of testosterone was dreadful, as was the stench of his oily hair.

'Whatever,' said Fenny. 'Hi, *Dad*.'

I forced a smile. 'That's better,' I said. 'Let's get you looking presentable. If you're to have your inheritance, like your brother and sister, then we have to convince the gods that you're not just a teenage dirtbag. Right?'

'Whaddya mean, inheritance?' The wolf's yellow eyes gleamed suspiciously. I could tell he wasn't stupid; unappealing he might be, but there was intelligence in those eyes. Right now, I wasn't sure whether this would help my cause or not; I just gave him my broadest smile and launched into my sales talk.

'Well, Jormungand got the One Sea,' I said, 'and Hel got the Underworld. It's only fair that you should have your own lands and dominions, but first you have to let Odin decide what kind of territory you deserve.'

'Ironwood,' said Fenris, without even stopping to think.

'Well, Ironwood's certainly a possibility,' I said. 'But have you considered—'

'*Ironwood*,' said Fenris again.

'I get it. You want Ironwood,' I said, with a grin to Angie. 'All right, I think we can manage that. But first, you have to come with me and swear your allegiance to Asgard.'

'My *what*?' said Fenris. 'Wolves don't swear. Wolves just hang out and . . . and, like, *devour* things.'

'Well, this time it's going to be different. I want you to be presentable. I'm not having you turn up in Asgard looking like something from under the bottom of a cave-troll's shoe. A haircut first – and perhaps some clothes?'

It wasn't an easy sell. But at last, with the help of Fenny's loving mother, I managed to get him to look . . . if not quite presentable, then at least looking vaguely human. I wasn't expecting him to score much of a hit with the gods, but I thought perhaps if they met him, they'd understand that he wasn't the monster they thought he was, and they might cut the kid a bit of slack.

Not so, unfortunately. To be fair, young Fenny was going through a bit of a rebellious phase, characterized by grunting, bad smells, obscene language, loud music in his rooms late at night and a generally uncouth approach to anything of the opposite sex.

Even Idun, who had declared him 'cute' when he first arrived in Asgard, complained about his lecherous comments to her and to her handmaidens. But it was when a practical joke (against Balder, as it happened) went wrong that Frigg's maternal instinct rebelled, and she went running to Odin to demand that the werewolf be restrained.

It wasn't a big thing, really. A youngster's prank, involving Golden Boy's lunch, some earwigs and a Chinese burn, but Frigg took the whole thing very seriously, declared that her son had been assaulted, and that if Odin didn't take action then she would get Thor to intervene in his place.

Odin had no choice after that. The werewolf had crossed a line. If only he'd come and told me that, then I would have understood completely. But he didn't. He said nothing, *did* nothing until I was out of the picture, and then, with Thor and Týr and the rest, he made his move against us.

I should have known he had something planned. A routine check on the Ice Folk, he said; rumours of a new warlord who might try something reckless. The Rock Folk had been restless, too, gathering in the foothills; perhaps I could find out what had caused their migration. Then there were tales of Jormungand sinking ships off World's End, and further rumours of Gullveig-Heid, raising the dead in Ironwood. And so on, with a whole list of tasks that would keep me away for at least a week – a welcome break, I thought at the time, from the responsibilities of fatherhood.

Meanwhile, in my absence, the gods prepared to drop the hammer on Fenris.

First Odin went to the Tunnel Folk and asked the sons of Ivaldi to forge him a set of magical chains. Then they threw Fenny a welcome party, and when they'd got him nice and drunk, Odin suggested some tests of strength to see what he was capable of.

Fenny, young and arrogant, saw no reason to suspect foul play. Drink, loud music and the presence of scantily clad female attendants had broken what defences he had. Faced with two thick, Tunnel-Folk chains, he broke them both quite easily, to the feigned admiration of the gods, but the last one was a narrow, deceptive steel band forged by the famous Dvalin himself – embedded with many runes and cantrips – and was almost unbreakable.

If I'd been there to comment, I would have warned the gods that my son, wild and uncouth though he was, was no fool. His finely tuned senses warned him that some kind of deception was afoot, and before accepting to try the third chain, he demanded a proof of Odin's goodwill.

'What kind of proof?' Odin said.

'One of you puts his hand in my mouth,' said the Wolf with a toothy grin. 'That way, I have something to bargain with if things start getting heavy.'

The gods exchanged glances. Finally, Brave-Hearted Týr stood up. Brave-hearted he was, I'll give him that, but also somewhat weak-brained.

'I'll do it,' he said, and slipped his right hand into the wolf's mouth.

If I had been there, of course, this would never have happened, but they were too clever – *they* thought they could handle the situation alone, with the result that, when *Naudr* bit, so did Fenny, and Týr lost his hand.

Odin showed no sign of regret. It was a calculated risk, and the gain to Asgard's security was greater than the loss. Týr got himself an ephemeral hand, all woven from runes and glamours, which, like a mindweapon, could be summoned in battle or at moments of need. The rest of the time he learnt to perform everyday tasks left-handed, and to bear with a lot of clumsy jokes. He'd never been a man of words, so we never heard what he really thought of having been Odin's sacrifice. But I like to think that, during the long nights, when his stump was itching like mad and the rest of the gods were fast asleep, even Brave-Hearted Týr might have sometimes questioned his loyalty.

They kept the Wolf in World Below, in a cavern deep under the ground. And when I came home, I realized that all the gods blamed *me* for the débâcle, whispering among themselves that I had been responsible for bringing Fenny into Asgard in the first place, and greeting Yours Truly with harsh words, cool glances and all the signs of hostility.

'What, no welcoming drink?' I said, arriving tired from twelve hours' straight flying.

'Oh, look who's back,' said Heimdall. 'Fathered any more monsters recently?'

I didn't give his words much thought, but when Frey turned his back on me, Bragi threw his drink on the ground, Thor saw me coming and growled, and Skadi, who was staying in Asgard on one of her infrequent visits, fingered her runewhip and *smiled* at me, I knew that something had happened.

'Where's Odin?' I said.

'In his hall. He doesn't want to be disturbed,' said Frigg, whose generally open countenance was pinched with conflicting emotions.

Even Sigyn, usually the first to welcome me, seemed distant. 'It had to be done,' she told me when I went to find her (hungry after my long flight, and hoping for a batch of jam tarts). 'That nasty werewolf son of yours was *such* a bad influence on our boys.'

Well, yes. I had to admit that was true. Vali and Narvi, so close to him in age, had taken to hanging around with Fenris. Perhaps it was his bad-boy appeal; or the tales he told them of Ironwood. Either way, I noticed that they had started to imitate him; letting their hair grow over their eyes and cultivating a wolfish sneer.

'Oh, they'll get over it soon enough,' said Sigyn, finally telling the tale of how the Wolf had been restrained for the good of Asgard. 'And so will you,' she added, with a playful smile, 'as soon as you've had a couple of these lovely jam tarts I baked for you.'

But suddenly, I was no longer hungry. The nest of wire inside my gut had tightened to an unbearable pitch.

They'd gone behind my back, you see: that was what really hurt me. They'd decided I couldn't be trusted, and had sent me off on a fool's errand, then blamed *me* for the consequences when their plan had backfired.

'Now, don't lose your temper, dear. You know that Angie person was no good. The last thing you want is a werewolf brat hanging around, causing trouble, reminding you of what you did to your wife and your *real* family.'

My *real* family. That was a joke. The accounts of Thor's journey to Utgard had left my sons under the impression that I was a giant loser. Fenny's incarceration had completed the job: now, in their eyes, I was the Man: a part of the oppressive patriarchal system; unable to understand the needs of a rebellious adolescent.

This was made abundantly clear to me as I went out to greet them. They'd grown since I last saw them, of course, and though obviously (favouring me), neither was as graceless or as uncouth as Fenny, both had managed to develop some of the werewolf's mannerisms: the slouch; the grunt; the silent contempt.

'So, how's it going?'

Narvi, the first and dominant twin, eyed me from under his long fringe. His eyes were like mine, his hair, too; his colours, wild and rebellious – it was almost like looking at myself when I entered the Worlds from Chaos.

Vali, the softer, friendlier twin, might have said something if we'd been alone, but in the presence of Narvi simply looked down at the ground in shame.

'No words of welcome?' I said.

Narvi shrugged. 'Hi, *Dad*.'

'I heard about Fenris.'

'Whatever.'

'I didn't know what was happening,' I said. 'Odin never told me.'

Too late I understood that having been taken for a fool by the General would do nothing to raise me in my sons' esteem.

I sounded weak and apologetic, which made me more angry than ever. Why did I even feel the need to justify myself to my sons? Since when did I care what they thought, anyway?

Narvi shrugged again. 'Whatever.'

Vali gave me shy look. 'What are you going to do?' he said.

I thought about that. 'I don't know.'

There was nothing I *could* do, short of freeing Fenny myself which, even if I could manage it, would hardly improve my standing in Asgard.

Narvi had already worked it out. 'He won't do anything, stupid,' he said. 'What, and piss off the Old Man?'

Well, he had a point, I thought. I'd lost the one supporter on whom I might have depended if things got ugly in Asgard. Even Thor might have hesitated to lay violent hands on a man with a werewolf at his side.

'Don't think I'm scared of *him*,' I said. 'But sometimes it's better not to jump at the first provocation. I won't be much good to Fenris if I'm chained right next to him.'

Narvi gave me the look again. You know that look – the one that says: *You can talk all you like, old man, but I know better, whatever you say.*

Yes, I know that look all right. I may even have worn it myself on selected occasions. That's why, of all human experiences, fatherhood is surely the most frustrating and pointless – because what's the point of experience if your children won't listen to what you've learned?

And so I went back to being Asgard's official whipping boy. If anything happened, it was my fault: from the loss of Týr's arm to the fact that Bragi's new ode didn't scan; to the failure of Sigyn's cakes to rise; to the fact that the Ice Folk were gathering in Ironwood. I was the wrong note in the symphony; the cockroach on the wedding cake; the bear with its paw in the honey pot; the razor blade in the cookie jar. I'd never belonged in Asgard but never had it been so clear to me how much the gods resented me; hated me; wanted me out. Even my sons.

Even Odin . . .

Yes, Odin. Now that he had what he wanted from me, the Old Man had finally dropped his pretence. His coldness towards me intensified; his birds were rarely out of my sight. I was puzzled, as well as hurt: especially as Odin still hadn't mentioned Balder, or his prophetic dreams. It made me wonder if all this was about something bigger than just me. It made me wonder if Fenris had ever been their primary target. But most of all I wondered how long it would be before someone suggested that the Worlds might be a safer place if I, too, could be kept in chains . . .

LESSON 3

Cake

Most problems can be solved through cake.

Lokabrenna

AFTER THAT, things went downhill fast. In spite of Fenny's removal, Frigg's anxiety for Balder had reached a point of near-obsession. If Golden Boy as much as sneezed, her concern went through the roof. She spent her time assessing risk; looking at loose flagstones in case Balder tripped on the parapet; hunting out toxic garden plants, as if Balder were suddenly going to start munching at the flowerbeds; peering suspiciously at items of sporting equipment; knitting vests in case Balder caught cold.

Finally breaking her silence, she set out to canvass everything in the Nine Worlds, seeking out potential threats and extracting from every creature – bear, bee, bramble – an oath sworn on its true name never to harm the Golden Boy.

'Why?' I asked her. 'What's the point? What do you think's going to happen to him?'

The Enchantress only shook her head. 'I don't know. But there's a shadow over us. It's not just Balder's dreams, or mine, or even the prophecy—'

'*What* prophecy?' I said sharply.

She looked away. 'Oh, nothing,' she said.

But when a woman says 'nothing', you can always bet there's something. Mimir's Head was an Oracle. *Had* it made a prophecy? And if it had, why had Odin chosen to keep it a secret from me, while telling Frigg all about it?

I remembered the way they had dealt with the Wolf, and decided to step up the scale of my investigation. Clearly, there was more to Odin's behaviour than a few bad dreams about Balder. Leaving Asgard again so soon would weaken my position still further.

And so I took a more direct approach. Bearing in mind Sigyn's belief that most problems can be solved through cake, I cut a slice of her fruitcake and went to stand on the Rainbow Bridge.

Hugin and Munin, like all their kind, were fans of sweet and sticky things. A handful of scraps and some patience, I thought, would save me a whole lot of flying around.

Sure enough, I hadn't been waiting long before the birds came down and perched on the bridge. The largest of the pair – Hugin, I think – strutted up and down expectantly.

'Where have you been?' I asked them.

'*Crawk. Crawk,*' said Hugin, flapping his wings and looking at me.

'*Cake,*' said Munin, the smaller bird, with a single white feather on its head. Its speech was clearer than its sibling's, and its golden eyes were shining.

'All in good time,' I told them. 'Just tell me where you've been snooping around.'

'*Ygg. Dra. Sil. Crawk.*' The larger bird jumped onto my shoulder.

'*Crawk. Cake,*' said the smaller bird, and I fed it some of Sigyn's cake – rather heavy for my taste, but packed with raisins and sugar.

'What about Yggdrasil?' I said. 'Why the sudden interest?'

'*Prophecy,*' said Munin. '*Crawk.*'

'A prophecy? What did it say?'

'*Cake,*' said Munin stubbornly.

'Just tell me about the prophecy!' I said, withholding the piece of cake. 'After that, you can both have cake.'

'*Crawk. Cake,*' said Hugin.

Munin pecked him on the wing. For a moment both birds fought, flapping their ragged feathers and *crawk*ing furiously. Then the smaller bird broke away and came to perch on my shoulder.

'That's better,' I said. 'Now tell me what you know.'

Munin *crawk*ed a couple of times. I could tell it was trying to speak, but the proximity of cake, and the beady eyes of its unruly sibling, seemed to make concentration difficult.

'*I know. A mighty Ash,*' it said. '*Its name is Ygg – Ygg –Ygg –*'

'*Crawk,*' said Hugin, alighting on my other shoulder.

'Yes, I know its name, thanks,' I said. 'So? What about it?'

Hugin pecked at the cake in my hand. I dropped it onto the parapet. Both birds descended upon it, flapping and bickering noisily.

'The prophecy, please,' I said sharply.

'*Cake! Stand!*' said Hugin, between beakfuls.

'What? Cake-stand? What does that mean?'

'*The Aff, Yggdraffil, cakeff where it fftandff,*' corrected Munin, its beak full of fruit cake.

'Yggdrasil? It quakes where it stands? Why?'

'*Cake.*'

'Oh, for gods' sakes!'

But I had run out of cake by then, and the birds were losing interest. They pecked up the last scattered raisins and flew off, still squabbling, towards Odin's hall.

Still, they had given me food for thought. A tremor in the World Ash was a tremor throughout the Worlds. And even if it *wasn't* a tree, the news that it was under threat didn't sound good to Yours Truly. Was this what Mimir's Head had foretold? *The Ash, Yggdrasil, quakes where it stands.* Was this why Allfather was so jumpy?

Well, I thought, *I'm about to find out.* Heimdall had certainly spotted me feeding birds on the Rainbow Bridge, and knowing his enthusiasm for spying on me and telling tales, I knew I could rely on him to take the story to a higher authority. Odin in one of his rages might give away more information than he intended. All I had to do till then was play innocent and wait for the storm to break.

Well, I was right about one thing, at least. Allfather *was* jumpy. As soon as he heard what I had done, he hauled me up in front of him and gave me the works – the Furious One in full Aspect; lightning, spear, flashing eye, the lot.

'Spying on me, were you?' he said. 'Trying to get inside my mind? Try that again and, brother or not, I'll thrash the sunshine out of you. I won't ask Thor or Heimdall. I'll do it myself. And I'll make it count. Do I make myself clear?'

'Clear as Mimir's well,' I said. This was no time for a smart response.

He looked at me with his one blue eye. 'I mean it, Trickster. What have you heard?'

'Nothing. Nothing important,' I said. 'Just some stuff about trees.'

'Trees?'

'Well, Yggdrasil,' I said.

The blue eye narrowed. Now it looked like a razor blade pushed into his cheekbone.

'Something's coming, isn't it?' I said. 'Did the Oracle prophesy?'

He gave a smile. Not a pleasant one. 'Never mind the Oracle. Knowledge doesn't bring happiness. As for the World Tree, forget it. Just because it loses some leaves doesn't mean it's dying.'

Leaves?

Gods, I hated it when the Old Man went cryptic on me. I thought of what the birds had said. *The Ash, Yggdrasil, quakes where it stands*. Well, that might explain the falling leaves. On the other hand, metaphorically, *we* were the leaves on Yggdrasil. I didn't like the sound of that.

'All right,' I said. 'No more questions.' (In fact, he'd answered *all* of mine.)

He seemed to relax a little at that. His Aspect went back to normal again, leaving him looking grey and old.

'You're looking tired,' I told him.

'I haven't been sleeping much lately.'

'Well, if you ever need to talk . . .' I began.

He gave me the evil eye again.

'Fine,' I said. 'I get it.'

'Just as long as you do,' he said.

LESSON 4

Destiny

A man too often meets his Fate whilst running to avoid it.

Lokabrenna

Well, I tried. I really did. But I was far from being reassured. All that talk about Yggdrasil; the Oracle; prophetic dreams . . .

It made me nervous. I needed to know. And so, one night, when my nerves were so drawn I was close to combusting, I went in secret to the spring where Odin kept what was left of Mimir's Head and looked into the water.

Yes, I know it was dangerous. But I was feeling vulnerable. The coldness of the Aesir; Odin's refusal to trust in me. I needed a friend like never before.

Instead, I got the Whisperer.

From its cradle of runelight, Mimir's Head looked back at me. I'll admit it was alarming. Over the years, the living Head had calcified, becoming stone, although the face was still mobile, expressing amusement and vague contempt.

'Ha! I thought you'd come,' it said.

'You did?'

'Of course. I'm an Oracle.'

I frowned at the submerged Head. I knew him by reputation but I'd never known Mimir in life. It now occurred to me that I wouldn't have liked him any more in his original Aspect

206

than I did in his current form.

He eyed me disapprovingly.

'So *you're* the Trickster,' he commented. 'I knew you'd come round here eventually. If Odin finds out, you're toast, of course. He'll kick you to one end of Asgard and back. He'll throw you off Bif-rost and watch you bounce.'

'He will if you tell him,' I said with a smile. '*Are* you going to tell him?'

The Oracle's colours brightened. 'Tell me why I shouldn't,' it said.

'Because you hate him,' I went on. 'Because he used you from the start, and lied to you, as he lied to me. And because you want to tell me something.'

'Do I?' said the Oracle.

'Don't you?' I said, and smiled again.

The Oracle glowed a little brighter. 'Knowledge can be a dangerous thing, Trickster,' it told me. 'Are you sure you want to know what the future holds for you?'

'I like to be prepared,' I said. 'Now talk. You know you want to.'

And that's how I was made privy to the Prophecy of the Oracle. Not that it helped me much in the end; prophecies tend to be incomplete, and Oracles have a habit of telling you things you only fully understand after the crisis is over.

Of course, it's all public knowledge now – Ragnarók, and what happened next. It's been public knowledge for so long that it's hard to remember what it was like, hearing it for the first time; the details of the terrible war that would tumble the gods and their citadel, and rewrite their story in bright new runes.

> *Now comes the final reckoning.*
> *Now come the folk of Netherworld.*
> *Now comes the dragon of darkness, Death,*

Casting his shadow-wing over the Worlds.

The Dragon of Darkness. Surt. *Oh, crap.* In my concern for the immediate future, I'd missed the bigger picture. Surt meant Chaos; which meant Ragnarók, the dissolution of Order. *That* was why the World Ash was shedding its leaves; that's what happens when seasons change. I told you all that was a metaphor, but the truth of it was clear enough: the time was coming when Odin's world would be swept aside, leaving nothing but Chaos behind, from which a new Order would one day emerge . . .

All very poetic, of course, but as a renegade from Chaos, I had some idea of what to expect if Surt ever got hold of me, and it wasn't mercy. As for the gods, it looked as if the side I'd chosen was set to lose. Where did that leave me? Should I run? Could I hope to escape the carnage?

'What happens to me?'

'Be patient,' said Mimir. 'I haven't got to the good part yet.'

'There's a good part?'

'Oh, yes.'

And as I listened in silence to the whispering from Mimir's spring, I felt a gradual coldness creep like death along my spine, and recognized the sensation as fear – a fear I'd never felt before.

'Odin would do that? To *me*?' I said.

'Oh, yes,' replied the Oracle. 'Why do you doubt it? He's done it before. He may feel a pang or two of remorse but that won't stop him from using you when he needs a scapegoat. Face it, Trickster, you're alone. You've always been alone here. Odin was never a friend to you, any more than he was to me. And as for the others . . .' The Oracle glowed in a way that was almost like laughter. 'You already know what they think of you. They hate you and despise you. The moment Odin gives the word, they'll be on you like a pack of wolves. Look what they did to Fenris. Look how they dealt with Jormungand. You know it's just a matter of time before you're officially declared an undesirable.'

'How do I know you're telling the truth?'

'Oracles don't lie,' it said.

'Well, how can we stop it from happening?'

Its colours brightened. 'You can't,' it said.

'But surely—'

'You *can't*,' it repeated. 'You've heard it now. Loki, this is Destiny. I know it's hard. But Destiny has a habit of finding you wherever you hide. Sometimes it even meets you as you go running to avoid it.'

'Is *that* a prophecy?' I said.

'What do you think?' said the Head.

And so I crept back to my bed, though sleep was slow in coming. I told myself that I didn't believe in Destiny, or prophecies, or dreams, but the Oracle's words still troubled me. Could I escape Surt's vengeance? Could I escape the End of the Worlds? Could I somehow save myself from the Old Man's treachery?

At last I fell into fitful sleep, and dreamed of snakes. You know I hate snakes. And then in the morning I went out to work, collecting every scrap of news or information I possibly could.

Nuts for the winter, like Ratatosk. That's all I was really collecting. A man should always be prepared for Last Days, and if Mimir was to be believed, those were the days we were heading for. Not that it showed as yet, no. Asgard's falltime was golden. There was peace in the Middle Worlds; Ice Folk and Rock Folk were both subdued. No enemy, no warlord, no renegade of the Vanir had come within a hundred miles of Asgard over the past six months, and Thor was getting slow and fat from lack of combat practice. There was nothing (except for Odin's aloofness and Frigg's maternal anxiety) to suggest that anything bad was on the cards. But it was. I *knew* it was. And knowing it changed everything.

Mimir was right. Knowledge *is* dangerous. All I could think of was the words the Oracle had spoken to me, words that I now wished I could unlearn. Was this what the Old Man felt? Was that why he was so alone? I sensed that perhaps it was, and if I could have confided in him . . .

But how could I think of doing that, knowing what I did now? No, my only chance was to find a means of diverting the Oracle's prophecy, or at least of escaping my part of it.

It was futile, Mimir said. I had already heard it.

And if I *hadn't* heard it? Would that have made it avoidable? It hurt my head just thinking about that one, which I guess was what Mimir wanted. So . . .

What problem *did* the Oracle have against Your Humble Narrator? Why was I such an integral part in its vengeance against the gods? I wasn't even in Asgard when Odin sent him spying on the Vanir. Of all the gods, then, surely I was the least likely candidate to attract his hostility?

Later I realized; it wasn't me. But I was Odin's brother-in-blood. Odin cared for me, *needed* me, which was why Mimir had set me up. Yes, he set me up – and in so doing, taught me the most important lesson I was ever to learn in my life:

Never trust anyone: a friend, a stranger, a lover, a brother, a wife. But most of all, remember this: *Never* trust an Oracle.

LESSON 5

Names

A named thing is a tamed thing.

Lokabrenna

WHOEVER SAID names can't hurt you was either drunk or stupid. All words have power, of course, but names are the most potent of all, which is why the gods had so many. To name a being is to subdue it, as I'd learnt on that first day, when Odin called me from Chaos. I'd been Wildfire incarnate, free and incorruptible. I became the Trickster; Hearth Fire; his creature, named and tamed.

Not any more, however. What I'd heard from the Oracle had given me a different perspective. It made me jumpy; suspicious. It made me lose my happy thoughts. Well, now was the time, I told myself, to start putting to good use some of the supplies I'd put by for later use; the scraps of information; the favours due, the little pieces of armour that would shield me at Ragnarók.

The most important of these, of course, was the favour I'd managed to wangle from Hel; a favour based on my promise to somehow deliver Golden Boy into her adoring arms.

Which was why I presently took wing, and went after Frigg on her continuing mission to name and tame everything in the Nine Worlds that might present a threat to her son. Rocks, trees, wild animals; a mother's love, it seemed to me, was endlessly anxious and tender, seeing danger everywhere, in every spark and splinter. Well, not *my* mother, obviously. But Frigg was never going to give up until everything – and I mean *everything* – that might damage her son had been rendered harmless.

'I name thee Oak, son of Acorn, and command thee and thy folk to obey.'

'I name thee Iron, son of Earth, and command thee and thy folk to obey.'

'I name thee Wolf, son of Wolf, and command thee and thy folk to obey.'

And so on, throughout the animal world, the plant world, the mineral world. It was the longest lullaby the Nine Worlds had ever known, and as a hymn to maternal love, was almost enough to touch my heart.

I said *almost*. I have no heart. Well, not according to history, which called me a number of hard names – *Father of Lies* being just one of them, as if the Old Man wasn't telling porkies long before I was a glint in the eye of whatever sparked me to sentience. Well, that's history for you, folks. Unfair, untrue and for the most part written by folk who weren't even there.

'I name thee Wasp, daughter of Air, and command thee and thy folk to obey.'

'I name thee Scorpion, daughter of Sand, and command thee and thy folk to obey.'

'I name thee Spider, daughter of Silk . . .'

And so on. And so on. And so on. Words are the building blocks of the Worlds; words and runes and names. And there was one *particular* name – a name the Oracle had given me – that had a special relevance to my situation; a name that, in the right hands, might even bring down an invincible.

I'd been following her in hawk guise for weeks and months. She was tiring. Her memory was failing her. And the little, half-wilted plant in her hand was so very small and helpless . . .

'I name thee . . .'

What's that? Could that be . . .

Mistletoe?

I tried to recall the exact wording of the Oracle's prophecy.

> *I see a branch of mistletoe*
> *Wielded by a blind man.*
> *This, the poison dart that slays*
> *Asgard's most beloved son.*

At first, I'd taken the stanza to mean something clever and cryptic. There's nothing very dangerous about a branch of mistletoe, and the phrase about the blind man had to be some kind of metaphor. But seeing Frigg with her mistletoe shoot, trying in her exhaustion to remember what it was, I felt an inspiration.

I shifted into the Aspect of a poor old woman of the Folk. Shielding my colours carefully, I approached Frigg, slowly, on foot, and greeted her with a toothless smile.

'What are you doing, my dear?' I said.

Frigg explained her mission.

'You're naming and taming *everything*? That's a lot of names,' I said. 'Still, I suppose there are lots of things that couldn't possibly be a threat. That little wilted thing, for instance . . .' I pointed at the mistletoe. 'Now how that could ever harm *any*one? I'm surprised it even *has* a name.' And I shuffled past with a little smile, leaving Frigg with her mistletoe shoot, watching me with a frown between her eyes.

At that moment a snake slithered out from behind a spill of scree. Frigg saw it and dropped the mistletoe, knowing the snake for a venomous one, and uttered the words of the cantrip:

'I name thee Adder, daughter of dust . . .'

And that, folks, was what I was waiting for; the tiny mistake that would give me what I needed. I waited until Frigg's back was turned, then shifted Aspect once again and flew back to Asgard, carrying the sprig of mistletoe in my claws. I couldn't vouch for Balder, but if things went according to plan, that small and insignificant plant might just have bought me a pass out of Hel.

*

In private, I studied the mistletoe. It didn't look much. But with a little work, it might make a suitable weapon. I dried the piece of mistletoe and strengthened it with fire. No runes; not enough to incriminate me with traces of a signature, but enough to make a sharpened point. Then I fixed it to a dart, and waited for a suitable time.

It was several months more before Frigg returned from her journey around the Worlds. During that time she had named and tamed everything she had encountered: insects; metals; animals; birds; stones and goblins and demons and trolls. The Ice Folk had given her their pledge, and the Rock Folk, and the Folk of the Middle Worlds. It was a testament to the peculiar affection that everyone had for Golden Boy that even our enemies gave their word that no harm would come to him on their watch.

Remained the gods themselves. Of course, Frigg only approached Yours Truly. The rest were beyond suspicion, as she made only too clear to me, whilst trying in vain to earn my goodwill.

'Why should I swear?' I told her. 'Thor hasn't had to swear an oath.'

'Thor is Balder's brother,' said Frigg.

'So? And he's not dangerous?'

Frigg sighed. 'I don't think he's a threat.'

'And I *am*? That hurts me, Enchantress. You're saying you don't trust me.'

The Enchantress looked sympathetic. 'We'd trust you a lot more, Loki, if you gave us a proof of goodwill. An oath of allegiance to Balder, for example.'

'Oh yes? Because my oath of allegiance to Odin means so much to all of you?' I said. 'I've given you people no reason to hate and despise me, and yet you do, don't you? And what if I refuse to swear? What then? You'll use my true name? Good luck with that, Enchantress. I have rather a *lot* of names. I doubt you know them all, and I'm not inclined to tell you.'

On came the waterworks. 'Loki, *please . . .*'

'So bring all the others here,' I said. 'Make them swear the same oath. Make them *all* reveal their names. See how *they* like to be named and shamed. Then, maybe I'll do what you want.'

She left, red-eyed and angry. Of course she wouldn't ask them. I could just see Heimdall's face – of Frey's, or Thor's, or Odin's – at being asked to submit to such a humiliating test of loyalty. She went to Odin and complained, but my brother-in-blood supported me.

'Loki's one of us,' he said. 'You can't treat him like an out-sider. I know he can be a bit wild—'

'*A bit wild?* He's Wildfire.'

'I know that. But he's served us well.'

'You could *make* him swear,' she said.

'No.'

'But the prophecy—'

'I said *no.*'

Finally, the Enchantress gave up. She came home to a feast of friends; a party in Balder's honour, with food and wine and party games. Of course, I wasn't invited. My refusal to swear the oath had ensured that I was *persona non grata*. Odin wasn't there, either; I guess he just wasn't a party person. But pretty much everyone else was there, all celebrating Golden Boy's quasi-invincibility.

The drink ran freely and pretty soon some of the gods were wanting to demonstrate Frigg's protective measures. After a show of reluctance, Golden Boy stood up on a chair – shirtless, of course, to make the girls sigh – and smirked as, one by one, the gods threw stones, then knives, and finally swords and spears, none of which did him the least bit of harm.

Some just bounced off Balder's skin; others vanished like soap bubbles in a flare of runelight. Even Mjølnir, whom Frigg had tamed, refused to perform. The gods all laughed. Honestly, it was revolting.

However, in the mêlée, I'd managed to gatecrash the party unseen, and now I stood in the shadows, watching and waiting my chance to join in.

Don't get me wrong. I had nothing much against Balder. Except for his looks, his smugness, his popularity and his inexplicable success with women, I had no particular grievance – but he was Odin's youngest son, and after my few words with Mimir, I was beginning to harbour a sizeable grudge against my friend and brother. Besides, Hel wanted Balder – and I knew a way to accommodate her, with significant benefits to Yours Truly, if I managed to pull it off. The only remaining problem was *how*.

Don't look at me like that. I thought you understood. I was fighting for my survival in the face of all of Asgard. The Oracle had shown me what fate was to be mine, and this was my only possible chance of escaping it. What could I do? On one side, there was Balder, who, let's face it, had everything. On the other, Yours Truly, with nothing but his cunning. It was hardly a fair fight and yet I knew that, if it worked in my favour, Golden Boy would get all the sympathy. Not that I was sure it would; and yet, I had to try. Didn't I?

By now the floor show was in full swing, and even some of the goddesses were vying with each other to see how many objects they could find to throw at Balder. Fruit seemed to be the favourite but however hard they tried, all it did was make him slightly sticky. Some of them wanted to lick him clean, and were kept at bay by Nanna, his wife, who was used to dealing with groupies.

At the edge of the little crowd, I noticed a figure sitting apart. It was Golden Boy's blind brother Hoder, looking rather mournful. I didn't blame him. Winter to Balder's springtime, he'd never been very popular, and Frigg, so proud of her *other* son, had never managed to hide her disappointment in his stunted, imperfect sibling.

I moved a little closer, still keeping to the shadows. Hoder sensed my approach, and turned his sightless eyes towards me. No one else had noticed me, and no one else was paying any attention to Hoder, who was confused by the laughter and noise, and whom no one had thought to enlighten.

'What's up?' I said. 'Feeling left out? Wishing you could lob a tomato at Mr Perfect over there?'

Hoder grinned. 'Well, maybe,' he said.

'No problem,' I told him. 'Here, take this dart. I'll show you where to aim. Now – *go!*'

As I spoke, I handed him the dart tipped with the piece of mistletoe. I watched as he aimed it at Balder, and then . . .

Pink!

The gods fell silent.

'Did I hit him?' said Hoder, turning his head this way and that. 'Hey, where did everybody go?'

In fact, the only one who had left was Your Humble Narrator, who saw the situation and wisely removed himself from the scene. But the mistletoe dart had struck home. Balder fell.

There was silence.

First they assumed he was playing dead. Then, as they realized the truth, it was too late to save him. He died right there, in Nanna's arms, while Thor, never quick on the uptake, still bellowed:

'Hey folks, let's try something else! How about we use my boxing gloves?'

Turns out the dart had punctured a lung, and Balder was dead as he hit the ground. As for Hoder, he never got the chance to find out what was happening. As soon as the others realized who had thrown the mistletoe dart, they were on him like wolves. I didn't see the result myself but I'd guessed it wouldn't be pretty, which made me all the more grateful that I had already left the scene.

No one had seen me arrive, or leave, and the only witness to the crime had just been summarily neutralized. Whatever the unforeseen consequences of my little practical joke, the upside was that I was in the clear; and my daughter owed me a favour.

Of course, Balder's death caused a terrible fuss, not least because they felt guilty about killing an innocent blind man in an irrational frenzy of rage. Not the best publicity for the gods of Asgard – and I made sure that word got round in all the appropriate places. They gave Balder a stylish funeral which, naturally, I did not attend. Nanna, his wife, died of grief and was burnt on his funeral pyre. Hoder too, redeemed by death, was given a rousing send-off. And Odin became even more remote, speaking to no one but Mimir's Head, and of course his ravens.

As for myself – I found that I didn't feel as good about all this as I'd expected. I hadn't entirely believed in the Oracle's prophecy – and yet Golden Boy had died just as the Head had predicted. That got me thinking about *other* events that Mimir had predicted, and the likelihood of them coming true. Then there was Hoder's ugly death – something the Oracle had *not* predicted but which perhaps I should have foreseen. In spite of everything, I felt just a *little* responsible.

And now I was trapped, no longer in charge of my personal destiny. Perhaps we were all Mimir's playthings, pieces on a chessboard. If he *hadn't* told me the prophecy, would I still have gone in search of the means of killing Balder?

Probably not. In fact, it wouldn't have crossed my mind if I hadn't already known what the Old Man was planning to do to me.

And Odin? His mistrust of me came straight from the Oracle's prophecy. At the time, the thought of betraying him had never even crossed my mind. I was innocent (well, nearly) until this web of deception descended on me. And now . . . well, now, I had no choice. There was only one path to follow. Admitting my guilt wouldn't save me. All I could do was carry on and hope that my daughter was grateful enough to offer me a means of escaping the destiny that awaited me.

LESSON 6

Tears

What do I care for Balder?
Don't expect me to weep for him,
who never would have wept for me.

Lokabrenna

MEANWHILE, the Enchantress marched straight into the Underworld to demand her son's return from the dead. She found Hel predictably difficult. My daughter had her plaything – though, typically, she still wasn't pleased. Balder dead was compliant, but dull. The spark had gone out.

Hel was jaded. In her hall of bone and dust, she created a court of the dead, clothed them in glamours, made them dance; and still there was no joy in her conquest. Balder sat staring by her side, as unresponsive as ever.

'Then give him back to me,' said Frigg.

But my daughter was stubborn. At least if *she* had Balder, she thought, then no one else could have him. And maybe she could find a way to make him love her, given time.

The Enchantress raged and pleaded. She promised and cajoled. She said that Hel was the only heart that could fail to be moved by Balder's death. 'The Nine Worlds weep for Balder,' she said. 'But you – you're as heartless as your father.'

Hel gave Frigg her dead eye. 'That sounds to me like hyperbole,' she said. 'But if it's true, then maybe you can change my mind.'

I didn't rate Frigg's chances. History is full of cases of folk who have tried to raise the dead, but usually they end in tears. This one also began that way, as Frigg set off to make good her claim.

'Weep for Balder!' came the cry.

'Weep for Balder!'

'Choose Life!'

The slogans spread like wildfire. Frigg's story could wrench tears from a stone, and did, throughout the Middle Worlds. At her command, everyone mourned; everyone wept for Balder. Flowers were tied onto trees in his name; women tore their garments; men hung their heads; small animals howled; even the birds played their part.

It was a kind of hysteria; people who hadn't even *met* Balder were suddenly stricken with grief at his death; sad songs were written in memory of him; total strangers bonded in grief.

But every trend has a backlash. At the moment of triumph, when all the Worlds wept for Balder, Frigg came upon an old crone living in a hovel in the woods.

'Weep! O weep for Balder!' she cried.

The old woman looked at her. 'Who?' she said.

'Balder, Balder the Beautiful. The People's Paragon. My son.'

'That's very sad,' the old woman said. Her eyes were resolutely dry. 'But why should I weep for him, eh?'

'Because, united in grief,' said Frigg, 'we can conquer Death itself.'

'What? So I won't die?' said the crone.

'No,' said Frigg. 'But *Balder* may live.'

'I'm sorry,' said the old crone. 'But this seems quite unfair to me. Why should Balder's death be any more important than mine? Is it because he was handsome, when I'm just a jumble of tired old bones? Or is it because he was young, and I'm old? I'll have you know I was young once. And I value my life at least as much as this Balder, whoever he was, valued his.'

'You don't understand . . .' Frigg tried to explain.

The old woman smiled. 'My dear, no one does. We all get a life, whatever that means. Go home. Grieve for your son. But don't expect me to weep for him, when he would never have wept for me.'

Frigg's eyes narrowed suspiciously. 'Who are you?' She fingered the rune *Bjarkán*.

The old woman shrugged. 'I'm no one,' she said.

'You're lying. I see your colours.'

Under the old woman's cloak, I grinned.

'Please. By all the gods,' she said.

'The gods can hang, for all I care,' I said. 'Go away and leave me alone.' And at that I closed the door in her face and grinned to myself at a job well done.

And that was that; Balder stayed dead, Hel had her due, and I had something to bargain with – something that, three hundred years later, would earn me an unexpected prize.

Still, all that was yet to come. For now, I had other things on my mind. The End of the Worlds, for example, as well as my own imminent death . . .

LESSON 7

Names, II

Sticks and stones may break my bones . . .

Lokabrenna

AFTER THAT, you might have thought I would have settled down for a while. Adopted a low profile, perhaps. Taken up a hobby. But there was something in the air; a scent of revolt, a whiff of smoke. War was coming. I wanted to fight. So shoot me. It's my nature.

It wasn't that I was remotely sorry for what had happened to Balder. Sorry isn't really a word that figures in my vocabulary. All the same, I didn't feel as good as you might have expected. I found myself growing restless. I couldn't sleep. I was irritable. I spent too long in bird form, trying to beat my increasing sense of imprisonment. I suffered terrible nightmares in which I was shackled and blinded, surrounded by venomous snakes that crawled all over my naked body.

No, it wasn't *guilt* I felt. But the joy had gone out of everything. The ball of barbed wire in my heart had grown to monstrous proportions. Food had no taste; sleep brought no rest; wine just made my head hurt. The threat of Mimir's prophecy hung over me like an anvil; I couldn't talk to anyone; I felt terribly alone.

It didn't help that Sigyn was cloyingly sympathetic.

'Poor angel, you look *terrible*,' she said, on seeing me looking less than fragrant after another sleepless night. 'What have you been *doing* to yourself? Come over, and I'll fix you something nice for dinner. The boys would love to see you . . .' And so on, and so forth.

My sons had become increasingly wild since Fenny's disappearance. Now they barely spoke to me, or to their mother, but spent their days lounging on the battlements of Asgard, throwing stones down onto the plain and jeering at Sól in her chariot as she raced across the sky.

As for the gods – since Balder's death my colleagues had been less than warm. Some of this was Frigg's doing; the Enchantress, although she had no evidence to support her belief that I was to blame for what had occurred, had nevertheless somehow managed to convey her suspicions to everyone else, with the result that no one (with the exception of Sigyn, of course) wanted to be seen with me.

All their grudges and grievances were brought out for an airing; Sif, the fact that I'd cut off her hair; Bragi, the kidnap of Idun; Freyja, that whole business with the sons of Ivaldi and the gold necklace; Thor, all the times I'd mocked him. No one remembered all the times I'd saved them from the enemy. The court of public opinion had judged and condemned me all in one. No one talked to me any more. No one even looked at me.

That hurt my feelings – no, don't laugh – even though I was guilty. They didn't *know* I was guilty; they just assumed it had to be me. As if I was the only one ever to have done bad things. As if I was dirt. It made me angry to think of it and, one hot night, when I'd had a few drinks alone in my dingy little rooms, I heard the sound of music coming from Aegir's undersea hall down the way. It sounded like a party and so I went to investigate.

I found all the gods assembled. Aesir and Vanir; boys and girls; Aegir and Ran, his glaucous wife; even the Old Man himself was there, drinking from a horn of mead and looking *almost* mellow.

Perhaps it wasn't the wisest move to try and gatecrash the party. But I'd been through some difficult times; the insomnia, Sigyn's persistence, my visit to Hel, the prophecy – not to mention Balder's death, that of his wife and the brutal killing of Hoder. Try to sympathize when I say I went a little crazy.

I opened the door into Aegir's hall and addressed the merry gathering:

'What, celebrating without me? Come on, Odin, let's have a drink.'

Bragi, who had been playing his lute, said: 'I think you've already had a few. A few too many, if you ask me.'

'But I *don't* ask you,' I said. 'I'm asking my brother Odin. Odin, who swore a blood oath that he would never pour himself a drink without making certain that I had one, too. Still, promises are like piecrust, eh? Always made to be broken. And speaking of pies . . .' I helped myself to a slice of something from someone's plate. 'Not bad,' I said, with my mouth full. 'Maybe a little greasy.'

Odin gave me his impassive stare. 'Come in, Loki. You're welcome.'

'Welcome? I don't think so,' I said. 'Face it, I'm as welcome here as a turd in a hot tub. Which is fine, because I hate you all. Especially you,' I addressed Bragi, 'because, apart from having the bad taste to hold a party without me, you're a terrible poet, a worse instrumentalist, and you couldn't sing in tune if the Worlds depended on it.'

Bragi looked as if he were ready to hit me with the lute. I told him to go ahead, it would probably do less harm to me than if he tried to play it. And then I turned on the others, who were watching me, open-mouthed, probably wondering what in Hel had happened to the silver-tongued Trickster they thought they knew.

Idun tried to take my hand. 'What's wrong?'

I started to laugh. 'What's wrong?' I said. 'How very sweet of you to ask. Sweet or stupid, anyway. With you, there's not much of a difference.'

Now Freyja stepped forward. 'Stop it!' she said. 'You're being offensive. Thor, can't you stop him?'

'That's right,' I said. 'Get somebody else to intervene. Preferably someone who's dumb enough not to realize you're using them. Thor's a pretty good choice – I mean, he *can* obey simple instructions, as long as you feed him properly . . .' At this point Thor gave a low growl, and I took the opportunity to deposit the piece of half-eaten pie onto the platter in front of him. 'Or maybe you should ask Odin? That is, if he can somehow forget that you sold yourself to the Maggots, and all for the price of a necklace – oh, shouldn't I have mentioned that?' I bared my teeth in a savage grin. 'It's the Chaos in my blood. It sometimes drives me to misbehave. *You'd* know all about that, Freyja.'

Freyja assumed her Crone Aspect. Her skeletal face was terrible.

'You need to get some beauty sleep,' I said. 'You're getting wrinkles. And don't drink so much beer tonight. You know it makes you fart in bed. Some men may like that kind of thing, but frankly, it's unappealing.'

I know, I know. I was on fire. I couldn't stop myself, which was, I suppose, part of the problem. Someone should have looked out for me. Someone should have *stopped* me.

Thor tried. 'If you want a fight, don't pick on a bunch of women. Fight like a man.'

'The way you did at Thrym's place, all dressed up like a bride?'

Thor took another step forward.

'Or when the old woman wrestled you to the ground at Utgard-Loki's banquet?'

Thor made a grab for me. I dodged and helped myself to wine. 'Slowing down a bit, Thor,' I said. 'Mind you, the amount you eat, I'm not surprised. You should work out – better still, get Sif to lend you one of her corsets—'

Sif gave a wail of protest. 'You animal! I do *not* wear corsets!'

That started me laughing, and once I'd started, I couldn't stop. I went round all the circle of gods, and told them exactly what I thought. The Folk call it a *flyting*, a ritual name-calling ceremony, and it became a tradition. One of my many gifts to the Folk. Anger is often cathartic, a healing process at moments of stress, although I suppose that, at the time, I should perhaps have given it all just a *little* more thought.

As it was, the wine must have gone to my head, because I gave them the works – told Frey he'd been an idiot to give up his runesword for a girl; told Sif she was getting fat; told Njörd he smelt of fish. I told Thor that his mistress Jarnsaxa was pregnant and expecting twins. I told Frigg that Odin had been playing away again. I may also have said something to Týr about the way he lost his arm, and I'm pretty sure I called Heimdall a 'pimped-up gobshite'. But it was probably a mistake to tell Skadi that her father had squawked like a chicken as he fell ready-roasted into the flames, and then to ask the Enchantress if Golden Boy was still as dead.

That brought silence to the room. Maybe I *had* gone too far. Thor picked up his hammer and levelled it at Yours Truly.

'Don't,' said Odin softly.

'I'd be doing the Worlds a favour,' said Thor.

'Go ahead,' I said. 'Bring it on. I'm unarmed and outnumbered. That ought to be odds enough for you. Or should I really be blind, as well?'

The others looked uncomfortable as they remembered Hoder.

'Well,' I said, turning to go. 'Much as I hate to leave, folks, it really has been a *very* dull party, and I have places I need to be.'

And so I walked out of Aegir's hall, and as soon as my headache had lifted – which was sometime later that morning – I took hawk guise and made for the hills. Call me over-cautious, but Your Humble Narrator was starting to feel that he had outstayed his welcome.

LESSON 8

Judgement

Run first, talk later.

Lokabrenna

TURNS OUT my instincts were right again. By the time the hangovers lifted and the sweet light of understanding had dawned, Yours Truly had been unanimously condemned by everyone in Asgard, not just of Balder's death, but of every crime imaginable.

Once more, everyone remembered something I'd done to offend them – with the exception of Sigyn, of course, who could never believe anything bad of me, and Idun, who could never really believe anything bad of *anyone*.

The rest of them made up for that, however. Skadi was particularly venomous, demanding my blood on the instant, and Heimdall was all too happy to remind them that he had never trusted me, and that if they'd listened to him in the first place, I would never have been allowed to gain a foothold in Asgard.

Finally, sensing weakness, he dared confront the Old Man.

'What are you going to do?' he said. 'Loki has declared war on all of us. Are you going to wait until he marches on Asgard with all of Chaos at his heels, or will you finally admit that you were wrong to take him in?'

Odin gave a low growl. Well, at least I imagine he did. Of course, I wasn't there to hear it. But I heard enough subsequent dialogue to be able to hazard a pretty good guess. Besides, I knew the Old Man better than he suspected, and I knew that sooner or later he would have to choose a side.

No prizes for guessing which side he chose. Not that I blame him – well, not much. The others were ready to turn on him if he didn't condemn me. Besides, I had outlived my usefulness, except perhaps as a means of uniting them in shared hatred. And at that point, I knew that the Old Man needed Order a lot more than he needed Chaos.

And so began the hunt. Of course, I knew what would happen if I were caught. I had Nine Worlds in which to hide, and runes with which to conceal myself. And I was good at hiding – but I was outnumbered, and friendless, and Odin had his ravens, his people, his spies and his Oracle.

They combed the Nine Worlds for my signature; tracked me out of Ironwood; tracked me to the Northlands; lost my trail in World Beyond; found it again in the mountains. I kept on the move, shielding myself; changing Aspect whenever I could. Eventually I found a place where I felt almost safe. I hid, hoping to outlast their rage until the crisis was over.

But the gods were relentless. First, they gave me an ultimatum, scrawled across the sky in glam: *Give yourself up. We still have the boys.*

From my hideaway, I sneered. Did they really think I'd fall for something *that* crude? They knew I was hardly Dad of the Year. And those boys were barely out of their teens. I knew Odin was ruthless, but would he really murder my sons, just for the crime of sharing my blood? Obviously, it was a trap. I wasn't going to fall for it.

Then came the birds. Those thrice-damned birds, who'd tracked me to my hideaway, a cave in the Hindarfell mountains. They circled, then came down and perched on an outcrop of rock close by.

I considered giving them a shot of my glam, but Hugin and Munin had Odin's protection, and I doubted even my best shot would have even singed their feathers.

And so I came out to meet them, first checking that they were alone.

'What do you want?'

The larger bird *crawk*ed. The smaller seemed to struggle for speech, pecking at the other one in what seemed like frustration.

'*Cake*,' it said in a rusty voice, its golden eyes shining hopefully.

'No chance,' I said. 'What does he want?'

The smaller bird – Munin – flapped its wings. '*Ack-ack. Come back.*'

'What, and leave all this?' I said. 'No, I think I'll stay right here.'

Munin flapped its wings again. '*Ack-ack.*'

Hugin joined in the mayhem, pecking at the rock at its feet, flapping its wings and *crawk*ing.

'*Loki. Two (crawk!) in Asgard,*' said Munin, who clearly had trouble with sibilants.

'Two sons. That's right.' I was getting impatient. 'And if the Old Man really believes that I'm going to give myself up just because he's holding them hostage in my place . . .'

'*Ack-acck!*' said Hugin, beginning to peck at the rock again. The pecks were slow and measured, each one roughly at a second's interval.

Peck. Peck.

Two seconds.

Peck. Three seconds. He was measuring time.

I looked at Munin wildly. 'What's he doing? What *is* this?' I said.

Munin said: '*Ack-ax-ty. Ax-ty ack-en.*'

'Sixty? Sixty seconds?' I said. 'Sixty seconds until what?'

But I'd already understood. The birds might have problems

with language, but I knew Odin only too well. Never forget that the Old Man was as ruthless as I was myself. He wanted to hit me where it hurt. And he knew me *very* well.

Hugin was still counting down. Twenty seconds. Twenty-five.

'Wait,' I said, feeling suddenly cold.

'*Come back*,' said Munin.

Thirty seconds. *Peck. Peck*. Each one felt like a hammer blow. I knew the Old Man was watching me through the eyes of those damned birds, trying to second-guess my thoughts, trying to outmanoeuvre me.

'I'm not going to fall for this,' I said. 'Vali and Narvi mean nothing to me.'

Peck. Forty seconds. *Peck*.

'You know you've got nothing to bargain with,' I said, forcing a brave, brash smile. 'Those boys belong to Sigyn, not me. Killing them won't change a thing. So go ahead, brother. Do the deed. Put them out of their misery. You're the one with the conscience, not me. So – do you feel lucky? Play or—'

And on that syllable, both birds took wing. With a sound like feathered applause, they rose into the ice-blue sky. And at that moment, a world away . . .

Don't ask me how I knew. I *knew*.

The thing was, he'd corrupted me with feelings and sensations. In my pure, Chaotic form, I wouldn't have cared for a moment, however many of my children he killed. But here, in this Aspect, weakened; alone; tormented by fear and guilt and remorse; hunger and cold and discomfort – none of them natural to a being like myself, not born to these sensations.

And the Old Man knew, of course. He was the one who had poisoned me. And he had known how to get to me, and thought he could force me to show myself.

What did they really expect me to do? Come howling back into Asgard, so they could shoot me down in flames? Declare war? Demand recompense? That's what a *warrior* would have done. That might have earned me some respect, according to their twisted honour code.

But no – it was too late for that. Odin had taken his revenge. Had I really believed he would? Honestly, I don't know. I'd always known he was *capable* of doing these things, but to do them to *me*?

And so I stayed in hiding, moving from the Hindarfell underground through World Below. The Aesir widened the search for me, sending Skadi to hunt me in the Northlands; Ran to comb the seas with her net; Njörd to search the rivers. Sól and Mani, the Sun and the Moon, roamed the skies in search of me; the Tunnel Folk looked for me underground; everyone was on the alert for the faintest gleam of my signature.

Frigg was especially tireless. Just as she had canvassed every root and blade of grass after the death of Balder, she now sent out a general call to seek and locate Yours Truly. There was talk of a reward, but mostly folk seemed happy to help. I'd known I wasn't popular, but not the extent of the hatred levelled at my humble self, growing ever more humble as the circle began to close.

I won't lie. I was getting scared. Everyone was against me. I'd holed up in the Northlands, in the valley of the Strond, on top of a hill from which I could see for miles. Under the Hill was a gateway that led to World Below and beyond; it was a kind of crossroads, with escape routes in every direction.

For months I lived as a fugitive, shielding my signature; saving my glam. I built a hut from turf and wood; I lived on fish from the river below. Winter was coming; I was cold. At night I was afraid to sleep, for fear that they might track me through Dream. In short, I was about as miserable as any of them could have hoped, and yet it wasn't enough for them. They wanted me to suffer more.

I don't know how they found me at last. Perhaps through Dream – I *had* to sleep. In any case, they came for me, converging on my hiding place like wolves on their prey.

I saw their signatures too late; a net of runelight, closing fast. Nine of the usual suspects: Heimdall, approaching in hawk Aspect; Skadi, in her snow wolf guise, with her runewhip in her jaws; Thor, with Mjølnir, in his chariot; Njörd, riding a kayak downstream; Frey with his golden boar; Freyja in her falcon cloak; Idun and Bragi on horseback, and of course, the General, mounted on Sleipnir, spear in hand, in full Aspect, flying his colours across the sky like a victory banner.

There was nowhere left to run. I shifted Aspect to that of a fish and slipped into the river. The water was deep; maybe I could hide among the stones of the river bed. But rivers were Njörd's territory; he must have seen my colours, somehow. He reached for the fishing net at his belt and cast it into the water. The weighted mesh fell around me like Fate.

I won't bore you with the details. Suffice it to say that I put up a fight, but that it wasn't nearly enough. The net was woven through with binding-runes, much like the ones that made up Hel's rope. I later learnt that Hel herself had aided in its construction, presumably as a means of getting back in with the popular crowd. Or maybe her resentment of me was enough to eclipse her dislike of them. In any case, the net was proof against even my Wildfire Aspect, and after several unsuccessful attempts to free myself of its choking mesh, I was hauled onto the bank, naked, freezing and dripping wet.

'Gotcha,' said Heimdall, unpleasantly.

I looked away and said nothing. I wasn't going to plead for my life; it wouldn't have worked anyway, and I wasn't about to give Goldie the satisfaction of seeing me beg. Instead I sat up as best I could and affected an air of unconcern.

'I say kill him now,' said Thor. 'Before he gets away again.'

'He isn't going to get away.' Skadi gave her chilly smile. 'We can take our time with him. Make it an occasion.'

'I agree,' said Heimdall. 'He deserves something special. Besides, Frigg will want to be there to witness his execution.'

The others seemed inclined to agree. Bragi wanted time to

compose a ballad for the big day; Freyja had a special outfit she wanted to wear and all of them wanted time to discuss the precise method of my dispatching.

Only Idun and the Old Man said nothing. Odin was standing apart from the rest of them, a hand on Sleipnir's bridle. But Idun had come to sit by my side; I caught the scent of flowers and saw that in the time she'd been sitting there, a number of nearby bushes had been coaxed into early blossom. It was a little warmer, too.

She looked at Odin and said: 'You can't.'

Heimdall gave a sneer. 'Why not?

'Because he was one of us,' she said.

Well, *that* was wrong for a start, I thought. I was never one of you.

I said: 'Go ahead and kill me. Just don't let Bragi play his lute.'

Idun looked at Odin. 'You gave your word. You know what that means.'

'*I* didn't swear,' Skadi said. 'Nor did the others.'

Heimdall agreed. 'He has to die. He's too dangerous to live. You heard what the Oracle said. When the time comes, he'll betray us to Surt in exchange for his miserable life.'

So, Odin had confided the Oracle's prophecy to Goldie, had he? I wondered why that surprised me. In fact, the Old Man had probably discussed it with everyone but me, debating its meaning extensively over the contents of his wine cellar. Conclusion: Loki, the traitor, having first attacked the gods in the most cruel and underhand way, would sell them over to Surt, in exchange for his rehabilitation.

I wish.

I could have explained at that point that Surt doesn't *do* exchanges. Exchanges, parley, truces, deals – Surt doesn't play by those kinds of rules. As for traitors, he deals with them just as he does with everyone else. The sea does not distinguish between individual grains of sand. It passes over everything, and there is no stopping it.

But Odin was looking thoughtful. Words, like names, are powerful things. Once given, there's no taking them back without risking serious consequences. Besides, we'd *both* heard the prophecy, though Odin didn't know about my conversation with Mimir's Head. Both of us already knew what was going to happen to me. Neither of us wanted it – but that was hardly the point, of course.

I looked up at the Old Man and quoted the words of the Oracle:

> *Now comes a fire-ship from the east,*
> *With Loki standing at the helm.*
> *The dead rise; the damned are unleashed;*
> *Fear and Chaos ride with them.*

'Sound familiar, brother?' I said.

His startled look was almost worth the whole distressing episode. 'Where did you hear that?'

'Where do you think?'

He sighed. 'You spoke to the Oracle.'

'Well, you weren't about to confide in me. I had to find out for myself.'

'And how much did it tell you?'

I shrugged. 'Enough to wish I hadn't asked.'

Once more, Odin sighed. Like it or not, we were both affected by the Oracle's words. We had *both* heard the prophecy – and once heard, it couldn't be unheard. Trying to go against it now would have been as futile as trying to make it happen – both courses of action being equally led by the prophecy. As the Head had told me, a man often meets his destiny running to avoid it, which meant that whatever Odin did, he would be playing the Oracle's game.

He turned to address the other gods. 'Killing him isn't an option,' he said. 'But he has to be subdued.'

'I can do that,' Skadi said, fingering her runewhip. 'I find the dead very cooperative.'

'No.' Odin shook his head.

Skadi made a rude noise.

'So what did you have in mind?' said Thor.

'Imprisonment,' Odin said. 'Until we know what the prophecy means, we can't afford to let him go. We need to keep him safe, somewhere—'

I interrupted: 'Wait! I know!' Once more I quoted the Oracle:

> *I see one bound beneath the court,*
> *Under the Cauldron of Rivers.*
> *The wretch looks like Loki. His wife*
> *Alone stands by him as he suffers.*

Odin gave me the evil eye. 'You're very well informed,' he said.

I smirked. 'Like you, I keep ahead.'

LESSON 9

Venom

Did I mention I hated snakes?

Lokabrenna

Aɴᴅ ꜱᴏ Your Humble Narrator, growing ever more humble as the sad tale unfolds, was dragged down into World Below, beneath the Cauldron of Rivers. Right at the source of the river Dream; on the borders of Chaos; the hinterlands, half in, half out of the waking world.

There springs Dream in its purest form; volatile, ephemeral. And that was where, deep underground, above a narrow, rocky vent that stank of sulphur and belched foul steam onto a trio of rocks the shape and size of a particularly uncomfortable chaise-longue, I was shackled and bound with runes that kept me from shifting Aspect.

Odin checked the bonds himself. They were quite unbreakable. He fixed me with his one good eye and said: 'I'm sorry it turned out this way.'

'When I get free, *brother*,' I said, 'I'll be sure to pay you a call. It's really the least I can do, don't you think? After all you've done for me?'

Heimdall grinned. Those golden teeth lit up the cave like a string of fairy-lights. I promised myself that if Mimir was right, and I *did* get the chance to meet Goldie in combat, I would

237

collect those golden teeth and make myself a neck-chain.

'You'll rot down here till the End of the Worlds,' he said.

I uttered something obscene. But, in a way, Goldie was right; it's just that the End of the Worlds was not as far away as they thought.

One by one, my erstwhile friends came to hammer the last few nails into Yours Truly's coffin. Bragi played a madrigal. Idun kissed my forehead. Freyja shot me a spiteful look and told me I'd got what I'd always deserved. Frey and Njörd just shook their heads. Týr patted me with his one good hand. Thor looked awkward – as well he might, after everything I'd done for him – and said:

'I'm sorry. You went too far.'

Lovely. What an epitaph.

By the end, there was only Skadi left. She stood very quietly by my side, watching me with a curious intensity. She'd let her hair grow while they hunted me, and it was pale as sea-foam, framing a face as deceptively sweet as that of a ravenous mink.

She stayed there such a long time that it unnerved me. What did she want? The others had gone. Was she planning to make good her threat, and kill me while I was helpless?

She must have sensed my unease. She smiled.

'We're one step away from perfection,' she said.

I didn't like the sound of that. Nor did I like the look of the thing she had in her hand. She'd been keeping it out of my field of vision, but now she raised it to the level of my eyes with a terrible deliberation.

'I brought you a little something,' she said.

'A snake? I asked for a *snack*,' I said. 'Still, I guess it's the thought that counts.'

Skadi gave that smile again. A little shiver went down, first my spine, then every hair on my body.

'Not just any snake,' she said. 'This one's a spitting cobra. It likes to spit venom at its enemies. The venom doesn't damage unbroken skin, but if it gets in the victim's eyes – you can bet that's going to hurt.'

I didn't much like where this was going. I said: 'What are you going to do?'

She smiled again. 'You'll like this. I'm going to put her right *here*.' She indicated an outcrop of rock just at the level of my face. 'You might want to try and keep still while I do. She can be a little jumpy.'

'Listen, Skadi . . .' I began, then realized that hearing me beg would only enhance her enjoyment. It wouldn't make any difference to whatever she did to me but I could at least spoil the moment.

And so I clamped my lips shut and said nothing, trying not to look at the snake. Snakes come in two general types; loathsomely sluggish and scarily speedy. This was one of the speedy ones. It thrashed and hissed in Skadi's hand as she pinned it to the rock. I hoped it would bite her, but it didn't. I guess it must have known instinctively that if it tried, it was bound to come off worse.

I looked at the snake on the rock ledge. It was right at the level of my eyes. I could see it watching me, its length full of tics and twitches. Its jaws flexed with rubbery hatred. It looked both mean and just stupid enough to assume that I was the one to blame for its current predicament.

I lay on the rock as still as I could and tried not to breathe. I knew that a sound – a gesture – could unleash an attack.

Skadi picked up a handful of stones.

Pinged one right off the rockface, just above the seething snake.

Said: 'You're going to have *so* much fun getting to know one another.'

The snake moved too quickly for me to react. A fine puff of droplets spattered my face. For a moment there was no pain.

Then there was.

I started to scream.

*

The pain went on for a long time. Blind, burning, beyond speech: I twisted and thrashed in my shackles. The snake did the same, hissing venom. A red curtain of anguish descended over everything. I think if I hadn't been chained to the rock, I might have clawed out my own eyes.

No, don't try to imagine it. Just think of Your Humble Narrator. All right, so I'd done a few things of questionable morality. But seriously? Did I deserve *this*?

When the red curtain began to lift, and I was able to use words again, I revisited the pleading option. My pride was gone; and my sense of shame.

'Please! Please! Take it *away*!'

But begging for mercy didn't work. Nor did screaming to Odin for help, or trying to turn my face away, or arching my back to try to get as far from the serpent as I could. As soon as I moved or raised my voice, the evil creature would strike again, and as soon as it struck, I screamed and thrashed . . .

'Please! Don't leave me! *Please!* My *eyes!*'

Behind me, moving away, I could hear the sound of Skadi's laughter.

LESSON 10

Punishment

*Punishment is futile. It doesn't stop crime, or undo
the past, or make the culprit sorry. In fact, all it does
is waste time and cause unnecessary suffering.*

Lokabrenna

THINK WHAT IT MUST HAVE BEEN LIKE for Your Humble Narrator. Chained to a rock in World Below; blinded and in constant pain. I have no idea how much time passed – Time works differently so close to Dream, and a few moments in the waking world can seem like an eternity. But Pain is also a country where Time works in a different way, and it might have been hours, or days, or weeks before I slowly became aware of a silent presence at my side.

At first I thought it was Skadi, come to torture me again. Then I *hoped* it was Skadi, come to put an end to me. Then I began to realize that it had been some minutes since the snake had delivered its last volley of poison spray, and that the burning in my eyes had begun to abate a little.

I was still blind, but now I could just distinguish light from darkness. I said:

'Who's there?'

No one replied. I could hear the slithering of the snake on the rock by my side, and the quiet breathing of someone who must have been standing very close. I said:

'Please. Help me escape. I'll do anything you want.'

I guess perhaps a part of me was still hoping it might be the Old Man, come to help me in secret after exercising his authority.

Dry-lipped, I said: 'Brother, please. I promise I'll never defy you again. I'll show you how to fight Surt. I know how to do it. Odin. *Please . . .*'

'It's me,' said a voice.

'*Sigyn?*'

I managed to open my eyes. They still burned but now I could see a shadowy outline next to me. The shape seemed to be holding something between my face and the serpent. As my vision slowly cleared, I saw that it was the large glass mixing bowl that Sigyn used to made cake batter. The sides of the bowl were already streaming with the serpent's venom.

'It's all I had to hand,' she said, looking at me tenderly. 'Silly old Snakey thinks he can get to you through the glass. He's a *nasty* one, isn't he? Nasty, mean old Snakey.'

Snakey hissed, as well he might.

Sigyn went on: 'Poor angel. You must be *so* uncomfortable. Still, I'm here now. Try not to move. You'll only hurt yourself, you know.'

My eyes were still streaming – with pain, I think, or perhaps they were tears of gratitude. For a moment the thought of release filled me with euphoria.

'Oh, Sig,' I said, 'I'm so glad you're here. I've been such a rotten husband. I promise you, that's going to change. Just get me off this rock. Please.'

'Oh, Loki,' she said. 'You're *so* sweet. And I really believe you mean it, too. But I can't let you go.'

'Say *what*?'

'Well, you're here for a *reason*, dear. Criminals have to be punished. And if I let you go, I'd be letting down Odin and all the others.'

For once, I was wholly lost for words. '*What?*' I repeated.

Sigyn smiled. Through a haze of tears I saw her face; tender, loving, immovable. 'Well, you *did* kill Balder,' she said. 'That's why Odin killed our boys. So in a way, you're responsible.'

I started to panic.

'No, I'm not! Sigyn, please! Let me go!'

'Stop moving. You'll knock the basin.'

I looked at her in disbelief. She looked serene – and quite unhinged. Had the deaths of Vali and Narvi finally brought her to the edge? Or was this the scenario she'd always secretly wanted – to have me to herself for good, helpless and in her power?

'I brought some fruitcake for later,' she said. 'If you like, I'll cut you a slice.'

'Cake,' I said. 'You brought *cake*?'

'Well, cake always makes *me* feel better,' she said. 'It's cherry and almond. Your favourite.'

'Please! You *have* to let me go!'

'I don't, and I won't.' Her mouth tightened. 'Now don't make me cross, or I might have to go for a little walk to calm my nerves. And if I do that, there'll be nobody to hold this between you and Snakey.'

I looked up at the mixing bowl, the snake's jaws horribly magnified through the thickness of the glass.

Snakey looked right back at me with maniac intensity.

I could tell he was only biding his time, waiting for Sigyn to lower the bowl, which was already a quarter-full of collected venom.

How many minutes, I asked myself, before she would need to empty the bowl? How many minutes before the snake, seeing its chance, would strike? How many minutes, how many hours before I was screaming in torment again?

Punishment is futile, of course. It doesn't stop crime, or undo the past, or make the culprit sorry. In fact, all it does is waste time and cause unnecessary suffering. Perhaps that's why it's the basis of so many world religions. I thought of the Oracle's prophecy.

The wretch looks like Loki. His wife
Alone stands by him as he suffers.

Oh, gods. And I'd thought the snake was bad. But to wait until the End of the Worlds listening to Sigyn's chatter, eating her fruitcake and watching the snake through the fish-eye lens of that mixing bowl . . .

I tried a last, miserable tactic. 'Please. I love you, Sig,' I said.

That's how pitiful I was. That's how sorry I was for myself. That's how wretchedly low I'd sunk – using the L-word *to my wife* . . .

She smiled again. 'Oh, sweetheart,' she said, and I knew that my last gambit had failed. In fact, my words had sealed my fate: she had me just where she wanted me. Needy, and helpless, and desperate, and hurt, and wholly in her power.

She looked at me with tears in her eyes, and her voice was tender as she said: 'Oh, Loki, sweetheart, I love you too. And I'm going to take *such* good care of you.'

LESSON 11

Escape

Never neglect the small print.

Lokabrenna

THERE FOLLOWED a long, strange, terrible time. Half in, half out of the waking world, it's hard to say how long it was, but to me it was an eternity of boredom, boredom interrupted by intervals of brief, but unspeakable suffering.

To do her credit, Sigyn tried her best. Mad as she undoubtedly was, and as impervious to my pleas as she was to my cajolery, she did what she could to help me.

Most of the time that consisted of collecting Snakey's venom. At intervals she emptied the bowl, at which times the evil creature struck. It also struck when she made me drink, which I had to do occasionally, or when she tried to feed me, or when she went to *powder her nose*. The result of this was that I was perpetually hungry, thirsty, in pain, or all three.

Sigyn was brisk and motherly, her tone like that of a nursery nurse with a fractious infant. She adopted exactly the same tone with me as she did with the snake, chiding us both for 'not getting on', and delivering stern little lectures. At other times she would sigh piteously over my sufferings, of course without ever accepting to free me of my shackles. I got the distinct impression that, despite all her complaints, she was happy. She had me to herself at last, and she wasn't about to let me go.

Time passed. I don't know how long. I learned to sleep a little between those intervals of torture. No one else came, and I gave up hope that Odin might one day relent and free me. He was, however, to some extent responsible for my partial relief; Sigyn had said how Odin had told her how to find me, and had given her permission to help me in whatever way she chose. But if anything, that made it worse; the knowledge that Odin, having put me here in the first place, should feel concern for my welfare now – or was it guilt?

Too little, too late. Did he expect me to thank him? No, I felt nothing but hatred now, for him and all his people. When I got free – and I swore that I *would* – I'd make them pay for what they'd done. And after that, I'd find Mimir's Head and kick it from here to World's End, and then bury it as deep underground as the Aesir had buried me.

Well, a man can always dream. Dreams were what sustained me then, between those terrible slices of pain. And Dream was so *close*; almost close enough to touch. I could hear it through the rock on which I lay; rushing through the Underside, bearing its load of ephemera off into the outside world . . .

Skadi's parting gift to me had a twofold purpose. One was, of course, the sheer pleasure of making me suffer. The other, I suspected, was to keep my mind from thoughts of escape. There's not really much you *can* think when your eyes are burning and blind, except for wanting the pain to stop. But during those long intervals when Sigyn held the snake at bay, I managed to regain some clarity, and my mind began to work again.

One thing I did was go over and over the prophecy of the Oracle. Especially the part relating to myself, and the precise wording thereof.

> *I see one bound beneath the court,*
> *Under the Cauldron of Rivers.*
> *The wretch looks like Loki. His wife*

Alone stands by him as he suffers.

At first I'd assumed that Sigyn was mentioned simply as the only one who might stay loyal to my interests. Now I realized that the truth was more literal – I was apparently stuck with her from now until the End of the Worlds. I could expect nothing more from her. I went over the fragment of text again, checking the small print for loopholes.

> *I see one bound beneath the court,*
> *Under the Cauldron of Rivers.*
> *The wretch looks like Loki . . .*
> *The wretch looks like Loki.*
> *Looks like Loki.*
> *Looks like Loki.*

I thought about that for a long time. Why that phrase? I asked myself. To fit the metre of the verse? Or for some other reason, as yet unknown?

The wretch looks like Loki.
I suffered. I screamed.
The wretch looks like Loki.
I slept. I dreamed.

LESSON 12

Dream

What is it that the slave dreams?
He dreams of being the master.

Lokabrenna

DREAM IS A RIVER that runs through Nine Worlds, even
Death and Damnation. Even the damned can dream – in fact,
it's a part of their torment. To escape, even for a second or two, to
forget reality and drift, only to be yanked back into the waking
world like a fish caught on a line . . .

Yes. In some ways that's even worse than to have no relief
at all. That second or two, on awakening, when anything still
seems possible, including the possibility that the past few
days – or weeks, or months – might themselves have been a
dream . . .

And then it hits you in the eyes. This is *real*. This is *now*. And
dreams are just ephemera. In such a case you might almost be
forgiven for trying not to dream at all, for refusing to swallow
the barb of hope that catches at the back of your throat. But I
had the germ of an idea. Not quite a plan – not yet. Not quite.
But the hope of escape had not yet quite abandoned me.

It was the phrasing of that verse. *The wretch looks like Loki.*
Not he *is* Loki, but he *looks* like Loki. *Looks* like Loki. Raising the
faint possibility that *Loki himself* may be somewhere else.

That would be nice, I told myself. If only I could make that work. But how could I *seem* to be in one place while actually being somewhere else?

Dream was the only answer. If I could somehow escape through Dream, leaving my physical Aspect behind, then maybe I could be free again. Free to rejoin Chaos, maybe; free of Odin's vengeance.

Of course, there would be serious risks. Dream is a dangerous element, subject to dangerous forces. Here, at its source, it could be lethal; a river of savage ephemera that could destroy a person's mind. On the other hand, everything dreams; and if I could manage to link myself with the mind of a suitable dreamer, then perhaps I could manage the seemingly impossible task of being in two different places at once.

Yes, I know. I was naïve. But I was also desperate. Ready to risk my sanity, my life, for the chance to get away. And so I practised dreaming; not as a means of passing the time, but doggedly, laboriously, as a convict scrapes away the floor of his cell with a sharpened teaspoon, hoping one day to dig a hole large enough to make his escape.

There are two kinds of dreaming. The kind that takes you in completely, and the lucid kind, in which you're aware of being between worlds and travelling. It was the second kind I sought. It took practice, and all the time I ran the risk of falling foul of one of the creatures that plumbed those depths, creatures all too eager to lure an unsuspecting dreamer before consuming him mind and soul, leaving his body to die in the waking world. A rare thing in the Middle Worlds, although it sometimes happens. But close as I was to the source of Dream, it was almost certain. And yet I considered the risk worthwhile. Anything to get off that rock, away from Sigyn and Snakey.

And so I began to sharpen my spoon. Gods, it was laborious. There were no days or nights here, of course. I slept when I could, which was seldom. Little by little, I came to know the perils and joys of that river and its islands of ephemera, some as small as a soap bubble; some as large as continents. I learnt to explore these islands; to skirt their dangers; to touch the minds of the dreamers who had created them. Little by little, I narrowed my search, all the time seeking a dreamer who would suit my purpose.

It had to be a strong mind, though not so strong as to resist my influence, or to try and consume me. An open mind; imaginative; not too constrained by moral issues. I tried many, only to find them all unsuitable in some way; and then, after an eternity of searching, I found the perfect one – or should I say, the dreamer found *me*. A strong mind, and imaginative, filled with familiar landscapes. A kindred soul, in fact, I thought; playing out scenarios that I almost recognized.

Some were tactile; comforting dreams of half-forgotten sensations. Dreams of sweet, cool water; of hands on my face; of linen sheets; of shady trees and the good scents of wet soil and vegetation. Trapped as I was, deep underground, barely able to breathe the air, always fearful, always in pain, always hungry and thirsty and sore, those dreams were my link to a sweeter world, and I embraced them fervently.

But as time passed I found the dreams becoming increasingly violent. The arc of a fountain of lava erupting from Chaos into the Worlds, bringing destruction in its wake. The journey of a flake of ash ascending from a bonfire. Dreams of fire; dreams of smoke; abstract dreams of Chaos. Burning buildings and fortresses falling into twilight; visions of the Folk at war; the Maggots; the Rock Folk; the Ice Folk; the gods . . .

At first it seemed almost too perfect. That violence, so akin to my own; I sensed the potential for a trap. And so I entered carefully, skirting the dreams with caution, occasionally adding a couple of small details of my own to see if he would take the bait.

Well, I say *he*. It isn't always easy to identify a dreamer. Dreams are complex structures, difficult as prophecies to interpret or understand. Identities are particularly hard to determine, as the dreamer tends to appear in many different Aspects. I took a different Aspect every time I entered Dream; one day a hawk; the other a cat; the next perhaps a frog or a spider. At first I had to force myself not to move too quickly, exploring the dreamer's landscapes without trying to make any obvious attempt at communication, or trying to make him reveal himself.

I'll admit, it was frustrating. But I knew I had to be patient. I'd found myself the perfect mind – clever, receptive, imaginative, and with just the right level of repressed violence to make us nicely compatible. I didn't want to frighten him (or her) away with my eagerness. I already knew so much about my dreamer; his thoughts and feelings; his intelligence; his imagination; everything but his identity.

And then, one night, I found myself more than just a spectator. At last, I had made a connection beyond the mere subconscious. In spite of my attempts to hide, the unknown dreamer had spotted me.

The dream was an oddly comforting one; a long, deserted summer beach, with trees almost up to the waterline and the scent of flowers and ripening fruit.

At one end of the beach, a small girl was busy building a sandcastle. *Could she be the dreamer?* I thought.

I moved a little closer. I'd assumed the Aspect of a little red-haired boy – an Aspect which I found both practical as well as nicely unthreatening.

The girl seemed wholly preoccupied with the task in hand; I ventured closer still, keeping in the background of the dream so as not to attract attention. But the girl had seen me. Her gaze was strangely penetrating, and when I tried to shift my ephemeral Aspect, to make myself inconspicuous again, I found that I couldn't. I was caught.

The little girl looked at me. 'Who are you?'

'No one. Nothing.'

'That's not true. I've seen you before. Won't you tell me your name?'

She *must* be the dreamer, I told myself. But like myself, she was lucid; clearly able to exercise control over aspects of her dream – and that included Yours Truly, trapped on a little island of Dream that might at any moment vanish into ephemera as soon as my dreamer chose to awake . . .

Perhaps, despite my precautions, I thought, I hadn't been quite wary enough. I'd relied too much on my camouflage, believing myself invulnerable. And now I was caught between realities, unable to shift, at the mercy of the dark intelligence I'd wooed for so long, and which, whatever else it was, was certainly *not* a little girl.

'Who are *you*?' I asked, to gain time.

'Heidi,' said the little girl. 'Did you see my sandcastle?'

I looked beyond her down the beach. The sun was going down, and the light was suddenly ominous. In its glow, the sandcastle looked even larger than before, and all at once it occurred to me that it looked a lot like Asgard.

I looked a little closer. Yes: there was Odin's hall; the walls; the turrets and bridges and towers and gates. There was my place; and Sigyn's; Idun's garden; Freyja's boudoir; all painstakingly built in sand, with the Rainbow Bridge arching out from the parapet.

The tide had suddenly started to turn. The wind, so clean and fragrant a few moments before, now smelt of mud and seaweed. In the glow of the setting sun, the waves were crested with frills of blood.

Once more I tried to shift my ephemeral Aspect. I was getting a bad feeling about this dream; the bloody light; the turning tide; the Sky Citadel built in sand. But again I found that I could not shift. The dreamer's will was stronger than mine.

I looked up at the sky. It was purple. The waves had reached the outer walls of the sandcastle. The bridge of sand fell almost at once; the battlements might hold longer.

'This is the bit I always like best,' said Heidi, in a bright voice. 'Watching it fall. Don't you agree? Watching as the sea takes it back, grain by grain, until there's nothing left?'

Silently, I nodded. Whoever she was, she had a point.

'Of course, these things aren't made to last,' Heidi went on in a dreamy voice. 'Order and Chaos have their tides. It's futile to resist them.' She looked at me. 'I know who you are. You're Loki, the Trickster.'

I nodded. 'Right. And you're Heid, otherwise known as Gullveig. The Sorceress. The mistress of runes. Cunning, greedy, vengeful. *Big* fan, by the way – those are my favourite qualities.'

She gave me a mischievous smile. Behind the little-girl Aspect she was complex; troubling. And, let's admit it, alluring; alluring as only a demon can be.

'I've heard a lot about you, too,' she said. 'You're clever, ruthless, self-obsessed, narcissistic, disloyal . . .'

I shrugged. She had me there, I thought.

'I've always wanted to meet you,' I said. 'But you're not an easy woman to find.'

Gullveig smiled. 'I was waiting for the right time.'

Interesting. 'Why?' I said.

'I want to offer you a deal.'

A deal. You'd have thought that by that time I would have learnt to read the small print. But after an unknowable time chained to a rock in World Below, I was hardly in a position to haggle. I thought of the Oracle's prophecy and said:

'This deal. Does it involve you freeing me from torment, putting me at the head of a fleet and doing to Asgard what the tide just did to your sandcastle?'

'Kind of,' said Gullveig.

I said: 'I'm in.'

BOOK 4

Twilight

The wolf at Hel's gate howls. The chain
Is broken; Loki's son runs free.
Ragnarók is come at last,
The Aesir's darkest destiny.

The Prophecy of the Oracle

LESSON 1

Heidi

Seriously. That thing I told you in
Book 1 about never trusting anyone?
That.

Lokabrenna

Aᴺᴅ sᴏ I ᴛᴜʀɴᴇᴅ ᴍʏ ᴄᴏᴀᴛ ᴀɢᴀɪɴ. What choice did I have?
The Old Man had abandoned me. The Worlds had unleashed
their dogs on me. And here was the Sorceress, Gullveig-Heid,
offering me a chance to strike back and to regain my place in
Chaos . . .

I would have been a fool to refuse. Anyone would have
taken the deal. Heidi was powerful, and she wanted revenge,
especially on those Vanir who had betrayed her by allying
themselves with Odin. Technically, I was the enemy, but I was
counting on the fact that my desertion from Asgard would find
favour in her eyes. And anyway, I was star-struck. This was the
legendary Gullveig-Heid, first mistress of the runes, for whom
I'd searched the Worlds in vain since Odin had first tricked me
into taking corporeal Aspect.

And the first thing I needed her to do was to release that
corporeal Aspect, currently suffering torment in a cave by the
River Dream. So I took what she offered me, without reading
much of the small print. And awakening now from the dream

state from which she had recruited me, I was so relieved to find myself free of Snakey, the mixing bowl, the chaise-longue rock and my rune-inscribed chains that I never thought to ask her for specific details of – for instance – just *what* had happened to Sigyn, or how I was to be reintroduced into Chaos's fiery fold. Turns out that wasn't the plan at all, but I imagine you've already guessed that. Used and betrayed by one set of friends, I was soon to find myself in virtually the same position with my shiny new demon companions.

In my defence, however, I was experiencing a number of exhilarating new sensations that had temporarily robbed me of my suspicion. Overwhelming gratitude; relief; release; the ecstasy of rubbing my eyes; the joy of drinking water without getting a faceful of venom; my reintroduction to food and drink (though I suspected cake would be off the menu for ever); the astonishing pleasures of bathing – first in cold water, then in warm, then in a multitude of different soaps, oils and various bath products.

Then there was Heidi – alluring, and with a demon's ability to take on any Aspect she (or I) most desired. Now she was golden from head to foot; a ring on every finger; eyes like those of a lynx and hair like waterfalls and rainbows. Tattooed all over in runes of gold, from her fingertips to the soles of her feet, sleek and lithe and wild and perverse and, like Angie of Ironwood, curiously attracted to men with red hair.

So shoot me. I took advantage. Not the wisest move, I'll admit, especially after what happened with Angie, but I'd been underground too long to deny myself the pleasure of a little harmless dalliance. Demon sex was a pleasure I hadn't had for a long time, and now I revelled in it again, as Order and Chaos prepared for war, burning up the winter nights in the fires of our passion.

Meanwhile, on my rock in World Below, a surrogate, an ephemeron made from runes and glamours, suffered torment in my place – just in case Skadi or one of the others came along to check on how I was doing. The ephemeron was not alive in any real sense of the word. It was simply an assemblage of thoughts and images selected by Heidi during my imprisonment, then given just enough substance – not difficult, so near to Dream – to deceive the eyes of the casual observer. Closer investigation, of course, would reveal the deception, but soon that wouldn't matter. War was coming; and before long the Aesir would have more on their hands than dealing with Yours Truly.

The plan was in three stages. One: preparation. Two: subjugation. Three: confrontation. Nice and clean. The first (and rather tedious) stage was actually almost complete, which meant that when I joined Gullveig's camp, the fun was just about to begin.

And it *was* fun – Wildfire, unleashed, bigger and badder than ever. Heidi and I had set up camp at the edge of Ironwood, where we could observe Bif-rost unseen. It was safe; there was plenty of game, and the river Gunnthrà that ran through the wood led straight down into World Below, providing a conduit for all kinds of beings to enter the Worlds through the River Dream.

This was the place from which our army would come, led by Heidi's incantations. Beings of all kinds would be summoned there, from the fears and dreams and tears of the Folk. You see, the human race had become a reservoir of power. Unsuspected by the gods, who still viewed them as little more than a fanbase, the Folk had an almost inexhaustible capacity to dream; to imagine; to conjure up the most intricate, the most explicit, the most enduring of fantasies – all of which the Sorceress could weave into the makings of the most advanced army the Worlds had ever known.

This was what she'd been doing during the years that I had searched for her. Living half in and half out of Dream, she knew how to surf its waters; how to coax them with her mind; how to ride the rapids that would have destroyed a lesser being. Gullveig-Heid was the most powerful manipulator of dreams that the Worlds had ever known, and it was through Dream that she planned to bring about the subjugation of the Worlds.

Of course, I'd be a key part of that. I knew Asgard's defences. I had lived with the gods for so long that I knew all their weaknesses, both strategic and personal. For instance, I knew that if we introduced certain elements into the fray (the World Serpent, or the Fenris Wolf, for instance), then members of Asgard's key personnel could be counted upon to drop everything, to leave their position, however strategically valuable, and to confront the enemy on whatever ground we chose. Timing is so important. And we had the advantage there; *we* could choose when the war would start, and how it would continue.

Oh, she'd been planning this for decades. I'd thought *my* dreams of vengeance grandiose, but next to hers mine were just the fleeting dreams of a sleeping cat. Gullveig had it all worked out: over the years she had entered the dreams of Ice Folk and Rock Folk, manipulating their chieftains; whispering hatred into their ears so that now they were almost ready to strike. She had entered the dreams of the insane; the murderous; the unhappy; the lost. Now all were converging on Ironwood – Ice Folk; Rock Folk; Tunnel Folk from underground; werewolves and witches and half-blood demons and bastard Firefolk from whatever little empire they'd managed to build during the reign of Order – while the unsuspecting Folk, Odin's beloved worshippers, assembled their warriors in the foothills and plains of Inland, driven by instincts as powerful as those of a nest of wild bees, swarming under the influence of some new, rapacious Queen . . .

Of course I was dazzled. Who wouldn't be? She was the golden Queen; I was the King. Of course, a beehive *has* no king, but I wasn't exactly following logic at the time. Heidi showered me with praise; worshipped me with her body; lavished me with extravagant gifts and placed me on a fire-ship at the head of a battle fleet that would launch, not across the One Sea, but through Dream, Death and Damnation itself.

That fire-ship. It was beautiful. Slim as a sword, and as deadly, it could glide through anything – air, or stone, or water. Its sail was like St Sepulchre's Fire; its skeleton crew was tireless. (And by 'skeleton crew' I mean a crew of actual skeletons, coaxed into life by a cantrip of *Naudr* and press-ganged into my service.) And when I was tired of playing with it, I could fold it up like a pocket knife and carry it wherever I went, or moor it in Dream, where it would wait patiently to be summoned.

As for the rest of my demon fleet, these were not *ships*, precisely. Instead they were *vessels* for my army, a motley assemblage of half-bloods, renegade demons, the undead and assorted ephemeral creatures, all summoned by Heidi through Dream and sworn to my allegiance. The creatures called me General and worshipped me in their slavish way, as I cavorted with Heidi, eating venison, drinking mead and looking forward to Ragnarók and the End of Everything.

> *Now comes the final reckoning.*
> *Now come the folk of Netherworld.*
> *Now comes the dragon of darkness, Death—*

This was the only part of the deal that caused me any anxiety. The Dragon of Darkness – aka Lord Surt – finally taking a physical Aspect to enter the Worlds and to cleanse them of that stubborn intruder, Life. Not what you'd call a happy thought. Heidi's assurances that, when the time came, he would recognize our role in the triumph of Chaos and take us back into the primal Fire all made perfect sense – at least, whenever she was around. When I was alone, I had a tendency to feel rather less certain about the whole thing. I wasn't even entirely certain that I *wanted* to go back permanently to my primary Aspect. I'd found too many things to enjoy in this corrupt, confusing world of conflict and sensations. I'd realized that one of the things I enjoyed most was challenging Order and breaking rules – and how in the Worlds could I do that if there was no Order to challenge? Even assuming that it was possible that I could be taken back into the heart of Chaos, that my radically altered being could even survive in that element . . .

Did I really *want* that? Had I *ever* wanted it?

Still, to Hel with the future. The present was well worth enjoying. This was the life, I told myself; wine, women, a vehicle suited to my personal requirements and a chance to thumb my nose at the gods. War was trembling in the air like a breath of springtime, and I could feel the Chaos in me leaping up to greet it. What if Surt *was* on his way? Eat, drink and be merry, I thought, for who knows what tomorrow will bring?

All right. Call it denial. I was enjoying myself at last. For the first time, I was a real god, and maybe – just maybe – it went to my head. But can you blame me, after all, with everything I'd been through? I was in my element. I had my fire-ship, Gullveig-Heid and an army of fanatical half-demon worshippers. What more could I want? I thought. What could possibly go wrong?

LESSON 2

Angie

One woman; trouble. Two women –
Chaos.

Lokabrenna

Acording to the oracle, it all happened in only a few
stanzas. In fact it took months for Asgard's folk to meet our
folk in battle. During that time, the General barricaded himself
inside, conferring with Mimir's Head and holding endless talks
with his people, as my new-found allies and I continued to set
the stage for the invasion of the Middle Worlds and its subjugation, an inch at a time.

The first hint of trouble came about a month before our
final campaign. We had a thousand fire-ships waiting to
attack through Dream. To the north of Ironwood, the Ice
People awaited our call, living under deerskin tents; and the
Rock Folk had taken the eastern side, adopting as their refuge
a labyrinth of limestone caves at the foot of the mountains.
Meanwhile, the Folk were assembling; little bands of warriors,
at first – no more than a few hundred at a time, armed with
swords and axes and shields and sometimes just farm imple-
ments – drifting in towards the south-west. There had been a
few skirmishes, but nothing more. The Folk were still uncer-
tain. Rumours of an impending war; omens in the winter sky;

nightmares; sudden deaths; ominous flights of migratory birds
– all premonitions of bad things to come for Mankind and the
Middle Worlds.

It was rumoured that Angrboda was in hiding somewhere
in Ironwood, leading a pack of werewolves that preyed on the
Folk that were gathering in numbers on the outskirts of the
forest. I didn't investigate the rumours. Angie wasn't my biggest fan, not after the way the gods had dealt with Fenris, and I
was in no hurry to introduce her to Heidi.

That's why when she arrived one night, unannounced, demanding to see me, I felt a shiver of apprehension. I was in my
tent; a marquee rather bigger than Odin's hall, inscribed all over
with fire-runes, draped in silk and tapestry and carpeted with
wolf skins. I was just opening a bottle of wine and listening to
the sounds of the night when in she came, looking warlike, followed by the harassed-looking demon guard I'd posted to avoid
just such encounters as this.

'I'm sorry, General,' said the guard. 'She just—'

'I can imagine,' I said. When the Witch of Ironwood comes
to pay a visit, good luck to the poor idiot who shows her to the
waiting room. I dismissed the guard with an absent wave.

'Angie! Love of my life!' I said.

The Witch of Ironwood has always favoured a youthful, innocent Aspect quite out of line with her true character, which
was as perverse as they come, and today she looked about
sixteen, fetchingly clad in black leather; wide-eyed under a
thick line of kohl; dreadlocks plaited with silver thread. Most
sixteen-year-olds wouldn't have been carrying a pair of perfectly matched double-bladed swords, curved as sweet as a
baby's smile and practically singing with sharpness – but then,
Angie was never typical.

'Is it my birthday?' I enquired.

She ignored that and instead looked around with interest
at my quarters. Noting the silken draperies, the embroidered
cushions on the ground, the candles, the furs, the food and

drink, she raised a bejewelled eyebrow.

'I suppose you think you've got it made,' she said, sitting down on a cushion. 'All this and the prospect of carnage, too. You must be in hog's heaven.'

I smiled at her. 'What's wrong with that? I've had an Age of pain, discomfort, humiliation and thwarted desire. I thought perhaps it might be time to experience some of the nicer sensations before the Worlds come to an end.'

'And *then* what?' Angie said. 'You think Chaos will take you back after everything you've done?'

I had to admit she had me there. There's a special antechamber of Dream reserved for renegade demons, and I wasn't in a hurry to see it for myself.

I said: 'Maybe, maybe not. In any case, I'm not planning to die. In fact, I have it on good authority that I'm going to bring down Asgard.'

'Good authority? You mean the Oracle,' said Angie, with a curl of the lip.

'It hasn't been wrong yet,' I said.

'But it hasn't told you *everything*.' Angie helped herself to wine. 'And neither has your new friend, that little madam Gullveig-Heid.'

Ah. I thought it might come to that.

'Feeling jealous, are we?' I said.

'Not on your life,' said Angie. 'I'm only keeping in touch with you for the sake of the children. *Way* to look after our son, by the way. I let you have him for the weekend and before I know it he's chained underground, awaiting Last Times and stinking of mead.'

'Ah. That.'

'Yes. *That*. If you hadn't messed things up, we wouldn't be having this conversation, and I wouldn't be joining forces with Pandaemonium's most poisonous blonde.'

'You're joining forces with Heidi?' I said. Well, I could see the advantages. Angie was the mother of Hel, which made her a force to be reckoned with. But why would Angie agree to the deal? 'Ah. Fenris.' It all made sense. 'So, Heidi promised to free him, did she? In exchange for your oath?'

She sniffed. 'I had no choice. He's my son. Besides, she freed *you*, didn't she?'

'Yes.'

'*That* was nice. So what does she want?'

'The usual. To bring down the gods, take over the Worlds, get bloody satisfaction. In fact, I've rarely met a woman whose tastes and ambitions were closer to mine – except perhaps for you, my dear.'

'Quite the philanthropist, in fact,' said Angie.

'Well, I wouldn't go *that* far,' I said. 'But Heidi's been very good to me.'

'And she's given you no cause to believe she might not be telling you everything?'

'Well, no,' I said. 'In fact, her general lack of guile and dishonesty may be the only flaw I can find in an otherwise perfect package.'

Angie sniffed. 'What about your wife?'

'My *wife*? What about her?'

Good question, I thought. In fact, it was the first time in months that I'd remembered Sigyn. I know it sounds bad. But I never pretended to be the ideal husband, or anything. Besides, when you're King of the Worlds, facing Last Times and surrounded by adoring lackeys and loose women, you tend to have more on your mind than flannelette nighties and fruitcake. But now Angie came to mention it, I realized that I'd never asked just what had become of my loving spouse when I'd been rescued from World Below, or indeed why she hadn't tried to pursue me into Ironwood with promises of apple pie.

'Because they bumped her,' Angie said, answering the question.

'*What?*'

'Obviously, your little friend didn't want her reporting

home. Quicker and far more efficient to simply get her out of the way.' She looked at me. 'Are you all right? You're suddenly looking kind of sick.'

'I'm just fine,' I told her.

And I was – it was simply that it had come as a surprise. The thought that Sigyn was really dead – sweet, harmless Sigyn; undoubtedly mad, with her passion for furry animals and her almost infinite capacity for baby-talk – was, like her fruitcake, almost impossible to digest. And the knowledge that Heidi had ordered her death without as much as a second thought, or even a word to Yours Truly . . .

'Are you sure you're fine?' Angie said. 'For a minute there I thought perhaps you were feeling responsible.'

I shook my head, which at that moment didn't feel entirely clear.

It was absurd, I told myself. After all, we were planning the End of the Worlds; Ragnarók; the Twilight of the Popular Crowd. What did I *think* would happen when Asgard fell? That all the survivors would kiss and make up over tea and little sandwiches? Of *course* the gods were going to die. If I was lucky, I might not be among them. But to succumb to sentiment at such a time as this was wholly inappropriate. And as for feeling responsible . . .

'You can't make a fruitcake without breaking eggs. I mean – you can't make an *omelette*.'

'What?' Angie said.

I tried again. 'Collateral damage, that's what it was. Choose your own cliché. Whatever. In any case, it wasn't my fault.'

'That goes without saying,' said Angie.

'So why tell me at all?' I said.

She gave that little-girl smile of hers. 'You may think Gullveig needs you,' she said. 'But as soon as your usefulness runs out, you'll be on the pile like the rest of them. I don't care if you trust me or not. Just don't go turning your back on her.'

When Angie had gone, I thought for some time about what

she'd said. Perhaps she was right, I told myself. Perhaps I hadn't been careful enough in my dealings with Heidi. Perhaps I'd let my pursuit of physical pleasures as well as my desire for revenge get in the way of self-interest. After all, what did I really know about her? What did she know of the Oracle? And what kind of deal, if any, did she have going with Chaos?

I went back to the prophecy. It wasn't much help. Heidi wasn't mentioned by name, although I remembered this couplet:

In Ironwood, the Witch awaits.
The Fenris wolf will have his day.

At first, because of the reference to Fenny, I'd assumed that the Witch was Angie. But now I began to ask myself if Heidi wasn't a better fit. If so, what was she waiting for?

Of course, I had no answers. All I had was the prophecy and Angie's unfounded suspicions – which could have been due to jealousy, or simple malice, who could tell?

And so I went on with business, telling myself I could always get out if things started to smell bad. But by the time I realized how, once more, I'd been manipulated, there was nothing left to do but run across the burning bridge towards whatever awaited me . . .

LESSON 3

Darkness

It's a crazy, god-eat-god world.

Lokabrenna

No one sees clearly during a war. History gives perspective. Perhaps that's why it took me so long to understand what had happened: our betrayal by Mimir's Head; my betrayal by Gullveig. And the role of Surt, of course; the pendulum of Chaos swinging back like a headsman's axe to cut us down like a field of grain. Oh, it was epic. Rousing stuff. Rivers of blood; rivers of knives; operatic feats of bravery and self-sacrifice.

The Oracle puts it this way:

> *I speak as I must. Three rivers converge*
> *Upon the gods in their domain.*
> *A river of knives from the east; from the north*
> *And south, twin rivers of ice and flame.*

In fact, that wasn't far from the truth. We'd placed the Ice Folk and Rock Folk strategically on the northern and eastern sides of Ida's plain, mostly as a diversion while the real business continued in the realm of Dream and to the south in Ironwood, shielded from sight by Heidi's runes.

Meanwhile, the Folk were still gathering, now in greater

numbers. Some had come from the Outlands on ships; some had ridden down from the north and from across the Ridings. They were disorganized, but they were many, clustering like ants around the edges of Ironwood; building their camps; lighting their fires; looking anxiously at the sky.

We made no move against them as yet. We had bigger fish to fry. Gullveig's plan was intricate; everything meticulously arranged to coincide at just the right time. Over the months, her minions had been placed in discreetly commanding positions all over the Middle Worlds, ready to act on her orders, and as soon as she gave the word, her plans had been set into motion; beginning with my liberation, Angie's recruitment, and the freeing of my son, the Fenris Wolf, who celebrated his coming-of-age by seeking out his erstwhile friends, the demon wolves Skól and Haiti, and conspiring with them to bring down the Sun and Moon chariots to plunge the Worlds into darkness . . .

That was the first blow. That darkness. Friend of outlaws everywhere; builder of fears and nightmares. In the uproar that ensued, the World Serpent thrashed up out of the sea, demon wolves overran the plains, and the hordes of Netherworld, at Heidi's command, began to surge up from Chaos's realm to overrun the Middle Worlds.

Some attacked the Folk through Dream, sending madness and violence. The rest came naturally, as it always does in times of crisis. Communities broke up; families turned against each other; opportunists took the chance to enrich themselves at the expense of their neighbours. People tend to blame Chaos whenever anything goes wrong, but in fact most of the time Chaos doesn't need to intervene. The Folk don't need any help when it comes to massacring each other. You name it, they did it – murder; rape; the sacrifice of infants – all the time blaming the sunless sky, when the darkness was already there, in their hearts.

And of course, they blamed the gods. That was the part I

enjoyed the most; that the Folk, who had worshipped Odin's crew in such a fawning, uncritical way should, at the first sign of Last Times, turn against him in mindless rage, razing his temples, toppling his standing stones, cutting down his sacred trees, cursing his name and all his works and turning instead to whatever crazed comfort was offered them.

All right, so the end result wasn't what you'd call advantageous to Yours Truly. But in this crazy god-eat-god world, you have to learn to move with the times. And when times are bad, when darkness comes, people always go back to fire. Fire never goes out of style. In time of war, in time of fear, fire is what unites us, huddled together around the glow of something warm and dangerous. Predictably, many of the Folk turned away from the gods of Asgard and started to worship me instead. They burnt their books to keep themselves warm; made firewalls against the night. Once more I had a new name – Loki Light-Bringer – and finally, I had some respect.

Up in Asgard, the General watched the collapse of the Middle Worlds. His birds were never far away, keeping watch, reporting home. In spite of the absence of Sun and Moon, I knew that he could see me. I bit my thumb at him from afar, grinning to myself. And then, one night . . .

Well, of course, it *might* have been day. By then there was no difference. In any case, they arrived at my tent in human, rather than raven form; Odin's Spirit and Odin's mind, finally wanting to make a deal.

I'd only seen them in their human Aspects a handful of times over the years. Odin's messengers favoured bird form, and even now their Aspects were more raven than human; both dark-haired and golden-eyed and with a tendency to crow when they got excited. Hugin was male, Munin female; other than that, and the white streak in her hair, they could easily have been twins. Both wore a great deal of jewellery: bracelets that jangled as they moved; rings in the shape of birds' skulls on their long, dark fingers.

Hugin was the most talkative; Munin seemed the most alert. Both were nervous, and rightly so; Ironwood was no place for them now, not with Fenris running wild and my army of Firefolk and half-blood demons so close by. But I guessed they had come to talk, and although I had no intention of cutting the Old Man any more slack than he had cut me, I wouldn't have missed this chance for the Worlds.

I shot them my friendliest smile. 'Come in.'

They followed me into the tent and sat down on the cushions. There was a dish of crystallized fruit standing on one of the tables. Munin *crawk*ed and took a pear, eating it deftly with small, nervous bites.

'And to what do I owe this visit?' I said. 'Is the Old Man lonely? Could it be that he's having second thoughts about throwing his brother onto the pile? And if that's the case, then why didn't he call by in person?'

'We speak for the Auld Man,' said Hugin, in his hoarse voice. 'Our words are his words.'

Munin *crawk*ed agreement and started on an orange.

'He wants ye to know it's not too late. We can still avert the prophecy.'

'Avert it? Why would I want to?' I said.

'Because ye want tae survive,' he said, 'and the only way tae do that is tae go against the Oracle.'

I had to laugh. 'So basically, what you're telling me is that Odin wants me back?'

'Aye. On certain terms.'

'What?' My laughter redoubled. '*Terms?* Has that eye of his gone blind? Those are rivers of steel, ice and flame, not three strings of tinsel. And if he thinks he can just say the word and I'll come crawling back to his side . . .'

'He thinks the Oracle planned all this. That Gullveig made a deal with him while he was in the Vanir camp. A deal in which she promised him revenge against the Aesir.'

'How very creative of Odin,' I said. 'But how could Gullveig have possibly known that Mimir would one day need revenge? When he arrived in the Vanir camp, everything was peachy. There was no cause for him to believe that his loving nephew was planning to sacrifice him to his ambition.'

'She's a Seeress,' Hugin said. 'She too may have made a prophecy.'

Ouch. That was too close to what Angie had already hinted at.

I shrugged. 'Never trust an Oracle. Doesn't prove a thing, I'm afraid.'

'The Auld Man says to tell ye that she's using you to get to him. And that when Surt crosses over, she's planning to use you to buy herself a place on the side of Chaos.'

I grinned. 'Is that the best he can do? The Old Man must be desperate. If I were him, I'd concentrate on choosing the outfit he wants to be buried in. That is, if there's anything left to bury when we've finished with him.'

Hugin shook his dark head. 'You're making a mistake,' he said. 'Surt will never take ye back. But Odin will, if ye help him now. It's not too late.'

I grinned again. 'I get it. This is a ploy to make me laugh myself into a fatal seizure. Nice try, Odin. But in this case, you're not paranoid. Everyone *is* out to get you. And when you fall from that parapet, the sound you'll be hearing as you go down will be me, laughing my head off.'

Crawk, said Munin morosely, helping herself to a pineapple.

'Does she not talk at *all*?' I said.

'Not much,' said Hugin. 'But what she says is usually worth listening to. And she says that the only way to stop the End of the Worlds is to combat Chaos with Chaos, which means to set free will against determinism. If we believe the Oracle, free will is merely an illusion, and all our actions were written in runes that were preordained from the beginning of time. But if we take matters into our own hands, then we can write our *own* runes, remake our own reality.'

'She said all that in a *crawk*?' I said.

'More or less,' said Hugin.

'Well, thanks for the offer,' I said. 'But I'm enjoying this too much. Tell him I'll see him at Ragnarók. Tell him to watch out for werewolves.'

After the ravens had flown away, I opened a bottle of wine and got drunk. Damn the Old Man. Damn them all. Because he'd got to me, of course, in spite of all he'd put me through. When Angie had tried to warn me, I'd dismissed her suspicions. But now they returned, and suddenly everything made sense to me. That Gullveig had worked with the Oracle – or perhaps even with Chaos – from the very beginning; that she had used Mimir's Head to manipulate Odin; to summon me; to bring about the end of the gods; and that she was planning to give me up to Surt along with all the rest of them as soon my usefulness had run out.

A cycle of betrayal, beginning and ending with Gullveig-Heid. Gullveig, who first came to Asgard to show off her demonic skills; who provoked Odin's envy and Mimir's death; and who then sent Mimir's Head back to Asgard, knowing that it contained all the knowledge Odin needed to plant the seeds of his own downfall.

Did she plan it this way from the start? Did Chaos put her up to it? Was it all part of a greater plan – one that ensured that from the first, Chaos held the winning cards? That sinking feeling of having been had – that feeling of belated realization as the pieces of the complex puzzle fall into place *just* at the time when you realize there's no going back . . .

There *has* to be a word for that, right? If not, I'll have to invent one. *Gullible.* I think that's it. It even has part of her name in it. And who *was* Gullveig, anyway? None of the Vanir remembered when she had first appeared on the scene. Was she one of them at all, or was she something different – an older being, from another place?

I speak now of the Sorceress,
Gullveig-Heid, thrice-burned, thrice-born,
Seeress, mistress of the Fire
Vengeful, bloated with desire.

And there she was, in the prophecy Mimir made to Odin. I hadn't paid much attention before, concentrating as I had on future, rather than past events. But there she was, in one stanza; Wildfire's mistress, out for revenge – but against whom? Odin? The gods? Or was this revenge for a *future* crime – a crime that would only come about *because of* her intervention?

It made my head hurt just to think about it. But could it be that all of this had been an attempt by Gullveig to lure me out of Chaos, to use my betrayal to bring down the gods, then to take my place by Lord Surt in the Aspect of Burning Ambition, surpassing even Wildfire in sheer destructiveness and guile?

Oh, gods. Could it be?

Er . . .

Yes, it made perfect sense. Really, it was beautiful. And yet I could not bring myself to go back to the General. Call it pride – that was always my downfall – but if it meant playing the Oracle's game, allowing Heidi to use me, even dying in battle, or worse – then so be it. I was ready. All those things were preferable to admitting that Odin might have been right.

And so I got bleakly, blackly drunk, and awoke with a shocking hangover to find that Heidi had finally given the word to move the troops out of Ironwood, onto the plain of Ida.

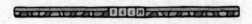

LESSON 4

Ida

When the going gets tough, choose your cliché.

Lokabrenna

WE WAITED THERE for nine days, making our camp on the open plain. It was cold; the sun's absence had brought on a fierce, harsh winter. Frost scoured the land; black winds blew; clouds of ash and smoke and dust mingled with the driving snow. Above us, Asgard's citadel looked like a cradle of brilliance, all shrouded in Northlights and shining with runes, with Bif-rost, the Rainbow Bridge, arching from the parapet.

It made me feel almost sorry that we had to bring it down. It was the last, most beautiful thing left in that dying, tenebrous world. But it was too late for regrets. We were engaged; the die was cast; the Gunnthrà was breached; choose your cliché.

This was the last part of Gullveig's plan: the final confrontation. The Ice People stood on the northern side; the Rock Folk to the east. To the west, the Folk still stood – or at least, what was left of them after Phase Two – ragged, hungry and afraid, but stubbornly holding to their gods. From the south, from Ironwood, came the rest of our army. Ten thousand strong; magnificent; spreading out across the plain in open defiance of Asgard. There were demons and trolls; werewolves and hags;

goblins and ephemera and human monsters and the undead. I had my fire-ship, my fleet to navigate between the Worlds; I had my crew of skulls and bones. And yes, I was fabulous. Even with the knowledge that Gullveig would betray me, that the Worlds would plunge into the abyss and that the best I could hope for was eternal oblivion, I was prepared to go out on a high.

Gullveig had stayed in Ironwood to supervise our remaining troops as they passed through from Dream and beyond. I stayed to shiver on the plain, enclosed within concentric rings of torches, braziers and campfires. Fenris came to join me, in wolf form; monosyllabic as always, but bristling with excitement at the prospect of a battle. His friends, Skól and Haiti, were there too, and they ran around as a threesome, snapping at shadows, devouring things and generally running amok.

Not great company for Yours Truly, who was getting restless. I'd waited enough. I wanted to fight. I hated hanging around like this, discussing terms and strategy. I wanted the cleanness of carnage. I wanted *certainties*. Is that so bad?

Looking up, I saw Odin's birds outlined against the battlements. Since their visit, they had not tried to contact me again. I found myself feeling obscurely resentful for this, as if Odin had abandoned me for the second time.

I asked myself, if he'd wanted me to come back home to Asgard, surely he would have asked me himself instead of sending those stupid birds? And, having failed to persuade me then, why had he given up so fast?

Damn him, I thought, and helped myself to another bottle of our dwindling stock of wine. There was no point in trying to save any of it; after all, the Worlds were due to end in less than nine days. Might as well end in a party.

Ten hours later, hung-over and feeling rather sorry for myself, I was rather regretting the decision. King of the Worlds I might be, but impromptu regurgitation and a thumping headache were not among the sensations I'd first signed up for in this Aspect. I found myself sorely missing my pure and elemental form, and wishing I could somehow go back, nameless, blameless, into Chaos.

No chance of that now. I was marked. All I could hope for was the chance to bring down as many of my enemies as possible – and, hopefully, Mimir's Head – before going out in flames. As for Heidi, I promised myself that if I could rob her of the chance of handing me over to Lord Surt, then I might even die happy. I had the germ of a plan – not great, but all I could think of at the time – and if it worked, I told myself that maybe, just *maybe* . . .

But I'm getting ahead of myself. That came nine days later.

I left my tent and my circle of fires and walked out alone to the edge of the plain, where the icy winds scoured the frozen ground and the snow was like iron filings. Even in my thick furs, I was cold; my feet were numb; my hands were claws; the air in my lungs was shards of steel. Across the plain, I could see my army; my hordes of ephemera; my legions of undead; my snakes and trolls and werewolves; my ships and vessels of dark fire.

Above me, Asgard. Defiant; doomed; flying its colours across the sky. I wondered if the Old Man was watching me from that throne of his. Then I stood in the wilderness and wished that I could see the stars, but the light from Asgard's battlements and the glow of the fires on Ida's plain had made them all but invisible.

One star still shone out. *My* star – the Dogstar – still made its mark. Then, as I watched, a bracket of smoke rose up from the plain and engulfed it.

Darkness beckoned. I had to obey. Call it Destiny, if you like, or predetermination, but my path was written in runes of stone, even though I knew it would lead to darkness. The Old Man had known even before he sent his birds that I would not yield any more than he would himself. The Aesir would fall. Asgard would fall. The Vanir would fall, and I . . .

Well. In any case, it wasn't my fault. I was as much a victim of this as any of the others. If the gods had trusted me; if Odin had swallowed his pride; if I hadn't listened to the Oracle's thrice-damned prophecy . . .

In his eyrie above Bif-rost, I knew Odin was watching me. I gave him the finger. *Damn him. Damn the lot of them.* Because I could have stopped it all, and the bastard knew it. But even so, his colossal pride prevented him from asking for help; instead he'd sent those ridiculous birds with his *terms* and his ultimatum, even though he needed me so badly that it was killing him.

All right, then. Let him fall. Let the stubborn old man fall. I wouldn't shed a tear for him. Let him fall, and let his last, desperate, dying moments be infused with sorrow and regret and the knowledge that his downfall was all because of his monstrous pride.

He'd driven me to it, I told myself. Hadn't he?

Hadn't he?

LESSON 5

Settling Scores

There goes free will.

Lokabrenna

O<small>N THE NINTH DAY</small>, we attacked. Nine is the perfect number. Nine Worlds: nine days, nine nights till the end of the Worlds. There is a curious poetry to such an equation. Nine days, nine nights. And on the ninth day, everyone died.

Everyone who matters, that is.

Of course, the sun didn't rise that day. Nevertheless, we followed tradition and attacked more or less at dawn. The Ice and Rock Folk launched a two-pronged assault to the north and east of Asgard, while the rest of our army gathered to wipe up the rest of the Folk and, as Heidi's people moved up out of Ironwood to challenge Bif-rost, I, in Wildfire Aspect, at the helm of my fire-ship, led my fleet across the plain to scour the land in a thin red line.

Finally, I knew what to do. I was in my element. Lighting up the darkness in glorious red-gold, deadly bursts; eating through wood and bone and flesh; clashing joyfully on steel. Within an hour, the snowfields of Ida were nothing but a grid of flame, and Bif-rost's gleaming parapet was alive with capering figures. Wolves howled; witches flew; ephemera surged out of Dream to take any shape they chose to take from the fears of those who assailed us. The gods were outnumbered ten thousand to one. Ice Folk here; Rock Folk there; Wildfire in the middle. And on the Bridge, our champions, howling their defiance and rage at the beleaguered Aesir; Fenris, the Wolf; Jormungand, lolling in his sheath of slime; and a host of vile ephemera dragged from the bed of the River Dream.

The air was black with smoke and ash; the plain of Ida slick with blood. Of course, in my Wildfire Aspect, I could not hear the blood in my veins; or smell the stench of carnage; or see the millions of ephemera flying like moths towards the Bridge; or taste the salt of sweat on my tongue; or feel the fear in the back of my throat like an animal trying to get out; or hear the howl of battle like the voice of ten thousand winds . . .

But there was carnage; delirium; joy – and a kind of purity. It had been such a long time since I'd last experienced the thrill of unbridled destruction, untrammelled by conscience, fear or guilt or any of those other feelings with which Odin had corrupted me. For the first time in an Age, I was free, and I meant to enjoy it to the full.

I launched my fire-ship at the Bridge. It cast a bloody pall across the plain. Cutting through Worlds like a razor, slashing between Death, Dream and beyond, releasing fragments of Chaos into the charged and rapturous air. All that stood between Asgard and us was that Bridge; cloaked in Northlights; gleaming like eternity.

And now, a figure came to stand halfway across its narrow expanse. Odin in full Aspect; spear in hand; colours flying. Sleipnir stood by him, in giant Aspect, his eight legs spanning the sky like a spider's web; a nimbus of flame around them both gave them a twin corona. I had to admit that at that moment there was something magnificent in the Old Man; something noble and melancholy that might *almost* have touched my heart – that is, if I had one. As it was, I dropped my Wildfire Aspect, the better to enjoy the scene about to unfurl in front of me. The noise of the battle fell silent. All eyes turned to the Rainbow

Bridge.

> *Now Odin comes to face the foe.*
> *Against the Fenris wolf he stands.*
> *He fights; he falls. Need I say more?*

The verse was as clear as Mimir's well, but still, I didn't believe it. Odin must have had plenty of time to study the Oracle's small print; to tease the weft of the prophecy into some kind of a safety net. I *knew* him. He wouldn't go gently; and although Fenris was powerful, a part of me expected – feared – that Odin's guile might still win through.

Behind me came an eerie lull as the hordes of Chaos waited. I watched him from the prow of my ship; naked; in human Aspect. Now I could feel the fire at my back; the chill in the air; the smoke in my lungs. All kinds of sensations flooded me – triumph; admiration . . .

Hope?

He looked at me from the parapet, his one eye filled with blue fire. And then he raised his battle-spear and launched it at the fire-ship.

Was he aiming at me? Who knows? If so, he missed his target. I saw the missile coming; swore; slipped back into Wildfire Aspect. The spear, with its shaft of laddered runes, passed right through the fire-ship and struck the fiery plain below in an icy eruption of glam. He took another step forward and slowly drew his mindsword.

'Fenris, are you ready?' he said.

There came a ripple from the ranks. The Fenris Wolf came forward. Fenris, the Devourer; thirty feet from nose to tail: fangs as long as a man's arm; fearless as hunger incarnate. For a moment, Old Man and Wolf faced each other in silence. I'd resumed my human Aspect to watch; now I felt the hairs on my neck stand up like a hedge of upraised spears. Behind me, all Chaos was watching; even the dying took notice. We all knew that something legendary was about to happen. And then . . .

They came together like drawn swords; their giant shadows leaping out against the cloak of the Northlights. Below, on the plain, the other wolves howled in unison, a chilling sound. Above them, eight-legged Sleipnir spun his web of runelight.

They fought. From Asgard's battlements, familiar figures watched the fight, their colours flaring – blue, red, gold. All my erstwhile companions: Thor; Frey; Týr; Njörd; Honir; Aegir; Heimdall. All of them watching in silence as Allfather battled the Fenris Wolf with the mounting desperation of a man who knows he is destined to lose.

It wasn't an elegant combat. The Old Man had his glam, his runes and his stubborn will to fight. The wolf had cunning and savage strength as well as his mother's protection. Both were bloodied and tired and torn; their breath plumed pale against the night; below them, Ida's plain was scorched and spackled with cantrips and broken runes.

But in the end, the Old Man was no match for the wolf's brutal cunning and vigour. Bleeding in two dozen places, he fell to one knee, and the wolf closed in to tear out his throat in a single bite.

But just as Fenris opened his jaws to howl his victory at the night, there came another figure onto the Rainbow Bridge.

It was Thor, with Mjølnir. His fiery tread shook the Bridge and brought stones tumbling from Asgard's battlements as, in his rage, he hurled himself at the Fenris Wolf, slamming violently into him and sending both of them hurtling off the edge of the parapet and into the thick of the enemy, who scattered to avoid them like crows at a handful of firecrackers.

Pieces of the Bridge showered down. Thor in full Aspect was far too much for such a delicate structure to take, and the walkway, already compromised by the assault, began to unravel, the thousands of runes that made up its length dispersing into the smoky air. Soon, it would be gone, leaving no means of escape for the gods and opening the way for my fleet.

Meanwhile, on the ground, the Thunderer and the Fenris Wolf were locked in mortal combat. For a moment, Thor had been stunned by the fall, and I'd hoped the wolf would finish him off; but then he grasped Mjølnir, and suddenly the fight was on. Accuracy wasn't Thor's strong suit, but he had strength to make up for it. Mjølnir flashed in his hand; the Wolf sprang back, snarling and baring his giant teeth.

For a time, they circled; Fenris dodging the hammer blows, Thor flailing at the enemy. The great hammer smashed into the plain, opening huge craters of fire wherever it struck; reducing flesh to cinders; steel to shrapnel; bone to dust. Wherever he struck, the Thunderer left a trail of carnage; fusing even the rocks to glass. At last, a blow connected, smashing the spine of my monstrous son, who died there on the battlefield, thrashing and snarling his hatred. One more for the Oracle.

Meanwhile, Thor was making his way across the plain to-wards my ship, using his hammer like a flail, cutting us down like ripe corn.

From afar, I heard his voice. *'Loki! You're next!'*

But he never reached me. My second son, monstrous Jormungand, had noticed the Thunderer's approach. Moving slickly across the plain, levelling troops with his powerful stench, the World Serpent now moved in on Thor, massive jaws flexing in slime and steel.

Thor saw him coming and turned to fight, but by then the snake had already half ingested him, drawing him into that giant maw as if he were a melon seed.

I said: *That's my boy*, or something close.

But Thor had Mjølnir, and Jormungand had only his mass of foul blubber. The mighty hammer struck three times, even as Thor stood wedged inside the monster's throat, its venom cascading over him as he sent the hammer hurtling through the back of the monster's head.

Jormungand gave a convulsive swallow. Thor hung on for dear life. And then, as I watched, the Thunderer staggered free of the Serpent's jaws, and Jormungand, dying and out of control, whipped the still half-frozen ground into a lake of mud and gore before sliding beneath the surface.

From Asgard's distant parapet came a cheer of victory. But the victory was brief. Thor took nine steps away from the place where Jormungand had breathed his last. Then, overwhelmed by the monster's venom, the Thunderer collapsed and died, just as the Oracle had prophesied.

There goes free will, I told myself.

After that, all Hel broke loose.

LESSON 6

Settling Scores, II

So what's the worst that could happen?

Lokabrenna

Having seen their two greatest heroes undone, the remaining Aesir and Vanir gave up any thought of strategy. They fought where they stood; on Asgard's walls, besieged from all sides by the multitude. Some of our troops had crossed the Bridge and were already chipping away at the battlements, unravelling the thousands of runes that made up Asgard's gleaming walls. Some attacked from the sky, as birds, or flying snakes, or dragons; some swarmed up from Ida's depths, clinging to the rock face; some attacked directly from Dream.

Bif-rost was seconds from falling, scattering in bright, glassy shards onto the battlefield. My fire-fleet stood ready to cross; arching brightly into the sky, consuming everything it touched.

I lost my sense of direction; in the turmoil of fire and smoke I caught glimpses of my once-companions, their shadows monstrous against the sky: Freyja in her Crone Aspect, slicing into the ephemera with a viciousness that came naturally; Týr, whose missing hand had been replaced by a gauntlet of glamours, reaping the crowds with his mindsword; Frey, who could have used his own sword if he hadn't given it away, flinging runes into the plain; Sif, in her Warrior Aspect, almost as fearsome as Thor himself, screaming revenge and murder.

I have to admit, they were good. With my help, my loyalty, they might even have survived the onslaught. *That* was what hurt me most, I guess; the knowledge that with my help, we could have beaten the prophecy. We could have held Asgard. We could have won. And in the heat of the battle, with fire to the left and ice to the right, and smoke and fumes and glamours and blood painting their own dark rainbow across the sky, Your Humble Narrator was suddenly seized with a kind of clarity.

I looked up at our battlements, now crumbling beneath the assault. I looked up at Bif-rost, its bright curve sagging with a legion's weight. Once more assuming my Wildfire form, I left my fire-ship and raced across the bloody battlefield, leaving a trail of fire in my wake, and leapt onto the Rainbow Bridge.

There I assumed my human Aspect; clothed in nothing but smoke and glam; ready to take on the enemy in the form in which they knew me best.

Why did I leave my fleet, you ask? Well, I knew what was coming next. Bif-rost was the final link in the chain that joins Worlds together. Gullveig had already opened the gates of Dream and Death. Only one remained: Pandaemonium – which meant that any remaining business, scores to settle, for instance, would have to be dealt with swiftly, if they were to be dealt with at all.

And so I crossed the Rainbow Bridge in the Aspect of Loki, the Trickster, just as the last shining filaments that held it all together dissolved like a soap bubble in the sun. I was unarmed, except for my glam; I'd never had much interest in weapons, and besides, this time I wasn't looking for a fight. There was one enemy left in Asgard who hadn't joined the fray, and for an excellent reason. He was – at least, technically – already dead, but that wouldn't stop me, I promised myself, from making him even deader.

The Oracle. That thrice-damned Head. Mimir's Head was to blame for all this. That damned Head and its prophecies. Why had we ever listened to them?

Well, if I had my way, I told myself, no one would ever listen again. I would bury the thing so deep that even the dragon at Ygg's root would have to strain to hear it. And so, with that intention in mind, I jumped lightly from the vanishing Bridge; shielded myself with a cantrip of *Bjarkán*; skated past a phalanx of ephemera; jumped onto the battlements; dodged a few little skirmishes and found myself in Asgard again, this time facing Odin's hall; its roof collapsing and blackened.

I went inside. It was empty. Odin's high seat was toppled and smashed. But Mimir's well was still untouched; the intruders had not yet understood the true nature of the enemy. So harmless, so apparently dead, so tranquil in its darkened pool, the Oracle lay in wait for me; glowing a little, as if in satisfaction, its calcified features shining.

I stood there, naked and covered in soot, looking into Mimir's well. Then I reached in and recovered the Head. Held it up at arm's length.

'You bastard,' I said. 'You disembodied stone bastard. So much for your prophecy.'

The Oracle looked smugger than ever. 'Hey, don't shoot the messenger,' it said. 'All I do is say what I must. The rest is up to you.'

I glared into the calcified face. 'Don't give me that. I worked it out. I know Heidi set this up. You were in it together.'

The Oracle glowed. 'You're a smart boy. I knew you'd figure it out in the end.'

I snarled: 'Let's see if you figure *this*.' And I tucked the Head under my arm and made for the battlements again.

'What are you doing?' the Oracle said.

'I'm going to bury you so deep that not even the Maggots will hear you.'

'Why?' I thought its tone wavered a little.

I laughed. 'Don't give me that,' I said. 'I'm pretty sure I'm going to die, but at least if I do, I'll go out knowing that *you're* where you deserve to be.'

'What, Hel?' sneered the Oracle. 'Go on, by all means, send me there. I've been waiting since the Elder Age. Or do you imagine I *liked* it here, being at Odin's beck and call, knowing that he'd used me – *twice* – and unable to do a thing about it?'

I grinned. 'I'm not going to send you to Hel. Hel's too close to Chaos. Chaos is too close to Heidi, whom I'd trust as far as I would trust a hungry seal with a barrel of fish. No, Old Man, I'm going to make sure you stay around for a *long* time.'

'What do you mean?' Its voice was sharp.

'You'll see,' I told it.

I've always been quick at casting runes. This time I worked faster than ever; there was a dark cloud in the eastern sky, darker even than the night, and if it was what I thought it was, I didn't have much time left. I cast a dozen runes in rapid succession, twisting them together like the strands of a fishing net. By the time I'd finished, I had something like a cat's cradle of runelight in my hands, which I pulled tightly around the calcified Head. Then I stood on the battlements and aimed it straight down, at a spot roughly five hundred feet below us, where Jormungand had made his last dive.

'Wait,' said Mimir. 'We should talk.'

'What about?' I said.

'Gullveig-Heid. I can tell you everything. I know—'

And that – that *very* moment – was when Heimdall chose to strike at me from behind, using a form of the ice-rune *Hagall*, knocking me sideways from my perch and onto the crumbling parapet. Mimir's Head went one way, bouncing off the battlements and down into the burning plain, and I found myself lying flat on my face in front of Goldie, armed to the chops, and clad in his showiest armour.

I said: 'Didn't you know it was a party? You should have made an effort.'

Heimdall flashed his golden teeth. 'Get on your feet, scum,' he said. 'I've been looking forward to this.'

I grinned. 'I always knew you cared.'

The cloud on the eastern horizon was getting closer very fast. I'd thought I might have a little more time – time to make a stand, perhaps; to jump onto the battlements and to scream my defiance at everything. Still, this was better than nothing. If I was to die in flames, I couldn't have chosen better company.

I assumed my Wildfire Aspect and leapt at Heimdall, all colours blazing. For a moment he clung to me, trying to find a hold on my fiery person. We struggled, he casting runes to immobilize me, I searing him with fire and flame.

Of course I didn't stand a chance. Heimdall was stronger, and armour-clad, and sooner or later I knew he'd get the upper hand. Just as I thought I had him – his face half blackened, his glam getting weak – Goldie cast *Isa* and froze me in place, yanking me from my fiery shape and back into my human form.

For a moment, time froze. I could feel the darkening air; smell the stench of the fire-pits; hear the Watchman's breath in my ear and see – was that a star in the lurid sky? Was that *my* star hanging there? I looked towards the east again and saw the black tip of a giant wing coming out of the shadow-cloud.

Then Heimdall looked straight into my eyes and stepped right off the battlements, carrying me down with him through the hot air towards the ravaged battlefield.

I grinned. He was *so* predictable. I'd guessed he would follow me from the Bridge to try and even the score with me. I'd guessed he would be quite prepared to sacrifice himself for me. And now he was staging a double jump, just as the end came into sight – secure in the grim satisfaction of knowing that, if he had to die, at least he'd taken me with him.

There wasn't much time to struggle. Even if I'd tried to escape, *Isa* would have held me fast. All I could do was watch the ground rushing up to receive me, looking very rocky and hard and cratered with smoking pits of fire.

So what's the worst that could happen? I thought. *Doesn't Hel owe me a favour?*

And then something swept across the land like the shadow of a monstrous black bird, and the ground disappeared; and the sky disappeared; and a cold like the ice of distant stars fell into sudden silence.

> *Now comes the final reckoning.*
> *Now come the folk of Netherworld.*
> *Now comes the dragon of darkness, Death,*
> *Casting his shadow-wing over the Worlds.*

And at the same time, I felt something snap inside me, like a little bone. I'd never felt the sensation before, but all the same, I knew what it was. They say you know instinctively whenever you break a bone, and in the same way I knew that what I'd just felt was the rune *Kaen*, giving up the last of its glam, reversed by a violent psychic blow.

And I knew Death wasn't my problem. No. My problem was a larger one. That cloud – that wing of darkness – was Surt in his primary Aspect. Surt the Destroyer; Chaos incarnate; the ultimate ruler of Netherworld, crashing into the Worlds through Dream . . .

I said: '*Oh, crap.*'

Then, night fell.

Oh, crap. As last words go, it wasn't what you'd call memorable. But as the icy darkness fell, I was dimly aware of a voice speaking to me very close, like the voice of the sea inside a shell, before the darkness engulfed me at last, body, mind and what passes for soul.

EPILOGUE

Always look on the bright side.
And if there is no bright side?
Look away.

Lokabrenna

Everyone thought I was dead.

Well, technically speaking, I guess I was – but Dream is a river than runs through Nine Worlds, and in the aftermath of Chaos's triumph, my physical and ephemeral Aspects were separated one from the other for good, and my ephemeral Aspect was dragged, not to Hel, where I had hoped for an early release – Hel had sworn an oath, after all, and such oaths are not lightly broken – but into Netherworld itself, the antechamber of Chaos.

There, Dream rules in its darkest form, and every nightmare is played out. Chaos isn't forgiving to those who try to defy it. Even less so to traitors – and I, of course, was both.

I shan't bore you with the details. Suffice it to say, it wasn't fun. A cell built from my deepest fears, and guarded by a demon especially chosen to keep me subdued.

A snake, of course. It's always a snake.

Not my finest moment.

But I was not alone there. Those who had fallen *before* Surt's arrival had been ferried straight to Hel; but when the black wing descended, and Pandaemonium was unleashed, some of the surviving gods were dragged into Netherworld alongside me, while the rest fell into darkness, or Dream, or Hel, or Pandaemonium. Gullveig-Heid took my place alongside Surt, who gave her a new, fiery Aspect. Now she was Burning Ambition; more ruthless and destructive than Wildfire had ever been. Well, I guess she'd earned it. I half expected her to call and visit me in my new cell – to gloat or to commiserate – but she never did.

I know. *Not* a happy conclusion, but you already knew how this would end. Everyone dies, or disappears, or fades into oblivion. Let's face it, that's how *all* stories end, once you reach the final page. There's no happy-ever-after for anyone, least of all the gods, who, if they're lucky, get to rule the world for a while before another tribe takes over.

As for Asgard, it too fell under Surt's extended wing, onto the plain of Ida, showering most of World's End with cantrips and broken rune fragments.

And the Folk?

Collateral damage, I fear. It's very hard not to step on the ants when you're fighting a war on an anthill. And then, when darkness came . . . well. Winter did the rest. A winter that lasted a hundred years, or so said the new historians – bringing new gods for a New Age of Order and enlightenment.

But I'm getting ahead of my tale. The Worlds as we knew them were at an end. Still, the Worlds have ended before, many times, and been remade. Nothing lasts. History spins its yarn, breaks threads, spins again, like a child's top, going back to the beginning. The Oracle knew that. That's what those last stanzas mean; a new world, rising from the ruins of the old. Of course, there was no chance of *us* ever getting to see it. Our time was done; the Oracle had made that very clear. And yet . . .

> *On what was once the battlefield*
> *A New Age dawns. Its children*
> *Find the golden game-boards*
> *Of bright Asgard, the fallen.*

See what the Oracle did there? That's what we call a teaser. A lure, thrown out at the end of a tale suggesting a continuation.

I wasn't about to argue with *that*. My story needed a sequel. Preferably a sequel in which I rose from the dead, regained my glam, saved the Worlds, rebuilt Asgard and was generally welcomed by all as a hero and a conqueror. A little far-fetched, I knew that. But in this ocean of mangled dreams, what else was there to do but cling to even the smallest of straws?

> *New runes will come to Odin's heirs,*
> *New harvests will be gathered.*
> *The fallen will come home. The child*
> *Will liberate the father.*

New runes? New harvests? The fallen, returned? That interested me strangely. Mimir was bound to tell the truth, though not always in the clearest of language. It struck me that if he had *really* wanted to enlighten us when he first made the prophecy, he wouldn't have chosen verse as his medium. Perhaps, I thought, there was something hidden in the text of the prophecy that Mimir didn't want us to know. If there was as much as the tiniest chance . . .

Hope, that cruellest of sensations, bringing release in the midst of pain, only to snatch it away again just as the sufferer dares to believe. How I hated it. And yet, I kept what little faith I could. I've always been an optimist. And those last stanzas spoke to me with a special intensity.

Of course, the Oracle's trick was based on the fact that everyone hears the prophecy that they most expect to hear; everyone assumes that the verse refers to *them* in particular. There was always the possibility that Mimir had put in that last bit just to torment Yours Truly; offering the hope of escape like the gold at the end of the rainbow, only to have it disappear every time I thought I was close.

Still, what other choice did I have? The final part of the

prophecy was still up for interpretation. And if I could find a way of reading it in my favour, then that was what I meant to do. Forget the Authorized Version. The Gospel of Loki would not be complete until every scrap of hope was gone. And so I waited in darkness, and dreamed, and thought to myself:

Let there be light.
Let there be light.
Let there be . . .

THE PROPHECY OF THE ORACLE

I know a tale, o sons of earth.
I speak it as I must.
Of how nine trees gave life to Worlds
That giants held in trust.

That was the first Age, Ymir's time.
There was no land or sea.
Just void between two darknesses,
No stars by which to see.

Till Buri's sons brought Order
From out of Chaos; light
From darkness; life from death
And shining day from night.

The Aesir came. On Ida's plain
The new gods built their kingdom.
Here they raised their citadel, their courts,
Their seats of wisdom.

Gold they had in quantity
From the folk in World Below,
They shaped the fates of mortal men
And sealed their own, so long ago.

From the Alder and the Ash,
They fashioned the first Folk from wood.
One gave spirit; one gave speech;
One gave fire in the blood.

I know a mighty Ash that stands.
Its name is Yggdrasil.
It stands eternal, evergreen,
Growing over wisdom's well.

I speak now of the Sorceress,
Gullveig-Heid, thrice-burned, thrice-born,
Seeress, mistress of the Fire
Vengeful, bloated with desire.

I speak of war, as now I must
Of war against the Aesir.
The Vanir, Gullveig's kindred
Cry vengeance for their sister.

Odin flings his spear. Now war
Is fast unleashed upon us.
Asgard's walls are broken down;
The Firefolk, victorious.

The Aesir meet in council.
But oaths are to be broken.
The Sorceress has done her work.
The Oracle has spoken.

But I see more. There Heimdall's horn
Lies underneath the sacred tree.
In Mimir's well, Allfather's eye
Was forfeit. Will you hear me?

I see your fate, o sons of earth.
I hear the battle calling.
Odin's folk prepare to ride
Against the shadows falling.

 I see a branch of mistletoe
Wielded by a blind man.
This, the poison dart that slays
Asgard's most beloved son.

I speak as I must. The funeral pyre
Sends smoke into the fading sky.
Frigg weeps bitter tears – too late,
Her son sits, silent, at Hel's side.

I see one bound beneath the court,
Under the Cauldron of Rivers.
The wretch looks like Loki. His wife
Alone stands by him as he suffers.

I speak as I must. Three rivers converge
Upon the gods in their domain.
A river of knives from the east; from the north
And south, twin rivers of ice and flame.

I see a hall on the shores of Death.
Acrawl with snakes and serpents.
Netherworld, in which the damned
Await the time of judgement.

In Ironwood, the Witch awakes.
The Fenris wolf will have his day.
His brothers howling at the skies;
The sun and moon will be their prey.

Night will fall upon the Worlds.
Evil winds will howl and blow.
A void between two darknesses –
What more would Allfather know?

Now crows the golden cockerel
To call the Aesir to the foe.
And in the silent hall of Hel,
A soot-red rooster loudly crows.

The wolf at Hel's gate howls. The chain
Is broken; Loki's son runs free.
Ragnarók is come at last,
Chaos rides to victory.

Now comes the time of axe and sword;
Brother shall kill brother.
Now comes the time of wolves; the son
Will soon supplant the father.

Yggdrasil, the World Ash
Quakes where it stands. The Watchman
Sounds his horn. In Asgard,
Odin speaks with Mimir's Head.

The wolf at Hel's gate howls again.
Loki's second son breaks free.
The World Tree falls; the Serpent writhes,
Lashing the waves in fury.

Now comes a fire-ship from the east,
With Loki standing at the helm.
The dead arise; the damned are unleashed;
Fear and Chaos ride with them.

Now comes the final reckoning.
Now come the folk of Netherworld.
Now comes the dragon of darkness, Death,
Casting his shadow-wing over the Worlds.

How goes it with the Firefolk?
And with the gods, how goes it now?
The day of Ragnarók is here.
I speak as I must. Will you hear more?

Flames from the south. Ice from the north.
The sun falls screaming from the sky.
The road to Hel is open wide.
Mountains gape and witches fly.

Now Odin comes to face the foe.
Against the Fenris wolf he stands.
He fights; he falls. Need I say more?
Thor will avenge the Old Man.

Now the snake that binds the world
Strikes in rage at wrathful Thor.
Thunderer wins the battle, but falls
To the monster's raging maw.

Once more the wolf at Hel's gate greets
Asgard's heroes, one by one.
Battle rages, Worlds collide.
Stars fall. Once more, Death has won.

I see a new world rising. Green
And lovely from the ocean.
Mountains rise, bright torrents flow,
Eagles hunt for salmon.

On what was once the battlefield
A New Age dawns. Its children
Find the golden gaming-boards
Of bright Asgard, the fallen.

New runes will come to Odin's heirs,
New harvests will be gathered.
The fallen will come home. The child
Will liberate the father.

I see Asgard built anew
Gleaming over Ida's plain.
I have spoken. Now I sleep
Till the world's tides turn again.